Joshua Hyde Library
305 Main Street
Sturbridge, MA 01566

WITHDRAWN

P9-CET-853

JOSHUA HYDE PUBLIC LIBRARY

Donated
In Memory of

James V. Gazzini

2010

THE MARRIAGE ARTIST

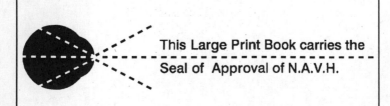

This Large Print Book carries the
Seal of Approval of N.A.V.H.

THE MARRIAGE ARTIST

ANDREW WINER

THORNDIKE PRESS
A part of Gale, Cengage Learning

Joshua Hyde Library
306 Main Street
Sturbridge, MA 01566

GALE
CENGAGE Learning

Detroit • New York • San Francisco • New Haven, Conn • Waterville, Maine • London

GALE
CENGAGE Learning

Copyright © 2010 by Andrew Winer.
Thorndike Press, a part of Gale, Cengage Learning.

ALL RIGHTS RESERVED
This is a work of fiction. All of the characters, organizations, and events portrayed in this novel either are products of the author's imagination or are used fictitiously.

Thorndike Press® Large Print Reviewers' Choice.
The text of this Large Print edition is unabridged.
Other aspects of the book may vary from the original edition.
Set in 16 pt. Plantin.

LIBRARY OF CONGRESS CATALOGING-IN-PUBLICATION DATA

Winer, Andrew.
  The marriage artist / by Andrew Winer.
    p. cm. — (Thorndike Press large print reviewers' choice)
  ISBN-13: 978-1-4104-3553-8 (hardcover)
  ISBN-10: 1-4104-3553-9 (hardcover)
  1. Art critics—Fiction. 2. Marriage—Fiction. 3.
Wives—Death—Fiction. 4. Suicide victims—Fiction. 5. Gifted children—Fiction. 6. Fathers and sons—Fiction. 7.
Jews—Austria—Vienna—Fiction. 8. Psychological fiction. 9.
Large type books. I. Title.
PS3623.I63M37 2011
813'.6—dc22   2010047525

Published in 2011 by arrangement with Henry Holt and Company LLC.

Joshua Hyde Library
306 Main Street
Sturbridge, MA 01566

Printed in the United States of America
1 2 3 4 5 6 7 15 14 13 12 11

For Charmaine,
my amazement

■ ■ ■ ■

We Lose Our Love to History, Part One

■ ■ ■ ■

WHERE WILL IT BE RECORDED?

Falling, in her final moments, Daniel's wife carries in her chest a heart burdened by the weight of her love for another man. She feels something, *every*thing — gravity? God? — gripping her heart, pulling the earth upward to meet it. The sidewalk is still far below her, discolored with patches of brown and black, but it is expanding quickly, rising as if to absorb her. She has little sensation of descent. This is what falling feels like. Around her the air, life-giving and loyal all these years, yields easily despite its wet summer night thickness. It is making way for her. It is assenting to her death.

Is she aware of her lover's figure, also falling, not quite beside her, some few feet away?

No, her *mind* is not on the man at all. In the greatest matters — love and death, sex too — our minds are rarely in concert with our hearts.

Of Daniel she is not thinking either. Not anymore. She has no more time. She is already a part of history. And history is the time of the dead.

Finally, she is left only with vision. There is the sidewalk. There is a discarded yogurt cup. There, a cigarette butt. Images of eternity.

Then it is finished.

Or that is how Daniel would imagine it, long after Aleksandra's body was found, near that of the artist Benjamin Wind, by a group of college students walking to a party. It had been an airless July night during which the heat bore down relentlessly on the city, pressing its inhabitants toward its sticky pavements. And there they were, two dark figures on the sidewalk, at angles too odd for sleep.

Because Benjamin Wind was something of a personage in New York, because — well, because he was in many people's opinion the best artist, in any country, of the last decade and probably the first great artist of the twenty-first century, and because Daniel had in no small way helped shape that opinion by championing Wind's work in a series of essays and reviews, because Daniel had called Wind's solo exhibition that spring "possibly the best showing of art by a living artist this reviewer has ever seen," and, finally, because the woman who lay dead next to Wind on the sidewalk outside his Bowery studio was Daniel's wife, the entire art world was lousy with gossip about the deaths. Certainly Wind and Aleksandra must have been lovers, it was suggested. Perhaps thirty-eight-year-old Daniel Lichtmann, the very art critic who had made Wind's career, discovered the pair in the middle of a clandestine liaison, forced his way into the artist's studio to find them beneath its outsize window, and precipitately tossed them out of it (precisely *how* Daniel had done so was detailed in numerous accounts, as various and tantalizing as they were apocryphal). Or had Wind, in the throes of some impassioned dispute, pushed Aleksandra from the roof of his building and then in despair followed her down? Or a question more interesting by half, even for Daniel: Had it been a suicide pact? Had the two, under the influence of a mutual death drive, sought a permanent embrace, an irrevocable consummation of their love?

Each of these speculations reached Daniel, despite his self-imposed isolation after That Day — that unnameable day in his life — but he quickly forgave his art world

11

friends. In truth, he was as in the dark as they were about the deaths (as were the investigators who, after plying him with questions and poking about in Wind's loft and a few other corners of the art world, came up with nothing), and it was all he could do to keep his own mind from fabricating the wildest ideas. He tried, typically, to retreat from reddened mental flashes of flesh and fucking and blood to the black-and-white world of words, with pitiable results. Late one night he found himself madly searching his shelves for a volume containing the last letter of the German writer Heinrich von Kleist, who had famously committed double suicide with Henriette Vogel in 1811. When he located the entry, he rejoined the heap of trash and uneaten frozen dinners on his bed and copied down the following line, in a spiral around an empty toilet paper roll, as an imaginary reel of Aleksandra and Wind's "flight" to their death played in his mind: "What strange feelings, half sad, half joyful, move us in this hour, as our souls rise above the world like two joyous balloonists."

If the two of them *had* been preparing in unison for death, there were no clues to be found in their obituaries — which were decidedly free of scandalous references.

Wind's ran a half page in the *New York Times.* That it drew generously from Daniel's published work on the artist's life and career, that it identified Daniel as the one who had coronated Wind "The Art World's New King," that it heavily quoted Daniel's own praise of a man who had probably taken his wife from him, made reading the obituary a cruel experience for Daniel — an experience he nevertheless drew out, in a spectacular all-night exercise in self-flagellation. Over and over again he read through the obit, fixating on the words he had once written and skipping familiar biographical details, two of which would become significant to his quest to find out what had happened to his wife:

Benjamin Wind, the first Native American ever to rise to the top of the contemporary visual arts, is dead at 37.

Mr. Wind is survived by his father, Herman, a full-blooded Blackfoot, who lives in Newport Coast, Calif., and his mother, Francine, of Bend, Ore.

In contrast to Wind, Aleksandra was relegated to the "Deaths" section at the bottom of the following day's *New York Times*

Obituaries page. Her brief death announcement had been provided by her family:

LICHTMANN — Aleksandra V. Beloved wife of Daniel. Beloved daughter of Salomon and Yulia Volkov. Photographer. Funeral services July 16, 10am, Weinberg-Lowensohn Memorial Temple, Queens, N.Y.

When Daniel read this, he was seated at the breakfast table that he and Aleksandra had purchased together at the Chelsea flea market. It was still early, he had been up most of the night, and his initial reaction to seeing her written about in this manner was rage — not at the "news" of her death, the cold reportage of it in ink on newsprint, but at the single-word description of her career: "Photographer." *Photographer.* How could this not be an insult to Aleksandra as an artist? Where was the mention of how valued she had been by the *New York Times* itself? He stared blinkingly at the obituary for several minutes before swiping the whole newspaper off the table.

Later that day, he was aimlessly making his way against the crush of Canal Street humanity when he realized that no amount of praise for her work would have captured

14

what was *truly* great about Aleksandra. If he
had ever been looked upon by a higher
sympathy, it was surely through her eyes.
Yet now that she was dead the world would
never know that capacity of hers. Because
history records what we *do,* not how we
love. No, the latter is one of marriage's im-
measurable burdens: to register — to somehow record — the other's care.

This, Daniel came to believe, was what
Aleksandra had tried to tell him one morning, only days before That Day, when he
had turned from their living room window
to find her silently staring at him. He was
frightened by the depth of sadness in her
eyes and did not immediately go to her. Nor
did she answer right away when he asked
her what was wrong. She regarded him with
a veiled look, as if guarding a mystery. Did
she know that she would soon be dead?
Abruptly her expression shifted, and he
began to be filled with true fear, fear that
she was about to tell him the saddest news
in the world. When she finally spoke it did
seem like the saddest news. "I'm the only
one who really *sees* your life," she said. He
mumbled some inarticulate response, but
she went on as if she had not heard him: "I
don't know how to love you more, Daniel."

When she was dead not a week later, when

15

Daniel learned that the dead take with them not only what we love in them but also what they love in us, this moment came rushing back to him. He would never forget how she had steeled herself then, after he told her he loved her. "You love me in a disinterested way," she said, her voice hardening. "That makes you my father. Not my lover."

But it was not true. He loved her painfully.

He had loved her painfully from the beginning.

Was there any other way for two people to love each other, in the beginning, when they were each married to someone else?

THE MARRIAGE ARTIST

Vienna, 1928. Inexplicably, for it has been a bitter and unrelenting December, tendrils of warm air — mysterious exhalations of breath, sweet and melancholy at the same time — worry their way down the Alpine promontories, following the fingers of the Vienna Woods into the gray capital. People, too, pour into the morning streets to take advantage of their city's Indian summer, unaware that the place is in its final flowering, the last of its artistic noons. They are unaware that the universe, having favored Vienna since Roman times, having held its walls fast against Teutons and Turks, having tolerated its Mozarts and Mahlers, its Klimts and Kokoschkas, its Beethovens and Brahmses, Schuberts, Schieles, and Schoenbergs — its gross husbanding of genius — is ready to leave their city out of its calculations. Unaware also that another breath will soon wash over the city from the north German plains, a breath not of the gods but of a human taint, carrying black archaic forces that will quicken the universe's leave-taking.

But the universe has not yet taken its eye off of Vienna. It is about to offer the city one final genius in the form of ten-year-old Josef Pick, though if the boy were to be told that the morning's strange warm air is an omen of this offering or of the bittersweet fate that awaits him, he would pay scant attention. His interest in the hot spell is more immediate: for the first time ever, his parents are taking him to see his grandfather Pommeranz, and the heat seems both to externalize his burning curiosity about the old man who recently moved here from Galicia, and furnish his father, now applying handkerchief to forehead, with one more reason why the three of them should turn around this instant and go home.

"Of all the days to visit the old Jew!" his father proclaims for the benefit, Josef is sure, of Taborstrasse's streetful of Jews, whose multitudes suck his family forward into the Leopoldstadt.

Josef has been to the Jewish district once before with his mother, but only to visit the amusement park at the Prater: they passed right through on a tram, and he does not remember seeing anything of the neighbor-

18

hood, certainly nothing like *this.* He steals a glance back at his father. Hewing to the sidewalk's edge several steps behind Josef, the man glares at the slapdash wooden carts filled with pickles and potatoes, cabbages and onions, at aged Jewish women who sit on the sidewalk without embarrassment, their wares spread before them on blankets, and at endless shopwindows festooned with makeshift banners announcing greatly reduced prices, grand openings, or going-out-of-business sales. Josef knows all too well what his father is telling himself: that none of this — no resident, no particular shop, no vendor, certainly no single beggar — has been here for more than five years, and not a one of them *will* be in another five years. How many times has his father ranted against "the provisional spirit of the *Island of Matzos,*" as he calls the Leopoldstadt — against its "fugitive, flagrantly commercial" aspect? "No enterprise can endure," his father always says, "when it's founded solely on financial aspirations, without respect for legacy and history. Just look at the bank for which I work: there's a *reason* why it has existed since the days of Baron Salomon von Rothschild! And why, alone among Vienna's firms, it survived the Great War and depression both! We haven't abandoned values born during Emperor Franz Josef's reign — the longest the continent's ever known, I might add! — a time before the War to End All Wars, when you could count on an institution to be in existence when your second or third child is born. A time when you could yet trust the human race!"

More distressful to Josef, though, are the traces of relief, of gratitude, gladdening his father's eyes. The man is surely also thinking how grateful he is that the Picks converted to Catholicism a generation ago. How grateful he is that his wife — Josef's mother — agreed not only to be baptized before marrying him but also to raise any child she bore as a Christian, as an *Austrian*. How grateful he is for having insisted this morning that Josef wear his lederhosen, green loden jacket, and white kneesocks — those symbols of national pride. How grateful he is that no one in his immediate family is *still a Jew*.

And this last thought, Josef understands painfully, is what makes the existence and recent proximity of Grandfather Pommeranz — his mother's father and an Ostjude, or Jew from the Eastern principalities — so bothersome to his father. The Ostjuden, who do not bother to wear a modern suit, who cannot be inconvenienced to shave their beards, who, most unforgivably, do not learn to speak properly the German of the Viennese or what his father calls "the sweetest, most sublime language ever to grace the European continent" — it is these scions of the shtetl, Josef has been told, who boldly violate the tacit compact of the assimilated not to reveal anything Jewish, who make no effort to do as the Viennese do, to fit in, to . . . *hide* . . . and who are thus to blame for Vienna's mounting anti-Semitism. He knows that his grandfather is a prime example of why the Ostjuden attract such hatred. Having been a failed rabbi in Galicia, the old man is now a failed rabbi in Vienna. A rabbi without a following — who has ever heard of such a thing? Who has ever heard of a rabbi earning his bread by trudging all over Vienna and begging its poor shop owners to allow him to bless their meats, produce, or appetizers in exchange for a few schillings?

It hurts Josef's stomach every time his father shares with him the latest joke from Café Central, where his father regularly meets his colleagues: *How many potatoes did the rabbi convert to Judaism this week? Does he do dumplings? I met a gefilte fish today on Kärntner Strasse who's having difficulty with his wife and could use the rabbi's blessing.*

21

"Wait till they discover the *worst* of it!" his father bellowed to him one night last week after returning home from the café. "That your grandfather, like a rabbi who wants to bring in more believers, tries to increase the number of meats he blesses each week! According to your mother, some of his foolish clients let the old man bless their meats *twice!*"

The old man's pitiful travails obviously pay little; why else would he shamefully accept the ten-schilling note Josef's father dispatches to him by courier once a month? It is almost enough to make Josef believe his father's assessment that all Ostjuden are not only crude and greedy but also doomed to failure. Yet as he pushes deeper into the Leopoldstadt's hectic center he senses something in himself competing with his father's disdain. Each scuffling shoe and bared ankle, each clacking heel and chafing trouser, strikes him as part of a triumphant symphony of momentum. But it is more than just the bustle that excites him. It is that these people *aren't* hiding — that here, Jewishness is altogether to be seen. Synagogues on each street corner, prayer houses in every other building, Hebrew lettering the permanent feature of many a shopwindow. And everywhere: the clamorous

22

swarming air of Jews, from the ultraortho-dox to the normal run of them. What is so wrong with this? Josef wonders. He does not see any difference between these people's scrappy struggle to succeed and the efforts of a pair of goldfinches who return each year to the same flimsy branch outside his bedroom window.

Suddenly, just as his father leads him into what must be the poorest and busiest marketplace in the district, an acute aware-ness of his lederhosen, kneesocks, and blar-ing green jacket causes him to shrink from the gaze of passing Jews — or rather from the sight of their clothes: every darkling caftan, felt hat, and tassel that hits him like a rebuke of his Gentile garb. Only his family's arrival at the door of Karmeliter-platz 2, a low-slung begrimed building tucked into a corner of the square, saves him.

"This," his father says in an incriminatory voice, "is where your grandfather lives."

Josef raises his eyes to the building's chipped walls, its sagging roof. It once might have been a family's home; now, hand-painted above the door: ROOMS TO LET — FOR MEN ONLY. Why does his grandfather live *here,* with other men who have no one, while his family's villa in Hietzing has several unoccupied rooms?

"Let's do this quickly," his father says. He leads Josef and his mother through the entryway and into a dispiriting concrete courtyard full of offense and stench and not much else. Josef, holding his nose, has never stood in so joyless a place, and he is troubled by a vague premonitory heaviness of heart for the old man he is about to meet. At his father's urging, he mounts the stairs.

In spite of all he has heard about Grandfather Pommeranz, he is not sure what he expects him to look like exactly, but it certainly is not the bluff, burly man in an obscenely ill-fitted suit who waylays him at the top of the stairs with a flurry of fake fisticuffs to his midriff, before locking him into a bear hug and hoisting him high into the air. From this vantage point Josef has just enough time and altitude to detect something septic, even vagrant, about the condition of the old man's black coat: the woolen fabric is threadbare and shiny along the collar's exposed edges, and the lapels are discolored by apparently repeated saturation (if the dank urinary odor is any indication) with the broth of unidentifiable meats and fishes. Dandruff covers the man's shoulders.

"The young Pommeranz!" Josef's grandfather declares to him in a stammering, Slavic-stained German.

"Young *Pick*," asserts Josef's father, joining them, along with Josef's mother, on the landing.

Grandfather Pommeranz lowers Josef so that their faces are level and close enough to make the old man's eyes appear to become *his* eyes and the old man's nose merge with *his* nose and the old man's breath, redolent of paprika and pickled herring, blend with *his* breath.

"He looks like a Pommeranz to me," says his grandfather.

Josef's mother, with a filial mixture of warning and affection, glares at her father. *"Papa . . ."*

"He is a Pick," insists Josef's father. "His name is Pick."

"But those eyes," the old man says, studying Josef, "those are *Pommeranz* eyes!"

"He is a Pick!" Josef's father reiterates, his voice growing uncomfortably loud. Josef catches his mother giving his father's arm an admonitory squeeze.

"That *nose*," says Josef's grandfather.

"Still a Pick!"

"And mouth —"

"Pick. Pick. Pick!"

The old man raises two hopeful eyebrows

at Josef. "What do *you* say, my boy? Pommeranz or Pick?"

Josef, feet still dangling off the ground, has been watching this duel with great interest. Grandfather Pommeranz's blowsy appearance, his challenging of Josef's father, his audacious wholesale claiming of his grandson, the old man's sheer pluck — these things captivate the boy. And to be so childishly fought over by two grown men, accustomed as he is to a household where children and adults occupy different universes . . . it is as if somewhere in his chest cavity the door to a prohibited and vacant space has been unlocked, and an unfamiliar, almost feral, excitement has taken up residence. Josef is thrilled.

"*Pick*eranz!" he abruptly exclaims.

His grandfather's expression falls. "Ah," he says with a sigh, and, for the first time, Josef notices the suggestion of a perplexed sadness in his bearded face. The old man's eyes, encased in drawn folds of faint and spotted skin, are still young and blue and full of spirit — defiantly married to the rest of his aging face as an airy optimism might be to utter resignation — but there is something about the tone of his "Ah," a delicate whiff of melancholy, that causes Josef again to experience a confusing sor-

26

row for this man who is his grandfather.

The old man's tone is the same when Josef's mother offers him a tin of apple strudel she labored over late into the previous night in preparation for this special visit. *"Ah,"* he says, glumly studying the flaked golden crust. "Another strudel."

The four of them stand there awkwardly until Josef's father breaks the silence. "I almost forgot," he says, producing an envelope and handing it to the old man.

Josef's grandfather takes the envelope and sighs again. "Ah, yes, another ten schillings."

It is in this dim mood that Grandfather Pommeranz leads the three of them into his flat, a cheerless cigar box of a room, cramped with furniture and saturated by a gamy, penetrating dampness. He pauses in the middle, a giant in his den, and picks at the frayed yarmulke on his head. "There is the table," he says gloomily, not bothering to point. "There are the chairs. A basin for washing. Stove for coals. The desk."

The sight of such dwarfish living quarters is new to Josef, and as his parents seat themselves, he examines the room with curiosity, passing an unmade bed in the corner to stand at a desk placed importantly before a window with a view of bustling Karmeliterplatz. It is then that he first lays eyes on the object that will change his destiny. Innocently, he lifts a piece of ink-embellished parchment paper from the desk and seals his fate with a mundane question.

"What is this?" he asks.

Hardly more than a decade later, when everything he knows will be gone forever — this life of his, the people in this room, Vienna itself really — he will look back on this moment and marvel at how randomly a life gets made. But then the rest of his memory of this day will come back to him, its queer weather, the walk with his pensive and distracted father through the Jewish district, his grandfather's underlying despondency, and all at once his life will look in retrospect like the correct if troublesome path, among many false ones, to the top of a baffling mountain — as if all his choices were made according to a larger uneasy symmetry. His life will seem as if it could not have been any other way.

"Ah," Grandfather Pommeranz says in response to Josef's question, though this time the note in his voice is not morose but rather excited. He joins Josef at the desk. "*That,* my young Pommeranz, would be a ketubah."

Josef holds the piece of parchment at arm's length, attempting to understand what, exactly, he is looking at. In size, it reminds him of the movie placards he often pauses to admire on kiosks, but he is confused by the byzantine complexity of pattern, symbol, and text that is inked and painted in many different colors across most of its pulpy surface (whatever the thing is, it appears to be unfinished). And despite clear evidence that this is the work of his grandfather — the desk is littered with dirty brushes and pen nibs, uncapped ink bottles, rags blotted with the very colors so finely wrought on the parchment — he finds it nearly impossible to believe that something of such jewel-like precision could be made by human hands, especially those belonging to the elephantine old man presently breathing malodorously over his shoulder. Initially, his eye is drawn to the miniature floral curlicues that interlock and form an unbroken border around the parchment — *this* makes sense to him. So does a golden coat of arms, centrally placed at the top of the page and surmounted by what he recognizes as two yet-to-be-colored turtledoves. But what does *not* make sense to him are the two side-by-side columns of text. That he is unable to decipher the Hebrew lettering is not what bothers him. Rather it is that no matter which way he holds the parchment

— up, down, or sideways — the words and lines are not correctly placed: when the two columns are visually weighed, they are not, finally, in *balance.*

"A ketubah?" he puts forth timidly.

His grandfather shoots his parents a look of disbelief. "What, I should explain to a Jewish boy what is a ketubah?"

Josef's mother starts to speak, but Grandfather Pommeranz has already turned back to Josef and begun declaiming against Jewish assimilation: "*Ketubah.* A marriage contract. What your father and mother were above obtaining. I would have made for them the greatest ketubah ever painted in Vienna! But apparently, they, like so many Jews I see in this city who claim to be Gentiles, who worship the café instead of God, have forgotten who they are. Theirs is a life carved from Christianity but, *God* help them, still shtetl stained! Just look at the two of them —"

On his right shoulder, Josef feels his grandfather's dense and sprawling hand willing him to turn and behold his parents. His father and mother stare at him from their seats at the lone table in the room, and there is something pitiful looking about them just now. He is unaccustomed to seeing their faces filled with such impassivity.

His parents appear to him like two fugitives who, having been freshly apprehended, stoically submit to a prisoner's fate.

"You see? I cannot earn a living because of Jews like them," his grandfather continues, forcibly squeezing his shoulder. "What use have they for synagogues or ketubot? They fool themselves into believing they are Austrians, forgetting that a Jew has no permanent home here, forgetting that we are all wanderers. Look!" — he whips the parchment out of Josef's hands and points at a line of text — "It says 'Danube River'; it does not name *Vienna* as the wedding location. There is a reason you only put rivers in a ketubah!"

"Why?" Josef asks.

An incredulous glow suffuses his grandfather's face, and the old man lets the ketubah fall back onto the desk. "But my *boy?* . . . As far as we Jews are concerned, Vienna can come and go, just like the Habsburgs. It is *we* who will endure. Like the mighty Danube!"

Josef has not previously heard Jews spoken of in this manner, but as entranced as he is by his grandfather's impassioned rhetoric, he cannot keep his eyes off the ketubah. A *marriage contract.* In all of his life he has never heard of such a thing. Of course he has seen many contracts before — the desk in his father's study is invariably covered with them — but they have always pertained to loans or business deals or money matters of some sort, and none of them are ever pleasant to look at. None have contained any decoration that he can remember, save for the bank's gold-embossed emblem of a double-headed eagle.

"You are still curious about this?" the old man asks him, indicating the ketubah with his forefinger.

Josef nods.

"Ah." The old man falls silent for a moment, as if in the grip of a fixed idea. "Tell me, my young Pommeranz," he abruptly enjoins Josef, "why do you think man and woman marry?"

Josef regards his parents again. Their inscrutable stares offer him nothing.

"Love?" he hazards.

"Love," the old man says, twisting the word into something sounding vaguely poisonous. "Perhaps. Yet this is not the only reason. Love may be pure, but marriage is not. Marriage — it is filled with knowledge! Knowledge of the spouse's flaws. Of *human* flaws!" His grandfather is staring directly at Josef's father now, his eyes lit with accusation. "Marriage is filled with *money.* With

motives. Calculations. Tabulations! Your father is a banker — he knows exactly how much money the Pick house draws from his account each month. He knows what my daughter costs him. What *you,* my young Pommeranz, cost him! *Please* — do not try to convince me that your father has not considered how many schillings he would save should he choose to divorce my daughter. I have been a rabbi for too long — I have seen too many of the goings-on in our wild human waters!"

The old man appears greatly offended by these financial calculations allegedly performed by Josef's father, and Josef watches him iron out the wrinkles in his vest — almost as if to purify himself — by dent of a fussy combination of tugs, pulls, and something amounting to massage. Having completed this rite, his grandfather presses his finger down, with an audible thud, onto the parchment on the desk. "That is why, my boy, the bride especially needs *this* — a marriage contract — to protect her should her husband get the crazy but not unheard-of idea to suddenly leave."

Josef looks at his parents. He is shocked by his grandfather's words, especially the mentioning of divorce. It has never occurred to him that his father would not want to be with his mother, with *him.* Can it possibly be true? He finds no answers in his father's face. The man's gray eyes, bright with anger and derision, are narrowed on Grandfather Pommeranz. And his mouth, normally a source of verbal foment, remains tightly shut.

His mother is a different story. Not the least of her usual charms is a playful manipulation of opposites: showing affection, she often feigns disapproval; preposterous fibs are told straight. Even her hair is a calculated study in contrast — severe in its raven color, worn short like a man's, and improbably placed atop a girly, coltish face. But Josef detects something different this time. Across her brow's porcelain surface a battle is being waged that is not under her command, a battle between anger at her father on the one hand, and . . . and *what?*

Grandfather Pommeranz draws Josef's attention away from her by again rapping his finger on the desk. "The ketubah protects the bride in *another* way," he adds. "Tradition has it that a wedding is the beginning of a journey. But this is simply not true. The wedding is only the preparation! No one is moving yet. You're only harnessing up the horses. Packing up what your life and love were — what *you* were. It is a

34

ceremony of saying *good-bye*. And then" — he snaps his fingers — "before you can blink even one eye, the new husband and wife are gone! And so is the moment — just like that. But a marriage? It catches the carriage of *time*. It is therefore natural that love changes because the *husband* changes, to say nothing of the wife!" Josef's cheek is buffeted by a gust of air as the old man whisks the ketubah off the desk and holds it up shakily for Josef's mother to see. "Man and woman need a ketubah," the old man declares, "to remind them of how they used to love!"

Something between a moan and a whimper, low in the register and barely audible, issues from the bosom of Josef's mother, and she turns her head — away from Josef's father, away from the ketubah. Josef strains to see her face. Is she crying?

"After all," his grandfather says with a growing fervor that seems directed at what Josef now perceives as his mother's puzzling new vulnerability, "marriage demands of us the *impossible*. It is a job for which there is no apprenticeship! — a riddle no one has ever solved. And the husband and wife, naively jumping into this great mystery, are left to shape it according to a vision they don't have. *This* is where the ketubah comes in! A good ketubah, in words both practical and poetic, in beauty that is symbolic and personal to the bride and groom, illuminates the mystery of the union of man and woman!" He waves the ketubah once more in the direction of Josef's mother. "A good ketubah helps give them a vision. A *start.*"

The old man, visibly exhausted from this last exertion, hands the ketubah over to Josef and goes to the window, where he leans against the sill and stares at the crowd below, his head slumped into his shoulders.

Confused by the behavior of the three adults in the room, Josef remains absolutely still by the desk where he is standing. He can hear his own breathing; his feet feel oppressively heavy in his leather shoes. When no one speaks for some time, he steps around the table until his mother's face comes into view. There is something clenched and bitter about her expression. Her eyes are cast down to the floor; they are not filled with tears. He looks over at his father. The man's attention is trained fiercely on an invisible spot sullying the opposite wall.

The two of them are *frightening* him. They no longer seem like his mother and father. Rather, they appear to him like two strangers — each engaged in their own version of the world — separate from each other, separate from him. It is this separateness that scares Josef the most. Dimly he perceives that this invisible gap between the three of them is a perilous place, and that he dare not step into it but instead do everything in his power to narrow it and seal it off. He looks down at the marriage contract in his hand.

It would be an understatement to say that, later that afternoon, when he asks to be shown how to illuminate a ketubah, his father is not pleased and his grandfather is. Nevertheless, despite the protests of his father and the heated argument that ensues between his parents — an argument whose ramifications are so numerous that his parents take it outside into the courtyard — Josef finds a chair and an advantageous position beside the desk from which to train his eyes on his grandfather, who sits himself down, dips a pen into a bottle of umber-tinted ink, and, while coloring in a turtle-dove wing, commences to spell out his aesthetic and religious philosophies with all the intelligence of a teacher, the integrity of a tailor, the moral indignation of a shoe-maker. This latter quality frightens Josef into mute attention, but when, halfway into the lesson, his grandfather claims that the most crucial ingredient — in any ketubah worth its salt — is mystery, Josef finds that he cannot remain silent any longer.

"Why?" he says.

His grandfather lifts his pen and turns to him. "What do you mean, *'Why?'* Are you here to tell me that you have solved the puzzle of life? What know you of the world, my young Pommeranz? Are you acquainted with it like a friend? Is anyone? What kind of God would He be" — his grandfather points the pen wildly in the direction of the ceiling — "if His riddles were so easy to master?" Shaking his head, the old man resumes drawing, and as he fights the paper with his pen so too does he seem to fight his own thoughts, his face grimacing each time some apparently elusive point evades him. Finally, with the marshaled defenses of someone whose feelings have been hurt, he continues: "There is a *reason* why He does not make His grace available to every lazy, opportunistic person. If He quickly rewarded each person who acted decently and embraced Him, then everyone and their mother would believe in God and try on goodness simply for the payoff!" He points out the window at the bobbing heads of Karmeliterplatz. "Imagine the connivers in

Leopoldstadt alone, all trying to prove their belief! Ah, but God is smart! He hides His messages behind the everyday things of this world, forcing us to spend a *lifetime* deciphering their patterns. There are no shortcuts to the truth! We must proceed slowly, and with our hearts. If you want to illuminate ketubot, my young Pommeranz, you must breathe sympathy for the things of this world. No matter how astonished you might become at what people are capable of, you must never forget how lonely an article is the human heart — so full of hope and aspirations, of illusions and sorrow and fears and pain. The ketubah artist tries to knit a few of these poor souls together, and in so doing binds them to the rest of humanity." Josef's grandfather holds up the ketubah dramatically. "This is not simply a *drawing*. Look here —" With his pen he indicates a line of Hebrew. "This specifies that the husband and wife are to undertake fleshly congress at least once a week so that they might produce offspring. It is a command! The ketubah not only binds man and woman: it also binds them to the children they have not yet produced and to the ancestors who were married before them. The ketubah, whose text has not changed for hundreds of generations, knits the dead to the living and the living to the unborn! *There* is your mystery."

Josef, staring now at his grandfather, feels caught in a struggle to correlate these elevated ideas with not merely the fussy filigree of line on the parchment but also the old man's brusque temperament and fingernails the color of egg yolks. His grandfather rants on, covering many topics that are beyond the limits of a ten-year-old boy's understanding, but one idea in particular grabs Josef's attention: the old man's claim that each bride and groom possess only one great mystery unique to them — that the rest of their qualities are merely *echoes* of other couples. As he watches his grandfather fill in the remaining elements of the ketubah — an Austrian flag, a griffin, and several vine-choked marble columns alternately separating and flanking the Hebrew text — Josef is dimly aware of a question forming in his mind. He can hear that his grandfather is still speaking, but his consciousness has quit interpreting the words, and when the old man finally sets down his pen and a silence falls on the room, Josef utters the only question that now matters to him: *"What,"* he blurts out, "is the great mystery of Mama and Papa?"

The old man's face registers surprise, but

as the motive behind Josef's question appears to dawn on him, his eyes take on a conspiratorial gleam. "Ah," he says, nodding, and then he pulls open the bottom drawer of the desk and retrieves a fresh piece of parchment, which he promptly places on the desk in front of Josef. He stands and gives Josef the pen.

"That is for you to discover, my young Pommeranz. It is time for my nap."

With that, his grandfather retreats to the bed in the far corner, his back curled away from Josef. Within mere seconds, almost as if he is playing a joke, the old man sinks into a deep, noisy sleep.

Josef turns to the desk, places his grandfather's ketubah beside the blank parchment, and dips the pen into a bottle of black ink. He is going to paint a ketubah for his parents, whose argument still continues in the courtyard below. It is clear to him now that they must have long ago fallen in love with each other but have been in a marriage that has not, for as long as *he* has been in the world, been a happy one. If his grandfather is correct, the fact that they did not procure a marriage contract is at least partially to blame. Josef has never handled pen and ink. He has never picked up a brush. When it has struck his fancy, he *has* doodled a dachshund here, a trolley there, to generally praiseful comments from teachers or friends. But his goal now is not to make a good drawing. That will not be enough. What he intends is nothing less than to repair his parents' love.

It is rough going, at first. Working in a silence broken only by his grandfather's snores and the plaintive dips and rises of his parents' distant arguing, he launches into a copy of the other ketubah's floral frame, but his pen falls into a disagreeable habit of releasing, without warning, vulgar blobs of ink onto the parchment's surface, a problem he finally attributes to his overloading of the pen's nib each time he dips it into the bottle. When, in initially trying to brush in a flower stem, he finds that the green ink is far too dark and saturated, it takes him four failed attempts to realize that soaking the bristles first with water will achieve the desired washed-out effect. These and other technical problems resolved, Josef soon abandons any notion of imitating the ketubah his grandfather made and instead concentrates on chasing the mystery of his parents' long lost love. In place of the traditional floral pattern that hugs the edges of his grandfather's design, he paints in a concentric arrangement of stylized squarish flowers reminiscent of the Jugendstil patterns his mother always points out on the facades of train stations and apartment buildings around Vienna. At the top of the parchment, he renders the double-headed eagle of the old Austrian empire, an icon so beloved by his father, and the emblem of his father's bank.

But as he continues drawing, Josef begins to lose any awareness of the particular images with which he is emblazoning the page. His right hand — the one holding the pen — appears to him almost as a distant, inspirited clay prosthetic limb, detached from his own flesh and tendering line and color in accordance with some mad doctor's instructions. And there *is* a madness to his thoughts, which come to him now as a tangle of shadowy remembrances of his parents: a certain look playing upon his mother's face on some distant morning; his father sitting alone in his study; the two of them engaged in a hushed deliberation on the balcony one cold winter afternoon. Then a strange thing happens. Possibly playing tricks on him, his mind conjures up images of his parents that he has never seen, moments he never witnessed, some seemingly before he was born. He pauses to wonder if this is the result of old photographs he might have once viewed and forgotten, but the thought is quickly transcended by the emotions these summoned images rouse in the deepest part of him: as if riding a magic carpet that floats back through his parents' love for each other, he feels the ghostly essence of dances long forgotten, of romantic talk that has lost its vitality, of affectionate embraces fallen away. And resuming his task, he finds himself adrift, wandering the wilderness of his parents' strange grown-up lives, haunted all the while by the ideas put into his head by his grandfather — about Jews and Gentiles, money and marriage and divorce; haunted also by his own new awareness of his parents' separateness. Yet for every question that nags at his being, for every confusion that leaves an uncomfortable dryness in his throat, his *hand* seems to have a large fund of answers, and though he is only vaguely following its actions, the lines it produces on the parchment cause him suddenly to hold his breath. The ketubah, he realizes with a jolt of excitement, is taking shape.

By the time he is finished, the light in the room has grown dusky and he can barely make out the lines on the parchment under his nose, let alone his grandfather's slumber-

44

ing figure in the far corner. He gets up from the desk and walks to the window. Karmeliterplatz is void of people now; a yellow streetlamp and a lone onion near its base are the only signs of human enterprise. Josef is exhausted and sleepy, and considers going in search of his parents when he hears their footsteps on the stairs.

His father enters the room first and in the dimness spots Josef by the window. "We are going home," he says curtly.

"Not before we see what the boy has done!" comes a booming, scratchy voice from the darkened corner. There is the sound of shuffling, of a squeaking bed coil, and then a lamp clicks on, submerging the room in a pallid light. Grandfather Pommeranz is already on his feet, recentering the yarmulke atop his head and blinking wildly at Josef. "Young man, show us your ketubah."

In the doorway, Josef's mother appears, looking disoriented.

"What is happening?" she asks.

"Your son has made something for you," Grandfather Pommeranz declares for the benefit of both startled parents. "Go ahead, my boy — show us!"

Josef is aware that his father is watching him askance, his eyes filled with sore re-

45

proach. Nevertheless, buoyed by his grandfather's stubborn insistence, he resolves to make his parents see what he has done before the three of them head home. He girds his spirit with a forced expression of confidence, and by means of heavy exaggerated footsteps he approaches the desk.

But when he sees the ketubah in the light, he freezes. He is stunned by its appearance. Not because of its beauty, or its delicacy, or the way color and line and shape subtly draw the eye toward its center (which he left blank, instead of copying the Hebrew from the ketubah his grandfather fashioned for another couple). Not because it resembles alternately a crown of jewels, a wrought iron gate, and the fanciful cover of one of the antique books in his father's study. Not, finally, because its hopeful symbolic shaping of his parents' love cries out from the page like a melancholic lament.

He is stunned by the ketubah because he cannot remember making it. It seems foreign to him, as if painted by someone else's hand.

"Show us!" comes his grandfather's command.

Josef reaches out, catches the feathered edges of the parchment, and, lifting it slightly, slips his fingertips underneath. The paper feels weightless. It flutters above his palms like an exotic bird that might take flight. He clamps his fingers and thumbs tightly around two edges, looks up at the three adults, and lifts the ketubah for them to see.

ALEKSANDRA

It was true. When they met, Daniel and Aleksandra were each married to someone else, and not entirely unhappily. Why, then, did they begin to see each other? Why would two people pursue a path that no matter how much pleasure it might lead to was guaranteed to produce pain? What makes people want to try something that will harm themselves (and probably others)? Is it because they actually enjoy suffering?

No, guessed Daniel, who had asked himself these questions nearly every day since the beginning of his relationship with Aleksandra: he imagined that people behave this way because they are worried. Worried that genuine, undiluted emotion will pass by if they do not reach out for it. Worried they will be cheated of life's thickness. Worried because deep down every one of us *knows,* knows that life is ephemeral. And so, unable to forget our fate, we mount our rebellion, our minor insurrections. We turn ourselves into tragic things, reaching for ruin and release from the start because we know we will find them at the finish.

He first met Aleksandra several months before the new millennium, during an autumn when, through none of his own doing, his star was ascendant. Due to a bitter internecine feud and several subsequent firings and leave-takings, he had managed to land a plum position as art critic for one of the nation's more prestigious periodicals, despite having written reviews for only a couple of local rags. And at a Chelsea art gallery that was between shows, the *New York Times Magazine* arranged to photograph him for a profile to be published under the doubtful title "The Tastemaker." (What an imposter he felt like!) The photographer was late, and Daniel ended up waiting for some minutes in the gallery's empty exhibition space, where, surrounded by white walls and treading on a white floor under ethereal light spilling from skylights, he felt he might have died and gone to some industrial heaven. Then he heard the sound of heels clacking cement, and turned to see a remarkable woman rushing toward him. Dark, full around the mouth, firmly built, she was bedecked entirely (as far as he

49

could tell) in Versace, whose ornate prints she bore brazenly. He could have taken her for an Italian, a Persian, or a Puerto Rican, had he not heard her Russian, which she was at that moment discharging into a cell phone with a ferocity and volume that filled the entire gallery. Behind her, a pretty, hostile-eyed young man (who Daniel would later learn had just finished a stint in the Israeli army) trudged into the gallery laden with camera equipment that he proceeded to drop near her feet. Daniel realized then that this riveting woman, who was obviously engaged in a heated phone argument, was his photographer.

"Life isn't like crossing a cornfield!" she shouted, in impeccable English, into the cell.

This struck Daniel as both an honest assessment of life's transit and perhaps the most arrestingly true utterance he had heard in an art gallery. Life was *not* as simple as crossing a cornfield. He stood there dumbly, and dumbstruck, as she concluded her conversation by yelling something in Russian, slamming the cell phone shut, and turning so that her dark flashing eyes looked straight into his.

"Aleksandra," she said, extending a hand. "Sorry, that was my mother."

"I assumed it was a client."

Her mouth smiled but not her eyes, indicating that his joke had fallen flat.

"When I was nine years old," she said blithely, "my mother took me away from the Soviet Union, but she succeeded in dragging some local Jewish customs with her, including fear of everyone and everything, and an obsession with money."

"What was that you said to her just before you hung up?"

" 'I'm your blood, but I don't have to bleed.' "

Daniel had never heard radiant anger expressed in such coolly poetic terms — not from the mouth of a living person anyway. Her words, her shining presence, seemed to him like a fragile membrane holding back so much vibrating energy.

Now her smile passed from her lips to her eyes. "And do you want to hear my mother's lovely response?"

He certainly did.

" 'You–are–a–*shit!*' "

Daniel simply stared at her, and she must have taken his silence as evidence of his astonishment. Shrugging her shoulders, she added, "At least we're in dialogue."

And there, in the first few words they ever exchanged, was contained everything about

Aleksandra that attracted Daniel to her, everything that would for the next year throw his life into perfect chaos: the Russian Jewishness, the insubordinate wit, her protean nature, the way she wore her burdens with either naked vulnerability or hard-bitten frankness that could be confused for callousness.

During the shoot itself, she was all business. She appeared absorbed in her camera and light meter, and rarely spoke except to direct Daniel to stand in a certain manner or to tell her assistant, who seemed easily irritated, to adjust the lights. Daniel would later learn that this was how she always operated — by losing herself in the work — but at the time he took her aloofness as a sign of her lack of interest, so he was surprised at the end of the shoot when she asked him to lunch.

They hardly said two words as they walked away from the gallery together, but some instinct told both of them, Daniel thought, to avoid the teeming eateries in the immediate vicinity of the galleries. In a quiet, unprepossessing café that served Cuban sandwiches, a waitress took their orders, then Aleksandra folded her hands in her lap, set her eyes again squarely on him, and said, "I can see by your ring that you are married. Before we talk about art, life, this lunch, or anything else, you need to understand that I have a husband."

"All I've done is order a sandwich," he replied partly in jest, "and I feel like we're already having an affair."

Her face suddenly reddened, and she looked at him with raw emotion. "As far as I'm concerned," she said, "we are."

Aleksandra's sudden certainty about wanting to be with him was terrifying because it confronted him with the very real possibility of infidelity. It also had the paradoxical effect of causing him to doubt he was worthy of such conviction, and left him feeling more an imposter than he had before her arrival at the gallery. Nevertheless, he began in the following weeks to meet her regularly, in a series of lunches where she captivated him with her comedy, her full lips, and the stories and dreams she shared with him. He learned she was a survivor not only of the Russian anti-Semitism of her childhood but also of the immigrant parents who took her away from it. She spoke passionately of the new body of work she was just then undertaking in Israel (and that would shortly bring her acclaim): photographs of Jews and Arabs who had been wounded, handicapped, and otherwise adversely affected by suicide bombings ("They are survivors too"). Daniel came to admire her utter lack of repression, which expressed itself in frequent admissions to him of her own lust (how these piqued his interest!) and selfishness, and in accounts of her nightly prayers asking God to help her be more kind and loving, even to those people — her mother, for example — who treated her cruelly.

Later, looking back on those first meetings before they slept together, Daniel would realize there had always been something about Aleksandra, some fatal (and fetching) quality that cast a retrospective shadow over all of his interactions with her. It was not simply her insistence that they had already begun an affair before having completed that first lunch: it was that a tragic ending to their relationship seemed a foregone conclusion. One afternoon during a meal, she removed a photograph from her wallet and slid it across the table toward him.

"My husband," she said flatly.

Daniel made no move to pick up the photo but instead let it lie on the table.

"I still love him," she avowed. "But now I know I am going to leave him."

This was the first mention of a possible sea change in either of their marriages, and it filled Daniel with a pang of culpability. If she did leave her husband, how could Daniel not be at least partly to blame? "Have you discussed it with him?" he asked, struggling to rid his voice of emotion.

Such a scene seemed to pass into her mind, but with a shake of her head she cast it out. "No. And I won't. I will just leave quietly, without saying anything. I am a Russian Jew, and Russians — let alone Jews — have too much pride to explain themselves."

Daniel took the photograph in hand. It revealed Aleksandra and a boyish-looking man standing on a tropical beach, arms entwined. The photo looked to Daniel like it had been snapped during a honeymoon: their eyes were filled with future. "Why are you showing me this?" he asked.

"I want you to see what you will soon destroy." She paused. "And what will probably destroy you and me. My husband is an innocent, Daniel. A very kind person. He has never fought with me — not once. There is a Russian saying: 'He who destroys another's innocence destroys himself.'"

"Why don't you stay with him then?" Daniel blurted out, aware of the tight ball of guilt that had lodged itself somewhere under his sternum.

"Because he's a boy, not a man. And I can't have a child with a boy." She took the photo from his hand and slapped it face-down on the table. "I want to have children with you."

For fear of disappointing and confusing Aleksandra that day, he did not reveal that his wife also intended to have children with him. How could he explain that — despite having mixed feelings about the woman — he had two years earlier jumped on board the procreation train with her?

Of course, he had not always had mixed feelings about his wife, and certainly not when the two of them had first been introduced at a mutual friend's wedding in the Puck Building. The ostentatious glamour of the event was characteristic of her world, and Daniel, who was eager to shed the remnants of his nine years as a poor university student, was seduced by this svelte blonde's extravagant grandstanding, her high finish. She was renowned in uptown social circles for her style, her arch spirit, and her mastery of the backhanded compliment and parting shot. He in turn seemed to satisfy some need she nursed to escape her affluent life. "You're my bohemian fling," she liked to remind him after sex, and, by allowing her misconceptions about him to stand — by not reminding her that he was just another overeducated middle-class Jewish kid from Scarsdale, New York — he traded on her desire for a quaintly impoverished, artily unconventional life and convinced her to marry him. The wedding, held at a friend's Montauk estate, was a mostly secular ceremony whose single reference to Jesus succeeded in casting Daniel's mother against his new wife. For days leading up to the marriage, he had begged his fiancée to winnow out the Christ mention (an act of deference to her attending Episcopalian family), but she had finally put an end to the matter: "Since when, Daniel, have you become sentimental about your Judaism?" His only comfort was that his father, who had been as Jewish as they come, was no longer living ("Thank God Dad is dead" was his exact thought). After a two-week honeymoon in Anguilla, he and his new wife moved into a recently renovated loft (paid for by her father) on Leonard Street in Tribeca — not quite bohemian, but still. Daniel's elastic sense of identity enabled him to adopt his new wife's version of himself as a brilliant starving intellectual, and at dinner parties thrown by her well-to-do friends he developed the habit of romanticizing his penniless student years. His wife, in return, grew attached to Daniel's version of her as a paragon of taste ("So well trained, isn't he?" she would gloat whenever he publicly advertised his admiration of her social skills). In this way, the salad days of their marriage were filled with love, to the extent that love means letting your lover understand themselves by way of misunderstanding you.

As for the true depth of their union, Daniel's doubting machinery remained idle for the better part of three years. Sure, he would privately note how often his wife's face had the remote, forgetful expression of someone who is saying one thing and thinking two or three other things. And, more duskily, he was aware of her whispered requests, during too many of their lovemaking sessions, for him to "finish." But he mostly ignored these signposts until finally, sometime during their fourth year together, he developed a close friendship with a female editor at the paper he wrote for. It remained just that — a friendship — but the intimacy of the thing (the exchanged confidences and confessions, the shared griefs and dreams, and, for that matter, the plain old expression of wonder at the myriad details of which their days were composed) threw into relief for Daniel the absence of any emotional intimacy between him and his wife. No matter how hard he fought to ignore it, his marriage had been harmed by these daily, sometimes hourly, conversations with his editor friend, and it left him susceptible not only to a desire for another woman (this, despite the fact that he did not find the editor particularly attractive) but also to making clear-eyed and cold judgments about his wife. He even went so far as to share his doubts about her with his mother ("Thank God your father is dead" was his mother's first response). Soon his wife's social sophistication began to look to him like a lack of self-knowledge, and he came to view her persona as exactly that: a persona. No wonder she worked in broadcast journalism, he found himself concluding. Since childhood she had had a lifelong love affair with the news, and now she covered it; but she did not *feel* it. She had no commitment to *life.*

Yet she did have a preoccupation with *creating* life. Increasingly, his wife was besieged by nightmares of herself as aged and childless. "Childless and sixty is not in the plan," she told him, and naturally her goal became his — a problem to solve. What a problem it turned out to be: two years of ovulation predictor kits, sperm tests, hormone tests, postcoital tests (he tried not to view the hostility of her cervical mucus to his sperm as a barometer of latent hostility in their marriage), ultrasounds, laparoscopies, ovarian stimulations, intrauterine inseminations, vaginal progesterone capsules, estrogen patches, semen samples (produced from endless dry wanking to shopworn, doctor-supplied pornography magazines in scores of fluorescent-lit medical clinic bathrooms across Manhattan), injections (into the fatty tissue of her abdomen and inner thigh and, more painfully, deep into the muscle of her buttocks), egg retrievals, in-vitro fertilizations, bed rests, monthly doctor's calls (informing them that they had failed to conceive again), and long, inchoate talks about adoption. Their infertility, which they had shared with no one, not even their own parents, had become for them a secret language, with which they were daily composing an epic. It was a private poem freighted with promise and prostration, enterprise and exhaustion. And it was unfinished when Daniel met Aleksandra.

After nearly five weeks of chastely meeting Daniel for lunch in the city, Aleksandra mentioned that her husband was away on business, and the following afternoon, for the first time, Daniel took the subway out to Queens where she lived. The Roosevelt Avenue station, where he would clandestinely disembark many times in the ensuing months, was its usual riotous self when he exited the train: garishly lit, noisy, crammed. Of all the subway stations in New York City, this one — suffused with the flavor and energy of Latin America and the Indian subcontinent — would become his favorite, because it would lead him to love, and to release.

Aleksandra was waiting for him when he emerged onto the street. Gone was the Versace. Gone were the heels. Gone was everything he had come to associate with her "look." Here instead was a woman in a faded sweater and old jeans, sans accoutrements, sans makeup, ultimately undefended. Daniel felt as if he were being taken suddenly into her intimacy.

She said nothing during their walk to her building. After a brief, awkwardly silent tour of her apartment, they found themselves in the bedroom, where Daniel nervously feigned interest in a black-and-white photograph, perched on a bureau, of several peasant Jews, ancestors from a long-ago Crimean shtetl. He was vaguely aware that Aleksandra was staring at him, but he did not make a move, partly because this was also her husband's bedroom, partly because it had been a long time since he had made love to any woman other than his wife. He was in the grip of some complex emotion composed of caution, craving, and a cowardly instinct to flee.

Aleksandra finally broke the silence. "I want you to see me as I really am."

When he turned and saw the embarrassed expression on her face (even as she tried to look proud) he was instantly moved, and took her in his arms.

"I've never been unfaithful to my husband," she said.

"I know."

Her mouth was parted, and he kissed it. Then, while she stood watching, he undressed her, and then he led her to the bed. Physical relations with his wife were never much more than a sociability or "insemination sex" — in either case an observation of form that too often ended with a pat on the shoulder and a disconcerting expression like "Good job!" So the tenderness of what happened on the bed surprised him. And there was something besides tenderness: a letting go of all those mornings spent in fluorescent-lit clinics, masturbating his sperm into sterile plastic cups.

Aleksandra, who while making love pressed her lips to the delicate skin under his jaw, shifted to one side of the bed when they were done and began to shake her head. She was crying, and Daniel sat up and asked her what was wrong.

"I can't believe —" Her chest shuddered and she let out a snort; she tried to dry her eyes but it was no use. "I can't believe my life has brought me to this!"

She broke out sobbing, and Daniel was left to surmise that she was crying out of sadness for the end of her marriage. He too felt like crying, because he suddenly and viscerally understood the magnitude of the betrayal he had just committed. In spending his sperm on another woman — in his imagination, a *fertile* woman — he had betrayed his wife doubly.

He continued to see Aleksandra through most of that fall and winter, aware that he had to make a choice, not only for the sake of doing right by her and his wife but also in order to salvage a measure of his self-respect, if not his sanity. Carrying on with both of them at the same time was causing him to become oversensitive, often to the smallest of things, such as his cell phone: every time he opened it he was confronted with a deceiver's message log, the names of the two women in his life appearing to repeatedly surmount and bury the other. And yet he could not seem to bring himself to make a decision. Each new time he made love to Aleksandra he told himself that he should leave his wife; but how, he would then ask himself, could he leave her — who almost nightly woke up crying from fear that she would never be able to conceive — for a woman who claimed to want to bear him *ten* children, and in her voluptuousness seemed destined to do so? The plain truth was that he secretly longed to have the decision made for him. On many evenings, in many restaurants, he would stare across a dinner table at his wife with a kind of pleading desperation born of exhaustion — he was tired of his own spectacular vacillation, tired of feeling heartbroken that the woman he had fallen in love with was in an apartment in Queens while he was spending yet another night in Manhattan alone with his wife — and he sometimes imagined that, if he could just offer his wife the right visual cue, she would suddenly put down her fork and ask him for a divorce.

After several months of this, he actually managed to convince himself that he was not in love with Aleksandra, that he could survive being in the world without her and make his marriage work. In a cryptic call, he told her (awfully) that he would not be coming to Queens again. And he changed his cell phone number.

Then came that terrifying, thrilling night when she appeared at a renowned art dealer's dinner that he and his wife attended. An important art opening had occurred that evening in Chelsea, and afterward the entire New York art world, it seemed, descended on a late-night café in the Meatpacking District. He had gone to buy a drink for his wife at the overflowing bar and there stood Aleksandra, whose absorbing red dress and curving frame sparked recollections that countered his resolve never to see her again. They greeted each other warmly if formally, then turned their backs to the bar and surveyed the crowd, in the manner, he could not help thinking, of two strangers at a party, who, after having earlier engaged in an intense and intimate conversation, awkwardly run into each other again and have nothing to say.

"How have you been?" he finally muttered.

"Happy. I've been out of the country. Far away from here."

The implication being that she had been happy to be far away from him.

"Israel?" he asked.

"Yes. In the desert." Directly in front of them was gathered a group of handsome, fashionably attired folks — random representatives of New York's cognoscenti — and she eyed them with traceable amounts of disdain. "Where they could care less about who's hot right now in the art world."

"I'm glad it was good for you."

"Life gets boiled down to the essentials in those villages. They live each day as if it might be their last."

"Still with your husband?"

"You have no right to ask me that."

From her vitriolic tone he guessed she was still living with her husband. He was about to apologize to her, for the question, for everything, when his wife appeared in front of them.

"Where's my martini?" his wife said to him as her eyes fell on Aleksandra with curiosity, derision, alarm.

He awkwardly introduced the two of them to each other, and Aleksandra was surprisingly gracious before excusing herself and leaving him and his wife to face each other.

"I'll get your drink," he offered.

"How tacky, Daniel."

"What?"

"That dress."

Was it fate that placed the restaurant's only two unoccupied dinner seats directly across from Aleksandra, at a long table lined with artists and dealers and their partners? Daniel quickly moved to claim the chairs, trying to ignore the look of displeasure on his wife's face as they sat down. Right away, he noticed the ceremonious stiffness at the table, a sense that each person was aware of participating in a performance, of being watched, of judgment right around the corner (in such an environment his wife normally thrived, but she was uncharacteristically quiet). Aleksandra seemed blessedly free from all this. And that freedom paradoxically drew all the table's attention toward her. Daniel was impressed by how powerful and self-assured she appeared as she ate and carried on a conversation with a middle-aged dealer from Cologne whose eyes kept falling to her breasts. Her voice, as she responded to one of the man's ir-

reverent questions about the Israeli occupa-
tion of the West Bank, boomed with authority and aplomb, and her Romanesque face,
fleshy, substantial, gorgeous, accorded her a
kind of gravitas. Finishing the last of her
prime rib, she entertained the table with
tales of her sojourns into the far-flung
regions of the Negev. But her stories were
more than mere entertainment, felt Daniel:
they were an implicit if unintentional challenge. The time she had spent photographing in Israel and the Palestinian Territories
had given her not only a surpassing sense of
the difficulties of social justice amid the
bloodshed and terror of long-standing tribal
warfare but also a greater weight in the areas
of human existence that mattered most —
the body, the soul, the expression of self.
And when she finished speaking, the rest of
the people at the table, Daniel included,
were left to silently contemplate the significance of their New York City striving.
Slowly, awkwardly, people reached for their
drinks and by degrees resumed talking.
Daniel, however, did not join in conversation or reach for his drink because he was
already intoxicated with the feeling of falling. In the improbable setting of a hollow
art world dinner, he was astonished to find
that he was back in love with this earthy

Russian Jewess.

His wife, who had been sitting quietly to his right all the while, had apparently noticed.

"Who is she, Daniel?" his wife asked, rather audibly, as she set down her drink. "You've been staring at her all night." She turned directly to Aleksandra, who had fallen back into conversation with the German art dealer. "Who are you?"

Their verbal exchange thus interrupted, Aleksandra and the dealer regarded her with blank, uncomprehending expressions.

"Who are you?" his wife repeated.

"What?" said Aleksandra.

One by one, each person seated around the table turned their attention to Aleksandra and his wife. His wife, for her part, was never one to deny an audience a good show.

"Who is this woman?" she declared loudly to all of them.

For what seemed to be minutes, no one replied. And then Aleksandra spoke up and proved that, in her, Daniel's wife had met her match.

"Who do you *think* I am?" she said, her eyes fixed coldly on his wife's.

His wife looked at him then, for help, for guidance, but he could offer her none. Murmurs had erupted around the table, and the German dealer, his curiosity kindled, sat up in his chair and peered out at the two women through a pink face positively aglow with excitement.

Daniel's wife stood up.

"Are you fucking this woman, Daniel?"

Daniel looked across the table. Aleksandra, who in confronting his wife only a moment ago had seemed every bit the warrior, now cast her eyes down at her lap, overtaken by shame, or self-reproach, or at the very least embarrassment at his wife's indecorous question. He could see her chest moving in and out rapidly as she breathed.

"Her name is Aleksandra," he said finally. There was a spoon on the table — he took it between his thumb and forefinger, briefly lifted it, then placed it back down beside his folded napkin. "And I am in love with her."

The effect this revelation had on his personal affairs was chastening and swift. He and Aleksandra filed for divorces right away and were married the following February by an old schoolmate from his Columbia days who had since become a rabbi at a progressive temple in Brooklyn. The ceremony took place in the living room of the modest first-floor apartment he and Aleksandra found on Greenwich Street in the

70

Village, and was attended only by his mother, Aleksandra's parents, and a spirited coterie of friends who had stayed loyal to them through their respective and at times acrimonious divorce proceedings. Daniel's mother, who was, if not exactly delighted that he was on his second marriage, at least relieved he was marrying a Jew, wore a stark navy blue dress and bold makeup and cried only when the rabbi acknowledged Daniel's father, dead now nearly a decade. As she wept she clutched a pendant housing the enormous emerald-cut diamond she had somewhat irreligiously paid a company to fabricate out of Daniel's father's ashes. Her behavior made public an aspect of marriage that had, in fact, been gnawing at Daniel's conscience in the days leading up to the wedding: marriage brought its participants into a direct relation with death, since, of the many promises people made, the most crucial was the promise to be together until the end. Daniel had broken this promise with his first wife and had been haunted by an image of her dying without him. What he could not foresee was that, on this most crucial promise, he would make good with the woman now standing across from him in an ivory dress.

"I advise you," the rabbi told Aleksandra

and him as the wedding began, "to ask yourselves what you want from each other, and to carry that question and its many possible answers inside you during the ceremony and each day of your future life together." What did Daniel want from Aleksandra? He wanted wilderness. He wanted sanctuary. He wanted Aleksandra and himself to inhabit a poetical province that contained both.

"Let it be a given that marriage is connected to the sacred," the rabbi proceeded, in an oddly rationalistic manner, "by the very fact that husbands and wives, as the co-creators of children's souls, necessarily enter into a partnership with God. Allow me, if you will, to quote a Christian: 'Love is humble and therefore rejoices that there is a power higher than it — if only for the reason that it has some one to thank.' That was Kierkegaard . . ." Amid all this reasoning, Daniel suddenly found himself in the same boat as his mother: he *missed* his father, a deeply religious man who when it came to God had never taken reason seriously, and who had once claimed, apropos of Daniel's religious skepticism (founded at the time on an unseasoned and *religious* dedication to philosophy), that if we knew with certainty God did or did not exist, we would have no use for faith. As Daniel stood staring into the face of a woman in whom he was now putting all of his faith, a woman he could not, in all honesty, really claim to know yet, he wondered if we can ever truly know anyone, and realized that his father had been on to something: perhaps unknowingness — dicey, formidable, common as air — was the thing to strive for.

To all who were present, the ceremony felt poignant and too brief. Daniel and Aleksandra were married in the waning light that escaped into the tiny golden living room, and they celebrated until well past two in the morning, when Daniel scrambled eggs for the remaining guests. Neither he nor Aleksandra could remember going to bed. But they each awoke early the next day after fitful sleep, and it was only then that Daniel realized they had indeed entered into a partnership with God, but not the kind the rabbi had described. By leaving their spouses to be with each other, they had begun a grievous engagement with guilt, the lost sleep of God in all of us.

In their first months of married life together, he and Aleksandra attempted to allay their guilt with justifications for the divorces. Daniel's was a determination to have a child with Aleksandra as soon as possible — at the very least, he thought, a child would represent a tangible good to have come out of the whole debacle. To judge by her insistence on frequent couplings during the middle of her cycle, and by her dogged early morning employment of an ovulation predictor stick, Aleksandra had arrived at a similar solution. They nervously traded a standing joke derived from the claims she had once made to him — "Ten kids," Daniel kept saying each time they made love, holding up all his fingers and smiling — but their desperation gave the lie to their attempts at humor. It was as if they each viewed their ability to procreate as the sole index of their marriage's worth.

Still, some secret part of Daniel actually feared success, feared that were he and Aleksandra to have a child, the baby would be a daily reminder of what he had been unable to accomplish with his first wife. The resulting prickings of conscience would, he worried, destroy whatever chance he and Aleksandra had of building a healthy and happy life together.

As it turned out, all their procreative efforts were futile. For reasons that an entire army of fertility experts could not discover, he and Aleksandra simply could not conceive. Nothing would seem to have indicated that they had a problem, except the incontrovertible fact of a negative blood test every month.

"It's God," Aleksandra said to him one morning in a cab. They had just come from the doctor and another negative test.

"What?"

"He's punishing us."

"Give me a break."

"You know it's true, Daniel."

She shifted slightly on the vinyl seat so that her body faced away from him.

"There's only the universe," he declared to her back. "And it's godless."

Was he being cruel? He supposed he was. But he could not stand the thought of heavenly judgment heaped on their self-recrimination.

Aleksandra was gazing out her window at Ninth Avenue's clayey apartment buildings. She touched her finger to the glass. "Then it's the universe," she said in a near whisper, "exacting its toll from us for what we did."

"That's it!" he yelled, and then kicked, with too much force, the metal base of the divider that separated them from the front seat. The driver, a young, weary-looking Haitian, favored Daniel in the mirror with his eyes, and their very somnolence seemed like a form of reproof. Daniel felt himself coloring. Something sick and hot swelled painfully in his chest. He rolled down the window on his side and was filled with embarrassment at his frustration, which prevented him from apologizing to her or the driver for his outburst. What ensued was a tirade into which Aleksandra poured all of her own submerged anger and disappointment, until Daniel abruptly abandoned the cab on a sullied street corner somewhere on the fringes of Hell's Kitchen and marched away, his mind bursting with all the unsounded arguments of the dumb and defeated.

It was the first in a long line of fights that proved to him the irreconcilability of guilt and love, and made him realize that in marrying Aleksandra he had really married two people: her and himself. He was staring into the mirror that real marriage — one containing intimacy — held up to him, and it reflected back his bare, unpretty self. He hated what he saw, but he did not have the strength to forgive himself or, for that matter, to change. It was easier simply to be angry. And to retreat. To become thoughtful, caring, but emotionally distant — a manner that was familiar to him, since he had employed it during the entirety of his first marriage. Aleksandra labored to love him for a good couple of years, despite what he had put between them, despite what was hurting in her. Only later, and certainly after her death, did he realize just how many times she had tried — with a reaching for his hand, or a whispered affection, or merely a look — to smooth over the fissures that separated him from her. In time, she simply gave up, and then adopted his strategy. And so eventually came her retort, in their living room only days before her death, that Daniel may have loved her, but in a disinterested manner that made him her father, not her lover.

That steely assertion was a first, but Daniel knew that it did not mark the end of their marriage. No, looking back during the days following Aleksandra's death, he realized that the end had come four months earlier, when she had accompanied him, at his urging, to a preview of what would become the artist Benjamin Wind's last showing. It was the show, Daniel understood, that had robbed him finally of Aleksandra. It was art that had performed the dark magic of ending his marriage.

WHAT EFFECT CAN ART
REALLY HAVE?

As her son stands there holding up the ketubah, Frau Pick stares at it with an amusement indistinguishable from despair. The brilliance of his creation is not lost on her — it seems as good as her favorite medieval illuminated manuscripts at the Kunsthistorisches Museum — but the source of her amusement, and of her despair, comes from her recognition that the ketubah's surface is only a pretty film covering a trembling depth in whose darknesses lies submerged her own unhappiness, not touched in twenty years. The beauty of what her son has made is remarkable, yet she is barred from the consolations of its art by a renewed longing it has loosened in her. A longing not for her husband, but for the man from whom she allowed her husband to take her.

Emil was the man's name, and after she finally abandoned herself to him in her nineteenth summer, he followed her to

Vienna from Kopyczyńce, the Galician town where both of their families had lived for generations. Descended from a lineage of red-bearded rabbis, Emil, who fancied himself a poet, was known for a certain indelicacy of manner, for his impolitic remarks, and for his pompous dress — qualities that immediately endeared him to Vienna's café society. She had left her village and her father to escape their Talmudic religious strictures and cultural provincialism, and to go on social outings with Emil during those first brisk autumn months in Vienna was to float from one high moment to the next, from salon reading to cabaret, from wine tavern to opera house, from painter's studio to architectural unveiling. Soon, though, she came to realize that much of this Viennese world was padded by people whose aspirations were seldom connected to actual undertakings, and whose enthrallment to café philosophy made them no less insular and narrow-minded than the most fusty hidebound old rabbi back home. And even if Emil was not one of these indolent café creatures who never realized their dreams (she had begun to suspect he was), there seemed to be no limits on life for him, and she understood that a limitless life would offer her no resting place, no wall

79

to lean against, and, more important, no door to stop him from leaving her.

It was during this time that she met, one evening at Café Central, the man who would become her husband. Emil's late arrival had forced her to take a table unaccompanied, and in a series of savvy gestures that took all of two minutes, her future husband approached and claimed a seat opposite her, identifying himself with a patrician air simply as a Pick (he was later taken aback when she confessed that she had never heard of the Picks of Vienna). His dress — a rich, anachronistic assembly of silk and tweed and leather, his fastidious deportment, and the imperious declarations with which he plugged the holes in their conversation gave her the impression that she was speaking to a Victorian man out of some Dickens novel. He politely excused himself when Emil entered the café ten minutes later, adding that he hoped she would allow him, again and sometime soon, to "bemire her fair table" with his presence "for a more lasting span."

Afterward, she could not get the strange encounter out of her head. The world of which Herr Pick had spoken — interest rates, Austria's wealth, the political situation in the provinces — seemed to be so solidly defined in contrast to the nebulous talk of Emil's friends (about the lyrical high art of Rilke or the pessimistic beauty of Schopenhauer) that it happily had not left her with the sensation of being outshined. Emil's fanciful approach to *everything* frequently removed the possibility of her own life being poetic. But in the light of Herr Pick's garden-variety talk, and under the gaze of his appreciative eyes, she had felt poetic just for being a woman.

That was not all. The mannerly Herr Pick came across as a man with a fate of his own; his life appeared to be governed. And she was starting to see that a life with Emil would be plagued by anxieties of the material and financial sort, and that because he rarely left the republic of his own soul, the worrying would fall to her alone. So she withdrew from her heart and from her body — both of which still very much belonged to Emil — and she shed Emil, along with her Galician accent, for an extended engagement with Herr Pick and the outward finish of life that he offered.

There was a price to be paid. She quickly learned that the Pick men, going back four generations at least, had been opinion and mood moguls all, and her new husband was no exception. By necessity she grew wary of her own opinions and shy in asking for affection, and she redressed her marriage's lack of intimacy by dedicating herself to the Pick villa (which Herr Pick had inherited from his father) and, later, to the education and civilization of their son, Josef. When her soul sometimes ached, she attempted to quiet it with tranquillity and stoic self-possession — two precepts of her new life. In this manner she made her peace, yet one subject to bouts of black despair. She came to believe that life mostly denies us what we want, occasionally granting us small rewards of a spiritual nature, rewards toward which we cannot strive. And so her secret life, which she did not share with her husband or son, was composed of a game of waiting — with silent alertness to the attainment of nothing. Thus was another vital village woman lost to the fastnesses of marriage in the metropolis.

As for Emil, she came to view her youthful longing for him as merely a young woman's obligation to her sex — the ritual "first love" that must be gotten past on the road to maturity.

Then, unaccountably in her fortieth year, she was afflicted with remembrances of him. What she remembered was not the restive, yearning timbre of his voice, or the benignly shaggy reasoning of his artistic credos, or even the specific endearments he lavished on her. It was his physicality. The woolen smell emanating from his chest when he embraced her. The way that, whenever he was angry with her, he would pull his hand through his thick hair so that its sharp upended tufts would put a point on his argument. Or, after every time she had given up her womanly warmth to him, his mildly astonished eyes. She remembered how he had ignited her whenever she was in his proximity. And painfully it occurred to her that such candescence must be the purpose of any person's life. Why else would she be *this* unhappy?

Still, what could she do about these pangs of old love? Experience had proven that an attempt to discuss these feelings — any feelings — with her husband would avail her nothing. In her more irrational moments she contemplated trying to find Emil after all these years. But the inertia of having for so long neglected what she most needed felt insurmountable. And so, since she found that she could not suppress these former urges, she decided that it was better to bear this final phosphorescence of her first love, in a kind of quiet daily keening, until in time it was tamed.

That was a year ago.

And now here she is in her father's flat staring at her son's ketubah, which, though painted with good intention, makes a mockery of all of her self-sacrifice. Its futile attempt at a restoration of her and her husband's love reveals their marriage for the false old shabby thing that it is. Its theme of union, its iconic promptings of passion, feel like an injunction on her to acknowledge the truth of their abiding separateness for the last twenty years, and the truth of her truncated love — the only real love she has ever felt — for Emil. Its highlighting of particular aspects of her and her husband's personalities — her passion for art, literature, and nature; the narrowness of his interests (which do not include her) — only throws into relief the fact that she has, in staying married to Herr Pick, wasted the vigor of her bloom. Her husband does not care to *know* her.

So the heraldic beauty of Josef's marriage contract is sadly nullified in her eyes. What is any marriage but a carcass if it has no heart? And what can she do now but smile weakly at this ketubah, with the self-reproach of a mother who knows she is being selfish in the face of her son's grand achievement, with the exasperation of a wife whose patience has been overtaxed by years of living in barren proximity to a remote man, with the *incredulousness,* finally, of a woman who has not gotten half of what she expected marriage would give her?

Herr Pick, standing to her right, is also staring at the ketubah with a kind of incredulity. It is not simply the artwork's rank Jewishness that nettles him so, nor that its creation constitutes an act of violence against the Pick family — one giant leap backward, toward the shtetl, that erases nearly two hundred years of striving. Nor is it chiefly the alarming brusqueness with which his son seems to have been co-opted by his father-in-law. No, this marriage contract represents a threat that is *personal.* Its iconography of banks and cafés, of money and the old Habsburg Empire, leaves him with the distinct impression that he is looking at a compendious, eerily accurate vision of himself — a vision so troubling in its implications that it seems to jeopardize the central truth of his existence.

Seeing his many lifelong obsessions corralled onto a single page — seeing his *convictions* made manifest — has driven an unfamiliar doubt into his marrow. His vulnerability to such doubt surprises him, because although his inward longing for the past has been the source of too many halting arguments with his republican cronies at Café Central, although it regularly sends him fleeing to the solace of his private library, where he glumly takes his ancient royal uniform down from the wall (often donning the coruscating brass helmet like an old fool!), his belief in the old values — longevity, security, stability — has remained stubbornly unswerving. Until this very moment, he has always believed that, considering everything Austria has so recently lost, his is a defensible, even virtuous, form of patriotism whereby one pines for a place in decline, when nothing, neither a nation's nerve nor future, is certain.

However, as portrayed by this, this . . . *thing* his son has painted, the old values he is so attached to seem — well, hollow. One particular image — minuscule, faint, nearly concealed by the lower left corner's distended veil of foliage — makes him feel downright foolish. It shows him standing before a gilt-framed painting of Emperor Franz Josef, which he inherited from his father and which has hung in the same place in his library (his *father's* old library) since he was a boy. There is nothing so unusual about him studying the old portrait: to pause to admire it is his habit, and Josef must have seen him doing so on countless evenings. But there is something uncanny about his son's rendering of it, a certain gleaming quality, which suggests that the gilt frame houses a mirror instead of a painting, a mirror that offers not his own reflection but an image of the long-dead emperor. Is his son implying that he, Herr Pick, fancies himself an emperor? What else could possibly be the meaning of this? Yes, he is certain that his son is mocking him. Yet all at once he is surprised to find himself thinking that the boy is *right.* What am I really, he muses, but publicly an unreconstructed monarchist, wasting the free moments of my life at the café longing for the good old days of Austria? And who am I in my own house but an intolerable paterfamilias given to haranguing my poor family at the dinner table with hoary jokes and the latest disappointing news of the republic? Why, he has to ask himself, do I keep a portrait of Franz Josef on my wall when in every lobby, lavatory, and lounge in Vienna (and even in my *own bank*) the old portraits of the emperor have been replaced by mirrors?

At this thought he becomes aware of just how insightful, how *sharp* this rendering of the emperor in the mirror reveals his son to be. The boy sees what he himself has not been able to: that he has been clinging to ideals and places, many of which are unstable or no longer exist, as a means of avoiding certain truths — truths such as his own mortality. He recalls an exchange he had with his son when first entering the Leopoldstadt this morning. They had just crossed the Danube Canal, and he was lagging behind his wife and son, contemplating a problem the bank was having with one of its larger clients, when he heard Josef say, "Papa?"

"Hmm," he responded absentmindedly.

"Where will we go next?"

Caught clinging to some high branch of his ramifying thoughts, he stared uncomprehendingly down at the boy's pale round face, until finally his wife offered: "Josef is asking where Grandfather's flat is."

"Yes," he said, clearing his throat. "Of course." He glanced up the boulevard then, and commenced to provide his son with characteristically exact instructions, all in the perfunctory bored manner of a provincial schoolteacher announcing the day's lesson plan: "We will walk straight ahead for two and a half long blocks. At Karmeliterplatz we will turn left, where, after taking twenty steps at most, we will turn sharply to the right, circumnavigating the northern portion of the Carmelite church. Then we will turn left and, finally, left again."

He remembers that the boy considered this for several seconds.

"And *then* what, Papa?"

And then what?

The question did not make sense to him at the time. "And then we are there," he said simply. But now, confronted with the brutal wisdom of this marriage contract, he is no longer certain that his son was inquiring about street directions. Perhaps the boy was seeking instructions of a much weightier kind, answers to questions for which there are no easy answers: What does one *do* with a life? Which path should one take? How might one live each moment? What will happen to us? To a man like himself, born of the old empire, a man whose bearing was hierarchically fashioned from a world where each citizen knew precisely what they would be doing each minute, each day, each year of their lives — to a man who deposits a not insignificant portion of his salary into a burial pension so that his grave will be regularly manicured and maintained in perpetuity — such questions are particularly threatening.

And then what? he thinks to himself, repeating the question rhetorically in his mind, and as he does so, his very breath is robbed by the image of a day in the future, perhaps a precious warm winter day just like this one, filled with people on the street and all their crazy longings — a day that will be empty of him.

And then what? He does not know.

Few men get through life without discovering that their certainties are founded on shifting sand. The experience, when it comes, usually sends them running for help, preferably to women. So Herr Pick, disarmed and frightened as he stares at his son's ketubah, suddenly directs his gaze to the imagery of his wife. Only then, as he takes in the passions of her life as captured by his son's delicate hand (the bright harmony of her figure out on a lone nature stroll and becoming one with the Schönbrunn's sylvan spaces; or her cheerful, lamp-tempered face as she takes tea at the museum; or her ineffaceably illumined eyes admiring the altar of St. Stephen's Cathedral), does he feel the greatest impact of this artwork's truth: he shares this page with Frau Pick, as indeed he has shared a house and child with her, but he has not shared *life* with her. The beautiful, distant woman represented in this marriage contract is a stranger to him, and it is his own fault. By perennially longing for what was, he has missed what *is.*

With no one to turn to for comfort, he is thrown back on himself to face this revelation alone, and he does so with the only weapon he has left: rage. Rage because, in this marriage contract, his son's prodigious wisdom — visibly superior to his own — has found its expression. Rage because in one fell swoop the child has arrogated to himself the position of top man in the household, stripping him — the boy's own father! — of his authority, of his very manhood. Rage because he has never felt so humiliated, so diminished. He has marched through fifty-odd years of living without meeting a single man who is, in his esteem, greater than himself. The heads of his bank, the acclaimed politicians and critics and architects of Vienna, the wit-parading habitués of Café Central — none of them has ever struck him as being in possession of abilities that he could not himself marshal. And a lifetime of social intercourse with such men had him convinced that a truly exceptional human being did not exist in Vienna, or in the rest of Europe, for that matter. Rage because for the first time in his life he feels . . . What *does* he feel?

He feels confused.

He feels — jealous.

His son will go on to achieve greater significance than he, this much is clear. And the boy will do it, most likely, by trafficking in the Jewish realm he so detests. All he can do now is stare at the ketubah in the manner of a person gazing at a measureless ocean, betranced, dazed, and dumb, his mouth falling open as if to engulf its grace.

Rage because he can forgive his son anything, except greatness.

If there is any person in the room who deserves to feel jealous, it is Pommeranz. His grandson has, in his first attempt, painted the finest ketubah that he has ever laid eyes on. Granted, the thing is rough in certain areas. The traditional halachic text, for one, is glaringly absent. No transparent wash of tea or diluted earth-tone color was laid down prior to its inking, thus depriving the ketubah of a traditional softening, or "aging," effect. And the parchment's porous surface has been the receptacle of, variously, three blotted spills, several greenish spatterings, and numerous false starts of line — errors that betray an amateur's handling of ink. But given his grandson's lack of formal artistic training and the obvious lacuna in his religious education — given his raising in a household where Jewish culture clearly has no place — such flaws are forgivable. Given the wholesale beauty of the ketubah, they are downright irrelevant.

The fact of the matter is, Pommeranz is stunned by how lithely this marriage contract is illuminated, and he spends several moments simply charting the unusual geography of its pictorial terrain. The entire contract appears to hang from the talons of a double-headed eagle, that celebrated symbol of the republic, as if his daughter's marriage to Herr Pick is dying in the clutches of the Austrian state — a particularly bold move, in his opinion, whose subtle critique of Jewish assimilation he cannot help but admire. And he is pleased to find that his grandson was paying attention to his lesson on the undeniable adhesion of money to all matters of marriage: the ketubah's imperceptible variegation of hue and its intricate latticelike tracery resemble nothing so much as a *bank note.* A pair of entwined lovers, clearly meant to evoke his daughter and son-in-law, are rendered not just once but some twenty-odd times, in slightly varied attitudes, beginning at the base of the ketubah and moving upward in sequence around two baroque pilasters, ascending according to some ripe musical rhythm. And arabesqued across the rest of the parchment is a riotous farrago of fleurs-de-lis, rosettes, garlands, plumages, frogs, various chinoiseries, military epaulets, beaded chaplets, books, Greek statues, mountains, rifles, and an incredibly accurate likeness of the Pick villa, whose grandiosity Pommeranz once viewed from the outside, with a fair amount of amazement, on a clandestine sojourn he undertook to the district of Hietzing in order to see where his daughter was living. This mad schematic that young Josef has crafted of Herr and Frau Pick's personalities settles in Pommeranz's mind like a hallucination of some leafy and remote Ottoman palace — chaotic, decadent, fraught with danger, and on the decline — into which his daughter and son-in-law have checked all of their personal belongings. My God, though, he thinks, how beautiful the thing is! Surely its images and motifs cannot have been *put* into place; they must have drifted into the composition on some light breeze, there to be caught, alive and vibrating, in the lacy delicacy of a spider's web. And therein lies the quality that distinguishes this ketubah from any Pommeranz has either himself painted or seen — the quality he has failed to capture, even once, in the more than two hundred ketubot he has made, the quality that cannot be taught someone, the quality he *should* be jealous of, the quality that gives him no choice but to submit to the boy's genius: the ketubah breathes with *life.*

Not a *description* of life — Pommeranz has illuminated plenty of marriage contracts that describe a style of living, of doing, and even of feeling. But his grandson's ketubah offers a style of *being.* And that style is love. Earlier, he belligerently asked his grandson what he knew of life. Well, here is the boy's answer. Here, in this illumination, he has unriddled life. Pommeranz cannot pin it down to any one image — the boy seems to have gone past the vernacular of marriage contracts. He has kidnapped the form. The thing has muscle. It has blood and fat. The boy tapped into something dangerous, vital. He traveled backward into his parents' love — God knows that only a burning carriage can take you to such a place! — and the ketubah plainly shows that he paid some kind of price. The savageness of its making, thinks Pommeranz, is evidence enough that the boy knows damn well his parents are unhappily married. But the boy proceeded anyway, with an open heart, and according to a motivation that was outside of himself — this is surely how great art gets made! Chances are the boy is some variety of mystic. Great-grandfather Moritz Leide Hersch, Kopyczyńce's only claim on rabbinical posterity, was said to be one. Perhaps the boy's freshly made ketubah, still wet but damply divine, arrays its elaborate offering of love not only for the benefit of this miserable pair but also the whole unhappy world. Its beauty, by touching this single marriage, reaches out to touch the hundred sadnesses in every marriage! As long as the boy doesn't give up on *this* marriage, he thinks, then there is hope for all of them!

Why then, Pommeranz is forced to ask himself, have his own ketubot fallen inexorably short? Does not the boy's ketubah make it obvious? Because he has been painting without this hope — without faith in love! Of course he *talks* about love and its centrality to marriage and life, but the truth is, his own acquaintance with love failed to advance many years ago, long before the death of his daughter's mother, in fact. Sometimes he even questions if he loves God Himself. The God of a world such as this is not so easy to love. Ah, but this is most certainly his own failing. So what does all this make him, the mighty old Pommer-anz?

He is nothing but the grand pedant of marriage contracts.

Thus, confronted with the real article, he breaks the room's silence with the words that only a pedant faced with a student genius can utter.

"Ah," he says. "Another ketubah."

And his words, combined with his daughter and son-in-law's *lack* of words, plant a disappointed and sorrowful expression on the boy's face as he is pulled by Herr Pick out of the room.

WHAT IS NOT SAID WILL BE SUFFERED

He was sorry about everything, except the fucking.

This was what Daniel longed to say to Aleksandra, at her funeral, as he sat sweltering in the tiny Queens temple, his gaze fixed on her casket. Somewhere a cantor was delivering an account of the Psalms, and the droning lament, acting in harmony with the complaint of an air conditioner, seemed to consecrate the veil of coitus that trembled before his eyes. Aleksandra was growing paler to him by the hour, but their fucking would not fade. Wedged between her weeping father and his own mother, he had the panicky urge to cry out to her. He nearly did bellow at the casket — the muscles in his calves tensed, ready to launch him to his feet — but in the end he was prevented from doing so by memories of their early unrestrained couplings, which washed over him afresh in successive waves, until by degrees he grew faint and he found it necessary to grip the sticky lip of the pew with both hands. Still, he had the sensation of being swept off by the unvanquishable thought that she, who had inhabited the ritually cleansed remains resting mere steps from where he sat, had chosen for a brief span to merge her flesh, and her few ticks of time, with his. As his vision penetrated backward through those initial years of their marriage, when they had so eagerly sought pregnancy and permanence, he simply could not believe that the body in that plain pine box had once hungered and hungered and hungered for him. All that blessed fucking! It had been their little toying with eternity.

Yet even as the run of his thoughts continued along these lines, so too did his mind begin to flash with memories of the two of them viewing Benjamin Wind's final show, until the frail levee separating these parallel mental streams gave way, and the one line of thinking bled into the other, and he could no longer distinguish between coming together with her on a bed and intersecting with her in the gallery, between the way she looked at him whenever they made love and the way their eyes met — calamitously — over Benjamin Wind's last sculptures. What he needed to know, more than anything else, was whether Benjamin Wind had been her lover by then. Had she already let Wind fuck her?

The exhibition was Wind's first in America in nearly three years, and Daniel had been invited to a private preopening survey by Wind's New York dealer, Patrick Carrigan. Unprecedentedly, Daniel knew nothing about the new artworks, and it lent an air of discovery and anticipation to the prospect of seeing the show. He wanted to share the experience with Aleksandra, who had always taken a curious if distant interest in the work of the artist on whom he had most staked his reputation. Relying on some fuzzy emotional calculus, Daniel hoped that their joint viewing of this major event might gently bandage the lacerations in their marriage, might provide a salve to some of their wounds.

But were his motivations for asking her to accompany him more complicated than he cared to admit to himself? Were they not in some way also linked to the fact that over the previous two years Benjamin Wind had contrived to postpone no less than six studio visits Daniel had scheduled with him? While Wind was a chronic canceler with pretty much everyone else (the head curator from the Museum of Modern Art or the kid delivering Chinese takeout), he had never, since Daniel had critically taken a shine to his work and helped elevate him to the artist-elect, given *Daniel* the runaround — until now. At length Daniel was made to feel he was hectoring Wind with his phone calls, and he gave up trying to see the new work. If there *was* any new work. As the date of the show approached, Daniel began to suspect there was not, or, if there was, that Wind was not happy with it. And this surmise — that all was not right with Wind, that something had gone wrong with his artwork — fluttered at the back of Daniel's mind when he invited Aleksandra to the private viewing at Carrigan Gallery. In a darker and unprettier part of himself, Daniel sensed that he actually wanted something to be wrong with the work — something *terribly* wrong.

Later he would concede that this negative desire of his, uncharacteristic in taking Benjamin Wind as its object, was born of an emergent fear of impotence. He had long been latently concerned about the perceived impotency of his profession, and he increasingly harbored a fear that Aleksandra would one day find the shattering impact of recognition in another artist. Then there was the impotency of their marriage: he had not made her pregnant and had for too long withheld any authentic offering to her of affection. Her respect for him seemed to be deteriorating as fast as the flimsy conjugal bridge they had erected over the widening chasm between them. In truth, however unconsciously, he wanted Aleksandra to come with him to the gallery for that most primal of reasons: because another man's failure would be his victory. What a relief it would be to write a *negative* review of Benjamin Wind's work. What a relief it would be to cement his superiority, in Aleksandra's eyes, over this extraordinary artist.

They were expected at the gallery at three o'clock. It was a crisp afternoon; the month of April still seemed to be cleaving to winter. Having only the day before returned home from Tel Aviv, Aleksandra was still exhausted and in no mood for the subway, so they bundled into a cab for the long ride uptown. Patrick Carrigan was one of several eminent American art dealers who in the early nineties had chosen to set up shop among Madison Avenue's pricey boutiques, and who, when the great Chelsea land grab occurred a little later (in which nearly all of New York's galleries fled SoHo for Chelsea's cheaper, larger digs), had decided to stay put. Daniel never minded the inconvenience of trekking all the way uptown to catch exhibitions at Carrigan because he respected the artists the man represented, and he tended to make good use of the subway rides, but the terrible silence that settled on the vinyl backseat of the cab where he and Aleksandra rigidly sat was unbearable. They had not made love the night before. A new development. Despite the emotional and physical distance that had opened up between them in the last few years, they had habitually made love directly after each of her homecomings from lengthy photography trips abroad. Granted, it had become a silent, measured business. To lie in bed together after many days apart was less to engage in passion than it was simply to listen to the other's breathing — the synchronizing of two old watches. But at least they were *familiar* watches. Last night, though, she had seemed to him a whole new brand, a foreign make he did not recognize. And through the bulk of his ensuing sleepless night Daniel had struggled to convince himself that she had been too tired — truly — to rouse her body to even a brief reacquaintance with his. Given her condition, it frankly surprised him that she was coming to the gallery at all. (Only later, in thinking back over the order of these events — for he was to think hard about them for the next twelve months — would he suspect that she had actually flown home from Israel *just* to see the exhibition.) And now this awful silence on their way to see Benjamin Wind's mystery work: Daniel was a man whose life was pledged to gleaning the truth in things, and he had to draw on all his powers of dissimulation not to see it — the deathlike quiet of the cab — as being inauspicious.

When they finally exited onto Madison Avenue, he caught her standing at the curb with her eyes solemnly fixed on him, and it made him pause. She looked away immediately, but not before her face offered up an expression so odd that he questioned for a moment whether it had actually occurred. No, he was sure of what he had seen: Aleksandra had given him a bright — fake — smile.

"You all right?" he asked.

There was a hesitation. "I'm fine," she granted a bit reluctantly, as if she were forty other more significant things too. And then she added, with what to Daniel's ear was a patent trace of falseness in her tone, "How about you?"

"How about me?" he echoed. "Fine — I'm fine." He grinned at her from a face that must have appeared strained, since he could feel his cheeks stretching.

"Looks like we are both fine then," she said.

"I guess so," he said cheerily. By now he had identified what was bothering him about her voice. Her words were falling heavily, were burdened with more of her Russian accent. It was what she did whenever she was uncomfortable.

She took a step backward. "Well — should we go in?"

They approached the entrance but were still out on the sidewalk when, through the extravagant curve of the "C" etched into Carrigan Gallery's glass doors, he was afforded his first glimpse of the show. He could not see much — a transverse interior wall, with Benjamin Wind's name neatly floating on it, obstructed most of his view — but what he *could* make out caused the sides of his throat to close up. It was merely part of a sculpture, an outstretched hand, or rather *two* hands engaged in a clasp, their fingers tightly intertwined, too hauntingly real, and it was enough to make painfully clear to Daniel that every one of his intuitions about Wind's new work had been wrong. If he had not been so well acquainted with Wind's materials (plaster, beeswax, resin, pigment, paint, hair), with his method of employing both contemporary resin technologies and painstaking casting techniques that had been practiced since medieval times, he might have mistaken the two clasped hands for flesh, bone, and blood. It was not simply Wind's knack for holding wax accountable to human emotion. There was something in the sensuousness of the beeswax itself, in the leftover traces of Wind's own hand that it permanently recorded, in the delicate bargain it struck between illusion and isness, that had allowed Wind to capture in the two sculpted hands — like Daniel's favorite figurative painters had always done in their paintings — how ultimately weird and tenuous an enterprise it was to inhabit a body: the extravagant price everyone paid for being mortal. In an instant, Daniel saw all of this and more in those two hands.

And then, when he and Aleksandra had penetrated several steps into the gallery, when he saw that the two hands belonged to the floating (*flying?*) figures of a woman and a man, when he saw that their clasped hands were representative — that Wind had filled all three of the gallery's cavernous

106

chambers with life-size figures paired off and joined by the holding of hands — when he saw that each pair of figures appeared to be *sprayed* in the air as if by some centrifugal force, when he saw how these sculptures of men and women and children seemed to be caught — as they eddied about the room and each other — in various states of ascendance, Daniel understood at once that Wind's show was not only a confirmation, and, really, a summation of developments in his earlier work, but also a monstrous upheaval representing nothing less than his attainment to greatness. How *foolish* he had been to invite Aleksandra. Panicking, he searched his brain for some pretense by which he could usher her back out onto the avenue.

But it was too late. Patrick Carrigan was already upon him in all of his chipper blondness, extending a hand, beaming an expectant smile, and Daniel was forced to exchange pleasantries and shoptalk with the man while watching helplessly as Aleksandra, like some marching automaton at the mercy of the show's magnetic pull, was sucked into the swirl of sculptures until her flesh disappeared into theirs and she was lost to the gallery's interior. "And don't misunderstand me here," Carrigan was saying, "I love Springsteen. You and I have talked about him before, right? Told you I saw him at Max's Kansas City. February 1973? You know I've been loyal to the Boss ever since, but this show, *this* show" — Carrigan made a sweeping gesture with his hand, as if to scoop up all the sculptures in the gallery — "is *better* than the *Rising* album, not that you can easily compare art with music! Anyway. I've said enough. Too much. Go. Enjoy. I let Benjamin know you were coming today. He was glad. He thinks the world of you."

Carrigan stood before him now with his hands in his pockets and his breezy air. He was smiling at Daniel with unqualified radiance. Was he not privy to the fact that Wind had cancelled on Daniel over and over again? Did he know that Daniel had not *seen* Wind for nearly three years? Was Carrigan fucking with him? Or had Wind failed to mention anything about the matter? This last possibility was not out of the question. Benjamin Wind *was* a very private person. At a loss for words, Daniel offered up another handshake, which the man accepted with gusto, and suddenly Daniel's feet were carrying him off in loud echoey pursuit of Aleksandra.

His immediate goal was to discover Aleksandra's reactions to the show. However, before he could even locate her in one of the two rear rooms, his attention was co-opted by the unusual power of the work in the first. Like all truly great artwork, the pieces demanded engagement, and he found himself being pulled, like Aleksandra before him, into the vortex of the swirling sculptures. Soon enough he lost himself completely in the work.

There were roughly forty figures in the first chamber alone. No contemporary deities this time (in past showings, they had been recurrent) — only humans here. Men paired with women, yes, but most of the couples were people who might otherwise never touch each other: old men held hands with other old men, toddlers with toddlers, teenage girls with prepubescent boys. Yet what most arrested Daniel's attention were three unusual aspects of appearance common to all of them. The first was their eyes: every one of them was closed. The second was how the figures were dressed: they wore elemental cotton garments, dyed monochromatic black or red or yellow or gray — garments of such simplicity and similarity as to seem like paradigms of clothing, rude embryonic versions of a uniform. Finally, their skin: each figure possessed the same stygian-hued pallor that was indicative of death, or sickness, or sleeplessness — possibly all three. Digested by the eye all at once, these details, thought Daniel, effected an alternately funereal and uplifting evocation of Matisse's dancers, or of the eerie truthfulness of Goya's severe "black paintings," or of the otherworldly sadness and beauty of every Jesus on the Cross hanging in every church in the world.

This last evocation — of the world's churches — forced Daniel to wonder again about Wind's many studio-visit cancellations. For all of Wind's apparently fierce attachment to privacy regarding this show, there was something so *public* about it. Viewing it was like visiting a great public place, a cathedral, a shopping mall, a train station or airport: the figures (was it their closed eyes?) were emphatically anonymous, people you might briefly glimpse in a crowd, but whose faces you forgot in the next instant. They seemed nameless to Daniel, unidentified survivors washed ashore on a tide of human flotsam.

Or maybe they had *not* survived. Daniel realized he was hesitant to look squarely at them — not just because of their lack of traits, but also because they seemed to be of the dead. Or almost of the dead. Was this

110

the source of the uncomfortable intimacy he felt just by being there in the room? He wondered if in these sculptures he were not figuratively witnessing, fortyfold, that most private of moments: the dissolution of the slender tie that bound each of these souls to their bodies. Yes, increasingly he grew confident that what he was looking at in every one of these clinging figures was the end of a life's tenure, when the reins are handed over to another driver (maybe *the* Driver). And it only made Daniel feel more like a voyeur that during their apparent dying each figure's eyes were closed. It made him feel exposed. With one foot already in the cosmos, the figures seemed to have a higher authority, as if Daniel could not hide anything from them. Here he was, still carting around his messy attachments — to the particularities of his personality, to the world of objects, to the people he loved. He almost felt dirty, as if he ought to purify himself for these dead or dying souls. The show was amazing.

And if it was, as Patrick Carrigan had implied, about 9/11, it was only tangentially so (in the same way, Daniel felt, that Springsteen's sad, sonorous album had been). Even assuming that Benjamin Wind had meant for the show to have such a pointed and singular meaning (and Daniel strongly doubted that he had), he would never have shared that fact with anyone, including his dealer: Carrigan was simply speculating, projecting — all too predictably — a dealer's esteem of topicality onto a show that looked to Daniel's eyes like a lament for the souls of all humans in all times. The Trade Center attacks had, in fact, occurred since Wind's previous American showing, but Daniel knew Wind well enough to understand that he avoided such literalness in his work. Sure, some of his earlier pieces had hinted at specific disgraces of the last two centuries (the genocide of America's indigenous peoples, for example), but such references to real events were always refracted through a prism of timelessness. They were summoned to the universal by their having been shaped into art. It was what lent the shows, this one included, an authentically spiritual footprint.

In the end, though, the cumulative effect of all these reflections was Daniel's abrupt awareness of his own insignificance. He felt affronted by Wind's achievement. The affront seemed at once personal, since Wind had refused — had he not? — to let him see the work, and *im*personal, because the work's greatness was even now pulling it far beyond the small arena of Daniel's private concerns. It already belonged to the world. This cold fact finally forced Daniel out of the chrysalis of his thoughts, and he stood there a few moments blinking and alone among the waxen sculptures, a foundling in a swarm of indifferent and dying strangers. Then quickly, very quickly, he exited the first room and went in search of Aleksandra.

He found her in the third and final chamber. She was kneeling on the concrete floor, her back turned to him, her head bent, keeping vigil beside two tiny sculptural figures that, suspended several feet off the ground, were either ascending or descending. As Daniel drew closer he saw that they were figures of newborn babies. Each infant had extended a delicate hand to the other, producing the effect that the two of them, fettered by their fine fingers, would not go alone to meet their dim or divine fate.

It did not take Daniel more than a moment to understand why Aleksandra had sunk to the floor at the sight of them. Over the last two years, she and he had worked sedulously to curb their habit of gawking breathlessly at every baby they passed on the street. The poignancy of seeing her now prostrate before these inert sculptures caused a congealing in his sinuses. He was grateful her back was turned so she would not see him in such a state, and it made it easier, when after a few seconds he had gathered himself, to reach out and touch her as an offering of reassurance that everything was going to be okay.

But her shoulder recoiled the moment his hand landed on it, and when she flipped around he was struck by the change in her since she had left him stranded at the entrance with Patrick Carrigan. Her face, raw and glaring, ablaze with the room's hard astringent light, had been redrawn by what she had seen: it was prettier, it was cleaner, it was, despite the pain seated in her eyes, all gelid reserve. There was nothing in it for him save coldness. That he would one day be the recipient of such a frosting from her he had long suspected, and he stood there with his eyes fixed on his icy companion, feeling that in a single bound she and he had traveled an enormous distance. And to his surprise, the shock of it all was mitigated by his relief of having finally arrived.

Then another shock hit. It began with a quiver that erupted across her forehead. She returned her gaze to the two newborns, and her face then was a difficult sight to see.

What had seemed all ice pack one moment seemed all melted snow the next. After a time, she looked up at Daniel and opened her arms, bidding him to come to her. And so he sank. Sank down beside her and let her squeeze his chest until something suppressed and locked broke from it, something that years ago in a different gallery had stolen into him at the very first sight of her — something that had never, despite endless threats and padlocks and eviction notices, moved out.

He and Aleksandra finally fell out of their embrace and, exhausted, found themselves sitting side by side and staring at the two sculptures. His head was a vacancy, his skin numb, his mouth dry, and it seemed to him as if they had just come to the end of one of their epic fights, the rare ones that would last all night and into which they would decant every last ounce of energy. Only after some time had passed, he had no idea how much, did he become aware that the fingers of his left hand were firmly interwoven with those of Aleksandra's right. And it struck him suddenly: the spectacle of them tranced there on the floor, holding hands like the paired sculptural figures whirling around them. What confusion, he wondered, would the scene cause a casual gallerygoer if at that very moment she were to stroll innocently into the room and happen on the two of them? Would she notice that they were distinguishable from the art only by their having reached the end of their flight? Would she guess that the thing was finished, their descending done? Or that what had grounded them finally was the gravity of their unredressed wrongs? Would she, moreover, understand that the two of them had momentarily forgotten that what they were looking at was art? Or that the effect of the wax infants was too personal, and that what rose before their eyes instead — what it seemed to them they were examining — was their own painfully intertwined lives?

This last question lingered in Daniel's consciousness even after he and Aleksandra had risen to their feet and begun, slowly, to pick their way through the sculptures toward the exit. They passed a flying motherly figure, at the end of whose outstretched hand flew a girl who could have been a young Aleksandra (or, more threateningly, one of her offspring). They passed pairs of men and women who could have been *them*. They passed *their* children. *Their* infants. The path through the three rooms was a path through a life that might have been, and Daniel felt each new piece as a potential peril.

"Well, what did you think?" asked Patrick Carrigan, bounding out of his office to intercept them at the front. He beamed at them with a face in which the charming and the vulgar handsomely merged, a face remarkable for an inquisitiveness born not of genuine curiosity but of a desire to ensure that all the world felt exactly as he did.

Daniel met Aleksandra's gaze and something passed silently between them — something huge and impenetrable and that bore heavily on the question but was impossible to air here.

Feeling obligated to speak, Daniel began: "I thought" — and then he caught himself. What could he possibly say to the man? That with this show Benjamin Wind had once and for all and in front of his wife bested him? That it had brought Aleksandra and him not only to tears, but likely also to a turning point in their marriage, the implications of which frightened Daniel to his core? Could he tell Carrigan, finally, that any show with the power to do *that* certainly rendered his opinion, and therefore his career, irrelevant? "It's incredible," Daniel blurted out, as much to himself as to Patrick Carrigan.

"*Right?*" Carrigan said, mimicking, but with a very different meaning, Daniel's shaking head and expression of disbelief. Then Carrigan turned to Aleksandra, his eyes exploding into an eager smile: "What did *you* think?"

Aleksandra stood there, red and winded, a little frightened, more beautiful than Daniel had ever seen her. He heard the vexation in her slightly delayed "Who cares what I think?" — which she delivered with a brusque offhandedness calculated to deny that the show had had any strong effect on her whatsoever.

"*I* do! I care!" Carrigan cheerfully declared, and Daniel found to his surprise that he was grateful for the man's artless insistence. However strong the dealer's interest in Aleksandra's opinion of the show, Daniel's interest was by an order of magnitude stronger.

"But I'm a photographer," Aleksandra protested, her voice quavering slightly and again bearing more of her Russian accent. "I'm not a very good judge of three-dimensional work." She was demurring, stalling for time. In the depths of her shining eyes Daniel thought he noticed an entirely different thread.

"Go on," Carrigan urged her.

118

She let out a substantial sigh. "I think it is" — her tone dropped an octave — "all right."

Patrick Carrigan raised his eyebrows. "All right?" he echoed loudly.

The echo bounced off the gallery walls, and, as the three of them stood there listening to it expire, Daniel could see Carrigan's appraisal of Aleksandra readjusting itself in the man's eyes. Carrigan stared at her now as from a speculative distance, like a psychiatrist might regard an emotionally disturbed patient.

It was time to go.

Daniel shook Carrigan's hand, coughed up some halfway apologetic adieu, and then he and Aleksandra were back outside, plodding slowly down Madison. The anomaly of them walking *slowly* in Manhattan, as if tourists, only reaffirmed what he already knew: they had just come through a tornado, and not just the one implied by the show's whirling figures. The day was already waning, its slanted light no longer reached the ground along the avenue, and the slate-colored shadows it cast the two of them into seemed to change the character of the street. The city felt wilder, the murmur of its vibrating life louder. It all squared with Daniel's sense of having emerged to find that he had to answer to a different lay of the land.

I think it is . . . all right. They echoed in his ears, these words of hers, promising him a ray of hope with their chord of dispraise, but the reassurance he tried to draw from them was being crushed by her mute, severe manner. Whatever the feeling had been that had caused her to take him into her voluptuous embrace on the gallery's cement floor, it was now returned to its cell beneath her rib cage, and the two of them passed a quarter of an hour in complete silence, adhering to their southerly vector down the avenue. He cast her a sidelong glance. She looked small and constricted, and was walking at an awkward distance from him, her path pressed so close to the storefronts that she had to step around open doors and menu displays. Walking usually settled him, but his breathing was shallow, and the exertion did nothing to calm his growing alarm at the amount of concrete and concealments that existed between them.

He needed to figure out his approach. He could not risk the wrong words. For a very long time now, he had not cared whether he had a perfect understanding of her. Perfect understanding of another person was a delusion, he had come to believe; the struggle to attain it was sheer vanity, a result of self-love gone awry: a person felt they were so worthy of another's perfect understanding of them that they would do anything — marry, take lovers, divorce, and fight and fight and fight — to bring someone else to it. What a waste of life! His first marriage, his affair with Aleksandra, his second marriage — in each he had done his own degree of such wasting. And his heart would sink whenever Aleksandra used to tell him that he did not *really* understand her. He would assure her of his interest, while being inwardly adamant that a marriage got along mostly on kindness and a healthy overlooking of the other's oddities — that it did not usually benefit from extreme nearness to the other's innermost meanings, which, anyway, were often too idiosyncratic or too privately painful to be understood by any soul not encased in the same blood and bones. But now, now that she was no longer asking *anything* of him, it was beginning to dawn on him that the very things about her that had in the past acted as irritants to his distancing efforts — her need, her asking of more from him, her weakness — were precisely where love resided. This human hunger — and in the end likely nothing else — was what made a marriage, or any authentic relation, stick. And now he wanted desperately to close the space between himself and her, on the sidewalk, in their conversations, in their eyes, in their minds. Now he wanted, selfishly, unselfishly, more than he had wanted anything in a very long time, a perfect understanding of her.

"You were right," he announced in the middle of the Seventy-third block, with a forced blitheness he regretted immediately because it advertised the fact that he was pursuing a particular tack with her. But as she had already turned her attention on him, he had no choice but to follow through, and so with a thickening voice he added: "It wasn't that good."

"It was amazing," she said simply.

At these words he was nearly breathless. He looked over at her. "I'm talking about the show," he said — just to be sure.

"So am I." She smiled at him sadly.

It was too much. He could feel his heart pounding in his ears. "It isn't *that* good." With this unfortunate repetition he had cornered himself, *revealed* himself.

She laughed at him then with an unbearable harshness. The laughter spread across her features like a fast-moving storm front, until it was all darkness. It gave to her face an odd, beautiful kind of power that frightened him. "It isn't that good!" she echoed, hauling up the words from some depth of dismay. What she said next seemed hauled up from their years together, the whole run of them, and yet was only raised to be flogged with a remorselessness that, while new in her, had something very old in it. She said, striking a note that would forever take its place in his memory, "Yes, Daniel, it *is* that good."

They were forced to stop for crossing traffic. With his eyes downwardly cast, he saw only rim and tire and asphalt. He stared long and hard into that buzzing blur until somewhere in it he also saw the irony of him standing here on Madison Avenue trying so hopelessly to convince his wife, of all people, that a show by his favorite artist was not any good.

Turning westward, they gained the edge of the park, where their loss of words had to reckon with the sequestered spaces, the boulder-haunted paths, the trees, the extravagant quietness of an evening coming down. They came to rest at the edge of the Conservatory Water, a wide, shallow pond ringed with willows and cherry trees and over which a fleet of radio-controlled sailboats, hardly visible in the dusk, were still skirting. When he finally glanced at Aleksandra, he saw that she was taking measure of him, calmly, from across a gulf, as if she were lounging on one of those sailboats shrinking away.

"How did he do it?" he said to her.

"It's a question I've been asking myself."

The ambiguity in her words, which did not so much constitute a reply as a musing, made it sound almost as if she had been asking the question of herself for a long time, much longer than just this afternoon. Was she referring to the quality of Wind's work, or to what the man's show had done to her and Daniel? Or to — what? And something else: the ambiguity seemed to strike a new note of freedom. She suddenly turned and looked out at the boats, and it left him feeling abandoned.

"I'm lonely, you know," he said.

A singular ejaculation of some sort — a "Ha!" or "Huh?" or "What?" — emitted from her chest, accompanied by an animal exhalation that blurred it beyond intelligibility, but its sharp, thin trill of disbelief was unmistakable. She spun around and glowered at him. "You've always been lonely, Daniel. You're existentially lonely. But I'm lonely too. Emotionally lonely. *Sensually* lonely."

For a few seconds it was as if they could

see in each other's eyes the exact dimensions of her loneliness. It was a vision of her unmet needs made flesh, a vision that radiated glimmers of her naked figure in the arms of other men. Then her eyes went dead. They simply ceased to admit light, and reflected nothing to him. The pale skin around her cheeks suddenly appeared drawn — she looked old — and he had the odd sensation that it would be the last time they would ever stand this near each other. It would not be, but it *would* be the last time, including the morning in the living room when they spoke shortly before That Day, that she would truly unbare herself to him, the last time she would allow herself to be pulled out of her self-possession. And for the next four months, beginning with their cab ride home from the park that evening right up to the day of her death, she was a *miracle* of self-possession.

It was in the beauty of this self-possession, and of his new freedom to love Aleksandra without a thought of any personal claim on her, that he lived during those lengthening spring days. In a very real sense he let go. The beauty followed him everywhere: across the gray pages of the *Times* that he scanned every morning, on his walks from their apartment on Greenwich to his magazine's offices near Union Square, to the madness of the hole-in-the-wall sushi house on Third Avenue where he often grabbed lunch with colleagues. He basked in it even when, during his monthly Sunday dinner with his mother at a Midtown kosher pizza joint, his mother proudly drew his attention to several grease-stained photocopies of her 1040EZ tax form, which she had just filed herself, saving nearly two hundred dollars in accountant fees. And if the beauty of Aleksandra's new footing engendered equanimity in him, it certainly did Aleksandra no harm either. By June her face, which that night in the park had appeared so weathered, now looked as if the weather had never come, or at least as if the storm had passed quickly and left it rain freshened.

But sometime around the Fourth of July weekend (which they spent at a friend's house in Sag Harbor, sleeping in separate twin beds), Daniel entered a state of clarity about his situation — a kind of sobriety of defeat. He felt like a politician waiting for election results late into the early morning hours when the exit polls were not auguring well for him. He was waiting for Aleksandra to announce the end.

The announcement came that July morning in their living room when he had turned from the window to find her staring at him. It was the longest her eyes had lingered on him since the day they had gone to see Benjamin Wind's show. He knew then, before she opened her mouth even, that his four-month period of calm had come to a close. It was the reason he was so threatened by her stare. And then she said it: "I don't know how to love you more, Daniel." In another time and under different circumstances, the words might have meant something else entirely — something good and wholesome and hopeful. But on this morning they were the election results finally coming in. They were, and the news could not have been worse, tantamount to the death of dreams and realities. A parting homage to his insignificance.

Why–didn't–he–just–*fuck*–her?

While Aleksandra's funeral service slid toward its conclusion, he was as defenseless against the question as he was against all these penetrating memories and the shame and anger they aroused in him. He was also defenseless against forces without: against his mother's incessant sighing and shifting next to him in the pew, against the massed weeping of mourners throughout the temple, and especially, most disturbingly, against Aleksandra's father, Salomon Volkov, to whom Aleksandra had compared Daniel mere days ago. Daniel had understood the bitterness behind the comparison. In a father, emotional reserve might pass as acceptable; in a lover, it was unforgivable. But there was nothing reserved about poor Mr. Volkov on this day: the simple, normally jocose man was displaying more emotion for Aleksandra in these few minutes than Daniel had managed to muster in years of marriage. He was showing Daniel up. And he was effecting a self-consciousness in Daniel that interfered with Daniel's own ability to grieve. Aleksandra had been wrong in calling Daniel her father. He was nothing of the kind. His feelings about her had never really been free from selfish motive — and they *still* were not. Whereas her father's grieving sprang from a paternal love that was pure and unassailable, Daniel could not avoid taking Aleksandra's death personally, could not help viewing it as a result of his catastrophic failure as a man and husband.

And this, more than anything else, was why the afternoon they had gone to see the show haunted him as nothing ever had. The way she had looked at him when he finally found her in the third chamber of the gallery — it was not, he only now understood, simply coldness. It was the look of a woman reasoning with her husband to let her go. It was the look of a woman sitting among her lover's artworks and asking, pleading, declaring: "How can I not be with this man?" It was the look one had after being *ruined.*

When the service ended, he led the soundless procession from the temple to Aleksandra's grave in a newer part of the adjacent cemetery, near neither a fence nor the looming expressway, for which he was grateful. He was grateful as well for the discreet efficiency of the funeral workers who had already transported and emplaced the casket by the time he and the others arrived. A shomer was still reciting the Psalms at the grave's edge. Things occurred quickly now. The rabbi said a few words, various members of Aleksandra's immediate family took up the shovel, threw their customary three shovelfuls of dirt onto the casket, and then, suddenly, it was his turn. He removed the shovel from the damp, fragrant mound of earth beside the grave (where each previous mourner had left it, according to tradition, so as not to pass along their grief), scooped up a bit of dirt, and moved to the edge. Until this moment, he had averted his eyes from the hole. Though it terrified him to look down into it, he opened his eyes wider, wide as the grave itself. Only now did he see what Aleksandra had done by dying: she had given him a whole heart, by breaking it forever.

He tossed the dirt onto the lid of the casket with a slow, distinct flick of the shovel. His brain would allow nothing to get between it and this action: I'm doing this, he thought. That is my wife in there. Those are my hands gripping the shovel. In this manner, he held himself together as he repeated this action twice more. But then he looked up to find everyone's eyes on him, as if in judgment, as if it *was* his fault this had happened, and when he turned and finally found the pair that belonged to that one, the only one, who was not judging him — his mother, who radiated with sympathy — he dropped the shovel and felt his lips give way to a blast of air, wet, hissing, and awful, that emitted from between his clenched teeth. His mother led him away, endlessly it seemed, through tombstones and trees, all blurred in his wet vision, until in the cramped parking lot beside the expressway she folded him into the passenger seat of her car. It was finally over.

Or so he thought. They were halfway through the Midtown Tunnel when, without taking her eyes off the bus in front of them, his mother calmly said, "Tell me how she really died, honey."

Daniel felt himself stiffen. *"Mom."*

"What." She said it more like a statement than a question, and he thought she was through, but he was wrong. "I need to know what happened, Daniel. What *did* really happen?"

"That's the big question, isn't it?"

She leveled a glare at him. "Don't you be rhetorical with me. I'm your mother. Not one of your art world friends."

"I'm not being rhetorical." It was all he could muster. It was the truth.

"Did she — kill herself?"

"Mom."

"Your own mother doesn't deserve to know whether your wife killed herself or not?"

"I–don't–know. *Okay?*"

She eyed him, obviously trying to discover in his face if he was being honest with her. After a moment she turned her eyes back to the road.

"I think she might have," he finally conceded, staring out his window at the lights of the tunnel streaking by. Although his mind had been relentlessly occupied with Aleksandra's death ever since it had occurred, he felt strange actually talking about it with someone. He realized he had not, outside of the police investigators, had a single real conversation about Aleksandra since That Day. This current exchange seemed a trespass, but it was also a relief — a letting-go made smoother and safer for occurring with his mother in the enclosed privacy of a car, with the added comforting carapace of the tunnel.

"But *why?*" asked his mother. "Why would a woman with everything in the world going for her do such a stupid thing?"

He suddenly felt cold. He leaned forward and shut the air vent. "Because I didn't make her happy. Because I pulled away from her — in the end."

"Oh, Daniel," his mother sighed in a tone full of disapproval and yet somehow also containing a lifetime's worth of understanding.

"And because then," he picked up, "in all probability, she sought comfort in Benjamin Wind."

"The man she was found with?"

"That one, yes."

His mother fell silent. She seemed to be turning it all over in her head. When she ventured to speak next, it was with an awkwardness of footing that she tried to

mask by measuring her words with a philo-
sophic pace: "Aleksandra took her life," she
began, "because her love for him was so
strong she couldn't *stand* it."

"No," Daniel said simply. "That's not it."

"Why not?"

"Because people don't really want to die
out of deep love for a person. That only happens in the movies."

"Oh, really?" He did not grant this a
response, and she had no need for one.
"Well, I think you've gotten too cynical is
what I think. And it's clouded your judgment. She fell in love with that man, and it
was just too much. I know that's very —
very — difficult for you to hear, honey.
Believe me, I understand. But there's really
no other explanation, now is there?"

He wanted to deny this an answer as well,
but he could not help himself. "There *is*
another explanation, Mom. And it's the
right one. It's the *only* one." And he proceeded with extraordinary precision to spell
it out for her. He explained how love, real
love, lifts the veil that people normally hide
behind. He demonstrated with several
supple metaphors how such a love shows us
in our nakedness, our despair, our culpability. He painted a picture of the shame Aleksandra had suffered after leaving her first

133

husband to be with him. He spoke of things from that time in their lives, difficult, painful things he had never related to anyone, and it gave him the odd feeling that he was enumerating wounds received during some distant battle campaign. He pointed out, by way of bringing his explanation to a close, that the shame they had endured was surely enough for one lifetime: perhaps Aleksandra, having fallen in love with Wind, simply could not brave it all over again.

Even as he communicated these things to his mother, he could detect a struggle ensuing in her face; it was the clashing of her pieties with his unangelic admissions, a reaction he had known ever since his early adolescence, when he first began to share his complicated and in particular paradoxical feelings with her. She had always had a certain reductive method of dealing with painful subjects. She treated them as fantastical tales, things that could happen only in books or in films or to other people whose underlying morals she did not agree with in the first place. "What, she killed herself because of some guilt?" she finally said with incredulity.

"Guilt?"

"G u i l t."

Daniel turned to her. She raised her

eyebrows as if she were truly, innocently, curious.

"Sure," he said, and with this assent he knew he was throwing in the towel.

"Well, that explains it. Poor girl. Guilt's always to do with the past. So of course it's going to take away the only thing that *really* brings joy to us."

What was his mother talking about?

"Mom, what are you talking about?"

"Well, about *beginning.*"

"Beginning," he echoed flatly.

"That's what life is, Daniel: beginning. Again and again. Each day. Each moment too. Don't look at me like that. And don't tell me I'm speaking in clichés either. I know what I'm saying. The feeling that you're always beginning. Aleksandra couldn't find it in married life — where it really is, by the way — so she went looking for it outside the marriage. People do it all the time. She expected something fresh in an affair, and all it did was put her right back in the same place she was in when she left her first husband to be with you. Even your mother, Daniel, understands the horror of finding yourself once again in an identical painful situation: I felt that way every time your father and I fought. Believe it or not, I almost wanted to kill *myself* in those moments."

Daniel found himself staring at his mother. She had managed to surprise him. Without turning her head she changed into the fast lane, and then seemed to think better of it when a car rode right up on her rear and flashed its lights. "The two of you should have had kids," she blurted out when they were safely back in the slow lane, wedged between two buses. "Then *none* of this would have happened."

Now he felt his blood rising against her. How was it possible that she could be so right, could express so clearly his very own thoughts, while seeming to say exactly the wrong words?

"We *couldn't*," he answered, and then immediately regretted letting out this old secret. It brought up a flood of feeling in him and made him long painfully for Aleksandra.

"What do you mean, you couldn't?"

He had started, now he had to finish. "I mean, we couldn't."

"Did you even —" She fabricated a verb with a nervous wave of her hand.

"What do you think?"

"I'm asking if you even *tried*."

"Yeah, I know, Mom. Of course we tried. We tried and tried and tried and tried and tried and tried. Do you want me to tell you all the different positions we did it in?"

His mother shook her head and muttered something silently to herself — a prayer or a curse, or a utilitarian union of each. It was another of her signals with which he was familiar: their talk was finished.

Soon they emerged from the tunnel and, in Daniel's first few moments of being back in Manhattan after Aleksandra's funeral, Midtown's sharp edges imposed clarity on him. He had not taken note of these buildings in years — not even when the World Trade Center collapsed and forced so many New Yorkers to contemplate Manhattan's *other* tall buildings. Over the course of their affair and divorces and ensuing marriage, he and Aleksandra had succeeded in diminishing the size of their surroundings while they enlarged the drama of their little life together. Now he suddenly could not imagine history or these canyons of concrete ever shrinking again. His insular life with Aleksandra, its pain and strife, its broken beauty, already felt like a world vanished.

Putting Aleksandra's affairs in order also proved corrective. It required that he interact with other people — the postal clerk, his lawyer, Aleksandra's agent and art dealer —

who were *not* stricken by recent calamity and therefore models of healthy preoccupation with daily and often trivial matters. And it made him more married to Aleksandra than ever, ironically, since he had to act as her husband all the time. With each new task completed, he felt that she was increasingly dead — or, more categorically true to his sense of it happening again and again, *continuously* dead — yet he had never so lived with her, he was saddened to realize. He dined with her and read with her, he listened to Brahms and Bowie with her, he strolled and sat and watched the evening news with her. She was there looking over his shoulder as he negotiated with the assorted and sometimes sordid people with whom she had had dealings. She was there too when he made his first forays back to the galleries, and when he began to write again. He had reentered life. He was pulling through, in his haphazard way.

And then he discovered the photograph. He had unintentionally come across it on Aleksandra's computer while tracking down several stills of commercial work owed to an advertising agency, and he immediately recognized the image as originating from the portable camera that had been a permanent fact of her purse. It was a close-up of her and Benjamin Wind standing before a slice of slate-gray wall. Into the right side of the picture protruded a massive, hand-cut lip of stone that Daniel guessed was part of some doorway masonry of European origin. The two of them were bundled in winter parkas and in each other's arms, and Daniel could tell from the strained angle of Aleksandra's left shoulder that she had held the camera out and snapped the picture herself. The image was dated the sixth of November of the previous year — when she was supposed to have been photographing in Israel.

Using the color printer attached to Aleksandra's computer, he produced a print of the image and then stood beside her desk for a long time, studying it carefully. Her right arm was not, as he had originally thought, wrapped around Wind: obscured almost entirely by Wind's puffy parka, it was actually tucked straight down against her own torso. This fact was important to Daniel — it meant everything to him at the moment — and his eyes kept returning to it. Both Aleksandra's and Wind's cheeks were flushed; wherever they had gone to snap the shot, it had been a very cold place. He set the print down for a moment, and on a Web browser brought up temperatures in New

York for the day the image had been made. A high of sixty-two degrees. Not exactly cheek-reddening weather. Just to be sure, he checked Jerusalem: *lows* in the midseventies. A quick tour of Paris, London, and Frankfurt revealed a Europe in the grip of an all-out freeze on that early November day.

What had they been doing in Europe?

A clandestine cultural getaway? A romantic week in Paris? Had Aleksandra taken Wind back to Russia on some nostalgia trip through her childhood? Until now, Daniel had not opened her e-mail. The regular mail that arrived for her troubled him enough; e-mail truly was for the living, and he simply had not been able to bear the sight of a single message arriving in her in-box. But he was overpowered now by a desire to know what Aleksandra had been thinking, and spent the next ten minutes searching the e-mail folders on her computer for correspondence between her and Wind. He was not able to find any. If she had used these accounts to communicate with the artist, she had scrupulously deleted the evidence.

He picked up the print again and examined their faces. Both of them were beaming broadly. As a smiler, Aleksandra had always been a natural — there had been permanent lines where her high cheeks pressed into her eyes. But Daniel could not recall ever seeing Benjamin Wind looking this happy, and it sucked the breath right out of his lungs to imagine the unimaginable things Aleksandra had done for Wind — surely on that very day — to make him so. Yet the more he studied the photograph the more clearly he made out a trace of sadness in her shining eyes. Had there still been some part of her, at the very moment she took this shot even, that was thinking of *him?*

He told no one of his discovery, including his mother. Each day over the next few weeks he looked at the photograph. Often, he moved it with him between rooms. And he developed a habit of folding it into his pocket and taking it along when he left the apartment. Increasingly as he scrutinized the picture, he came to focus on Wind's face, until finally the artist's liquid dark eyes, his fighter's nose, his smiling feminine full-lipped mouth, were all that he saw.

Who *was* this man who had taken Aleksandra from him? What did Daniel really know about him? Despite the fact that he had been haunting Benjamin Wind through his work for years, the answer was almost nothing.

THE VOWS

The bewildering afternoon at Grandfather Pommeranz's flat comes to demarcate a great divide for Josef and his parents, between the days when the old man was a source of mealtime conversation and many a cheap joke, and a new phase in the Pick household, notable for a deliberate eschewal of the man's name and marked by truncated discussions, blank stares, furious pockets of silence. So increasingly removed from the family lexicon is Grandfather Pommeranz over the ensuing months that everyone, including the maid, Fraulein Oeser, is nearly frightened to death when he suddenly materializes one morning in the villa's portico. That the sole purpose of his visit is to convince the Picks to allow Josef to return to the Leopoldstadt, unaccompanied, so that the two of them can spend an afternoon in the Prater, there to ride the giant Ferris wheel, catch a marionette show, and generally partake in the giddy esprit de corps that only a grandfather and grandson can cultivate, surprises Josef the most, because he was certain that his grandfather never wanted to see him again. The old man was so clearly unimpressed, after all, by his one attempt at ketubah illumination, and Josef cannot blame him: the thing failed to fix his parents' marriage, as the increased soundlessness of the villa's rooms seems to prove.

From his daughter, Grandfather Pommeranz wins approval of his scheme — Josef's father is conveniently absent — and on the following Sunday Josef embarks on his first one-man outing across Vienna, a trip made more challenging by a stupidly cold winter storm that has arrested the city and shellacked its surfaces with ice, defeating everything, including the stones, which appear to be contracting, even retreating, into wall and pavement. Josef could not care less. The journey to his grandfather's building, requiring him to solicit directions from the conductor of his trolley, several random passersby, a Tabak clerk, and one absurdly flinty Polizei officer, gives him his first engagement with strangers that does not occur under the critical gaze of his father, freeing him of the monotonous weight of causing a father pleasure or pain. Lifted by this, he pauses on the landing outside his grandfather's door to linger a few moments in the damp half-light, fancying himself a cabaret star savoring the moment in some backstage shadow after bringing the house down. At last, he sounds the door with several hard raps.

"Ah!" comes Grandfather Pommeranz's unusually chipper voice from within. "Enter, Young Pommeranz!"

Josef finds the door unlocked. Inside stands his grandfather, beaming at him expectantly, arms outstretched, but Josef does not go to him because beyond Grandfather Pommeranz's shoulder and seated at the table are a man and a woman, both unknown to Josef.

"This," Grandfather Pommeranz says, stepping aside, "is Herr Brotman and Fraulein Rozen."

Josef stares at the strangers. He is confused as to who they are and why they are here. Will they also be going to the Prater? (He hopes not.) The man, who has not removed his hat and who sits not *in* his chair but *on* it in a tensed-muscle manner that suggests he might at any moment spring *off* it, looks Josef over as if he is a breeding stallion for sale. In the space of a single instant, the man's eyes — engaged in a kind of savage inartistic scrutiny — take in Josef's entire person, starting with his trunk and moving outward toward his extremities. The woman, on the other hand, does not regard Josef at all. Her severely bowed head, indicator of fear or embarrassment, prevents her eyes from studying anything more interesting than the worn leather satchel she holds fast in her lap. Like Grandfather Pommeranz, the two of them are poor and new to Vienna — this much Josef guesses from their bedraggled rural clothes and from the way life has prematurely aged them *in parts:* in their eyes he can see the remnants of youth, but on their faces the end of the world looks already at hand. Joy, anyway, does not appear to exist within or without either of them, and like every peasant Josef has ever seen, they each seem to wear the practical problem of life like a second suit.

"And *this*," Grandfather Pommeranz proudly declares, putting a hand on Josef's shoulder, "is the young maestro!"

It is then that Josef notices the ketubah on the table — the one he painted for his parents all those months ago and inadvertently left behind in the commotion of his family's hasty exodus. The discovery is disconcerting. On heightened alert, his

145

senses detect something breathy hanging in the air, a remnant whiff of an earlier conversation, and he is possessed by the distinct feeling that his grandfather and the two strangers were talking about him before he walked in.

The man lifts his hat long enough to smooth his thinning hair with one hand, then uses the same hand to gesture at Josef. "But he is all of ten years old," the man complains to Grandfather Pommeranz in words laden with Yiddish and poverty. "I don't care how good he is. Such a sum of money I will not pay a *child*. For half a schilling we can buy a lithographed contract from any shop in the Leopoldstadt."

At this, the woman suddenly raises her head, and she and the man look at each other bitterly, as if silently resuming some ongoing debate.

It takes a moment for Josef to grasp the meaning of all this. Amazed that his virtually virginal ketubah-painting services are being offered for an unknown price, he watches his grandfather attempt to take advantage of this impasse between the pair of impoverished Jews.

"You aren't paying the *boy*," his grandfather tells the man, and then points to his own chest. "You are paying *me* — his

146

teacher."

"Nevertheless," the man says, removing from his coat a shabby pair of gloves, standing as if to go, and motioning for the woman to do the same, "twenty-nine schillings is far too much."

"Far too much — for love?" Grandfather Pommeranz asks with a sly insouciance.

The man looks at him. Then at the woman. She has once again lowered her head. Josef's grandfather does not wait for the man's answer. "My boy, *young maestro,*" he says, abruptly turning to Josef with an expression on his face so solicitous and theatrical that Josef, who is stunned by the amount of money he is attempting to exact from the visitors (enough to buy a small *horse*), feels compelled to assume the role of maestro, and straightens his posture and lifts his chin ever so slightly, doing his best to affect a ten-year-old's version of haughty amour propre. "My Viennese wonder, oh brilliant painter of love," his grandfather continues, "tell our soon-to-be-wed guests just how many *days* it takes you to compose your masterpieces of marriage."

Josef is astonished by this situation. He tries to espy somewhere, *anywhere* in the old man's face — his eyes, his mouth, his bulbous red nose — a clue as to what his answer ought to be, given that he has only ever painted *one* marriage contract, in a matter of hours, if not *minutes*. His grandfather's visage offers him nothing but a wide, fatuous smile, and so Josef, by dint of an on-the-spot calculation that takes into consideration his only two givens — the formidable price his grandfather is asking and the old man's clear emphasis on the word "days" — arrives at what he feels is a reasonable answer.

"Seven hundred and eighty-two days!" he proclaims.

He says this, for greater effect, with proudly closed eyes — after the manner of Furtwängler, the incomparable conductor of the Philharmonic, whose baronial jeu de theatre on the pedestal recently held Josef in thrall for the better part of Beethoven's Seventh when he and his mother attended the Staatsoper.

His grandfather's only response is to stare at him aghast. Ever so slowly, the old man turns to the visitors. "Well . . ." he begins, obviously searching for words, "the boy can do *yours* more — quickly," adding, as if a brilliant idea suddenly occurs to him, "especially under my strict supervision."

Evidently sniffing weakness, the peasant Jew tries to press his advantage and commands Josef's grandfather to lower his commission. A heated negotiation ensues, which, because its outcome bears on whether he will have to produce the second marriage contract he has ever painted in his life, Josef watches with rapt attention. On the amount of twenty-nine schillings his grandfather remains intransigent. The younger man, hanging on his face a wooden mask of defiance that seems hollowed from some hard and ancient tree of vanity, refuses this price with upturned nose and wave of hand, as if a bad piece of fish is being offered him. He refuses to name an acceptable price as well, and Grandfather Pommeranz calls his stubbornness "unwarranted — an act of total effrontery" and repeatedly challenges the man and his fiancée to please leave the flat if they intend to so insult the Pommeranz name. After some minutes, however, and no hint of any backing down on the part of the strangers, his grandfather contrives by a plainly painful spasm of will to produce a new price: twenty-*eight* schillings. The peasant Jew stares frostily at him. Then, with a punctilious flourish, he tugs the gloves off his hands and returns them to his jacket pocket. "A fair price," he allows. Josef's grandfather, assuming a chivalrous look that suggests the ketubah is being given

149

away as an act of prodigal charity, replies, "Indeed."

This baffling business is hardly concluded when the man's fiancée abruptly opens up her satchel and pours its contents — dog-eared bundles of old photographs — onto the table. She looks up at Josef.

"My life," she says simply.

Josef glances quizzically at his grandfather.

"Do not be shy," the old man tells him, gesturing suggestively for him to approach the table. "It is time to get acquainted with Fraulein Rozen."

"Why?" Josef asks aloud, in his confusion directing the question to all three of them.

His grandfather grins at the visitors. "My *grandson* — always with his sense of humor!" He gives Josef a sharp look. "What, you are going to look into your crystal ball and illuminate our clients' ketubah from pure conjury? Go on, now — you know the routine."

Josef does not know the routine, there *is* no routine, but he nonetheless walks to the table, whereupon the woman smiles at him and pats the seat of the chair next to her in indication that he should sit down, which he reluctantly does with a child's natural aversion to the falseness of a stranger's sudden display of cozy familiarity.

The woman, loosening the strings around the bundles, proceeds with considerable ceremony to place photographs of gray ancestral faces onto the table one by one and with a kind of slap, as if disencumbering herself of memories. While her fiancé begins debating Grandfather Pommeranz on the merits of Vienna's chief rabbi, she plies Josef with names, dates of decease, and historical anecdotes that Josef feels can only have meaning for her or another living relative; nevertheless, as he examines her pictures he is aware that she is watching him with a familial pride so primeval that he can imagine her striking out at him if he fails to openly share in it. Not without an element of embarrassment and boredom does he thus affect interest in every dead, vacant-eyed member of this strange woman's extended family.

But when the photographs of these figures accumulate into ten neat rows, their heads and bodies sprouting like ghostly flowers out of long-ago landscapes, his pity is unexpectedly excited, and by degrees he is brought to feel powerfully for this grown woman carting around her dead for the sole purpose of joining them in marriage to those of a husband. How in the world will he paint a ketubah for her? How can he possibly do for this stranger what he could not do for his own parents?

The futility of it causes him to lift his eyes and bristle at the vision before him — of his grandfather solicitously engaging the other stranger, now trying to warm his hands by the stove — a vision from which Josef draws a sense that a lingering vapor of truth may yet curl through his father's cruel pronouncements on his grandfather. Disappointment in a favorite family member is difficult enough for any child to bear; it is redoubled if it bears out the warnings of a parent, and Josef throws up a boyish resistance to the notion that his father has been right all along. The effort colors the rest of his interactions with the strangers his grandfather has forced on him, and if, during the fiancé's review of what he thinks their ketubah should convey, Josef too obviously retreats within himself, it is not because the man is long-winded, or because his ideas, having to do with the continuation of his family lineage and the purchasing of a Moravian farmhouse, are a muddle of sentimental adages and saccharine hopes, or even because the man's mental map of his future marriage contract contains no ground in which to bury his fiancée's dead. It is not the poor man's fault. It is Grandfather Pommeranz's fault. This finally comes home to Josef as a series of painful, disorderly, and conflicting emotions, and by the time the couple quit the flat he sees that his grandfather in the end is ready to do *anything* — bless meats, take advantage of peasants, exploit a grandson — to make money.

"Can you believe such people?" Grandfather Pommeranz says as he locks the door. "Daring to haggle over a *schilling!*" The old man goes to the misted window and, wiping a hole through which to view the couple as they traverse Karmeliterplatz, airs his annoyance at their avarice, takes exception to their lack of decency, and, while extolling his *own* decency, numbers the many injustices committed by the pair of peasant Jews during their time in his flat. This subject exhausted, the old man's speech takes another line of thought entirely. That line being wealth. "We will be *rich!*" he lets out all at once, abandoning the window and grabbing Josef by both shoulders. He suddenly looks around and lowers his voice, as if the other tenants in the building might be in league to despoil him — *"Rich,"* he whispers, "thanks to the gift that God in all of His merciful benevolence has finally brought to my doorstep! A proper harnessing of your artistic powers, my boy, mystical

153

or not, to the marriage machinery of Leopoldstadt, where weddings are *always* in the offing, is going to bring the schillings pouring into Karmeliterplatz Number Two!" He lets go of Josef abruptly. "Now, let us get you to work."

"No," Josef says. And he takes a step backward.

"What?"

"No."

"No? *No?* What do you mean 'No'? You are not telling me 'No.' "

"Yes."

"Yes?"

"No."

Grandfather Pommeranz yanks the yarmulke off his own head. "Please explain, Young Pommeranz."

"No, you lied to me. No, we were supposed to go to the Prater. No, you only said 'Ah, another ketubah' last time. No, I will not make another marriage contract."

All of this, he yells.

Surprised, alarmed even, by the frankness of his own words and yet propelled by their general thrust, Josef resumes his retreat from his grandfather, whose wild eyes scour his face. Josef's left hand finds the doorknob, and before he knows it he is on the landing. He looks back: the old man is

154

standing there, staring blindly into the crumpled yarmulke in his hands.

It is only Josef's second time in the building, but already it appears to be his destiny never to leave it neutrally. Last time: pulled away against his will. This time: he pushes his own way out, reintroducing himself to the market of Karmeliterplatz as if suddenly emancipated from a cage he was fettered to by a short chain. Freed from narrow walls and low ceiling, from the close smell of clothing and bodies and breath in a heated space — freed from his grandfather's will — he falls into a run. The temperature has dropped emphatically since he arrived. Breathing, he feels that he is taking a burning liquid into his chest. He speeds past the scarved bellowing vendors huddled against Karmeliterplatz's frigid wind and pushes up Taborstrasse toward the canal. At the Marienbrücke, where a flurry of snow hits the bridge and the buildings and him, he does not take the tram. No decision is involved in this, no choice exercised. He simply does not take it. Oblivious to his protesting lungs, a pulse beating loudly in his head, he runs mindlessly in the direction of home, veering left here, right there, a practically unconscious creature, more wolf than boy.

He is more dead than alive when he collapses against the Pick villa's snow-dusted door some time later (he has no idea how much later: being in a frozen state he has no ideas). For what seems like eternity, nothing happens. The falling flakes quietly establish themselves upon him, a white weight pressing him down. From below, he senses a cold wetness rising up through his clothes as if to engulf his body. He will drown just off home dock. But at a certain point he becomes aware of voices, and soon of limbs enfolding him — a life ring of elbow and arm. Then he is being lifted . . . for a brief moment, he is convinced that he is weightless, even floating in water, until his body is met by a firm cushioned surface, and gravity reclaims him. He feels himself brushed by soft fabrics and human hands, by successive waves of radiant heat. And then he feels nothing. Rescued, he has already left port, aboard a ship calling at distant, dreamless shores.

On awakening, he opens his eyes to find himself locked in an embrace with the parlor's antique settee, with whose oaken arms and silken skin he has taken up an almost intimate relation. Thought returns to him haltingly. The dark brownness of the parlor, its thick muffled air and high wood ceiling, the fireplace's glowing embers and the dim china lamps quietly illuminating every deep, richly polished surface — they register in his brain as kindred things, elements of a kinder world. He raises his head, and his attention is drawn to a particular corner where two figures are duskily seated. He cannot make out their features, but he instinctively feels their intense regard. Only when a lamp is abruptly clicked on does he recognize his mother and father, whose presences seem more remarkable for being together in the same room.

"I never want to go back there again," he blurts out. So automatically, so *instantly* do these words fall from his mouth that he has to pause a moment to allow his thinking, still operating at half speed, to catch up.

"My God," his mother says. "What *happened?*"

The question seems to melt the unthawed regions of his brain, which hemorrhage a torrent of memories of *exactly* what happened in Grandfather Pommeranz's flat. In this manner he rediscovers a tear-producing anger at his grandfather resulting less from his disappointment at not being taken to the Prater's amusement park than from his having been brought to the point of yelling at the old man. And it is this — his having yelled at his grandfather — that leaves him prey, now that he has an audience, to that peculiar need for sympathy that befalls any person in the aftermath of giving someone dear a piece of one's mind. He tells his parents *everything.*

But as he speaks, he becomes conscious of a smile mounting to his father's cheek. It is a smile that tells Josef, as nothing else can, of his father's desperate need to have his opinions about Grandfather Pommeranz vindicated. At each new detail Josef shares, the man nods proudly, regally, as if saying, "You *see?* Did I not tell you?" Yet his father's need appears to run deeper than mere vindication: the man's eyes reach out to him with a child's hunger — to be admired, loved back — a hunger displayed so nakedly that it permeates Josef's own hunger for sympathy. He loses all sense of his mother. It is only he and his father now, locked in some spinning amusement park ride that his grandfather never took him to, twirling around each other's need in a cage from which kindness is centrifugally flushed. Naturally, his father carries more weight, and Josef finds himself at pains to tell the man exactly what he wants to hear. He exaggerates his grandfather's wrongdoings, making them sound more extreme, if only to bring his feelings about the old man into some sort of balance with those of the tetchy, stubborn, insatiable person seated across from him.

This filial effort continues over dinner and then over the following weeks, creating a new and knotty alliance with his father that reintroduces to the Pick villa the old habit of mocking Grandfather Pommeranz and, more important to Josef, yields a first invitation to accompany his father to Café Central.

The evening begins with a trolley ride into the inner city and seems filled with hidden promise. Josef sits beside his father on a rattling bench, watching out the window as darkness descends on frantic Mariahilferstrasse and the night comes to life. His father's cologne, woody, grown-up, alive, washes over him with a wild unfamiliarity: he realizes that he has never before noticed the smell of this man who has always been there. Without turning to look at his father, he breathes in the man's scent, giving himself up to this new closeness with him.

Café Central's windows radiate a golden glow, and when they enter, he and his father are greeted by the headwaiter's stoic and surprisingly hostile stare. Josef asks his father if the waiter does not like him, but his father disabuses him at once of the idea that there is anything personal to it. It is the waiter's way, he tells Josef, of saying "Good evening" according to the immemorial habit of all coffee house waiters in all times. But Josef is not convinced. It looks personal to *him*. And it is the first sign that the evening will not go as he expected. Never has he seen a man treat his father with anything less than reverence, and as the offending waiter leads them past tables ringed with loud, smoking patrons, Josef steps gingerly — skeptically — across the marbled floor, his eyes drawn upward by the rising smoke and pale green pilasters to the heavily arcaded ceiling that hangs threateningly over everything.

They are led not to their own private table but one already inhabited by five of his father's friends and their respective tobacco pouches. He has never met these men, who, in their archaic manner of dress, in their moustaches and fleshy jowls and substantial paunches, bear such striking resemblance to his father that they give him a start. When his father introduces him around the table, several of the men pretend to try to draw him out with jokes chosen, it seems to him, with no stronger motive than to hear their own voices or the others' laughter. In a short time they forget about him entirely and fall into a dizzying display of sociability, each in turn locating the pipe lost in his whiskers and raising the volume of his witticisms with the goal of imposing his personality on the table. The conversation turns primarily on Austrian politics — in particular the empire's fall from majestic, nearly unknowable heights to a shrunken country given over to self-interest, sexual perversion, and, more worrisomely, Socialists and Jews. Josef wonders if the other men are aware of his father's Jewish blood. He wonders if the others might also be hiding their Jewishness. An argument follows — not among them, but collectively against the current Red-leaning doings of the government. Josef notices how easily his father and the others enkindle themselves with ideas they do not appear to believe in; he begins to doubt even his father's belief in the old empire, which the man mentions repeatedly with a false reverence usually reserved for a deceased parent. And despite the fact that the other men — who, like his father, seem to hold powerful positions in various of Vienna's businesses and banks — speak from unequivocal positions of authority, Josef, even at his young age, can tell that theirs are the arguments and cynicism of

161

men who have no control over their world. Their quips, their cackles, sound very like cries.

When the headwaiter is suddenly among them removing empty glasses, the men jeeringly ask the man for *his* opinion on the current state of Austria's political affairs. Josef senses that they have asked the waiter merely for the sake of feeling better about themselves, and he turns to see what the waiter is going to say — to see if the man will speak at all. The waiter pauses in response to the question, the tray of dirty glasses frozen in his hand. His stony expression remains unchanged from when Josef first beheld it, giving Josef the sense that the man will die with this face. At length, and drawing from some vast deposit of waiter knowledge, the man answers simply: "Has it ever been any different?"

Josef's father and the others exchange uncertain looks.

"The boy," the waiter adds, meaning Josef, "will likely want a Sacher torte."

After the waiter leaves, a grave silence encloses the table, and Josef watches the men search the rings of smoke they loose into the air for how they feel now, for what they ought to say next. He catches a few of them sneaking glances at one or the other

162

— hard, awful glances. They don't actually *like* each other, he thinks. They seem bound to the table by nothing more than a shared anger at the world, leaving him to wonder if his new friendship with his father — if the reason he is sitting here tonight — is due only to *their* shared anger, at Grandfather Pommeranz. When, toward evening's end, his father puts an arm around him and sounds out for the benefit of the other men a litany of complaints about "the old Jew," Josef has his answer. He has granted his father a new purchase on him. A negative alliance — the price of sympathy.

Herrengasse, by daylight the path of Vienna's multitudes, is an empty corridor of stone and shadow when Josef follows the men out of the café that night, holding in the deeper reaches of his heart a disappointment he cannot explain to himself in any utterable way. Is it that the evening awakened him to the fact that his father is not unique, but part of a class of men? Is it that for four endless hours they all sat in sharp judgment of the world? Is it what they revealed about male friendship, its camaraderie cut with hostility and deception? As he and his father slowly walk away from the others, Josef longs to put distance between himself and the adult male behavior he just witnessed. But he cannot. If it is not already a part of him, he feels life pushing him toward it, as if he is marching down some long dark defile, a thousand men behind him, a thousand men in front.

A taxi is hired at Michaelerplatz to convey the two of them back to Hietzing. When they pass the emperor's former residence, his father, sitting beside him in the backseat, lights his pipe and stares silently up at the hundreds of darkened windows. After a while, he tamps out the embers.

"I have ceased sending checks to your grandfather," he suddenly says.

He looks at Josef fixedly and seems about to say more, but then he turns away, and nothing else is said between them.

By the time they arrive at home, his mother has retired for the night, but Josef finds that she has left a letter, addressed to him, on the secretary in the foyer. It is from Grandfather Pommeranz, and, before his father notices, he conceals the letter in his jacket pocket and carries it up to his room, where he opens it under his desk lamp.

My Dear Young Pommeranz:
I hold your marriage contract in my hand as I write this. It is not just another ketubah. It is, with the exception of you,

164

the most blessed thing my eyes have had the privilege of beholding. Please visit me again, so that I may take you to the Prater.

May God watch over you, my child.

                                    Your Grandfather

P.S. Blessed 42 chicken legs today. Also: 35 gizzards, 12 gefilte fish.

Lured back by the letter, Josef once again finds himself mounting the stairs to his grandfather's flat — this time on a Saturday — having told his parents he is hiking in the Vienna Woods with several of his soccer mates. But when he reaches the landing, he comes to a halt. Not only is his grandfather's door wide open, but it also seems to have been flung with a violence that has separated it from its hinges. The thing looks flayed. And the lock, torn from its socket, is lying on the floor, its greasy metal organs shamefully exposed.

He rushes into the flat to find the place all but ransacked: overturned furniture and broken crockery strewn across the floor, splayed books and torn pages everywhere in heaps, and a lone strip of pickled herring, apparently the object of someone's wild throw, flush against the windowpane. An awful smell dominates the room. He turns his attention to the corner, where, asprawl on the collapsed ruin of the bed, a figure lies concealed in a shroud of blanket. Stepping toward it, he burns with amazement and fear.

"Grandfather Pommeranz?" he hazards.

Several moans issue from the heap. Josef moves quickly to pull back the blanket, revealing his grandfather's ashen face. The old man has been beaten. He looks at Josef with crestfallen eyes, a blood-soaked yarmulke hanging pathetically from a strand of his hair. "I wanted to take you to the Prater," his grandfather offers weakly.

There is a purpled depression in the middle of the old man's forehead, and just below it a nasty tear from which blood is leaking. Josef instinctively bunches a section of sheet in his fingers and reaches out to dab the cut.

"Never mind!" his grandfather says, swatting his hand away. "Hear my words, Young Pommeranz: against the diabolical imbeciles who hold this world enchained, you will have to become God's gladiator!" The old man lifts his head to deliver this admonition, and the effort leaves him dissipated. He sighs and sets his gaze on the night lamp's exposed bulb — somehow still illuminated — and in its glow he seems to see his attacker's face all over again. "There are certain men of bad, bad character, my child — the Leopoldstadt is filled with them."

Josef looks around the room. Little of his young life has been given over to pondering the cruelty of the world. That it should enter this place — this ridiculously small flat where his grandfather lives — rends something untouched and slightly miraculous inside of him, something he has always held without knowing it: a belief in the reliable goodness of people. "Why," he asks, as much to himself as to his grandfather, "would they come *here?* Why would they want to hurt you?"

As if the matter were as plain as day, his grandfather replies, "Why do they hurt anybody? They wanted their money back."

Josef catches at these words. He gives his grandfather a single, searching look.

"And they were Jews," the old man puts in. "Would you believe?"

Josef stares at him. "You *borrowed* from them?" he finally asks.

His grandfather sighs again; his tired eyes fill with resignation. "Spectacularly."

"How much?"

"You wouldn't believe."

A tight coil of frustration — at his grandfather for taking the money, at his father for discontinuing his monthly checks to the old man — registers its presence in Josef's stomach, and he has to turn away. He gets up and walks to the desk, which lies on its side. When he bends down to right it, he notices a new, half-completed marriage contract on the floor. It is the work of his grandfather and obviously intended for the two impoverished Jews Josef met last time he was here: he can tell this by the sketchy attempts at representing the woman's old photographs of relatives and by the lonely farmhouse that sits near the top of the page. But what is striking about the unfinished ketubah is that it is otherwise an exact replica of the contract Josef illuminated for his parents. His grandfather was copying *him.*

Josef lifts it off the floor and turns to the old man, who stares at the thing in sorry recognition. "Would," Josef begins, "twenty-eight schillings —"

"Be enough to stop this?" his grandfather interrupts, gesturing at the room's broken mess. "Not even close," he says glumly.

A silence overtakes the room.

"But it would be a *start,*" the old man adds.

Over this suggestion their eyes meet for a

tense moment. Then, for lack of a better idea, and in the manner of many who have attempted to rein in the unruliness of confusion and anger, Josef busies himself with straightening up the desk and chair. This fussy display concluded, he takes a seat, his gaze fixed on his grandfather's half-completed forgery, which he has placed before him. Into whatever part of his heart he secretly reserved for the old man (beginning the day he first heard the words "Grandfather Pommeranz") his grandfather has driven a thin, invisible wedge. If he cannot hate the old man, neither can he like him purely. It occurs to him that this is exactly how he feels about his father. His mother too, most likely. And so it is that Josef experiences his first conscious recognition of the deep, the thorny, the bizarre pull between family members that most people call love but, more often than they would care to admit, resembles tolerance.

The intruders crushed three of his grandfather's ink bottles, whose vital contents were absorbed thirstily by the floor's porous wood planks, but the rest of the bottles are otherwise unharmed, and Josef begins assembling these and other painting utensils — brushes and pens and rags — into a usable order around the unfinished ketubah.

"You are upset at me," his grandfather calls out from the bed.

Josef does not respond. Selecting a medium-size brush, he saturates it with black ink and begins where his grandfather left off: a plinth of stone serving as the base for what appears to be a fountain. This he helps to a certain nobility in a matter of seconds by topping it with a statue of Neptune that he has always admired on the Schönbrunn palace grounds.

"But how I loathe the word 'contract'!" the old man declares, with a stagily indignant tone that betrays his embarrassment at the situation. "It makes marriage sound like paying so many taxes! Contrary to what these Christian countries would have you believe, it isn't the government, after all, who has authority over the institution. Any pious Jew will tell you that God is the only one who oversees marriage. You have only to read Proverbs: 'He who finds a wife has found happiness and won God's favor!' In any case, young man, do not finish that ketubah for me: finish it for *God!*"

Josef wants him to be quiet — all of the old man's talk is only increasing the tightness in his stomach. He focuses on the nib of his pen, grateful for the way it releases ink onto the parchment with a perfect fidelity. Moving on to the border, he picks up its leafy pattern with a furor. But halfway around the left side of the page, he sets down the pen.

It is no use. The marriage contract is hopelessly ugly. The thing is unfinished, yes, but its essential failings are settled beyond repair. He pushes the ketubah aside.

This his grandfather notices from the bed and acknowledges with a groan. "Another failure!" he mutters. Then he proceeds to enumerate *all* of his life's failures: to please his wife while she was alive; to secure one of the three synagogues in his village; to convince the Polish Jews there — who preferred their spirituality unvarnished, who were mistrustful of ornamentation when it came to matters of God, and whose poverty already lent enough poetry to their lives — that they should shell over the zlotys for the fancy marriage contracts he had learned to illuminate from a Sephardic Jew; to compete, finally, with the modern ketubot so degraded and cheapened by mass production.

Josef tries to ignore all these laments. In the bottom drawer of the desk he finds a clean sheet of parchment. He stares at length into its white blankness, contemplating the peasant couple anew. It has been a long time since he met them, and he attempts to remember the woman's recollections of her dead relatives, the man's longings for the Moravian countryside. A few details repeat themselves in his mind. He begins to hear the quality of their voices. He starts to draw.

Illuminating this fresh ketubah feels awkward at first, unreal. His mind seems asleep, and he has a vague sense that he is drawing a dream, a vision stretched to the limits of what he can remember. By slow degrees, the couple's haggard faces become part of his bewilderment, the making of their ketubah like some nocturnal crossing. Yet it is working. Working so well, in fact, that he begins to wonder if memory or even forgetfulness is where beauty gets made. He has never drawn anything this well from real life — not flowers nor dogs nor the birds outside his bedroom window. Is it because there was no distance between those things and him? In making this marriage contract, his memory is bringing the man and woman back to him, but not the same man and woman he met. Time has broken them up, left certain elements behind, remade them into something new, into something that belongs to him.

So absorbed is he in drawing that hours

pass like minutes, and it is only when he pauses to shake out his hand that he realizes his grandfather has been craning his neck from the bed, stealing glimpses of the new ketubah's progress. When their eyes meet, a guilty glow suffuses the old man's face and he self-consciously looks away. His pride seems wounded, and he tries to hide it by extemporizing about Josef's chances of being a successful illuminator in Vienna, where, he explains, there are many Sephardim, enough to support the Turkish Temple, the most spectacularly ornamented synagogue Europe has ever seen, and where even the Polish Jews' tastes run to the ornate, the macabre, and the decadent. "But you have to create a name for yourself, young maestro!" his grandfather warns him with a touch too much defensiveness. "You need to build a reputation! You must work hard, and *fast,* and —"

"It is done, Grandfather."

The old man regards him with puzzlement. Josef holds up the ketubah for him to see.

"Oh," his grandfather mutters, casting his eyes downward.

"Don't you want to look at it?"

"I suppose so."

Josef stands and walks the ketubah over to

him. The old man reaches up and takes it delicately into his hands. He examines it closely for a long while.

"Only an *image*," he says at last, "can fill us with a pure joy." Then he surrenders a weak smile and hands the ketubah back to Josef. "Your creation, Young Pommeranz, is better than those whose union it establishes."

As was the case with the one he illuminated for his parents, Josef has nearly no recollection of the ketubah's making, and so it is with virginal eyes and a raw kind of curiosity that he takes a good look at this second marriage contract occasioned first by money, then by memory, at last by imagination. Across its wispy, dreamlike surface, life and death are rendered frankly inseparable, as if the living and the dead have always occupied the same space without complaint. But space in this ketubah does not appear to be of this world per se. Rather, it is displaced behind an inky blue film that covers everything like a veil. The bride and groom, whose likenesses are gestured at in transparent, nearly disappearing, washes of ink, peer out from the open doorway of the groom's fantasy Moravian home, which lies nestled, sunnily, verdantly, forever inaccessible, among some tentative chestnut trees. Darkly immured in the earth beneath the house are many of the faces, remembered or imagined, of the woman's dead relatives. Yet her ancestors' dubious privilege of being dragooned into her marriage contract is brightened not only by their companionable arrangement in tight seedling ranks underground, but also by the release of many of them from the dirt and senseless decay: first as blooming yellow florets in a tussock of dandelions and then as gossamer ball angels raised by the wind to the impure geometry of the living. Their ascent describes a wide upward arc around a nave containing the ketubah's traditional wording (which Josef painstakingly copied, without understanding its content exactly, from his grandfather's failed contract). If the text represents the couple's vows and vision of their future married life, the sky is a fabric of seraphic, thickly flowered souls whispering advice at its edges. These angels come to rest, finally, in a dovecote made handsome by its Moorish details and forming a sort of celestial vault at the top of the ketubah. Josef is pleased.

"I should sign it," he says.

"What?"

"To create a name for myself and build my reputation."

The old man winces with disdain. "One does not *sign* a ketubah. Art is a devotional activity, my boy, the aim of which is to glorify God, not the individual! God gave you your special gift that you might give it *back* to Him. Ketubot are not opportunities for self-advancement, but for pious meditation — for continuing a tradition that traces back to the ancient Hebrews! You, Young Pommeranz, are part of a sacred line of numerous, *nameless* artists."

"But if I don't sign it, no one will know that it is mine."

His grandfather sits up painfully, snatches the ketubah, and shakes it at him. "The entire painting is your secret signature! *Everyone* will know that is yours."

And his grandfather is right. That week, the peasant couple retrieves the ketubah Josef made for them and are overjoyed — *overwhelmed* — by its beauty. Within days three requests to meet "the new prodigy of marriage contracts" come in, and, after a difficult discussion with his mother in which he apprises her of her father's current state of destitution (and, to her dismay, her husband's discontinuance of financial assistance), Josef spends the whole of the following Saturday in his grandfather's flat

176

speaking with two new couples. Like the first pair, all four of these men and women are poor and labor for hours on end to share their lives with Josef. And although Josef gives them the impression as he listens that he is laboring right beside them, he is in fact drowning in boredom, having sounded the depths of each bride and groom within minutes of meeting them — having almost at once limned the layout of the marriage contract he will make for them. He and his grandfather contrive to limit Sunday's meeting with the third pair of clients to a more reasonable, practicable half an hour, and some consequent ketubah illumination confirms his suspicion that the less time he spends with customers, the better the resulting ketubah. He need only garner a flashing sense of the couple to be married — the length of a woman's ropy hair, for instance, or the officious manner of her fiancé's pronouncements — to let their particulars pass into his memory, from which he can later coax a comely contract. This yoking of his memory to his customers instills in him an oddly familiar feeling that he is trespassing — not only into other people's lives, but also into their dreams. He remembers when he has felt it before: on evening sojourns with his mother through the darkening residential streets of Hietzing. His mother is invariably remote during these outings, lost in her thoughts, and the two of them never speak as they pass dwelling after dwelling. Instead, they peer through glass windows into small, illuminated rooms where strangers, unaware that they are being observed — that they are becoming part of one boy's childhood memories — sit eating or talking or reading, caught up like fish in the dream bowls of their own lives.

Josef garners more commissions over the ensuing months. And his father is brought into a reluctant acceptance of his return to Karmeliterplatz 2, where he spends nearly every weekend, learning to write in Hebrew and Aramaic, receiving new clients with dispatch, shadowing forth marriage contracts in increasing numbers and for increasing prices, most of which earnings go toward keeping his grandfather afloat and chipping away at the old man's outsize debt, though Josef is careful to bring home enough schillings so that his father cannot argue against his success. The ketubah he painted for his parents — his first and the only one he ever fashioned from a pure heart — becomes, for lack of another one, a sample of his style, and each time his grandfather hauls it out to show to potential

178

customers, it takes on more pathos in Josef's mind for not hanging in Hietzing. There is simply no place in the world for an unwanted marriage contract.

As the asking price of his ketubot increases, so do the number of customer requests for specific imagery. If Grandfather Pommeranz had him convinced that Jews should never become attached to any city in Europe, Josef sees no evidence of such a trend in his clients, who, beyond their typical requests for the tree of life, olive branch–carrying doves, cupids with trumpets, Stars of David, shields, crowns, jutting Alps, Doric columns, or Venetian gondolas, express a vigorous interest in ketubot that reveal how *proud* they are of their city. This is how Josef comes to lard his marriage contracts with distinctive Viennese imagery: buildings like the Secession, Rathaus, Hofburg, and Burgtheater — one pair of Jews even requests St. Stephen's Cathedral; faces of Vienna's famous, from Schubert to Empress Sissi; and the Art Nouveau patterns of Otto Wagner's train stations and Gustav Klimt's paintings. "They are becoming tourist maps of Vienna!" his grandfather grouses about his ketubot.

But the old man cannot complain about the results. Within a year, Josef is known throughout the Jewish district as the "Mozart of Marriage Contracts." Enthusiastic strangers — his first fans — sail up to him on the street, asking if he is the boy working miracles at Karmeliterplatz. Many of them are more affluent Jewish couples, aglow with love, who have heard from their friends that purchasing a ketubah from him is "the thing to do these days." Josef, alas, is in vogue.

By the time he is a striking young man of thirteen — and has been bar mitzvahed in a humble ceremony officiated by his grandfather and attended only by his mother — commissions pour in from all twenty districts of Vienna and beyond. "Even from assimilated Jews!" his grandfather cries. "My beautiful, handsome grandson — he will reconvert the Jews with his paintings!" Such praise caresses Josef's eardrums like a sweet adagio: if his art can make Vienna's assimilated become Jews again, what else can it do?

What else can it do?

It can bring him admiration is what else it can do. And respect, and praise, and . . . love.

Yes, love — something that has been on his mind lately. Lately, the knowing gleam in the eyes of the young couples who come

180

to see him intimate at love's larger promises — not the kind of love he feels for his grandfather, not the kind between siblings, or parent and child, or friends, but an altogether different sort that seems part of a secret world, more infinitely magical, carnal, ungovernable. Lately, more than one of the brides-to-be — it is always a younger one, by all appearances closer to Josef in age than to the man she is going to marry — has given Josef long and frank glances while her fiancé endlessly orates about himself. Josef's eyes inevitably wander, such times, to the lambent slope of the woman's neckline, and then downward, to the modeling of her big or small bosom. His mind wanders as well. He imagines kissing her mouth, imagines it tastes of honey: heavenly and sexual, possibly poisonous. The ketubot he paints for these couples display a distinct favoring of the bride and a tendency toward rendering her man graceless. Lately, through the thin wall behind his grandfather's stove, he has heard the sounds of a man and woman doing vague, untoward things to each other in the next-door room — has heard the man, while doing these things, shout in clear High German: "I love you so much I want to throw you off a *cliff!*" Listening to such sounds, such proclamations, Josef feels that

181

he is witnessing some new kernel of man's capability. Lately too he has found himself becoming aroused when he inks in that part of the marriage contract's text detailing the Judaic objuration, taken by the groom, of providing his wife with sexual satisfaction. He imagines all the fornication he is facilitating with his drawing, the fettering of his pen to the procreation of the Jewish race.

Lately, his eyes fill with an impossibly beautiful vision of his *own* wife — who, he fatally maintains, will be offered up to him by the world to come. His vision of her does not contain specific physical details, such as the color of her hair, or eyes, or even the general shape of her face. This is not how his dreams work. His imaginings of the future arrive in his brain much like his memories do: cleansed of what is not important, distilled to essences, pitched toward the wondrous. What he feels when he envisions being with his wife is his own disappearance. He is convinced that he will have to withdraw in her presence, even efface himself, creating enough room in the world so that her grace can pass into it. Not surprisingly, he dreams of illuminating their future ketubah. The contract will be pale, diaphanous, nearly not there. He will push its spareness to the point of its own collapse, then halt at exactly that moment. He cannot picture it containing the standard text but instead a blank space in the middle — like the ketubot he used to hand over to his grandfather before he learned to write the ancient words — a space burning so brightly it cannot be gazed upon directly.

All of this takes shape in the back of his mind. In the meantime, a new voluptuousness adheres to the actual ketubot he paints for his ever-increasing customers. His past contracts have been innocent of a sexual patina, but now the odd nude female figure, displaying an outslung hip here, a munificent buttock there, makes an appearance on the page. And inspired by the erotic paintings (which his mother recently showed him at a gallery in the inner city) of Vienna's own Egon Schiele and Gustav Klimt, he smuggles into a number of new ketubot renderings of very fetching women — in various states of undress — being groped and embraced by men whose distorted, elongated figures suggest striving, accommodation, all-out worship. This new vein of his work seems to have fresh appeal for his male clients, who are suddenly less interested in quarreling about his grandfather's exorbitant asking prices for his marriage contracts. When these men come to retrieve their ketubot, Josef catches them studying his other works-in-progress with deliberation, seeking some kind of pleasure by proxy, he thinks, in the images of enraptured women. His grandfather, despite the resultant increase in profits (which, significantly, facilitated the recent clearing of his debt), upbraids Josef for this "unfortunate" turn in his work.

When, in his fourteenth summer, Josef receives a ketubah commission from the Rothschild family (who still lend their name and money to his father's bank), Josef finally smells an opportunity to win his father's admiration, the absence of which he has felt as one of the main bitternesses of his new-found success. The meeting he arranges with his father one Sunday evening in the man's study is surcharged with all the weight of an emergency measure. He finds his father waiting for him, arms akimbo, before the vast sepulchral darkness of the cold fireplace. Seeing Josef, the man smiles at him tentatively but does not move from his position, his eyes betraying an effort to suspend his bewilderment at how estranged he has become from his son. In a voice that seems choked by judgment and longing, he queries Josef about his gymnasium studies, his swimming and soccer practice, the latest

American film — topics of little interest to either of them that only throw into relief what does not exist between them. All at once, Josef sees sharply what he has not seen before: his father cannot recast his constitution and *like* him. What prevents him from saying it? *I don't like you.*

For form's sake, Josef goes ahead and shows his father the check made out to him and signed by a Rothschild. His father removes his spectacles, and as he examines the check, Josef notices the forces of resentment assembling defensively over the darkening terrain of his face.

"*My* son!" his father finally spits out, lips trembling, as if he is roundly condemning not just Josef but also himself. "My son: The *Marriage* Artist!" The last three words he announces in an amplified, caustic tone that seems intended for some imaginary tribunal of judges in the room who share his condescension. In Josef's ears, the words sound like "con artist" — as if Josef is a man who has been married twenty times, a man who manipulates women into joining him at the altar.

Without meeting Josef's eyes, his father holds the check out to him. *"This,"* he says, shaking it, "I cannot abide."

Josef takes back the check and looks

boldly at his father. Whether it is the man's disbelief that the Rothschilds — Vienna's first truly assimilated Jews, whose urbanity, worldliness, polish, and power he so esteems — would do something so *Jewish* as ordering a ketubah, or his jealousy that Josef now has a more direct relation to the Rothschilds than does he despite his having worked some twenty-odd years for their bank, or some combination of both, Josef does not know. What he does know is that *it* — whatever it is that once knitted him to his father — is gone.

He will never make himself vulnerable to the man again.

The next Sunday, his grandfather once again shows a pair of potential clients the ketubah Josef painted for his father and mother. When the nosy fiancée happens to ask whom the sample contract was made for, Josef exchanges an awkward glance with his grandfather.

"For a couple who are now dead," Josef asserts firmly.

Later, he will view it as no accident that this is the exact moment when he is alternately born as an artist and robbed of his convictions about marriage. His father's rejection of his artistry, and Josef's subsequent rejection of his father, unclenches him from the confines of bourgeois expectation, thus freeing him to be a true artist (to the degree that an artist defines who he is by what he is opposed to) — and freeing him from the biggest bourgeois expectation of all: marriage. If his father and mother are dead to him, then so is marriage.

There are other moments. Frau Glückstadt — one of his first clients from four years earlier — suddenly appears one afternoon in his grandfather's flat, holding the marriage contract Josef painted for her all that time ago. "I'm returning it," she tells Josef, slapping it down on the table.

"What's wrong with it?"

"What's wrong with my *husband?*"

"I don't understand."

"I've divorced him."

Josef is confounded by this, and he stares into the ketubah. Its foreign shapes, though clearly products of his own hand, seem to mock him from across the years.

"You put so much effort into it," Frau Glückstadt goes on in a blank, matter-of-fact tone, "I figured you would want it back."

"Don't you want to remember what you once had?" Josef asks. He does not really know what he is saying.

"For that, I do not need your contract —
I never did," she says harshly. "I married
Manfred in my heart, not just on your silly
paper. Once you do that —" She breaks off,
her chest heaving. She wipes her eyes. "I
have another piece of paper," she begins
again, "given to me by the rabbi. It says that
Manfred and I are divorced. Do you think
that means anything to me either? Do you
think that helps? There *is* no real divorce —
you cannot divorce yourself from *memory*."

She is not the only one of his clients to
divorce. Through his grandfather and the
Leopoldstadt's thick gossip chain, he learns
of others. When he thinks of this, when he
thinks of his own parents, marriages look
capricious to him, unstable and slightly
grotesque. He marvels that so many people,
nearly everyone it seems, rely so heavily on
such a thing in order to make it through
life. No wonder they come to him for
ketubot: they need to get the beauty of marriage down on paper to guard against its
grotesqueries. *Only an image can fill us with
a pure joy.*

But his images appear increasingly inef-
fectual. The couples do what they will, he
finds, regardless of what messages and com-
mandments his ketubot convey. He has been
aware from the very beginning that certain

of his clients do not love each other, and they are always the most thorough in their instructions to him, the most zealous. He used to think that, through his paintings, these passionless couples could achieve conjugal bliss by fiat. Now he sees that thoroughness is simply something they can do well together.

Nearly *three hundred* marriage contracts. His activities in Karmeliterplatz 2 have offered him a binocular view of love, and the humanity that has come to him through its doorway has assumed one sad, wholly wearying sameness. He feels that he is merely some visa clerk working the fortified border between the married and the unmarried. He is a stamper of passports, collector of names, loser of his own dreams.

His final disillusionment appears one August morning in the form of Herr Wiener, a bellicose, cigar-smoking man of substantial weight and age (well over seventy years, to Josef's eye), who comes to the flat, his twenty-year-old fiancée and teenage son in tow, to seek Josef's services. The three strangers are well dressed in the extreme, more neat and careful of their persons than Josef is used to seeing in his customers. They appear reluctant to avail themselves of the flat's scruffy furniture, leaving Josef regretful that he so casually told them to sit wherever they wanted. Herr Wiener makes the first move: perhaps sensing that any of the modest wooden chairs at the table cannot possibly support his enormous body, he takes a seat on the corner of the bed, which lets out a wail of protest and is embarrassingly unmade by Josef's grandfather, who had to run off to Klosterneuburg for the day to visit an ailing friend. The man gestures for the other two to sit at the table — the young woman obligingly does so, but the boy, who has not removed his green, wide-set eyes from Josef since he first entered the flat, refuses and remains standing.

By way of introducing himself, Herr Wiener explains that he has lived in Vienna all of his life, becoming at the end of it a very wealthy man, the result of having worked his way up from tailor's assistant to owner of the city's second largest textile factory. "This will be my sixth marriage," he boasts, blowing a puff of smoke from his eyes and pointing his cigar at his son. "His mother but recently passed away. Lost two sons to the Russians, a daughter to influenza, eleven children total" — again he points the cigar at his son — "of which *he's* the last. Twenty-two grandchildren, I have, all of them living within a tram ride of my home in the ninth district."

That is how his story begins. For fully three more hours Josef is subjected to the vagaries, the progressions, the triumphs and tragedies of Herr Wiener's life, and he finds himself thinking how appropriate is the man's name, which means "Viennese" or "native of Vienna": the measureless meters of fabric fathered by his factory, the immodest amount of wives, his obscene millions, the very meat that has fed and fattened his children and grandchildren and the ponderous pink and white flesh of his descending double chins — all mined in various ways from Vienna's abundance. "Now," Herr Wiener says at one point, waving his cigar to draw in Josef's flagging attention, "this next part is important if you are going to get this ketubah right." Josef pretends to listen, but he is too distracted, even perturbed, by the man's desperate need to share his long history, a desperation that makes him wonder if the man sees his marriage contract as some kind of warrant against death — against the world's disinterest, its short memory. Is *this* why everyone comes to him for ketubot? Is marriage nothing more than an effort to ensure that they will not be forgotten?

These questions leave him feeling uncomfortable when, later that afternoon, he accepts a deposit of twenty schillings as a token of his agreement to illuminate Herr Wiener's contract. So dazed is he by the moment that he is hardly prepared for the odd thing that happens as Herr Wiener and his fiancée turn to exit.

The son asks if he can stay.

"What?" Josef says, assuming that the boy is addressing him.

" 'Course you can stay," Herr Wiener bellows from the landing. "Then you can learn how to draw marriage contracts."

With that, Herr Wiener and his young fiancée are gone, and Josef finds himself the doomed companion of this strange, neatly dressed boy who has stared at him for the bulk of an afternoon. Now Josef returns the boy's stare. If Herr Wiener, over his long life, has partaken heartily of Vienna's provender, this son is as frail and pale as the pitiful wood chair in which he refused to sit. The boy's head, so narrow and diminutive as to seem like some sort of prehistoric throwback, accentuates the protruding yet delicate ears on either side of it.

"I don't want to draw marriage contracts," the boy says bluntly.

"Neither do I," says Josef.

"Let's get out of here."

"Where will we go?"

They will go to the Prater and ride the giant Ferris wheel, at the top of which the sun, sinking behind the distant Alps, will transfer to their cheeks its dying flush. "I hate my father," the boy will announce to the air. Josef, noticing how the sun glows pinkly through the boy's translucent ear, will wonder if sons soured on their fathers always find each other out, before replying, "I hate my father too."

They will go to the darkening banks of the Danube and witness an old Jew pulling a perch from the water before rapping its head twice on the frame of his bicycle and dropping it into a sack. "What about your mother?" the boy will ask. "Do you hate *her?*" Josef will push the toe of his shoe into the mud. "No." Then the boy will turn to him, as if about to cry. "I loved my mother." The moment will feel awkward and uncomfortable. "I love mine too," Josef will offer, and the boy's eyes will travel all over him, a smile overtaking his lips. "You and I are going to be best friends." At this Josef will let out a large laugh and boldly declare, "No we're not." "Yes we are."

They will go to St. Stephen's while Mass

is under way and steal into the cathedral's submerged atmosphere, two divers plumbing the ocean's depths. High above, the stained glass will behave like a watery surface, refracting and diffusing the last of the day's light. And in the side shadows they will find a truncated pew, wedged darkly between Gothic staircase and stone column, an underwater crevasse in which to rest and monitor their breath and the marine murmuring of Mass. "What is your name?" Josef will whisper. "Max Wiener." "Max of Vienna," Josef will say. The boy will fix him with an angry gaze. "Don't ever say that again." "Why not?" "The Jewish nation is my only home." "There *is* no Jewish nation." "There will be."

They will go to the top of St. Stephen's south tower after prevailing on a deacon, who mutters "crazy Jews" as he flips the light switch, to give them fifteen minutes to make it to the top and back down. And the stairwell, at that hour nearly all blackness, will lend their ascent up its spiraling stone steps a giddiness re-electrified with each surprising appearance of a blaring white bulb. They will scream and shriek in the beginning but soon fall into a silence broken only by the echo of their shoes. The circular room at the top, mysteriously unlit, will reward them with four modest holes in the thick stone giving out onto views of night-time Vienna, and they will peer out each one, silently changing places, aware of the deacon waiting for them below. Josef will linger at the sight of the Leopoldstadt. In the foreground, on this side of the Danube Canal: the squat spire of St. Ruprecht, the oldest church in Vienna. Beyond the illuminated barges of the canal, down Tabor-strasse, past Karmeliterplatz, past the Prater and the Danube River: only blackness, where the Great Hungarian Plain begins. "I'm never getting married," Max will announce all of a sudden. Josef will turn and look at the boy's vague silhouette. "I'm not either." And as his words are borne up by the gathering darkness with a redoubled weight, he will realize that this is truly how he feels. "Then let's make it official," Max will say, jingling coins in his pocket before pressing one into Josef's palm. "What is this?" "I kissed it — now *you* kiss it." "Okay." "This" — Max will hold up the coin they each kissed against the faint city light filtering in — "is *our* contract." The emphasis on "our" will lead Josef to think that the boy — this Max Wiener — might mean the two of them have secretly married. But Max will suddenly scream "I'm never getting married!" out of an opening, casting the coin into the night air where it will drop onto the nearby tiled roof of the cathedral. And before Josef will even be aware of what he is doing, he will lean out another window and let Vienna know that he too is never going to get married. "Never!" he will shout repeatedly. Two Jewish teens at the top of a cathedral yelling for all of 1933 Europe to hear that marriage will never be an option for them. Never. NEVER! *N E V E R!*

WE LOSE OUR
LOVE TO HISTORY,
PART TWO

THE ARRANGED MARRIAGE

She waits, Hannah Engländer, in a line stretching across half of the Leopoldstadt, to marry a man she has never seen. He has yet to appear, despite his promise to do so when the new marriage office, separately established for Jews, opened for business this morning more than an hour ago; the two of them were to become familiar while standing in line, and she is surprised to find herself harboring feelings of impatience and anger and worry — *already* — toward her future husband. Against her better judgment she stares with envy at the other young couples in front of her on the sidewalk, even though she knows they are here for the same awkward and desperate purpose: to make a hasty marriage — to anyone — in order to maximize the immigration permit to Palestine that one member of each couple has somehow obtained. The permit — she has one — is good for a husband and wife. Her envy is stupid: most of them are friends who will divorce as soon as they, *if* they, set foot in Palestine. Still, clasping her small purse in both hands, she cannot cease to look deeply into their faces. She wants to know what *they* think about wedding in such a manner. She searches their expressions for signs of how she ought to feel marrying a stranger. But their nervous eyes, ever leveled on the building's portal at the front of the line, tell her nothing.

Her acquaintance Max Wiener, who convinced her to go through with this, and who is accompanying her through the line with the sole intention of introducing her to her husband-to-be, is not telling her anything either. He will not even reveal — *still!* — the man's name. No, to the very end, for purposes she has not yet discerned, he is guarding his friend jealously. She considers demanding that he tell her — before she takes one more step in line — whom she is about to marry but decides against it when he suddenly leaves her side and crosses noiselessly to the curb, where he lights a cigarette and stares down the street. Whoever the man is, his unexpected absence is working a slow evolution in Max's extended ears, reddened now with emotion, and in his pale green eyes, which Max, full of some

200

private injury, abruptly turns back onto the people in line with a silent indignation. He does not dignify Hannah with his gaze, and she is embarrassed by how easily this bruises her. It is, finally, her own fault for finding herself in this situation. Shortly after Vienna's synagogues were burned to the ground several weeks ago, Max approached her with the proposition, having discovered that, like him, she was a permit owner. She agreed, and took no issue with his odd request that his friend's identity remain unknown to her until the actual marriage. In fact, she told herself that it was better the transaction be conducted in this manner. She wanted no confusion. After all, her motivations for agreeing to the proposal were entirely impersonal: she merely intended to help another soul get out of Austria; the civil ceremony would be nothing more than an expedient, a common-sense calculation. She certainly has no real interest in marriage. She knows herself too well.

Marriage means sex. About this she has never been illusioned, though neither has she necessarily ever viewed sex with antipathy. She simply has not rated it important. Sex strikes her as a paltry production unless it results from a union aspiring after the divine. Plato, her only real teacher, insisted as much. And among the number of men who attempted to exert an amorous influence on her, none awakened in her body the sacred sense. When she turned nineteen several years ago, she became aware of the effect her appearance and manners had on men, and she did not dislike it *altogether.* For a while she even attended to her looks, but she began to notice several curious consequences. The more energy she directed toward the physical presentation of her person, the more she coveted beauty's slippery surfaces. More troublesomely, she realized how unsoothed she was by the increased attentions of Vienna's men — even the attentions of the sophisticated ones she met at the university, who were all dazzled by themselves and driven to clarify things about her that she did not wish to have understood. These men who approached her for coffee after lectures, and who tended to lead weightless, dissolute lives, were often openly ardent toward her and tried to hurry her past the reservations she held about sex by pressing her to reveal what, exactly, she was afraid of.

How could she tell them she was afraid for their souls? That she feared for them not because they frequently bedded the more willing population of female students (she had no use for the word "sin" when applied to unmarried sex) but because she could see, had *always* seen, the eternal dust coating everything. How could she tell these vital young men that even in their eager eyes she saw life continually thinning? How could she tell them that she loved them? That her heart breached at the very thought of them, not because she was attracted to them as individuals, but because they were part of all autumnal things forever folding into oblivion.

She did not dare share this with them. Her suitors were too urbane, sarcastic, caught up in the whorl of wit and modern thought. She could play that game as well. Though she found it tiring, she could appeal to the perversely intellectual. She often told them that for her the carnal act itself fell squarely within the realm of the possible, whereas she was only ever attracted to love that was *im*possible. They liked this challenge, until she informed them that because of this preference her one great love was God. Incredulous, they inevitably tried to argue that she had no way of proving God even existed. Nietzsche's name tended to be mentioned in these protestations. True, she always conceded, God was unprovable, impossible, an infinite idea. But whether He existed or not, we had to *try* loving Him — it was our only chance to love that which is outside this brief world. "Don't you think," she would ask them, "that the perishing ought to be permitted to love a pure and lasting thing?"

Few who heard this argument displayed a genuine interest in discovering what underlay it: an uncompromising vision of the world in which evil was actually the oxygen of a spiritual existence. The half dozen men who *did* (interestingly, they were never Jews like her, but rather Catholics) had to implore her to speak about beliefs with which she was reluctant to part. How could one speak about such things without sounding ridiculous? When on the rare occasion she finally submitted to their entreaties, she tried, usually over coffee at Café Landtmann, to be as clear as was possible: Absolute goodness, she felt, was nowhere to be found in the world; if it existed at all, it was billeted in an uncataloged corner of the universe, a corner she was tempted to call God (and here, by way of illustration, she would sometimes slide her coffee to a remote corner of the table). God so separated Himself from the world that we might be as far away from Him as possible, thus making our effort to love Him as great as that distance — as great as His love. To ensure that any real love of Him was not small and false, He provided the world, before absenting Himself from it, with a thick pall of time and evil (here she would sometimes push together everything else on the table — the cream, the spoons, the salt and pepper — until they formed a rough wall down the middle). She therefore felt in the deepest reaches of her being that affliction and suffering had to be viewed as a gift from God, a grace, because they mirror — or rather they *are* — the agony of trying to reach Him across such a divide.

Whenever she finished unbaring these painfully personal feelings, her admirers always paused and then asked her where she came up with her ideas. She was savvy enough to see what they were seeing: an odd yet fairly attractive female classmate with whom they felt they had chances (a Jewess they could imagine nude and couchant on some student bed), who was espousing unusual, possibly crazy ideas that just might lead to erotic fumblings in the dark. Nevertheless, she tried to answer them honestly; they were lost in their lust, but she was lost in her way too: *all* people's endeavors were fumblings in the darkness that is the world.

Her ideas? she would say, *well* — if she had to ascribe them to anything it would be to her many soundings of Greek thought and her experiences helping those citizens of Vienna who were less fortunate than she. When still a gymnasium student, she had begun volunteering at the Rothschild Hospital and had requested to be assigned to the most desperate cases: the terminally ill, the psychotic, the suicidal. She had also joined several Zionist groups (which ultimately led to her receiving one of the scarce immigration permits to Palestine) — not because she believed Jews were the Chosen People (*every* soul plucked from the shadow realm of eternity and born to the diverse beauties and indignities of the world had been *chosen*), nor because she believed they were owed their promised land (she did not believe any human is owed a thing); no, she merely wanted the opportunity to counsel the impoverished-but-intrepid Eastern Jewish youth who made up the bulk of the groups' membership, and, frankly, she had been certain for many years already that the Jews' tenure in Europe was about to expire, a certitude that would soon enough become a certainty.

Since she did not take pleasure in drawing attention to her own suffering, she never

told her wooers that her belief in the centrality of suffering to any meaningful life had
far less to do with Plato and her social work
than with a persistent melancholy she had
had since birth, and the concomitant nightmares and headaches that relentlessly
troubled her dreams and days. She did not
mention the perils of nights, nor how, waking at terrible hours, she had only her
reasoning to rely on as a means of penetrating the darkness. Why discuss these things
when she had learned to love her lot, this
trouble, and the extra content it gave?
Above all else she held her headaches high-
est: their unstilled pain humbled her head
and purified her days; they sentenced her to
a life without falsehood. Her headaches had
the size and power on which a faith could
rest. All of her visions — of God's mercy
coming down to her through affliction, of
loving Him through pain, of receiving His
grace in the form of grief — appeared to
her only when her brain was being squeezed
by great unseen hands.

Her suitors ignored everything but her
"unusual" beliefs, which they attempted to
use as justifications for why she should go
to bed with them. Since we were all time-
blighted creatures caught in the agony of an
ephemeral world, they would say to her,

since God was so *far* away, what did it matter whether she slept with them, for a night, here below? Why not simply have some fun?

It was sometimes all she could do to prevent herself from breaking out into laughter in the face of one of these poor fellows. There was a charm to their resolve, and witnessing it elicited from her a certain tenderness for these single-minded men. She had enough humor to throw reason right back at them: Pleasure or happiness, she would retort, when one saw how much these were products of chance and circumstance, bore the stamp of their opposite — human misery. She would therefore never *pursue* a thing like happiness or love; these would have to come to her and only in a very specific form. If, for example, love came in the form of desire for her, she could not abide it. The men always wanted to know in what form would love have to come for her to accept it? Her answer never changed: "The only one that reflects man's true condition — absolute affliction." It was here where the conversations ended.

She soon wearied of these interminable coffees. And before long she lost interest in the attention to her appearance and in people's stares — men's and her mirrored own.

What does it mean *now,* her rejection of all those men? She asks herself this while scrutinizing the other young women in the line. Their situation is grim; each is not exactly exchanging spoony stares with her partner, but they at least look like they *could* fall in love. The couples' shoulders are pressed close together, their hands hang within a finger's reach of each other. Why has she never been moved by a desire to secure for herself at least some semblance of this normalcy? What has prevented her from inventing ways to at least *appear* the same as others? Following an ideal: what a monstrous thing to do. And right up to the end at that. How like her only to allow herself to be married under these circumstances — anonymously, by force, waiting in a *line!*

And her partner is not even showing up.

"It's almost noon," she finally announces.

Max, back in line with her now, is all breath and indignation — his little show of resentment at having to respond. "He'll *be* here," he answers curtly without looking at her.

They are keeping their voices to a whisper. Although the two brown-shirted storm troopers, who earlier entertained themselves by berating people in line for half an hour, have disappeared and only a regular police officer is positioned at the street corner, she and Max, like the other Jews around them, do not dare risk revealing that there is anything unusual about her marriage. For the first time all morning she grants herself permission to really look at the entrance up at the head of the line. The plain building's portal frightens her. It is doorless, a black ruin edged with a thin lip of molding. Far from appearing as a threshold to matrimony and the future, it resembles a gateway leading in an entirely different direction, an exit out of life, the very vanishing point of human love. The couples in front seem to be entering a dying person's mouth. "He isn't going to come," she says.

Having uttered these words, she experiences mingled relief and sadness, and wonders if she has been lying to herself. Did she really agree to this civil marriage in order to be of service to another Jew — or is there another reason, some unacknowledged need? She suddenly feels uncomfortable in her body. An alien sensation, this. Has her soul finally removed itself beyond the reach of her flesh, leaving her here to marry, to do God knows what with a man? How else to explain this new vulnerability?

Max steps out to the curb again and peers

down the street for several seconds before meeting her gaze, *finally,* and returning to the line. "Maybe he was picked up," he murmurs.

It is the first verbal concession to a concern they have each privately held all morning: that Max's friend — sometime between now and yesterday afternoon when he briefly rendezvoused with Max in a café on the Praterstern — was apprehended by the gestapo, who have been loading the city's Jewish men into boxcars, often at random, and shipping them off to Dachau.

She looks at Max and her eyes tear up, surprising her; it is one thing to make doubt-ridden statements yourself but an entirely different thing to have your pessimism confirmed by another. She tries to diminish the severity of the implication weighing on both of them by offering a joke: "Maybe he decided he can't marry a stranger."

Max's response comes as a shock to her: "A stranger is all he *can* marry."

What? Could his friend possibly share her *exact* reservations about marriage? The idea makes her heart quicken and she begs Max to elucidate, but he simply stands there beside her as if lost to his thoughts. She notices then how *thin* he truly is. Not only does he look alone on the sidewalk despite being mere inches from her, he also looks alone in his *suit,* which hangs mostly unused and unfilled by his frame.

"A long time ago," he begins. He pauses to raise his eyes, and the sky's unvarying blue, so seemingly indifferent to the details deviling them here on the sidewalk of Zirkusgasse, fills his pupils until they appear blind to all but the problems of the past. "A long time ago he made a vow."

"A vow," Hannah echoes. She hesitates. "To — another woman?"

"To never marry."

She blinks at him. She was not expecting this, and for some reason it strikes her as an affront.

"The truth is," he tells her, "we both made the same vow."

A sudden and inexplicable anger takes hold of her. "Why aren't *you* marrying then?" she blurts out. "You have a permit. You've been sermonizing about the Zionist cause — how we need to get everyone we possibly can to Palestine. Why don't you marry someone as well?"

The question seems to fall on Max like an enormous weight. "It would be impossible," he says simply.

She hardly hears this. Her mind can think

212

only of the man who should be standing here beside her instead of this frustrating acquaintance of hers. "And when you approached your friend with your idea, when you told him about my permit, did he agree to the wedding" — the image holds her up a moment — "as easily as I did?"

"On the contrary. He refused at first."

"Even though it meant possibly saving his life?"

"It took me four days to convince him."

She considers this for a moment, more intrigued than ever by this mystery man. "He made a vow," she begins slowly, as if solving a riddle, "a vow you also took and are sticking to. You convinced him to break it, and now I'm a part of it. What you're telling me is that your friend is a noble man, and we're conspiring to corrupt him."

Max abruptly turns on her as if she is the sole repository of all the world's evils. "I–will–*not*–leave–Vienna–without–him–do–you–understand?"

He has been ungentle with her before. Almost immediately on meeting him two years ago at a Zionist training farm he was overseeing outside of Vienna, she noted his stormy mental weather during social interactions; conversations with him resembled nothing so much as messy romantic entanglements in that they began passionately, were rarely completed, and often came to a crashing halt. He would hardly know a person before attempting to exert influence on them, all the while displaying a touchy adoration that blew hot and cold. And though Hannah had readily agreed that the need to get the Jews out of Europe had become a reality, she was always repelled by Max's exhortatory tone and his pitifully simplistic and circular reasoning whenever he spoke of the Jews' return to Zion. She was amazed to see how many members of their Zionist organization cottoned to his personality and its unpredictable geometries; it was a lesson in the blind need people had to follow someone who simply assumed power. Because she rejected *any* cultivation of power, and because she easily bested him in every argument about Jewish nationalism or religion (he was an impassioned atheist), she paradoxically aroused in Max an attraction to rivalry and rejection, and he pursued her friendship with avidity. In fact, he affected to be in love with her, pretending that she was his inamorata. He was terrible at it, of course. At the endless lectures on Palestine he invited her to, at meetings organized by every offshoot of the Zionist movement in Austria, even at dinners in his father's large house in the ninth district, declamations against the National Socialists and the odd pat of his palm on her shoulder formed the core of his overtures to her. Nevertheless, she continued to meet him socially; she liked that he never tried to convince her to sleep with him, and there was something about him that left her with an ungraspable sorrow whenever they parted. He seemed to her to be the loneliest living thing she had ever come across. Still, her frustration with him grew in proportion to the number of hours she spent in his company, and she was ready to disown him after only a few months. He struck her as the only human in existence whose weaknesses did not reveal the person. And when she was not a victim of his unwarranted emotionalism, she had to withstand his stolidity, both of which behaviors blinded him to the most important needs — the subtle, internal ones — of other people, hers included. So she let their friendship lapse into a pale acquaintanceship until, with the help of the Germans, their association found its final form: he would help her to help another, by bringing her a man to marry.

But in light of what he has just so irately revealed to her — that he will not go to Palestine without his friend — she wonders if he is not so much helping her as he is helping himself. And a new fear enters her thoughts, a greater doubt about the man he wants her to wed. In all the time she has spent in Max's company, why has she never met this person before? To what shore is she being ferried?

"Tell me his name," she says to Max.

It is as if she has committed an insurrection, the way he looks at her. "No."

For a moment they lock eyes. Then she hoists her purse onto her shoulder and steps out of the line.

"What are you doing?" he asks, only now practicing restraint with his tone.

"Leaving."

"You can't do that."

"Then tell me his name."

He just stares at her, as determined and recalcitrant as ever.

"Good-bye," she says, turning away.

"Josef Pick."

She stops and swivels around to face him. Other people in line are watching them now, but Hannah, buoyed by the fillip of energy that her small victory over Max has granted her, does not care. Triumphantly, she reassumes her place in line, doing everything she can not to allow a smile to overtake her stoic expression. "Pick? I've heard of that family. They're well connected, aren't they? I would have guessed they'd already left Austria by now. What's your friend — this Josef Pick — still doing here?"

"It's his father," Max answers. "He won't leave. If you can believe it, the old man loves Vienna too much."

She believes it. That the city's charm has long cozened its Jewish citizens into a false sense of belonging is nothing new to her. How could its abundance of culture *not* be seductive — particularly to the bourgeois Jews who have created so much of it? As for herself, she was deprived at a young age of any illusions about the Jews' place among the Gentiles, by her Russian Jewish mother's pogrom-stained stories, stories portraying Jews as outliers among a populace compelled to rise up against them with frightening regularity, stories of murder and pillage and a thousand inconceivable things — stories told nearly every day of her childhood that amounted to a dark summary of the Jews' entire European history, and, more personally, to a permanent disabusement of the nearly religious devotion to Vienna held by so many of her Jewish friends and compatriots. Unlike them, Hannah could see the city's operettas and waltzes, its salons

217

and society, only as a cruel theater that seduced its Jewish actors into a stupor, while overhead the stage lights whitely shrieked away, and the songbirds darkening the chestnut trees sang of the tragedy's ominous ending.

Hannah was not surprised last March by the sudden Nazi incursion, nor by their recent ransacking of synagogues and stores and homes that, overnight, has left Jews once again puddled at the entrances of every foreign embassy in town. Hitler and his men have merely pierced the proscenium. They are the new opera troupe, who happen to have a heraldic allegiance to Wotan, god of war and death. To her, the German entrance onto the Vienna stage is nothing less than a stylized reintroduction of the primeval world — into a city that first expelled it all those centuries ago when Aurelius and his Romans, encamped on the Danube, beat back the barbarians. Into a city that has been continually expelling it ever since, through royal decree and decadence, gymnasium-born pedantry, and good old-fashioned bureaucracy. Now that the very people brought up on those fruits of civilization have opened their arms to the barbarians once again, the real theater — the oldest drama in the world — has begun.

Like all conquerors, the current ones cannot see that in the end we are all the conquered, and that therefore they are not so much creating human affliction as they are revealing it. What with their freshly created titles, their crabbed rulings and involuted laws, their vain shiny surfaces, and their erratic fury, the Nazi bureaucrats and bullies fancy themselves princes of a new order, but they are only bringing ancient news.

"So his family has stayed," she says, picking up the thread of their conversation, "but surely if he's a friend of yours he must be a rabid Zionist — why doesn't he have a permit to Palestine like you?"

This clearly aggrieves Max, who folds his arms tightly against his chest and stares vacantly at the building's entrance. "Believe me" — his tone has turned querulous now — "if he hadn't so adamantly refused the Zionist call, he and I would already be in Tel Aviv by now."

"I suddenly like your friend a lot more."

"Don't fall in love with him."

A curious thing to say. "Why not?"

"It won't do anyone any good."

She searches his eyes. "You mean it won't do *you* any good," she ventures, wondering what she is saying.

But he is unhelpful, implacable. "Don't fall in love, Hannah. It doesn't suit you."

"What do you mean by *that?*"

"I mean you *destroy* love — that's what I mean. You let men fall for you, but you stall them off. You don't ever requite their attentions . . . no, that would be too beneath you, because men are real and you can't love something real. You can only love nothingness. Isn't that what you try to do to men — turn them into nothingness? Cajole their love into friendship by exciting their desire then refusing to satisfy it? It's how you kill them, cut them down, so that you can then so piously resurrect them. But I think it's even more than that: it's how you *keep* them. You arrest them in all their libidinal bloom. That way, you don't suffer from anything except your own indifference. You recast any inclination you have to love into an inclination to *be* loved. But you don't know what love even looks like. You have an approximate idea at best. That's why you focus all your love on your god — you can only love an approximate thing."

As Hannah listens to this invective, she tries to present a face of deep consideration, but the truth is that Max's words are so unexpected, so virulent and mean, that it is all she can do just to reconcile herself to the

220

scale of the indictment. As for the particular points, several of them hit her as cruel truths, while others she can only hope are dismally wrong. She is aware of her failings when it comes to love, but she would never intentionally cause another soul to suffer. Since Max's interest in her has never been enough to merit this display of wrath, she can only conclude that he is in great pain. Then it comes to her: as much as he needs to bring off this marriage, he regards it as an offense, or rather a threat, to himself. She suddenly turns and looks at him. His great pain — it is *heartache.*

Reflexively, she throws her arms around him, feeling, as she squeezes what little there is of his slight upper self, the bony spur of his shoulder jut into her bosom. There before her is his pinkened ear, and into its folds she whispers: "You *love* him."

"He is my friend," Max insists, his voice frail and disembodied. "He is my friend."

She does not immediately withdraw her hold on him, and to her surprise neither does he make a move to evade it. Resting her cheek against his shoulder, staring down at the hopeful new shoes worn by the couple in front of them, she wonders at the strangeness of fate. That her arms are around, of all the men she has known, the one who as a general thing has never welcomed her affection; that she and Max could pass right now as a loving couple waiting to get married; that this little balloon of tenderness between them has risen only out of a recognition of his feelings for a man; and that she is supposed to *marry* that man! strikes Hannah as a series of small ironies brought to perfection. Yet overriding these musings is a deeper sensation that has been spreading inside of her ever since she and Max joined the other couples in line: Hannah is covetous. It pains her to admit this to herself, but toward Max's friend she harbors a possessiveness that has increased both with the hours that have passed without his appearance (Max is *right:* she can love only nothingness!) and, more bothersomely, with the revelation of Max's amorousness toward the man. The truth is, despite her compassion for Max's situation, she cannot help but feel glad, no, *victorious* that this Josef Pick, to judge by Max's undeniable heartache, does not return his admirer's affections.

Max suddenly slips from her embrace under the pretext of having to step out to the curb again in case Josef Pick is looking for them in the dizzyingly long line. He stands out there forever, back turned to her, feet lolling precariously on sidewalk's edge, leaning his upper body over the street as if longing to leave; occasionally he takes a quick glance at her over his shoulder, reminding her of a boy who has swum rebelliously far from shore but because of some survival instinct keeps looking back at the land. When he finally rejoins her, there is a trace of resentment in his eyes and an extreme awkwardness between them. The minutes pass slowly, stretching, it seems, into hours, until time becomes intolerable, a tyranny, and all at once it occurs to her that the Nazis have succeeded: they have stopped time by fiat. With nothing else to do, she watches several smartly dressed women come down the sidewalk, the day's shopping weighing down their shoulder bags; they march past her and the rest of the line, heels clicking, eyes fixed on the tasks lying ahead. Non-Jews, clearly. The business of life must go on, the bread must be bought. Either a vast hidden bewilderment is at play, Hannah speculates, or Vienna's Gentiles truly *are* unamazed by the alterations Hitler has hung on their city, truly are undisturbed by the embarrassment of Jews ringing its blocks.

Abruptly, Max's outstretched thumb jabs deep into the tender flesh at her hip bone.

"It's him," Max says.

It's him.

She is struck by her reaction to these two words; they might as well have been: "It's Him." Her breathing stops and her vision contracts, reducing the wide, scary world to a few blurred objects below: there are two shoe tips, there a purse, and there, clutching at its leather straps, a pair of trembling hands. It takes a moment for these things to register as belonging to herself. What is happening to her? And why, since she is suddenly certain that she has waited *forever* to hear these words? It's *him.*

Max jabs her hip again. *"Wave,"* he urges her. "Do it now. He doesn't know what you look like. I'm not here." Before she can grasp all this, he slips discreetly behind her in the line, but not without provoking the ire of the couple standing there, whose complaints he quiets instantly with a threat to kill them should they not shut their damned mouths. *"Now!"* Max commands her, nudging her in the back.

Hannah's ears are roaring. Pulling herself together enough to make her first move, she dares to raise her eyes, and her courage is met at once with confusion, because, near the distant street corner where Max's attention has been focused, there are *two* men, each appearing to scrutinize people's faces as they slowly make their way past the line. Should she wave? The two of them are walking abreast of each other, their bodies so close as to give her the odd impression that they are holding hands. But as they draw a bit nearer it becomes clear that one is being conducted down the sidewalk by the other, who has a pistol in his opposite hand. Now she waves.

And she shouts — "Here!"

The men come to a halt. They have spotted her. Words are briefly exchanged between them, then they proceed swiftly in her direction — in sync, it seems to Hannah, with each terrible throb of her heart.

When they are still ten paces away, she is shocked to see that on the surface they resemble one another: though of differing heights, each man is slender, rangy, and pale of cheek, with something undomesticated — a seeping intensity in the eyes — darkening his features. She is shocked because one of the approaching men, the one wielding the pistol, is a gestapo officer in plain clothes. But for a few silvery appointments on his lapel (including a tiny swastika), he and the other — is it really her Josef Pick? . . . she gives him five frantic glances: yes, it *has* to be him — could be taken for ill-assorted brothers.

But there is no brotherliness in what happens next. The officer pushes Josef's delicately boned face right up to hers, so close that she can see the brush of whiskers on his chin and the thick hairs falling loose like a black wing over his forehead — so close that she can look into his uncommonly radiant caramel eyes as the officer presses the tip of his pistol into Josef's temple and yells, for everyone in the line to hear: "This Jew insists he is to be married to a woman with a visa to Palestine — but he could not produce her name for us! I would have put this Jew on last night's train to Dachau if I wasn't so curious to see his bride-whore — because only a *whore* would marry a man who didn't know her name!" The officer turns his eyes on Hannah. "Are you the whore who is going to marry this man?"

Josef's eyes shine at her with amazement and fear. In reply, in a single instant, she feels every part of herself rise to him. All of her womanly instincts, all of her spirit, all of her animal protectiveness — they are his, irrevocably. As if he sees this, everything in his aspect becomes fixed and clear. His face is bloodless now, brilliant and hard and strangely inexpressive. It fills the air like a banner of victory. No wonder Max protected him jealously: this is a man to be guarded, a dazzling person. Hannah cannot look away.

"I said are you the *whore* who is going to marry this man?"

She reaches out and takes his hand.

"His name is Josef Pick," she announces, still transfixed by his eyes. "And, yes, I will marry him."

CONTACT

If Daniel knew *anything* about Benjamin
Wind, it was surely this: that it had been no
small feat for a Blackfoot to conquer a world
that was, at least in the eyes of its fiercest
critics, a cliquish, sometimes-secret society
whose impenetrable workings could seem
downright cabalistic. Skeptics maintained
that Wind had done it by appealing to an
art world that prided itself on its inclusion
of minority voices, but Daniel did not buy
this, because the truth of the matter was
that the art world remained all too dominated by whites and Eurocentric leanings.
Others attributed the critical and commercial excitement that had girt Wind's
work to excellent buzz or even his feline
good looks, and Daniel saw these arguments
also as silly. Perhaps the most tenable theory
put forth by Wind's disbelievers was that he
had achieved success by remaining that
most elusive of figures: the artistic anchorite.

He *had* held a healthy intolerance of fraternizing, which paradoxically won him large adoration from an art world that equated aloofness with brilliance. But by Daniel's reckoning, Wind had deserved the money, adulation, everything the art world had thrown his way, because his art had passed the aesthetic test, period. And yet it had revealed nearly nothing of the man: Wind's work was honest, it seemed to emanate from an unchecked heart, but in its conquest of your psyche it had all the impersonality of a coat of arms.

Of Wind's personal life Daniel knew still less, since personal statements never issued from the man's mouth. It was as if Wind had believed it inconsiderate to burden others with his vicissitudes. Conversations with him therefore had seemed light, at times even trite, or, worse, confessional on Daniel's part, because Wind's reservedness had had a dilating effect on him: Daniel would do most of the talking, inevitably vomiting up whole lava flows of unnecessary, frequently unseemly autobiographical details while Wind sat there listening and trying to avoid his eyes.

Daniel had assumed that Wind's Blackfoot blood laid claim on his mannerisms. Greeting anyone, the guy had always looked as if he were reluctantly parting with a majestic privacy, and this quality, perhaps more than any other, led people to black conclusions about him. Men were inclined to label him arrogant, and many would wonder aloud if Wind were not a homosexual, citing his manner of dress (he was invariably well-groomed) and, of course, his beauty. Daniel imagined they had envied him because they could not know him — a feeling he himself had experienced in Wind's presence, right up to the end. The artist had certainly been complicated, even problematic — life seemed to put forth greatness in no other variety of person — but he had been kind. Daniel had liked him.

Even in retrospect Daniel could not see anything calculated about Wind's un-knowability. The man had carried it like an uncurable illness, from which people — women in particular — continually rushed in to deliver him. Was this how he had initially drawn in Aleksandra? *How* had Wind taken her from him? If the show had sealed the deal, when had the negotiations begun? And had death been written into the deal from the beginning? More ominously, had Aleksandra tried to terminate the contract? Had That Day been a consequence of such an attempt?

It was in the pursuit of answers to these questions that Daniel decided he would attend, several months after Aleksandra's funeral, the upcoming memorial service for Benjamin Wind at All Souls Church.

"What business do you have going to that horrible man's memorial service?" his mother asked during their regular weekly phone conversation, after Daniel had confessed his intentions to her. "I can't believe you're even *thinking* of going to that thing. Don't you *hate* that man now?"

It was a good question, actually. One he had been considering for weeks — ever since he had found the photograph. And to his dismay, all of his consideration kept leading back to himself. He hated Benjamin Wind to the degree that hate included every other sentiment: envy and admiration, love and disbelief, shame and understanding, the need to convince and control. Wind's work had been *his,* Daniel's, work. Wind's last love had been *his* last love. Did he hate Benjamin Wind? His ability to hide from himself had never been so little at his command. Sure, he hated Benjamin Wind. He hated Aleksandra too. He hated and hated them.

"I hate *myself,*" he ended up telling his mother.

"Oh, *Daniel,*" she said with real feeling.

He heard something in her voice then that went back to before he was a conscious person, a note infused with all the years of a mother's caring for her son, and it made him erupt into tears. He cried unabashedly, with no awareness of time, while his mother listened patiently on the other end and interrupted the long pauses only to offer an occasional soft murmuring of his name.

When he had finally composed himself and the conversation resumed roughly where it had left off before his declaration of self-loathing — that is, with his mother again pressing him not to attend Wind's memorial service — he found that he was a lot less clear about his reasons for planning to do just that. She put forth so many counterarguments, she said so many things — she had *always* said so many things — that it was statistically impossible for a few of them not to be true. He was tired, his head felt hollow after his little display of emotion, and he could only answer her that he was going to the service for *something.* He did not know what it was yet. He might *never* know.

All Souls Church, a stone distillate of crisp Georgian geometry, commanded its corner of Lexington Avenue and Eightieth Street like any good Unitarian church ought to: modestly, firmly, with Spartan self-possession. It stood a mere two hundred yards as the crow flies from Carrigan Gallery, and Daniel, mounting its shallow steps, could not fail to see irony in the proximity of the church, where he would now join others in ritually remarking Benjamin Wind's death, to the site of the artist's greatest triumph in life (over the art world, over *him*).

Daniel could not fail to see *many* things as he passed under the austere massive white transom of the church's door, because to arrive at the memorial service of a man you had come to hate as much as admire was to unseal your senses, to be on high alert. He saw that his presence was unwelcome. He saw that he was crashing a party whose hosts had deliberately not invited him: his entrance into the sanctuary, which required him to breast several tides of unfriendly guests, was more intrusive than if he had unexpectedly barged into Benjamin Wind's house while the singularly private man had still been alive. More unsettling was his impression that he was intruding not only on Wind's turf but also on Aleksandra's. The small eternity it was taking him to find a seat, the incriminating soberness of the sanctuary's symmetry, the darkly victorious clouds pressing on the windows, the protest of the church piano, the eyes and gossip penetrating from every pew, even an usher's effete attempt to make him feel welcome — what were these but warnings to be reasonable about this, to submit to the facts: Aleksandra may have married him, but she had died with Benjamin Wind. Could he accept that death was the stronger bond, or worse, that his marriage had not been what he had believed it to be — not necessarily a lie, but something narrower than love? Did he have the courage to admit that he had confused his instinctual urge to impregnate Aleksandra with the higher summons and the thick dailiness that are marriage? Did the photograph he was carrying in his jacket pocket this very minute — the one showing Aleksandra nestled close against Benjamin in some European city — not tell him everything he needed to know? Could this memorial service actually add anything that would magically make him understand? In other words, should he not simply go home? As it was, Aleksandra's premature death would hound him the rest of his days; had he really come here to be divested of every last illusion he held about his marriage to her? Did he want to carry *that* loss until the tomb?

Maybe he did. If it brought him closer to the truth, it could be worth it. And yet, what would the truth about Aleksandra and Benjamin really buy him? Would it not reinforce what he already feared might be the truth about living: that if you were lucky enough to be allotted any length of it, living always resolved your life's best things (in his case, Aleksandra and Benjamin) into its most painful? Illusion or truth — between the lines of which of these stories did he want to find his life?

His friends and colleagues were now watching him. In their eyes he was clearly diminished, not ennobled, by his choice to attend the service. It had reduced him to the status of the cuckold, the dope, perhaps even damaged his professional standing. His art world comrades, usually so flip, had abruptly adopted a Renaissance ethos of honor and saving face. He was in violation — an embarrassment to all of them. Had he any *pride?* their stares seemed to ask. In ruder ages, he would have been expected to piss on the grave of his wife's lover; no one would have flinched if he had disinterred the man's remains and dragged them through the streets. These were different times, it was an urbane world, but the least he could do was avoid the humiliation of paying respects to the man who had been fucking his wife.

The glance of mock pleasure at seeing him cast by Patrick Carrigan did little to help. *"Daniel,"* Carrigan said, sandwiching Daniel's hand between both of his own. "Coming here like this, it — it must be hard for you." The man's tone was all sorrow, stretched as long as his face. "It isn't!" Daniel broke out at him, and then tried to couch his embarrassment in declarations of how much time had passed since "the thing" ("That Day" was a phrase he would never allow himself to speak) and by boasting of a sangfroid he did not own. He attempted to withdraw his hand but Carrigan maintained an unconscious clamp on it, which threw Daniel's free hand into dire confusion: it moved to unfix its imprisoned sibling, but, to its utter horror, found itself suddenly established atop Carrigan's wrist in a four-layer embrace that could only be described as intimate. The free hand propelled itself away with uncalled-for violence, before describing a ragged arabesque in the air and finally bivouacking on Daniel's hip.

Carrigan released Daniel's hand. It was clear that behind the comprehensive smile smeared across his face he was drawing ungenerous conclusions about Daniel.

"I'm going to sit down," Daniel announced.

"Yes," said Carrigan.

Daniel beetled his way toward the pews, pretending to be confused by the crowd, preoccupying himself with the falseness of finding a seat. The ridiculous physicality of the Carrigan encounter and the incoherency of his own conduct had instilled in him a negative resolve — it had nerved him to stay. He would ache out the rest of the service, other people's judgments be damned. In the rear of the sanctuary he found privacy and a good view of the proceedings. The sun had broken through the windows and a hundred cheeks in front of him were at once pale with it. Did any of them belong to someone who represented the reason he had come today? A number of them certainly belonged to people who had just given him a very stiff reception, but he was surprised that he bore no ill will toward them. It had something to do with seeing the backs of their heads, which aroused his compassion. It was like looking out at an ocean of exposed, eyeless creatures that were dumb to his scrutiny and defenseless against attack.

The church pianist suddenly stopped playing and a minister approached the pulpit — two signals that sent a dampening hush through the sanctuary. Daniel found himself focusing on the two front pews where he assumed Benjamin Wind's family were sitting, though if he was looking directly at Wind's mother or father he would not have known it, and since he could not see their faces from where he sat anyway, his interest in Wind's family became tangled up and ultimately lost in a monotony of hair.

One figure, however, did catch his attention: a bespectacled man of extreme old age, to judge by his frondlike limbs and the insubstantiality of his frame. He was seated in a wheelchair parked close enough to the edge of the left front pew to be associated with whoever of Wind's family was stationed there. Still, Daniel had strong reasons to doubt that any such association existed. For one, the man wore a yarmulke on his hairless and freckled scalp, and, as far as Daniel knew, there were no Jews in Benjamin Wind's bloodline. More curious, and the reason Daniel's attention was drawn to the frail old fellow to begin with, was that Daniel recognized him from Aleksandra's funeral several months earlier, where he had not spoken to the man (he had not spoken to anyone at Aleksandra's funeral) but had assumed him to be some distant relative of hers, a tertiary uncle to whom Daniel had never been introduced. Why, then, was he here? Was it plain curiosity, of the sort that had seemingly driven half the art world to a Unitarian church early on a Saturday morning? Or was he, in addition to being one of Aleksandra's relations, an art collector — an owner of Wind's work? This theory was not as implausible as it sounded. Various of Aleksandra's large family — immigrants now dispersed all over the eastern seaboard — had made fortunes in simple, unemphasized trades like groceries, warehousing, and ship lading. Daniel could easily imagine this guy hearing through the Jewish-family grapevine that Benjamin Wind's work was a "smart buy." And it *had* been a smart buy, particularly now that the artist was no more. The longer he mused on the mysterious old Jew, the more Daniel was convinced he was correct. If this uncle had attended Aleksandra's funeral because of blood, he was here because of Mammon. The old man's proximity to the front pew was merely structural: he appeared to be nearly blind — no doubt he was also deaf — and in need of being as close to the pulpit as possible in order to savor his prosperous good turn ritualized.

That ritual's leader, the fair-haired gentleman now adjusting the height of the pulpit's microphone, was clearly one of the church's young ministers. He was scrub-faced and spotless in his black vestment, and he strove eagerly to meet the eyes of at least one person in all four corners of the sanctuary. "Welcome to this holy space," he began, "where we gather to give thanks for the life of Benjamin Wind."

And this, surprisingly, was all it took to send Daniel into a sudden paroxysm of grief — not at the end of Benjamin Wind but rather at the end of Aleksandra. During her own funeral, he had not heard one of the rabbi's words. Her death's bite, still so fresh then, had been fatal to his faculties. It had torn him away from words, demoted him to the stone world of senselessness. But here at All Souls, where he sat, improbably, at the service for her late lover, it was a different story. Simply by evoking Benjamin Wind's name the minister had opened the door to death, and Daniel stumbled right through the threshold. Through the threshold and into the *fact* of it: the meaningless blind necessity of it, the paramount irreversibility of it, the wicked joke of it, the scientific silence of it. Death — it was not even nonbeing, but instead a big, blank, alien nothingness that refused every vision of souls or permanence or Aleksandra. And to Daniel's dismay, his only current means of escaping from its vacuum was this rookie minister's voice. So he listened carefully to the man's words. They were his only hope now. They might even be what he had come for.

The minister told a few anecdotes about Benjamin Wind (gathered in haste, no doubt, from obvious art world sources like Patrick Carrigan), but with these second-hand accounts, intended to be humorous, the guy essentially struck out — two half-hearted laughs were all he managed to extract from the pews. Yet the young minister had come prepared to meet a hostile audience, and his next move seemed a defensive one. By way of proving that he was not so different from any art world denizen, he advanced what Daniel understood to be the proverbial bread and butter of Unitarian Universalism — its recipe of tolerance mixed with a catholicity of religious strands, including atheism — and peppered it with a few feigned off-the-cuff hipster art world shibboleths. "I believe Benjamin Wind, as both an artist and a Native American, would have approved of this place for his death memorial," he an-

nounced. "Here in this cathedral conse-
crated to openness and diversity, we are the
bad-boy artists of the religious world. Long
ago, we recognized that we had to decon-
struct the conventional walls separating the
established religious traditions and create a
new conceptual space — a kind of nonprofit
artists' collaborative where we played a
creative and curatorial role in bringing
spirituality to a broad spectrum of people.
Think of Unitarian Universalism as as-
semblage or scatter art — an alternative,
all-encompassing context for the sacred."

This did bring many, though unintended,
laughs, and Daniel found himself all at once
feeling protective of the man at the pulpit.
The guy was trying. Sure, there had been a
comical overreaching to his introductory
words, yet their rootedness in reality had
already had the effect of comforting Daniel.

But his comfort, to say nothing of his allegiance to the minister, came to an abrupt
end. "I've spoken about Benjamin Wind the
person. Now I'd like to say a few words
about his art, which it was my pleasure to
study over the last few weeks in preparation
for today's service. What a profound body
of work Benjamin Wind produced! My
mind and my heart were sent in many directions — most of them wonderful — while

242

looking through the books and catalogs and reviews of his sculptures. And that's what I want to draw your attention to right now: the *wonderful* in Benjamin Wind's work. For I don't believe that Benjamin Wind's was the 'Art of Dying.' "

From the moment he had set foot in the church, Daniel had sensed a subtle antagonism directed toward himself. He was mostly willing to attribute the feeling to the handiwork of his own tired mind on the lookout for someone to blame. But he was not imagining *this,* the minister's allusion to the title of the review — "The Art of Dying" — that he had written of Benjamin Wind's final show. He was not imagining the minister's eerie reassembling of exact quotes from the piece.

"I don't believe," the minister continued, glancing down at his notes, "that 'the most pressing question in Benjamin Wind's art is death.' I don't side with the theory that this eminent artist gave 'shape to the world's suffering.' Nor that it is necessarily any artist's obligation 'to be on such intimate terms with death.' It seems a dangerous pursuit to me. Who knows where it can take us, or those dear to us? Are we not obliged, morally and spiritually, to look toward the light? It is *that* question which guides my viewing of Benjamin Wind's life and art."

These thinly veiled assaults on the review's speculation about dying seemed to insinuate that Daniel had presaged Wind's and Aleksandra's deaths. If Daniel was alarmed, he was also bewildered. The very aspect of the review with which the minister had taken issue was not at all what had been important to Daniel when he had written the thing shortly after he and Aleksandra had attended the show. Every critic waited a lifetime for such perfection, works of art about which he could write: "At last — greatness!" But for Daniel the review had been both a politician's concession speech ("A race well run. My opponent deserves the presidency. I wish him well . . .") and a surrender missive from a defeated general ("In the face of such superiority, and given the sheer number of dead, I regrettably . . ."). It was elegiac in tone, yet its paragraphs were also suffused with confusion. For all that Daniel had been able to identify the show's effects, he had not been able to understand how Wind had come to make this new work, and the review had unraveled into an extended airing of the question: "What had happened to Wind in the past three years that had so transformed his art?" Daniel had made a few stabs at guessing. Perhaps, he suggested, Wind had become overwhelmed with his escalating fame or the public's growing obsession with his Blackfoot identity, and his work's new turn was an attempt to remove himself from his art's equation; or maybe Wind had been feeling *old*. Now that Daniel thought about it, he saw that the minister was right about the review's inaccurate interpretation of Wind's show, but it had nothing to do with labored divisions between death and life, or the dark and the light. It had to do with Aleksandra. *Of course* his review had been a misunderstanding; it conveyed everything but what Benjamin Wind's show had really meant to Daniel: the end of his marriage. It was the strangest art review he had ever written.

When the minister did, at last, turn his comments to Wind's death, their brevity came as little surprise to Daniel: "Benjamin Wind has found a solace and stillness, and we trust that he is now held, as he was his whole life, by love. The love that upholds the universe, the love that sustains all that is. We know love is stronger than death — we know it is what survives."

That was it — everything he was going to say about the subject. And it sounded like a bowdlerized version of death to Daniel, who, no matter how self-deceiving he might have been in the rest of his existence, was for these few minutes a funeralgoer with a large stake in the person being eulogized, and therefore a barometer of truth. When he thought of Wind, when he thought of Aleksandra, when he thought of his father — when Daniel thought of anyone he had known who was now dead — what survived of them was not only love. What survived also were the echoes of all the resistance they had thrown up to life (and therefore to death). Sure the love, but also the rage, the refusal, the running, the shouting, the punching, the probing, the flailing, the crying, the sprint of sex, the furious hunger to *be.* When Aleksandra and Wind had hit the pavement, it was the releasing of *resistance.*

Had they attained peace? The rookie minister had his answer, but Daniel could not join him on it. And as the man steered his ocean liner of a eulogy safely into port and offered up its cargo of diversity with a benediction that spanned the globe ("Shalom, Salaam, Namaste, Blessed Be, and Kin-na-ye" — the last being "Amen" in Blackfoot), Daniel could not help but wonder if the most important freight had been jettisoned at sea. He was thinking of the tetchy question of how — exactly —

Wind and Aleksandra had died, with its specter of suicide, or murder, or both. Did not death, the last, the most important act in a life, bring into a final alignment all of one's previous actions, lending them their ultimate meaning? How could Daniel make sense of his marriage to Aleksandra, of anything she had ever said to him, if the circumstances of her death remained unknown to him?

In no condition to engage in a sincere exchange or especially small talk after the service, he fled to the church's adjoining garden, where refreshments were being served. There, despite a drastic drop in temperature and clouds overhead that threatened rain, lingered a share of attendees he did not recognize, Wind's family and friends. They were eager to discuss anything but the deceased, and it was a relief to Daniel, who was smarting, he only now realized, from the sheer number of times he had had to hear Benjamin Wind's name said aloud. The realization sent him to the bar. He found his first vodka tonic not quite what he needed, and the second what he needed still less. Only then, as he stood to one side, engaged in a stuporous staring contest with a marble bench, did it occur to him that someone might tip the minister off about his presence, and that the man might be on the lookout for him, might even try to do something as unpleasant (for Daniel) as pursue a conversation, regale him with pointed questions about Benjamin's art, or, worse, defend the things he had said in his eulogy.

"A lie — all of it," came a slightly accented voice.

It was the old man in the wheelchair. Daniel had failed to register the man's rolling up beside him, yet he was hazily aware that the guy had actually been shadowing him ever since the service had ended. To his relief, the man's motivations were visibly free of animosity; in fact, the stranger seemed distracted, nervously interrogating the lowering sky one moment, staring at the church entrance the next, until his gaze would wander away miserably among the people hovering near the alcohol. His pale green eyes were dismal with some private irritation, and Daniel found it odd the way the old codger had sidled up to him only to sink into his own thoughts. He was curious to know if the man was, as he suspected, a relative of Aleksandra's (his yarmulke, European accent, and peculiar Old World mannerliness certainly suggested so). "A lie?" Daniel echoed solicitously. "What —

the memorial service?"

"Such garbage have you ever heard?" the man said with a chuckle. He smiled up at Daniel with the side of his mouth.

It was then that Daniel's uncrystallized attention was finally pulled into sharp focus. What *was* it about this guy? He was so old, yet his eyes, nearly washed of their pigment, appeared unable to hold anything so colored as a past. If Daniel was not mistaken, the problem was love — something the matter with his appearance told him that the man had not gotten enough of it. His look was that of a plant deprived of light, his aged face a register of all it had never received. When Daniel peered into its creases, he felt he was staring at violent retreat.

But then, in the unlit reaches of the man's eyes, he thought he detected the semblance of something that contradicted everything he had just noticed. Something immense was being stored there, like a hope detained — a presence that was silent and stubborn, bent on permanence. And the man's slipshod clothing, especially the collar of his white shirt, did speak of a history: they were damp and intimate — they seemed to conceal certain facts — like the foxed pages of a diary.

Or maybe Daniel was just drunk. "No, I

haven't heard such garbage," he answered, and he meant it. Then he added, with the hope of drawing the old man out: "You don't seem that upset by it."

"Ha!" the old man snickered. "When you have spent a life becoming depressed by the smallest of nothings, you grow impervious to the heaviest blows." The man set his gaze on the second story of the apartment building looming over the garden, and Daniel followed his eyes to a lone uncurtained window. For a few seconds, they each remained looking into the window as if it were a portal to the world of heavy human blows in general.

"Which was the heavy blow?" Daniel pursued. "The lies — or Benjamin's passing?"

Whatever smile had clung to the man's face suddenly fell away. "You're the critic," he said. "I recognized you from Aleksandra's funeral."

The familiar use of Aleksandra's first name: he *had* to be a relative. "And you are —"

"I have read your review of Benjamin's exhibition."

"Yes" — Daniel had not expected the conversation to take this direction — "as has everyone else at this service, apparently."

Through his thick glasses, the man kept a grave pointedness on Daniel. "What you wrote . . . what you have thought about Benjamin — all of it — is wrong."

"Really?" Daniel exclaimed so loudly that other people turned to look at him. His transparent sarcasm had miscarried, making it embarrassingly obvious that he was both overwhelmed and intoxicated. Nonetheless, he could not seem to muster any other means of defense against this old man's criticism. "That makes two of you, then," he continued. "You, and the minister."

"You have no idea what it is that you're talking about."

"No, I guess not."

"Perhaps you are aware by now that something very big — with tragic consequences — came into Benjamin's life before he died."

Daniel could not imagine that the man was referring to anything other than Aleksandra, and he was not about to concede any ground. "Mr. Wind spoke of his misfortunes to no one," he retorted.

The old man changed color then. He seemed to be trembling. "That," he said, looking fiercely up at Daniel, "is because

251

everyone — including you — is partly to blame."

"What are you trying to imply?" Daniel demanded.

The man lifted one of his shaky hands and removed his glasses. Without them, his eyes appeared unhoused — medieval and visionary. "You ask in your review what happened to Benjamin. You ask what he was doing the last years that could make such a change in his art." The old man became flushed with feeling, as if overcome by an embarrassment, which, ignited by some spark of his memory, exploded into a howl of anger scarcely smothered: "*I* can tell you what he was doing!"

Daniel certainly did not need to be told that Wind had been fucking Aleksandra for the last two years; from the gleam in the old man's eye, this appeared to be exactly what he was about to convey. "No thanks," Daniel said.

For a moment, the man studied him with a smile on his lips that Daniel thought was condescending. "Okay," the old man finally said, slightly raising one hand in a signal of defeat. "*Okay.*"

Now that he had thrown in the towel, the man looked deflated and weak, woundable, and Daniel suddenly felt ashamed of how he had acquitted himself with this elderly person; to anyone who might have been watching, he had passed for an asshole at best.

As it turned out, someone *was* watching. The old man signaled to an elegant woman standing not six feet away, who was there to assist him, to judge by how swiftly she approached the back of his wheelchair, took hold of the handles, and kicked up the brake release. It was obvious to Daniel that she had been waiting there the entire time — within earshot — for the man to conclude his business with him. She was younger than Daniel, and touched the old man tenderly with her fingers, not as a lover but as a mother might, or the child of an overly needy parent. Daniel could see that she had known the guy a long time — she read his needs without him having to speak — and he would have guessed that she was his granddaughter, except her features bore no notable resemblance to his. If anything, she looked the man's opposite. His skin was dusky, his eyes round, while she had the kind of pallor that reminded Daniel of the frailty of living things, and two astonishing, nearly Asiatic, eyes full of an intelligently arranged warmth.

The man was now introducing him to her

("this is the art critic I was telling you about"), and the woman — if he had heard it correctly, her name was Carmen — let the moist darkness of her gaze fall into his just long enough to fill him with heavy regret at having right in her view treated the old man with such disrespect. He stood there very stupidly, aware only that his cheeks were now betraying his embarrassment, if not an uncomfortable enchantment. She was awfully good-looking.

"Are you okay?" she asked.

He was alarmed to find the question penetrating straight to the tear-making center of his self. The morning's confrontational exchanges had left him susceptible to the slightest display of empathy, and he fought an irrational urge to disclose to her everything that was inside him, all his pent-up pain. He managed to restrict himself to a nod of the head, as a signal (a lie) that he *was* okay. But when she resumed the task of removing the old man from the garden patio, he was overcome with a sudden sense of panic.

"Mr. Lichtmann, I want to thank you," the old man called out as the woman — Carmen — wheeled him away, "for all you did for Benjamin. He wasn't easy — I know. I only wish I could have done more to help that boy. The sad truth is I hardly knew him myself."

After they were gone, Daniel went for his third vodka tonic. He nursed it slowly as he stood there, encircled by the jabbering art world cavalry, truly despairing of both his head's confusion (what was he doing noticing a woman's attractions?) and the day's seemingly wasted effort. What was he to make of it all? And how was he to deal with the echoing images, now reverberating in his skull, of the old Jew and his lovely assistant? It was that odd feeling he sometimes experienced after intense encounters with people: they haunted his emotional engines like so many ghostly backfires. He was, he knew, a disaster of sensibility.

Yet when a cold drizzle began to fall a few moments later, he barely managed to register the fact, because it had occurred to him that the old man's parting thanks were the words of someone who had cared for Wind — deeply, personally, historically. The pain Daniel had noticed in the man's face: it was the pain of family — not *Aleksandra's* family, but rather Benjamin's. And the startling, unspoken revelation behind the voiced lament ("I only wish I could have done more to help that boy. The sad truth is I hardly knew him myself") was that this old Jew —

a relative, somehow, of Benjamin Wind — had come to the memorial service for exactly the same reason as had Daniel: to learn something about the dead artist.

The implications were so arresting (Wind was a *Jew?*) that Daniel could have stood there all morning getting wet. Yet his feet were already propelling him toward the church door, not to join the crowd now seeking shelter, but to locate the old man and his assistant, these strangers who had all at once become the two most important people in his life.

Theirs were not among the animated faces filling the sanctuary. He checked the street outside: nothing but two sodden, branchless trees that seemed to mock him. Back inside he tried the men's room — nobody there except, *Christ,* another art critic! — and then began exerting all his weight on the ungiving handle of an adjacent door when he felt a tap on his shoulder.

It was the rookie minister.

"I've been looking all over for you," the man said with a smile.

Daniel straightened up. He could feel his cheeks oxygenating.

"You *are* the driver, right?"

"Driver — ?" said Daniel.

"Oh, I'm so sorry . . ." The minister's face

now colored too. "I thought you might have been the car service I called. The poor grandfather — he and a woman with him were caught in the rain trying to catch a cab."

So Daniel had guessed correctly: the old man *was* Wind's family — his *grandfather* — and they were still in the building.

The minister must have noticed his eyes briefly light up at these two pieces of news. "You were in the pews during the service," he said, squinting at Daniel. "Are you —"

"Family," Daniel sputtered.

"Family?"

"Yes," he said with relief. It was not a complete lie, in his mind. He *was* related to the deceased, just not the one being memorialized today. And in some dark way Aleksandra's final "act" had married Daniel to Wind, forever. Besides, his half-truth was necessary to what he had to say next: "I'm actually looking for the grandfather."

"I should have known." The man nodded at the door handle that had failed to yield to Daniel's 180-plus pounds. "That's the utility closet. The rec room where I've got him resting isn't the comfiest, but it beats sitting on a cleaning bucket. Follow me."

The rookie minister: Daniel's friend after all.

Daniel entered the recreation room by himself and found it to be little more than a linoleum-floored waste — of card tables and folding chairs — containing an echo and a musty smell. Off to one corner, Wind's grandfather was shivering in his wheelchair, his clothes soaked through, Carmen bent over him and administering a folded napkin to his neck. The old Jew looked sad and dispossessed, an effect heightened by the room's prosaicness. The tower of coffee filters on the kitchen counter, the refrigerator humming nearby, the warped Ping-Pong table abandoned against the opposing wall — they almost gave the impression to Daniel, having come by way of the sanctuary, that he had entered a chamber of disgrace.

What happened between him and Wind's grandfather during the next five minutes — it was all the time they ended up having before the car service came — was for the old man the end of a very long journey, as Daniel was about to learn. For Daniel — who, stripped of pride, walked straight up to the old man, pulled out the photograph of Aleksandra and Wind, and, shaking it before the man's eyes, asked if *this!* was what came into his grandson's life before he died? if *this!* was what his grandson was doing that created such a huge change in his art? — for Daniel the five minutes with the old man would, he was certain, become part of the meaning of the rest of his life. When the man stunned him by responding in an accent that now clearly gave him out as a Jew of Germanic origin, "I stranded that boy twenty years before his birth, when even his *father* was only a child! Your wife, that sad woman — you abandoned her when Benjamin was still unknown to her! The two of them are gone while you and I . . . we survive. You must believe me when I tell you that it is always the *survivors* who are the guilty ones!" — when the man told him this, Daniel saw he had slipped into a room as fateful as it was ugly, as life changing as a hundred better rooms never were.

And so, after Carmen discreetly removed herself to a nearby chair, Daniel sat down in one directly opposite the old man and started to listen. He had no awareness that he was holding the man's hand — no awareness of the morning, or of any of its sounds, whether the hum of the refrigerator, the building's far-off creaks, or the voices beyond the double doors. The whole of existence had been pressed into this old man's fragile voice, through which life in all its force was now speaking plainly to Daniel — he had merely to wait. Its first piece of news:

259

What had secretly altered Benjamin Wind's art was not Aleksandra. "She came to Benjamin's life only *after,*" the old man said.

Daniel cleared his throat. Hearing someone speak with knowledge about Aleksandra's relationship with Wind returned him to the same feeling — of shock and strange relief — he had experienced finding the photograph of them together. "After what?" he asked.

The signature of some specific hurt cut its lines deeply into the man's brow. "I am referring to Benjamin's discovery of my existence."

Daniel could only stare at him.

"What I am saying," the old man added, "is that my grandson never knew — until we finally met two years before his death — that I was alive. He had no idea that, living in Los Angeles, sometimes within only miles of him, was a man who was his grandfather, a man who never passed a single day without sadness for not being able to see him. During my grandson's growing-up days in California, his years finding his way in the world as a young man, and during that liberating time in his life when he discovered himself as an artist in New York, he had been told over and over and over — by my own son — that I was dead."

260

The old man looked at him as if trying to discover whether or not Daniel recognized the magnitude of his revelation.

"Herman — that is my son's name —" he continued, his cheeks now shaking, "he had convinced Benjamin, for complicated reasons which would take too long to explain, that they were Indians." The old man was pointing a finger at Daniel. "Do you understand? I do not mean from India — I mean Indians! Like so . . . cowboys and Indians, bows and arrows and tomahawks? If I ever happened to be mentioned, if on occasion my grandson naturally asked about his dead grandfather, it was said only that I had belonged to the tribe. The *tribe!* Can you imagine when I finally meet my grandson (which was no easy meeting to set up, let me assure you) and he sees *this*" — the old man patted his yarmulke — "and he hears the European accent? Can you imagine when I tell him that the tribe his father and I and *all* his ancestors belong to — the tribe Benjamin himself belongs to — is *not* the Blackfoot, but the Hebrews? I will never forget how he looked at me. He did not see his own flesh and blood before him — he saw a Jew! A small–old–*foreign*–Jew. My *own* grandson: there was hate in his eyes! A kind of hate I had not seen since *1944!*"

With a painful hatred of their own, the old man's eyes now stared into a distant corner of the room, as if it were inhabited, Daniel presumed, by Germans and Gentiles. "It was here in New York. I flew in — I spent a week at a hotel preparing. Then I made the phone call. He did not believe me, of course, when I told him it was his grandfather speaking. Still, I convinced him to meet me on neutral ground — in a Greek coffee shop. It might as well have been a local tavern in the Tyrolean mountains. Sitting there in the booth after I told him who he really was: never had I been so self-conscious of my head cap, my Semitic features, as I was under the gaze of my grandson's eyes. I felt he wanted to kick me out of that diner and onto the sidewalk — as had happened to me so many years ago in a very different time and place." The old man lifted a hand in Carmen's direction. "*She* was there. It was an impossible situation. But what choice did I have? You see, my son, Herman, shared *nothing* about Benjamin with me (he shared nothing with me, period), and, besides, he was not talking to Benjamin by that point, or rather Benjamin was not talking to him — not for years. I was forced to follow my grandson's life through the magazines and newspapers from my room in Tempe. I read many, maybe all, of your own reviews of his work. You have no idea how important they became to me. Ask Carmen. She tracked down each one and brought it to me. How can I ever repay her? I read them as if they were dispatches from the son I never had, proudly reporting back to me on my grandson's achievements. I held the pages carefully in my fingers — I studied every sentence you wrote, pausing on your verb choices, analyzing each adjective, looking for clues, digging out the deepest meanings, trying to see — to *see!* — my grandson through your descriptions. Over time, I came to understand that you admired my grandson very much. Line after line after line — each formulation, each argument, each complex pattern of language: filled with tender admiration! Your reviews were nothing like those I read by the other critics, who seemed to examine art as if they were doctors diagnosing a great disease in order to cure people of it. I cannot say I comprehended every idea you put forth about Benjamin's art: despite a youth spent devouring philosophy, despite an adulthood marked by an increasingly desperate drinking of the best intoxicants our theologians have to offer, I am simply not that intelligent. But I do have enough wisdom, if only of the kind sharpened by negative experience, to recognize love. Yes, it's true: I believed that your reviews were love letters. Not of the romantic sort. I am not speaking of the love that can exist between two men — but of that which exists between two souls. In this way, I was certain you loved my grandson. From my room in the desert, I often imagined you associating with him in the New York circles — who knew? perhaps you were the best of friends. These thoughts brought me comfort. You have no idea what it means to pass day after day without hearing from your own son, your own grandson — from *anyone* who is family. I felt buckled to an airplane flying toward a country called Oblivion. I woke each morning only to spend my hours rehearsing existence in the other eternal silence where I will be soon enough. But when Carmen would place before me an art magazine and I would see your name at the top of the review, a warm feeling would take hold inside me. It was like seeing a son's name in print. I have waited many, many years to meet you, Mr. Daniel Lichtmann."

Now that he had fallen silent, the old man was unable to look Daniel in the eyes. Daniel, moved deeply by what he had just heard, could do nothing but stare directly into the face of this man who had just confronted him with a truth he had tried to bury ever since Aleksandra's death. He had loved Benjamin Wind's soul — had summoned so much of his thinking, his heart, and more preciously his time (half his adult life!) to a nearly mystic contemplation of it. The old man, implausibly, from across an entire continent, through the pages of the art reviews, had found him out.

And it caused Daniel to tell the man now how much his grandson had meant to him. He once more praised the greatness of Wind's artistic achievement, and, because he knew it would be the last time he ever did such a thing, he said *everything.* The man listened to him with all of his attention, nodding at certain statements, closing his eyes briefly at others, until Daniel was finished speaking, and they sat there simply smiling at each other, even after the minister had leaned his head in to inform them that the car had come and was waiting out front. Only then did Daniel realize he was clutching the man's hand. He looked away, feeling self-conscious.

The old man let go of his hand, and, as if on cue, Carmen took hold of the rear of the wheelchair and kicked up the brake.

"That photograph," the man said to Daniel. "The picture of them you carry with you. I know very well the wall they are standing in front of. *History* was made in that house. And then it was wiped out by the Germans. I sent Benjamin there to discover who he was. And your wife, she went with him — to Europe, just as she came with him to Arizona and then California. I am sorry to tell you this. She came to the West, Mr. Lichtmann. Not only to be with him when he joined me again but also when he performed the difficult task of paying a visit to the man whose face he had promised himself never to lay eyes on again. I am referring to his father. My son. Herman." He reached into his coat pocket and extracted a wrinkled business card. "If you also choose to come west" — he handed the card to Daniel — "please visit us."

Daniel sat there blinking at him. His ears were hot and ringing; he could feel resentment gathering in his clenched jaw.

With a lifting of his hand, the old man signaled to Carmen that he was ready to go. She swung the wheelchair around so that for an instant she was standing before Daniel. He felt himself looking up at her urgently. He wanted to say something to her, tell her they could not possibly leave — not yet. But her eyes seemed to avoid his.

As she wheeled the man toward the double doors, Daniel became aware of the card in his hand, the one the old man had given him. In desperation he searched its face and was confused by its ornamental design. It looked nearly hand-painted, as if it were some kind of wallet-size illuminated manuscript. Then his eyes landed on the name printed in bold calligraphy across the bottom. MAX WIENER, it read. *Wiener,* not Wind. *Wiener,* a person from Wien — Vienna.

"Max of Vienna," Daniel found himself saying in a frantic effort to say anything to pin the man down and keep him there.

Instantly the old man signaled and the wheelchair halted. He directed Carmen to turn him around and push him halfway back across the room toward Daniel. His eyes were filled with reproach, and beneath his resolve was an incomprehensible savagery.

"Don't ever say that again."

A WIFE IN THE WORLD

As far as Hannah is concerned, the civil ceremony is their second wedding. Their first was presided over by the gestapo officer as he berated them in the line a little over half an hour ago, with Max standing behind them as their witness. In all her life, she could not have hoped for two better weddings. How *perfectly* the one has ended up complementing the other: evil and passion from the Nazi, absolute indifference from the civil servant, each wedding weaving her and Josef unimportantly into the fabric of existence. The gestapo officer, so ceremonious in his inquisitorial vetting of her documents, so deeply concerned in his railings at Jews for populating Palestine with the offspring of prostitutes, disabused Josef and her of any illusion of privacy, dutifully reminding them that they stood in the historical dimension. Whereas the hired bureaucrat now officially marrying them —

a woman from some very northern German place, to judge by her right-angled accent — sits immovably behind her desk like a stone representative of God's unconcern. She makes it clear by her rote reading of the state-sanctioned vows that the stale air of her office will allow no sentiment; her lack of the human touch is so extreme as to give Hannah the impression that the gestapo officer's veins carry the warmer blood.

Repeating and affirming their civil vows, Hannah and Josef make no eye contact, as if falling in line with the bureaucrat's example of disregard. They do not need to see each other, Hannah realizes, because they can detect in the quality of their voices everything they could ever want to know about each other's investment in the proceedings. Hannah, her eyes fixed straight ahead on the swastikas clinging to the wall, is moved by the way Josef transforms the vows' instrumentality into a reserve for profound human expression. There is a dignified control to his tone, yet at the same time his voice is afire with life, applying tenderness to the all but flat and frigid words. It is the sound of a man repossessing himself and the ceremony's significance. In his mouth, the words seem oriented toward the future. They even make her hear the good of the world.

The ceremony is brief, naturally. Afterward, their marriage certificate bejeweled in all four corners by the official red stamp of the Third Reich, she and Josef leave the room as if having just visited an accountant, outwardly imparting to the occasion no more meaning than they would the completion of a year's taxes. Josef is temporarily waylaid in the hall by a friend also about to be married, and Hannah is first to exit the building. There, waiting impatiently, covering her with stares of what can only be envy, is Max.

"Where's Josef?" he stammers. "Is he all right?"

"He is extraordinary."

"I was hoping you wouldn't say that."

"I'm very sorry, Max."

She reaches for his hand but he flings it away angrily and asks: "What is happening here?"

"What *has* happened," she corrects him.

He seems about to lambast her but Josef catches up to them, and Max sinks into a sullen attitude of betrayal as he regards his friend.

"Now what?" he asks finally.

The very same question rests on Hannah's lips. Will she and Josef simply part now that the deed is done, go their own way until the business of getting out of the country requires that they meet again? She seeks out Josef's eyes, finding to her relief that they are waiting for hers. And right then, in a single exchange of glances, it passes between them that their civil ceremony was no completion. That, in fact, it has begun a business far more urgent even than escaping Hitler's house of horrors, a business that may not let them part ways again.

"What?" says Max. "Why are you two looking at each other like that?"

"Let's walk," Josef says.

For the rest of the afternoon, Max shadows them around Vienna, prating on about Zionism, about tree planting in Palestine, about nothing, pausing only during Hannah's brief communications with Josef, and not without making a display of his newly organized resentment of her. He purposely barricades himself between the two of them, separating them as an insolent child would his parents. Consequently, she and Josef hardly look at each other, as if they are each ashamed, or hoping that the anger and judgment emanating from this boy between them will pass like a juvenile tantrum. So as to soothe the child, they speak nothing of the profound thing they have just done, nor of any of their subsequent feelings, but instead exchange entirely factual information with each other, mostly concerning the emigration status of their respective families, and in this manner she and Josef find each other around Max's pale, hot head. She tells him about the impossibility of obtaining a visa for her Russian-born mother when every country's Russian quota has already been filled; and she reveals that she has no idea where her father is, since he divorced her mother when Hannah was only a child and failed to maintain contact with either of them. Josef's mother, she learns, has been for several weeks in the Rothschild Hospital on account of a weak heart. Not helping the woman's condition any is the fact that Josef's father was recently fired from his bank as a result of Aryanization, and that all of his assets have been frozen despite his baptism and claims of Christianity. Hannah is surprised to hear that the man disinherited Josef three years ago, the result of his bitter disapproval of Josef's relocation to a flat in the Leopoldstadt belonging to Josef's maternal grandfather. She is further surprised to hear that Josef has been living there alone for some time due to the *grandfather's* disapproval of Josef's decision (what a rebel she has married! — *good*) to quit illuminating Jewish marriage contracts in favor of making modern paintings, a decision that precipitated the grandfather's return to his home village in Poland.

It is just after dusk when the three of them mount the stairs to the very flat in question. She watches Josef struggle with his keys — charmingly, she thinks — and then, the door finally pushed open, her nose makes friendly contact with the vapor of oil and turpentine and a hundred other sources less immediately rewarding. The flat is a remarkable place. In its center are two tiny beds, only one of them used. With the exception of a small stove and washbasin, and several deferential lamps wilting from the walls, they constitute the only pieces of furniture in the room. Everything else, every bit of floor, wall, even ceiling, has been given over to the demands of painting. A well-used easel commands the foot of one bed. Everywhere cans are filled with brushes, knives, and colored fluids. Curled tubes of paint lie strewn on the floor like dead fish beached upon some lakeshore. Rag and garment alike are paint-stained, heaped here and there in indistinguishable piles. But all of these things are subordinate to, indeed surrounded by, the fifty-some large and small paintings, floating pell-mell across the room's walls and ceiling, of women being sexually gratified by men — the sight of which sends Hannah's heart racing.

"Welcome to Josef Pick's Museum of Conquests," Max blurts out with a meanness of tone directed clearly at her.

Hannah turns and finds Josef staring at her. His expression is unreadable. For a brief instant her eyes fall on the two beds in the middle of the room.

"Is it true?" she asks.

While retaining a certain ambiguity, Josef's reply seems to lean toward the affirmative, but she is touched by the firmness and sincerity with which he holds her in his gaze during its delivery: "My grandfather exploited my talents before I knew what a talent was. When I recently wrote to him that I painted all those ketubot to pay off his loans, he sent a return letter claiming that I had made them for God, and God alone. Now I'm painting for *myself*."

"Not for God, as well?" she asks.

Josef pauses. He seems to be trying to understand her. "Do you think He would approve?"

"I don't think He would approve or disapprove."

He looks at her then with an unblinking amazement, as if certain that she is referring less to his paintings than to the act so unambiguously represented *in* them. For her part, she is not so sure she isn't.

Max, who during this exchange has been glaringly mute and distant, suddenly speaks up. *"Wonderful,"* he lets out with a breathy sarcasm addressed to Josef. "I arrange for you to marry the one woman in the world who stood solidly opposed to sexual relations of any kind, and now she is going to screw you."

Hannah and Josef simply stare at him. It is obvious to all concerned that he should have left them to be alone several hours ago, and he now stands before them like a tiresome guest still tethered to the floor long after the party has ended.

"Do you take me for an idiot?" he continues, his eyes now swinging wildly between them. "How odd that I, who brought you two together, who *scripted* the entire sham to begin with, feel like a bit player with a silly part. All my altruism, my dedication to the Zionist cause" — he turns pleadingly to Josef — "all my concern and love for *you,* my dearest and oldest friend . . . what does any of it mean, this hard work and self-sacrifice, when I know that the two of you are about to screw?"

With this, and with a painfully authentic

expression of self-pity blazing out of his clenched face, Max exits the flat, slamming the door shut behind him.

For a minute Hannah and Josef stare at each other from across the room. Then Hannah begins to undress. She starts with her sweater, her blouse and brassiere, then unzips her skirt, and, stepping out of her shoes, carefully pulls down her skirt and panties and garter and stockings — until she is completely exposed. Josef is watching her, his face slightly turned.

"Max was right, then?" he asks.

"I know what marriage means."

He steps around the two beds, somehow unbuttoning his clothes at the same time. Suddenly he is standing there shirtless before her. She cannot look away from his chest. "Then you and I think it means the same thing," he says.

"We'll see."

He takes her hand. "Do you want me to turn the paintings around?"

Only now does she meet his eyes, having detected a flatness in his voice, as if he made the inquiry by rote. "Is that what all the others requested?"

The question seems to stiffen him. He appears resolved not to answer it. So she leans into him, until her cheek is against his breast, and she feels his hands on her back. "Do to me," she says, "what you did to them."

And he does.

He does *more* than what he did to them.

He does it, with her consent, with pain, that very first night of their marriage, on the two narrow creaky beds faked up to resemble a large one. And then he does it each subsequent evening, when a newly instated Jewish curfew, and a need to return again to the sully of sex, compels them back up to the tiny room.

He might have married her to save himself, she thinks, but he makes love to her like a man trying to destroy himself. As if to express his impatience with how long it is taking to obtain the ridiculous number of forms required before they can leave the country, as if the act is merely another aspect of the dissipated days of Germany's takeover, or another result of escalating social interdictions against the Jews, as if Josef himself is attempting to add his own kind of effort to the shouting and the pistol shots, the searches and arrests and seizures — to the crazy things happening in the hobbling world outside — he takes her loudly, greedily, she might even say violently.

He does not appear to enjoy it. As far as she can tell, he is at pains to *conquer* pleasure, prove its futility to the onlooking lovers in his paintings. Thus his probing of her is never an escape. Even in the carnal act, they have not passed beyond the reach of Hitler. The Nazis have simply made them more primitive lovers, eliminated conscious-ness from their passion. Indeed, all of her thinking, her faculties of speech, are ar-rested by the things Josef does to her on their makeshift bed above Karmeliterplatz — until she is forced to consent to being a thing.

And she is grateful.

She has tried her entire life to become a thing. How else to love impersonally, as God does? How else to know His nothing-ness? He does not love as a person loves, but as a mountain boulder is brown. It is why she has so valued her headaches, as-sented to their violation — as she assents to Josef's — with all of her soul. Their pres-sure explodes the walls of selfhood. Suffer-ing under them, she can harbor no false-ness: the pain, like Josef's pounding, pushes it out, taking with it any illusion of being someone. She is *glad* Josef's paintings are not turned around: they remind her that she is not unique. And it seems to her that, could she only remain in bed with Josef all the hours of the day, she might maintain this fleeting silencing of her individual being.

Fleeting, for she has to admit that he is pressing into *someone*. Someone is being forced to love with her flesh. Someone is amazed by the bizarre logic of finding herself so physically free amid the most unfree time in Viennese history. Someone is delighted to hear her name uttered as a sexual cry, to have every odd corner of her body emphasized, to have to tell a man who expresses a wish to kiss her anus that he is sweet like a dog. Someone likes how that man finds his way into her without his eyes, likes how the contours of his body repay her scrutiny, the unconscionably wide back, the gleaming white throat that still looks to be in the throes of childhood. Someone is even attracted to the slightly sour smell of his breath — a sign that he is alive, digesting — though this makes her hurt for him, makes her wish she could *hold on* to him. It is painful to think, as she catches another glimpse of the washbasin opposite the bed, and its tiny mirror whose framed glass fills with their bodies each night, that their lives will be no more permanent than a flash of skin in a darkened room. All of her effort to get beyond time: it feels like a sin to her now. Let limits into your *heart,* she tells herself. What did *you* ever have to say about eternity when you did not yet know its opposite: a shoulder's sweep beneath a linen shirt, the sound of a belt coming off, the mineral richness of a man's mouth? The truth is you want to *engrave* yourself making love to him on that mirror's glass. You want it to be the room's newest and final painting, a record of a love that happened once.

Then, three months after marrying him, she gets her wish — a record of a love that happened once, perhaps the only tangible record life has ever offered. Among the many things she feels after having her pregnancy confirmed by a doctor at the old hospital in the Malzgasse (the one hospital besides the Rothschild still open to Jews) is the irony of the fact that she did not truly experience the brunt of the Nazis' very public invasion until now, when she has been invaded by something entirely private — an embryo. The prospect, suddenly, of bringing a child into the world makes the doings of Hitler and his men even more personal and menacing to her than they were before.

But they are not the only threat to come

stealing into her life as a result of her pregnancy. Her mother, who was originally given to understand that Hannah was marrying a stranger solely to help him emigrate to Palestine, is outraged one afternoon when she first notices Hannah's slightly swollen belly. Availing herself of the full crudity of her native Russian tongue, the woman harangues Hannah in words that eerily echo those bellowed that day in line by the gestapo officer: "Good, now the Land of Israel will be resettled by whores and their children. Don't bother trying to get me a visa — I'd rather die here at the hands of Hitler than see the Holy Land be so disgraced. Go. Go back to your 'husband.' Don't worry about me. Perhaps I will just kill myself this afternoon. Then you can leave for Palestine tonight."

Hannah and Josef do not leave that night. Nor the night, nor the week, nor the month after that. Much to the consternation of Max Wiener, who appears as unhappy about Hannah's pregnant belly as her mother, and who keeps pressuring them to flee with him, they are resolved not to emigrate until they have seen to it that their parents can get out — a task whose spreading difficulty is not made any easier by the declining condition of Josef's mother (the Reich requires each emigrant to provide a certificate of good health, and the poor woman has had to be transferred from the hospital to a Jewish sanatorium in the ninth district), or by his father's obstinate insistence, despite all evidence to the contrary, that the threat of war and "the whole Hitler thing" will blow over. They do not leave by April of 1939, when, in order to make way for an "Aryan in need of a home," Josef's father is kicked, literally, out of the Pick Villa, in whose high-ceilinged chambers three generations of Christianized Picks slept soundly, and forced like any regular Jew from the outlying districts to decamp to the Leopoldstadt — the "Island of Matzos" so detested by him — there to live not in Josef's flat (the proud old man ignores his son's protests that he room with Hannah and himself) but in a meanly furnished place still more confined, not the least because it is already being tenanted by three other very Jewish families. Neither do they leave by May, when Britain issues a decree concerning Palestine called the White Paper, which instantly reduces Jewish immigration to a trickle and, disastrously for Hannah and Josef, illegalizes the use of an immigration permit by anyone other than its owner — she can still go, Josef suddenly cannot. The only way for him to get to Palestine legally now is to purchase a capitalist's visa, but the price is well beyond the amount of money he has remaining from his years of painting ketubot, and anyway he and Hannah are relying on his savings to survive.

By September, when Hitler invades Poland, Hannah is great with child, and great with concern for its journey, within her womb and without. She is great too with emergent doubts about her marriage to Josef Pick. He has been pressing her nearly every day to leave on her own for Palestine. And in spite of his promises to find his way out — and to find her there — she is amazed, no, she is hurt, that he would want to separate, especially when she is carrying his child. It is as if now that the purpose of their marriage has been rendered irrelevant, he has no use for her.

She hates feeling this way. And she can convince herself that his pleading with her to leave only reveals a practical concern for her survival, but she and he have not been separated yet, and her body — *it* she can convince of nothing. As her abdomen hardens, the shape of her sensual life with Josef has assumed contours much less firm, a development that for her cannot have happened at a worse time. Before, when there was nothing growing inside of it, she had no difficulty ignoring her body and its demands, deeming, as she so loftily did, that sex was not important. But now that her body is bearing the product of sex and regularly speaks to her of ache and tiredness and hunger and . . . life, she needs to have its desires listened to. It is not that Josef ceases making love to her entirely, but she has noticed his increasing avoidance of the subtle instances — a certain exchanged glance, the right word spoken, the catching of a wrist — that can lead them to bed, and even when they do come together she sees the look of fortitude on his face. In turn, she stops giving herself to it utterly, and she nearly has to marvel at how two people, earlier so avid for each other, can fall into such disenthralled lovemaking. It is *almost* work.

One evening, lying in bed after enduring his inattention through another dinner, she finds herself warily eyeing — over her protruding belly — all the slender women in Josef's paintings. They stare down at her like a tribunal, enclosing her in their circumference of sex.

"Turn the paintings around," she says.

Josef looks at her from the stove where he is making tea. "What?"

"They are mocking me."

His eyes perform a quick tour of the paintings. "Don't be silly."

"Then they are mocking *us*."

With a pained expression he relents, and very slowly takes down each painting and leans it face-in against the wall. And it is not lost on Hannah, who watches him from the bed tortuously, that it was less than a year ago when she first walked into this flat and allowed him, right before they made love, to leave the paintings face-out. What a turn things have taken.

Then, another turn.

It comes several weeks later, when, after a trying day of filling out forms at three different foreign embassies, and of worrying about the baby's unusual paucity of movement inside of her, she and Josef return home to find, among several pieces of mail handed to them by Herr Hörler, the building superintendent, an envelope from Poland. Its postmark, already bearing the Reich's swastikas, reads "Kopyczyńce." Grandfather Pommeranz has written Josef another letter.

In the stairway landing, Josef gives the envelope a little shake in the air. *"This,"* he says, smiling playfully at Hannah, "we're going to enjoy."

He puts tea on as soon as they enter the flat, then halves the remaining portion of a torte they have been nursing all week (recent rationing has transformed the enjoyment of sweets into a rare indulgence), and, once they are both seated side by side on the edge of the bed, opens the envelope while raising one brow coyly at her. She has not seen him this happy in months. With torte in his mouth and an air of amusement he begins reading the three-page letter aloud: " 'My Dear Young Pommeranz —' " He pauses. "Can you believe the old man still calls me that? 'My Dear Young Pommeranz, I was disappointed not to receive from you a reply to my letter dated the second of November 1938, but your mother, despite her illness, has brought me up to date on your recent activities, including your hasty nonreligious marriage to an unknown woman' — *Ha!*" Josef exclaims, smirking at Hannah — " 'and the pregnancy that has resulted from this unfortunate union.' " He looks up gleefully. "*See,* I told you we were going to enjoy this."

Hannah tries as best she can to participate in Josef's ironic interpretation of the letter, but it is hard. This Polish grandfather has somehow in the very first sentence of his missive gone straight to the heart of what has been secretly worrying her for weeks.

" 'Your father, Young Pommeranz,' " Josef continues reading, " 'often had occasion to deplore your mastery of the art of ketubah illumination, and I am aware of how severely he wounded you all those years ago when he contemptuously called you "The Marriage Artist," but now I must say, having married in this fashion, you *are* a marriage artist. It has never been more clear to me how unfortunate you are to be living in a permissive city like Vienna. Such a personal catastrophe as you now find yourself in certainly wouldn't have happened in Kopyczyńce. But you got what you wanted, my child, haven't you? A marriage marked by no significance. I did not forget our many arguments about marriage, especially when you became so embittered after painting hundreds of ketubot. How you hated it that every Hans and Franz got married! How you came to despise the *sameness* of the marriage contracts! It all became dreadfully prosaic to you, my young Pommeranz, a matter of filling in the blanks of each ketubah you created. You marveled at how people could put such significance into a particular day of a particular year in a particular place, when the very next day, yet another marriage, or two or three, even,

287

would be made in the very same synagogue. As you grew older, especially when you began to make those modern paintings of yours and to spend time at cafés with all those bohemian women and their raffish artist friends, you came to idolize the peculiar. You wanted your love to be unique. But I must tell you, Grandson, and this comes from an old man who has failed pitifully in his rare endeavors to balance the two, that love is a unity of the unique and the universal. Don't make the mistake of equating uniqueness with greatness. The latter only comes when you find the universal within the unique.' "

Josef stops for a moment and exchanges glances with Hannah. She cannot tell what he is thinking, but his earlier irony seems to have dissipated.

"He's right, you know," she suddenly lets out.

"Is he?" Josef replies defiantly. An angry sarcasm overtakes his features. "About me being 'a *marriage* artist'?"

"He loves you, Josef."

He turns and stares down into the letter's pages, his eyes filled with hardness.

"Keep reading," she says, resting her hands on her round belly. "I want to hear the rest."

After a while he clears his throat and picks up where he left off: " 'In spite of my misgivings, I still hold out hope for you, Young Pommeranz, and even for your marriage. The path you have chosen is unusual. As you well remember from your many dealings with eager young couples, most newlyweds are drawn into marriage because they believe it is good, and they end up being chained to it because it becomes necessary. From what I can gather from your dear mother, you and your bride began in exactly the opposite manner: by chaining yourselves to each other in marriage because it was necessary. May you learn to be drawn to your marriage because it is good.' "

Again Josef hesitates — this time without lifting his eyes from the letter. She is staring at him. "Keep reading," she says.

" 'Young love struggling with adversity — I've seen it my whole life, I see it every day right here in Kopyczyńce, and it is *still* the most affecting thing I have ever witnessed. Often, I am moved even by the sight of two people who are entirely unsuitable for each other entering into a marriage. The majesty of that kind of mistake can often trump the mistake itself, render it surmountable; you have only to look at history, your own family's included, to see the truth of this.

Thus, in the end, it cannot *hurt* you to be married, Josef, even to a stranger, just as it cannot hurt you to have to care for a new child. Both will liberate you from the despotism of arrogance and one-sidedness that a man is inclined to develop when he lives, as I have for too long now, on his own. That particular form of tyranny was probably what made the flat at Karmeliterplatz too small for an old man and his grandson, but I'm sure the place is just the right size for a young man and his new family.

" 'I've been thinking, of course, about what drove us apart, and why I eventually had to leave. Granted, I am guilty of too heavily resenting your forsaking of sacred art for its secular siblings — but I think you do yourself a disservice when you write, as you did in your last letter, that you only bent yourself to the task of ketubah illumination to save me from my "lender lowlifes," and to keep me "in pickled herrings." I've tried to understand your move toward modern art, and the meaning of your statement that you realized only later, after you discovered the French artist Manet and his contemporaries, that by working on ketubot, in the total isolation of our Karmeliterplatz flat, you traced the entire history of modern art on your own. I suppose it is true that, if the signs and symbols and words of the marriage contracts came to hold no significance for you, then they could mean anything. That this is what led to your "modern" work only confirms to me how meaningless such work must be. And it must have given you pause when your new paintings were mostly ignored by Vienna, when you found it impossible to find a gallery willing to sell them, knowing that you left behind a practice where *every one* of your paintings was sold, before it was even produced, and for which your reputation soared above the city's Jewish districts. Nevertheless, I believe you when you claim that you never felt such a lifting of weight, so light and free, as when you made your first painting that was *not* a ketubah. But let me say something now, Young Pommeranz, that I've never told you before, and that, given the current state of things, I've never been so certain of: whatever they may say about these famous modern artists, you are this century's greatest painter of love. And you are the last great illuminator of Jewish marriage contracts that Europe will ever see.' "

Josef and Hannah slowly turn their eyes to each other. She says: "Keep reading."

He flips the page over and continues: " 'Word has reached here of the happenings in Vienna. I am particularly glad that I was not there to see her synagogues burning, though a similar fate now seems to be on the horizon for our own modest temples here and in the surrounding towns. With the entrance of Hitler's tanks into our country, the Polish people are in a sudden fever to get rid of their Jewish neighbors. The use of force seems to produce an intoxication in men. I can't see an equivalent force to counteract it, other than nakedness. If the Poles and the Germans were deprived of their murderous garments and uniforms, and Jew and anti-Semite alike had to face each other unclothed, the fever might subside. As a religious man, it surprises me that my Catholic brothers cannot distinguish the evil in themselves and all around. It only increases my long-held conviction that the moral landscape of the modern world is becoming featureless. My Jewish friends in Kopyczyńce are of two minds about Hitler: either that he will be stopped very soon, or that he will never be stopped. Both opinions seem to me to be attempts to lessen the fear associated with the anticipation of badness. It is easier to imagine a miracle, or to live under ongoing pain, than it is to accept that evil is going to come, no matter what.

" 'Take care of your mother, Young Pommeranz. She may be dying. Take care of your father also. Despite not raising you as a Jew, he did do some good for you. Surely, my boy, you have always known that yours was a childhood of extreme privilege. Whether poor or wealthy, a person senses the surfaces of their station in life in the same vague way the tongue is familiar with molars in the back of one's mouth. Just because your father disinherited you does not mean you should disinherit him: now that he has been reduced to nothing (how your mother, from her convalescent bed, worries about him living in that tiny flat with all those strangers), go see him, Josef. And give him some of that money I know you still have stashed away from all the ketubah commissions. I would send him money myself if I had any. It would be the least I could do to repay him for his generosity with me all those years ago. Here I am struggling in fact to make last week's rent, though with any luck (don't tell my landlady I used the phrase — she is waiting eagerly for my payment, she does not want to know from luck) I'll have it by tomorrow. May God watch over you, my child. Your Grandfather. P.S. —' "

All of a sudden Josef lowers the letter to

293

his lap. Confused by this abrupt termination of his reading, Hannah instinctively takes his free hand.

" 'P.S.,' " he tries again, holding up the letter — but it is no use, he seems unable to continue.

She waits a few seconds, then asks if he would like her to finish reading it aloud. When he nods his assent she gently retrieves the letter from the clutch of his grip and, locating the postscript at the bottom of its final page, reads it to him: " *'P.S.,'* " she repeats, in as reassuring a tone as she can muster, " 'Blessed three chicken legs and one gefilte fish today. In fact, also seven perch heads, two pigeons (dressed, but not yet plucked), and the tail of a squirrel. It has come to that.' "

These words have a strong effect on Josef. She sees his chest heaving and tries to comfort him, but the letter has affected her too. He has only ever spoken of his grandfather intermittently, usually with an anger that truncated the topic before she could see a full picture of the man. Now these pages, saturated in truth and composed with a grace that caught her by surprise, have brushed in color where there was only a preliminary charcoal sketch, and added a light source that alternately illuminates the man's love for his grandson, highlights the edges of his thinking, and indicates where his shadows may lie. But, more important, they have deepened her perspective on Josef. "Show me one of your marriage contracts," she blurts out.

He pulls away and looks at her with suspicion. "Why?"

"Josef," she says, her voice rising with incredulity before she has good sense to restrain it, "wherever we go in Vienna, people recognize you. They come up to you, even now when all is so terrible for them, and their faces light up when they mention the ketubot you painted for their weddings. And your grandfather — he thinks you're Europe's last great painter of marriage contracts. You've been hiding something from me. I need to see one of these things. Everyone *else* has."

There is a measurable pause.

"I don't have any left," he replies.

She searches his face. "You're lying to me."

"I made them for people's *weddings.* They got married. They *took* them," he says, shrugging as if the matter is plain as day. When she does not respond, he adds: "And now the Nazis are causing them all to be destroyed."

She waits. He glares at her. Pinched with irritation, he works his lips.

"I have *one,*" he says at last.

With a devastating sigh, he hands her his half-finished plate of torte. Then he kneels beside the bed and pulls out a dust-coated artist's folder. "It's the first one I ever painted," he mutters, unfastening the leather tie. The folder suddenly splays out across the bed and yields up its contents: two blank sheets of paper that Josef promptly removes, and the ketubah in question, which takes Hannah's breath away. Wrinkled and yellowed, it has the appearance of having been touched by thousands of hands, and at first her eyes convince her she is beholding some fragment of Egyptian papyrus covered in delicate symbols and hieroglyphs. But in the next instant, as the disparate images coalesce in her vision into a recognizable narrative, a second impression hits her, this time not of age but of scope: the ketubah seems to be not only a map of one couple's marriage, but also a whole breviary of human matrimonial conscience — a portrait of love in a perishable world. Her attention, following the drift of the ketubah's imagery, is drawn toward its center, whose arresting emptiness seems to have sucked the contract's text into a primordial nothingness, as if the act of marriage were an emigration to eternity. "I did it for my parents," Josef adds, hitting a note of disparagement, "twenty years after they got married. But my father wouldn't allow it in the —"

"Why did you marry me?" she interrupts.

He turns his eyes on her with immense concern, not for her, but for himself — as if she has committed a grave trespass with the question. "What?"

She feels an awful embarrassment filling her cheeks as she stares down at the ketubah. She knows he married her as a last-ditch effort to flee the country, but that is not what she is asking him right now. "If you find *this*" — she indicates the marriage contract by shaking her head at it — "so appalling, so horrible that you made a vow never to do it yourself, why did you marry me?"

He colors instantly and stammers: "Because I'm *against* marriage, that's why."

"Meaning?" She has begun to shake.

"Meaning I don't *believe* in it anymore. Meaning that's why I was able to go through with it, with someone I didn't know, like it was so much red tape."

She looks him full in the face. He is actually smiling at her, mockingly, spitefully, and she wonders how it is possible to love someone and absolutely hate them in the same instant. It takes all of her powers not to react with a fury she will regret. When she finally speaks, her voice is calm: "Only a man who has faith in something can have it broken — *that* is what your grandfather really did to you. Forget about him using your talent for money. The real calamity is that he robbed you of the joy of your own marriage — a joy that was your right, your due, after you added joy to so many other marriages with your ketubot. Don't you see, Josef? If you once believed in it, your faith can be mended."

"No. There is no mending. *None.*" He is on his feet now and pointing angrily at the ketubah on the bed. "I painted that to mend my parents' marriage, and later my grandfather had me believing I was mending the Jews themselves. But all of them — my parents, the Jews who came to me for my contracts — all of them eventually taught me there was no mending anyone. And then I began to ask myself, Why are they all *broken? Hitler* obviously knows they are. Is it as simple as my grandfather's or Max's claim: that it is because they were separated from Israel all those centuries ago? Is *that* what is wrong with us? I never stopped asking those questions, even after I quit making the contracts. And then, when Max told me about you and your permit to Palestine, I thought, 'Maybe there's truth in those claims. . . . Why *not* marry to escape that brokenness? Why not use marriage to get *back* to Israel?' Only then did I recognize a version of marriage that felt honest to me . . . utilitarian to the core, directed to a purpose, a bureaucratic —"

"Stop!" Hannah cries. "Just stop!"

He freezes in front of her, a column of thunderstruck rigidity, and she seeks something in his face, a trace, a sign, anything that will make her feel better. "What did I say?" he asks — a shirking of responsibility that reveals only the same disaffection that has been building in him for months. Never has she felt so far from him. She buries her head in a pillow and releases all of her sadness into it.

"Hannah? Hannah?" he calls out.

"Go!" she wails.

She feels the bed sink and the weight of him next to her. "Hannah?"

"Go *away*."

He will not go away, and she is secretly grateful because she has no idea who she is right now. Her feelings, her behavior: they perplex her, they *exhaust* her. She keeps her face pressed into the pillow well beyond that moment when the emotion that necessitated its use in the first place has subsided. When he begins gingerly to stroke her hair, she starts telling him things, first of her love for him (with the hope that he will not stop showing her this small tenderness), then, encouraged by his caresses, of her fears. She reveals that initially her idea of marriage was not so different from his, and that she only half-realized how important it really was to her after living with him, when her idealism began to give way under the erosion of events, their lovemaking, and certainly under the weight of their pregnancy. She tries to explain how, now, his devaluing of marriage only makes her value it more, how it causes doubts in her about the fact that he did not choose her as his bride (*Max* did) but instead chose to marry as a general thing toward a very specific end. None of her actual words come out well, and what does come out cannot change the fact that she is hurt, and embarrassed, and saddened to find that she has become a pathetic, silly person. Frustrated, she lets her voice fade away into the pillow feathers. At first his stroking of her head persists bravely, then tentatively, until by degrees it comes to a stop altogether and she lies there waiting and unsure, blinking into the fabric.

"It's better I didn't choose you," he suddenly whispers, his warm breath filling her ear.

"You're just squeezing out words to fill the silence. You don't know what you're saying."

"No. I know exactly what I'm saying. It's better I didn't choose you."

There is such conviction in his words this time.

"Why?" she asks, her head still turned into the pillow. "Why is it better you didn't choose me?"

"Because love, and *this*" — his fingers find her belly — ". . . they're unchosen."

She rolls onto her back and looks at him. And in the moment before she takes his hand and presses it to her cold cheek, she sees their life together — the talking and sharing, the eating and loving and arguing, the sleeping and waking and worrying, *all* of it — reclothed by the tragedy of their circumstances. Then, so as to supply the vision with another tragic image, she moves his hand from her cheek to her swollen breast, and after that, lifting her skirt and pushing her panties aside, to her cunt. His fingers find what they want there, and quickly, by unbuttoning his trousers and turning her onto her side facing away, so does that other hungry, hard part of him.

"Paint a ketubah for us," she whispers, staring at the wall as he takes her, ardently, from behind.

"No," comes his reply.

She feels the child inside of her finally let out a kick. And she thinks of what the gestapo officer said. She thinks of what her mother told her. The phrase "offspring of whores" fills her ears. She tries to look back at Josef, but her body will not let her twist far enough, and she can catch only a side-long glimpse of his dark moving shape. Weakened by the effort, by her doubts too, she allows her cheek to fall back to the bed.

"*Am* I your whore?" she lets out.

But even as she asks it, the words send an electric thrill through her body. And there is certainly electricity in his delay, and then in his firm response, first from his body, and then from his mouth:

"*Yes.*"

RESERVATION

Start with the Indian. Such was Max Wiener's advice when Daniel, hoping to learn more about what might have led to Benjamin's final show and his relationship with Aleksandra, phoned the old man at his home in Arizona a few weeks after meeting him at the memorial service. "Should you want to understand really what happened to my grandson," Max said, his ripe glissando voice crackling in Daniel's receiver, "you must do what *he* did: visit his father, Herman — America's one and only Hebrew Indian.

"It will not be easy," Max added. "Herman is a scientist. Such a successful scientist! So thorough when he looks into things. My son had to find always a clean solution to problems. He hated messiness, including in people. And trust me: he is very good at walking away from what he does not like. If Herman suspects that you understand *any-*

thing about him, if he discovers you have talked to me . . . What can I tell you? — he will shut the door in your face. The man erased me. Erased all Jewishness from his life. Even from his *name:* 'Wind' instead of 'Wiener.' I am sure I will go to my grave without once seeing him again. In any case, it must be obvious to you that, should he agree to meet you, and should he mention the woman Benjamin brought to their reunion, you cannot reveal to him that she was your wife."

Armed with this cautionary information and a belief that he was haltingly nosing his way toward the truth about Aleksandra's death, Daniel called Herman Wind in late October, claiming that he was writing a book on Benjamin's art and life. To his surprise, Benjamin's father came across as civil, interested, and faintly sad, and by the end of their phone conversation an interview had been arranged, to be held at Herman's home in Newport Coast, California. Three weeks later Daniel was caught blinking and bleary-eyed by Orange County's bright parade of castellated villas. Could he, in repeating a trip Aleksandra had taken to this area two years earlier, reexperience a moment from a part of her life that had been hidden from him? He was as uncertain about his motive for asking this question as he was about its answer, because while he viewed his impulse to reconstitute Aleksandra's past as the product of his hurting love for her, he also could not help but see it as an act of concentrated jealousy — an assault on emotions that had never belonged to him, and a rage against her right to have had them.

Still, he was determined to repeat Aleksandra's path. Before leaving New York, he had ferreted out all her business receipts from the period roughly corresponding to the time that she and Benjamin had visited Herman, and he had spent the better part of a night probing to the bottom of them. His compensation for these efforts had been a single receipt, from the Starbucks in Newport Coast, for one Grande Caffè Latte with soy. In conducting her affair with Benjamin, Aleksandra had been fastidious. Daniel vaguely remembered her "flying to L.A." around the same time, on one of her many photographic assignments in that city. Benjamin must have paid for everything — their flights, their hotel room, their dinners and breakfasts. . . . The latte was an error, a result most likely of her lifelong caffeine addiction. He imagined her asking Benjamin to make a last-minute stop at the Starbucks just before heading to his father's house, imagined the artist waiting in the car, racked with nerves about the difficult meeting ahead, while she ran inside and made her one purchase of the trip. It was probably the only time she had been alone — the only moment of the whole tricky sojourn when they had not been together.

Which was exactly why Daniel, after arriving at John Wayne Airport, drove straight to the very same Starbucks and ordered a soy latte. Newport Coast, as it turned out, was not a city per se but rather a planned development. Newly terraced and treed, newly nailed and newly gated, it was the last garrison before the ocean, the end of America. Max's son must have done very well in science to afford a home here. Nonsensically, occupying the priciest piece of the development's land (closest to the beach) was its commercial center, a glorified strip mall that fronted the Pacific Coast Highway. Here the Starbucks was located, and, with almost an hour to go before his interview with Herman Wind, Daniel sat down at one of its outdoor tables in order to contemplate, over his bitter drink, the profoundness of being in the same space that Aleksandra had occupied.

It was odd to be so laden with longing in

this place — not just the Starbucks, but this whole development that seemed the one spot in the world not connected with anything unpleasant. Daniel felt like some brooding German émigré who had just arrived, fresh from Hitler's Reich, amid the palm tree–packed Pacific Palisades. But even the Palisades and the rest of Los Angeles had its share of sorrow. Here, some other principle was operating — the elimination of decrepitude. Awash in piped jazz, he found himself staring at barefooted men in baseball caps and baggy shorts happily emerging from European luxury cars or from elephantine vehicles that looked ready for desert warfare; every one of these gadget-encumbered boy-men was attached, it seemed, to either a cute bulgy-eyed dog, or a cute towheaded toddler, or a cute young woman (wife? girlfriend? daughter?) wearing an ironic T-shirt — sometimes to all three — and every one of them carried an expression in which simplicity and drive were easily blended, a look that suggested a commitment to nothing in particular, except a belief that the world was their inheritance. Did it take a residential development that destroyed the distance between what a person is and what they dream of being to make a man like Herman Wind, a Jew posing as an American Indian, feel at home?

Daniel carried the thought out to his car, then past the guarded gate and up the hill to where the man himself lived. The house, a large faux Mediterranean, winged and groin-shaped, made a disappointing first impression — an effect of false parapet and functionless battlement, of incongruous Mansard roof and chimney hood in the Moorish style, of stucco sameness to every other home on the hill. Daniel stood there in the driveway looking at the residence, and for an instant the sight of it reduced Aleksandra's betrayal of him to banality. Affairs were not always inspired things. He suddenly felt stupid for being here. Stupid — and ashamed, as if Aleksandra and Benjamin were behind him, leaning against the hood of his car, watching him in judgment. Theirs was a love that had surely known no moment of peace, and here he was still troubling them with this obsessive personal pursuit of his. He considered getting back into his car, driving straight to the airport, and going home.

But then his eyes caught sight — between two enormous Grecian urns commanding the bridge to the house's portico — of a square patch of the Pacific. And it spoke to him, that "peek view," of something beyond the banal, and it reminded him that Benjamin and Aleksandra had been driven here by forces that lay underneath the surface of things, driven here by the kind of questions that defined a life, by the same search for meaning with which Daniel, in his own way, was now occupied. He went and knocked on the door.

Despite being ensnared in the fixity of late middle age, the face that greeted him was in every way save the eyes an uncanny echo of Benjamin Wind's. The full lips, the pugilistic nose, the faint knifelike smile that told you nothing. Differences did, in the next instant, however, reveal themselves: the head of hair was still considerable, but considerably peppered with gray; the cheeks looked hollowed by age — by discontent too. And then there were the eyes. While they seemed to possess the same reach of intellect as the eyes of Wind the Younger, they were lighter. This difference in value of color seemed to represent a lessening of some human value that Daniel could not quite identify; it made looking at the man's eyes for more than a moment intolerable. And yet Daniel was forced to look at them, because they had taken hold of him straightaway and subjected him to both a pointed appraisal and a clear show of dismay.

"Did I get our meeting time wrong?" Daniel asked, so thrown by Herman Wind's expression that he forgot to introduce himself.

"You're on time," said Herman after some hesitation. "Just didn't expect to encounter anyone associated with Benjamin again."

The man treated Daniel to a quick look of watchful amiability, then extended a hand. His grip, when Daniel took it, was wooden, firm if forcedly so, more reflective of tactfulness than warmth, and, as the two of them exchanged their names and handshakes, several perceptions washed over Daniel. The first was an instant recognition that he hated Herman Wind. Hated him at a gut level. The second was a realization that his hatred was not simply some animal intuition. It was the shock of meeting in the flesh a man who had so occupied his thoughts ever since Max had spoken of him at Benjamin's memorial service. Everything Daniel knew about Herman Wind — his falsity, his "killing off" of his father, his audacious lying about who he was and, more damagingly, about who his *son* was — became so present to Daniel that the vision of the real man before him was as of a monster. A monster who had had the privilege of seeing Aleksandra — *his* Aleksandra — with passion and love and worry in her eyes for his son. Daniel's hatred arose also from his fear that he was about to learn things that could reorient his entire picture of Aleksandra and Benjamin. His antipathy was the inevitable resistance one put up in the face of knowledge. Daniel hated Herman Wind, finally, because he understood that he was not justified in his hatred of this man, because he knew very well that these feelings had more to do with himself — and it made Daniel, as Herman invited him inside, hate the man all the more.

If the exterior of Herman Wind's house was adorned with a thousand silly embellishments, its interior was all modern minimalist gleam. He led Daniel through one cold room after another where no accent of life remained. Daniel was no stranger to austere spaces, the white box having long been the exemplar of the New York gallery and loft, but there was not even a hint of humanity in this man's house. Its rooms were not merely dehumanized: they felt *dispeopled.* The place was . . . bloodless.

"I don't believe in hanging anything on the walls," Herman announced when he caught Daniel staring into a blank cube of a bedroom. "For the past five years, I've been practicing Zen Buddhism, which I don't consider a religion. It's more a practical philosophy, and I find it has a lot of parallels with the Blackfoot outlook. Anyway, the point being that I want nothing in my house to distract from the present."

The allusion — to art hanging on walls — reminded Daniel of the small wrapped gift he was carrying in his briefcase: a signed copy of the catalog he had written for Benjamin's midcareer retrospective at the Guggenheim Museum, and, because Daniel wanted to see Herman's reaction to it, a copy of his review of Benjamin's final show. When Daniel pulled it out, Herman eyed the package reticently and received it with a fraudulent courteousness ("Oh, well, thank you . . . thank you kindly"), making a little production of leading Daniel to the kitchen and, pausing before an island of brushed steel, tugging at the ribbon and parting the wrapping paper. With an oddly clipped "I see" and "Thanks," he flipped through the catalog's pages, and he only briefly looked askance at the review before placing both into a drawer and making them disappear. He seemed exceedingly pleased with himself at having performed this neat vanishing trick. "It's all history now," he declared, looking up at Daniel.

"I didn't notice you at the memorial

312

service," Daniel said.

"That was for the art world. Jess and I, she's my second wife — we held our own ceremony right after Benjamin died. Had him cremated. Scattered his ashes in a place in Montana that's important to our family. What can I get you to drink?"

"I'm fine, thanks," said Daniel. "A Black-foot place?" He could not help himself. Max had prepared him for Herman's imposture, but Daniel was surprised to find that his own sense of protest was put on high alert almost at once by Herman's bald lying about who he was. Some degree of misrepresentation, he understood, played a role in nearly all human relations. But this was different. He was looking into the face of a fellow Jew — the son of Max Wiener, a European immigrant — who, for some forty years running, had claimed to be a Blackfoot Indian from Montana. The blatant *bifurcation* of it, thought Daniel, the rational irrationality. Granted, life had not been exactly perfect for a Jew in the America of the fifties and sixties, but why choose a race that was even *lower* in the country's hierarchy of disempowered minorities? Why not do what any Jew wishing to cast off the burden of otherness had done for at least the last two hundred years — become a

313

Gentile? Was it some kind of bold end-run around anti-Semitism, an attempt to pass over American Gentiles and head straight for native rights in order to stake an indigenous claim?

"*Used* to be Blackfoot land," Herman replied lightheartedly, flashing Daniel a big, impenetrable smile while his hands found their way into his pants pockets. "Everything up there was. Now it's in the park boundary, on the mountain, not too far from the rez. Both my parents' ashes were scattered up there as well."

Incredible the lies, the storytelling, the casual tossing off of "the rez," as if he had actually grown up on the Blackfoot reservation. Listening to this bullshit, Daniel found himself taking the side of Max, despising Herman as a brother loyal to the father might. He had never encountered someone who denied belonging to the clan *outright,* and, as they shifted to several chromed Italian chairs in the living room, he had the sensation of conversing with the guard of a graveyard, a man who was going to do everything in his power to prevent him from getting his hands on whatever he had come to unbury.

"So you're an art critic," Herman threw out, trying to take his ease in his chair but instead settling into an attitude of defense. Or perhaps it was offense, for with his next statement he fired his first salvo. "I prefer science. It doesn't distort."

"It also doesn't provide meaning."

"You don't need to look at art, Mr. Lichtmann, to understand how base humanity is."

Daniel eyed him firmly. "No, I can find that everywhere I look."

A new spark — of malice and intent — entered Herman's face. He was taking Daniel in now, trying to discern what Daniel wanted from him. "What I meant," Herman said, leaning forward in his chair, "is that we should strive to see the world as it is. We shouldn't distort existence."

"A completely undistorted existence, Mr. Wind?" Daniel found himself asking. "Who really lives that way? Do *you*?"

He was sure he had gone too far with the question, risking the man discovering that he knew much more about him than he was letting on, and, to the extent that he could sink back into his ungiving chair, he tried affecting retraction.

But Herman rose to his challenge instantly with a defense of his meditation practice, which he claimed not only offered him an "unobstructed view of reality" but also the potential to attain limitless happiness. In a voice rank with propriety, the man spoke of sitting silently here in his house for hours and noticing every thought that came into his head, spoke of how, over the course of the last five years, he had liberated himself from all attachments. No longer clinging to life, he had given away all his old items and assembled a new home in which no object — no single piece of furniture — evoked his personal history, a home in which there was otherwise no physical evidence of a past. And as he said these things, Daniel could not help thinking, particularly in light of the man's relationship with his dead son and still-living father, that he had succeeded in making Zen sound like so much selfism, a vast excuse to turn away from obligations.

"But enough about letting go of the past," Herman said suddenly, brushing a non-existent speck of dust from the arm of his chair and fixing his eyes on Daniel. "You must have particular questions you want to ask me."

"That I do." From his briefcase Daniel pulled out a notepad, a gesture that was merely for show, as there were no questions written on it. He did not require notes to remind himself of what he really wanted to ask. What he really wanted to ask was if this man realized just how much he had fucked up Daniel's life. Did he understand that Daniel's wife had been drawn to his son because the only thing more compelling than a talented unknowable man was a talented unknowable man who suddenly comes to know himself? "I was wondering," Daniel began, pretending to read from his pad, "if you might be able to shed a personal light on your son, particularly on anything that might have shaped his art."

"Where should I start?"

Daniel hesitated. "Well — the past."

Herman looked at him hard for a moment, then seemed to acknowledge Daniel's attack with a barely perceptible smile. "You want to hear something no one else will tell you about Benjamin?"

This sent a jolt all the way down to Daniel's feet. *Yes,* he indicated, with a nod of his head.

"I think Benjamin got his appreciation of materials from *me,*" the man began, and it was already enough to dash Daniel's hopes of learning something that would help him. "Ever since I can remember," Herman continued, "I always had a special relationship to the ground and, weirdly enough, to falling. Took a real interest in the properties of soil, and especially the laws of gravity, and later I managed to parlay that into a pretty rewarding career in aerospace technology. Worked in L.A. for years and eventually ended up becoming involved in the ceramic tiles that coat the space shuttle, and other stuff having to do with landings."

"Must have been wonderful to see your son's excitement about what you were doing," Daniel offered.

"Oh, sure. Wonderful."

That Herman was at ease talking about science and philosophy and his career, but slipped into an economic shallowness whenever he tried to speak out of the experience of a father, told Daniel as much as he needed to know about how close the man had been to his son. The direction of the conversation required a fast readjustment — a bending back toward the big question. "In your opinion," Daniel asked, again providing the impression of reading from a prewritten question on his notepad, "what did Benjamin's *ethnic roots* have to do with the kind of art he produced?"

"Well, they played — some part in it." The man's reply came out clipped, an attenuation of something rich and revealing that had been on his lips. And it suddenly came to Daniel: the real meaning of Benjamin Wind's last show. It had not only been

318

about death. It had also been about memory
— and its vanishing. What a shock for Benjamin to learn that his memories were based
on incorrect information. It must have been
akin to having his memories ripped away
from him, a blank slate his only reference
by which to judge the present. No wonder
the faces on his final figures had seemed
anonymous.

"You mentioned that your parents' ashes
had been scattered on the old Blackfoot
grounds," Daniel pressed on. "When did
they pass away?"

Herman threw back his head as if doing
the math. "Father died almost forty-five
years ago, Mom a few years after that."

What a *charade.* But Daniel went along
with it: "So Benjamin never knew them. Did
you nevertheless stress tradition? What kind
of relationship did he have to his heritage
— to where his family came from?"

"I took him up there in the summers.
Showed him the important stuff. He knew
who he was."

"When's the last time you saw him?"

"Oh, couple years ago."

"Can you tell me a little about it?"

Herman seemed to be turning this request
over in his mind, his eyes set on a distant
point out the window. Then he came back

with: "I don't feel comfortable revealing that information."

Now Daniel gave up all appearances of referring to his notepad. "This will sound a little weird to you," he told Herman, "but there's a rumor floating around New York that Benjamin Wind was actually a Jew."

The word "Jew" exploded in the stark white room like a black paint ball.

Herman was staring at him now, eyes narrowed into thin, mistrustful slits.

"Will there be more of you, Mr. Lichtmann?"

"What do you mean?"

Herman rose to his feet. His next words came spitting out of his mouth: "I mean that from the minute you walked into this house your visit did not feel like that of a stranger, but rather of someone from the family. To be more specific: from a part of the family I consider to be history. I *saw* the way you looked in my rooms for signs of that history. It was exactly what Benjamin did when he walked in here two years ago. Each of you had the same look of disappointment — it was uncanny. I think we both know I'm talking about Max. Don't lie to me and tell me you haven't met with him. It was obvious to me ten minutes ago. I only needed to hear a few of your questions to confirm my suspicion. Max is a slave, you know. He's attached to a time, to a world that no longer exists. He can't accept the passing of things. Why do you think he built a storage empire?" Herman paused here and smiled down at Daniel. "I can see by your expression that he hasn't told you where his wealth has come from. Perhaps you didn't even know he was wealthy — the way he dresses and acts, who would? In any case it's true: the man owns the biggest conglomeration of self-storage chains in the country — he essentially *invented* the business to begin with. Made a fortune out of doing what he has always done anyway: try to hold a vanished world together by storing its chairs and paintings and photos and papers. But what he still hasn't learned is that a world isn't composed of its objects. He tried shuffling some of the stuff he saved onto me — things from Europe that were important to him. But I threw them all away. I wanted nothing to do with his memories. Those things, that world — it wasn't fair to burden me with them. Will there be no end to what we take on of our parents' baggage? We already get enough of the psychological burden. We've got our own era, our own reality, we don't need to carry their old memories as well. Let people be who they want to be. I'm certain Max has a thousand more objects stored away. When the old man dies, and if any of it comes to me, I'll throw those away too. I didn't expect you, Mr. Lichtmann. I thought that when Benjamin left my house, it was the end of it. I can see clearly now that it isn't. It's as if, now that Benjamin is dead, Max has sent you in his place. Again, I want to ask you: Will there be more of you?"

Daniel got up from his chair so that he was standing opposite Herman. "No," he answered coolly. "I believe I'm the last of them."

"I'm relieved to hear it. This is extremely unpleasant for me. I'd ask you to leave right now if I wasn't so curious to understand why you really came here. Here's a suggestion: Why don't we lay our cards on the table? Perform a little exchange of truths. You tell me something I can believe, and I tell you something you're *not* going to believe."

All at once, Daniel felt the whole encounter — their weird, aberrant conversation — come into tight focus, as if an examiner's dagger of light was directed straight at his face.

"I'm here because I know your son didn't arrive alone when he visited you that last time," he said.

Herman seemed to read the meaning of this. "His girlfriend —"

"My wife."

They held each other's gaze. Something meaningful — a first real understanding — seemed to course the air between them. And for an instant, there was a break in Herman's ardent coldness. His mouth, where all the man's emotions had seemed cauterized, relaxed a little at the corners, and his eyes, which had been so full of self-regard, now radiated, just a bit, in Daniel's direction.

"She stood out there," Herman suddenly said, indicating, with a dip of his head, the wide deck beyond the glass. Daniel turned to look. "Stood there for quite a while actually. She was really taken with the view. Said it reminded her of a place she'd been as a child. 'Odd'-something."

"Odessa," Daniel said.

"That's it."

Daniel remained standing there stiffly, his eyes frozen on the deck's rail. Herman was now telling him something else that Aleksandra had said, some unimportant remark about the house. Then he was telling Daniel where she had sat, what she touched, what she saw. And Daniel tried, tried as hard as he could to imagine it. But it was hopeless. Her movements in the house two years ago, detailed in Herman Wind's dry and deliberate tone, saturated Daniel's vision with all the pixeled opacity of a computer screen. Herman could not tell him how she had *felt,* so he was telling him nothing.

"Did they seem — happy?" Daniel tried to make the question sound factual, but there was a high, breathless pitch of curiosity in his voice, and he felt like a schoolboy asking a science teacher to explain who had started the big bang.

Herman's answer was as unhelpful as any a science teacher might provide to such a question: "You can imagine that, given the impetus for Benjamin's surprise visit to me, I was not exactly in a frame of mind to record the relative happiness or unhappiness existing between my son and — and your wife."

It was then that a woman wearing a tennis outfit and visor suddenly manifested at the kitchen counter, a bag of groceries in her hand. "Here's *mine,*" Herman said, offering Daniel an adamant smile that indicated their conversation was over. "Jess, this is Daniel Lichtmann. He came to interview me concerning a book he's writing on Benjamin's art."

Jess was an attractive, if somewhat plain, blond woman who appeared to be in her late forties, and who betrayed a perfect cheeriness as she came into the living room and shook Daniel's hand. Her tanned shoulders shone and Daniel picked up a hint of sweat and exertion in the air as she tried to convince him to stay for drinks and her special nachos, a request that both he and Herman found ways to rebuff. She gave Herman a soft slug on the arm for not telling her that Daniel was visiting during her doubles match, beckoned Daniel to come back any time if he had more questions, and, in less than one minute, generally made up for the lack of warmth that her husband had displayed over the course of the afternoon.

A few seconds later, Herman was accompanying Daniel silently out to his car, and then, as they shook hands, he laid his cards on the table. "Be careful with Max. Not everything he says is true. Here's one example. Max is not my father."

Exactly as Herman had predicted earlier, Daniel did not believe this, and it showed in his voice. *"Really?"*

"Really."

There was a pause. Whatever existed now between Daniel and this man — whether it was dislike, disbelief, or fellow feeling — could not be discerned in Herman's stony face, and Daniel was sure that his own aspect was no more revealing. They were two men standing in a driveway, trading poker faces as if they had not just revealed to each other the embarrassing details of their existences.

"Good-bye, Mr. Wind," said Daniel.

"Good *luck*," Herman said.

Only as he was driving away did it occur to Daniel that Herman had astutely avoided broaching the one subject that most obviously should have been discussed between the two of them: the question of the sudden side-by-side deaths of Benjamin and Aleksandra. Surely the man had to wonder why his son was unexpectedly found dead with the woman Benjamin had brought to his house. An opportunity had fallen into his lap to speak about it to the only other person on the planet as connected as he was to the mysterious deaths — and he had passed it up. The evasion nearly felt blasphemous to Daniel. And utterly, stupidly tragic. Herman Wind had not liberated himself from anything. His beliefs, his house behind gates — what were these if not small kingdoms of confinement? What was the arrogance in his eyes if not the pride of a slave? No taste of freedom had ever been as close at hand as that which came knocking on his door in the form of his own son two years earlier, and Daniel today. But in both instances the man had acquitted himself like a true veteran of captivity, fighting to preserve the walls that held him in. Daniel felt like an indecent visitor who had pried awfully into a constructed universe, and he was relieved, driving through the gate, to be getting off this particular reservation of the rich. As much as he loathed red-eye flights, it was a further relief to be sitting some hours later in an airplane headed back to New York, where the decent and indecent were given equal rein, and where enough sorrow flowed down its old streets for even Daniel to feel like a native.

The tired disappointment he felt on returning home without a single clue regarding the mystery of Aleksandra's and Benjamin's deaths never left him in the weeks that followed. It did not help that he was getting behind in the business of his life, was, in fact, running out of money. Running out of favor with his boss too, who warned that his position with the magazine might not survive his grieving process: "This isn't a sinecure, Daniel — you have to *produce*."

So he produced. He visited the galleries with diligence, wrote, read, and drank without moderation. But they were undistinguished, his days, his drinks, his new reviews. Especially the reviews: stock considerations so falsifying they hardly merited the scant money they fetched. He even stooped to repurposing phrases from reviews he had published years ago. His job had no claim on him. His obligations, his past passions . . . they had been ejected from his field of vision and supplanted by the smile on Benjamin Wind's face in the photo Daniel still kept in his pocket.

Over the next few months, Daniel pursued every possible connection to that face he could find. He followed up on his awkward California visit with "America's one and only Hebrew Indian" by phoning Max Wiener to ask whether there was any truth to Herman's claim of having no blood connection to him. He was only ever able to reach Max's Arizona answering machine, on which he left several versions of the question, but his calls were worrisomely never returned. What if Max had become ill, or worse? Daniel tried phoning the Hebrew Indian himself to see if there had been any "bad news" about Max, and he left messages to this effect on his voice mail, but Herman could not be troubled to call him back — no great surprise, given the poisonous note their meeting had ended on. Max, though — the old man had been adamant about maintaining contact with Daniel; if he was not ill or dead, there had to be another explanation for his silence. What if he *had,* in fact, been lying about his relationship to Herman and was too ashamed to face the lie? And if he was not Herman Wind's father, and therefore not Benjamin Wind's grandfather, *who* was he? These questions only made Benjamin Wind an even greater enigma to Daniel, who was coming to feel that the more he pursued the truth of Aleksandra's involvement with the artist the more distant that truth lay. Aleksandra herself had already become ghostly to him, and even that, her spectral presence, now seemed to be vanishing as he sped toward it.

There did remain one unexplored link to Benjamin Wind: the artist's mother. Like Max, Herman had not spoken of her, though this was unremarkable given the distance he obstinately maintained between himself and his past. From the obituary of Benjamin, Daniel knew the woman's name and city of residence. A few clicks of his mouse put him in possession of a phone number for the lone Francine Wind in Bend, Oregon, and after annihilating the better part of another February afternoon not writing an overdue review, he dialed it. But the Winds, even the discarded ones, were all dedicated non-answerers and, as Daniel was to learn after leaving a nice message for Ms. Wind of Bend, rooted non-returners.

Frustration made him go to his bookshelf some weeks later and pull down the catalog for Benjamin Wind's final show. He had looked at it countless times since That Day, but had never made it past the bewitching photographs of the whirling figures. This time he did, and what he found on the very last page astonished him. Sandwiched between Patrick Carrigan's acknowledgments and the identification of the photographer and printer was the following line:

The artist wishes to thank A.V. and
Clifford Fatheree.

Daniel was pierced by the sight of Aleksandra's initials, and it took a minute for his eyes and his thoughts to land on the second name. Who was Clifford Fatheree?

He put the question to Patrick Carrigan when he phoned him the next morning, but all the dealer could offer him was that the last name sounded "kinda Blackfoot." Fatheree was not Blackfoot, as Daniel's investigation on the Web quickly revealed, but a variant of an old Creole name. The Web also revealed that a Clifford Fatheree — the only Clifford Fatheree he could find — lived in the Bronx; in addition to an address, there was a phone number, which Daniel tried.

A man instantly picked up and trumpeted *"Yes?"* as if he were saying "God here." It stunned Daniel, who realized he had not planned what he was going to say, and he hesitated.

"*Who* is this?" the man said angrily into the phone. That sentiment was echoed by a woman's voice in the background: Daniel could hear her repeatedly ask, between trying to quiet a crying baby, who was calling.

Daniel identified himself, proffering as credentials the magazine for which he wrote, and then asked if he could speak to Clifford Fatheree.

"Hold on," the man said, forcing Daniel to sit there at his desk, phone to his ear, listening to a hushed argument unfold in the background. Finally, there was the sound of the phone being taken up and a long intake of breath. The subsequent exhalation — equally long — was the name "Clifford Fatheree," spoken into the phone as a question by the woman, followed by: "He don't live here no more." There was a click and the line went dead.

Daniel called back, and when the woman answered, he asked if she could please tell him where he might find Mr. Fatheree. But she repeated what she had told him before — "Clifford don't live here no more" — discharging the words like a woman who dealt in obstruction and elision as a matter of course, like she was prepared to repeat them a thousand times. And then she hung up on Daniel again.

He puzzled over the strange phone encounter for the better part of a week before deciding to go ahead and mail a clipping of his review of Benjamin's final show to the address he had found on the Web, along with a note to Clifford Fatheree asking what he might know about it. But after he had posted the letter a sense of hopelessness swooped into his being, a feeling that all of this was only an exercise in avoidance, a desperate search for some outside cause of Aleksandra's and Benjamin's deaths so that he did not have to face the possibility of their suicide.

And then Francine Wind surprised him by calling from Oregon. He had nearly forgotten about leaving a message for Benjamin Wind's mother, and had certainly given up any hope of the woman ever returning his call, and so was doubly surprised by how willing she was to talk. In fact, she was unguarded with him, disarmingly free with the details of her personal life in the breezy manner of an old hippie. She was also, as a result of what she revealed (and did not reveal) about Benjamin and Herman Wind, electrifying, scarifying, shattering.

Her son, Benjamin, she claimed, had regularly kept in touch with her right up to the end, but something about the way she spoke of his memorial service, her generality perhaps — a detectable note of at least several removes in how she chose to describe it — signaled to Daniel that the woman was presenting a filial closeness on Benjamin's part that was largely of her own imagining: "Oh, I found it to be very moving. Very moving. Specially that preacher's homage to diverse cultures. That made this mother very proud, Daniel — can I call you Daniel? It confirmed what I'd always hoped for my son. I taught him to make a beneficial impact on each place he went, and it was clear to me from what I saw at the service that he'd had a good effect on New York City." It was disheartening to Daniel, this unknowingness, and he could not help receiving her subsequent statements about Benjamin skeptically, until she made this one: "Benjamin didn't kill himself. That I don't believe. The way he sounded last time we spoke — he'd just come back from Europe. I said to him that he was talking like someone who was in love, and he didn't deny it. He seemed so taken with what life was bringing his way — despite everything."

Despite everything? Daniel had no idea how much this woman knew about Benjamin and Aleksandra — or himself. His phone message to her had been left under the pretext that he was writing a book about her son. He had only identified himself as an art critic who had recently interviewed Benjamin's father. But it would not have been difficult for her, particularly if she had read any of the newspaper accounts, to put two and two together and connect him — Daniel — to the photographer woman with whom her son had been found dead. If she knew, she clearly did not want to talk about it.

What she wanted to talk about, much more than anything to do with her son, was her son's father: Herman Wind. The low-grade hatred that attached itself to every thought this woman shared about her ex-husband made it clear that, inside Francine Wind, their long-vanished marriage had a negative permanence. "It was not a real marriage of any description," she told him, and then she described it, for the next forty-five minutes, while Daniel paced his apartment cradling the cordless against his ear. Almost at once, she assumed the air of some put-upon academic recapitulating a particularly vexing moment in history in which Herman Wind had been the key player, but Daniel's ear perked up only when she asserted that Herman was "the atheist of love" — an epithet that struck Daniel with its unexpected piquancy and aptness, given his own brush with Herman Wind.

"Atheist of love?" he echoed, staring out at the street from the tiny window in his kitchen.

"He didn't *believe* in love, Daniel — only sex. It's like, in his mind, he believed he'd purified love of its artificial meanings, and the result was a lot of sex. *Too* much sex. Don't get me wrong, I enjoy sex as much as anyone. But he stripped it of everything. There was no spiritual component. Instead it became a physical transaction. Like we were sprinting together. He was an athlete about it, all efficiency and rhythm. Rhythm is important, I know that, but not if you have to *think* about it. Even his *breathing* seemed calculated. No, it was just pure sex — but it never *felt* pure."

"I think I know what you mean," Daniel put in, mainly so that she would not worry he was being quiet due to an uncomfortableness with the intimacy of her revelations. He went so far as to add that he had dated women like that, though it was untrue. Even the businesslike manner of his first wife during their later couplings had been cut with a vulnerable, metaphysical longing for children.

"But his atheism produced more than just disattached sex," Francine continued, as though she had not heard him. "It extended to the way he looked at everything in his life, including his own family. I mean, the man told me they were dead! *Dead!* And I *believed* it all these years. That goes way beyond the usual for men of his generation. I've had enough relationships with baby boom men to know that many of them tried to shed the past, especially their parents' past. But Herman is sick. Really sick. When we first set up house together he wouldn't let me put up photos of my family — he didn't even want the old chairs of my grandmother's to be around. He tried to put them in the garage, and they were beautiful antiques! It's like he saw newness as a panacea for all emotional disorders. He didn't even like to *shit* — and I think it's because his shit reminded him of what was already behind him (no pun intended). I know I'm a bit New Agey," she said, her voice starting to shake, "but I think you'll agree, Daniel, that the depth of a person is connected to how much of the past is in them. I mean, even if you don't believe in past lives: people can have a *feeling* about them that seems old, older than they are. But not Herman — he was all surface to me once I really got to know him. Unfortunately, very unfortunately, we were already married and with child by then."

Her tone had grown somber with the latter statement, and she lapsed into silence. "Maybe that's why he's taken up Buddhism," Daniel suggested. "Because it rejects the importance of the past in favor of the present."

A cackle came over the line. "Well he certainly didn't take it up to find *meaning* in his life." She already sounded stronger, and no matter how thorny the conversation was turning out to be for Daniel, or how much he wished the subject had stayed on Benjamin, he realized that it felt satisfying to actually be discussing Herman Wind with someone who knew what he was talking about, and the longer they spoke, the more he wanted to keep Francine on the line. She represented, after all, a direct link to Benjamin and therefore to Daniel's dilemma. But it was also more than that. She was speaking from a place that was acutely familiar to him, the land of the left behind.

"I heard about his new obsession with Buddhism," she picked up. "And I wasn't surprised. He's hated death ever since I've known him, so he chose a religion that tries to erase that hatred. He probably grew tired of carrying all that hate around. Anyway, it suits him better than the whole Blackfoot lie he made us all buy into. Every Jew in Oregon is a Buddhist now, and I imagine it's true all over the country, so he's got lots of company. And he needs rules to follow. I guarantee you his Buddhism isn't a reflection of some midlife quest to find out what his purpose on this planet is. He never asked those kinds of questions — not once. No, Buddhism gives him another set of rules to go by, just like his science, like the self-help books, the relationship books he was always buying. I still know how it goes with him:

he's got a lot of fear. Lots of doubt and guilt too. This is only the latest toolkit to help him accept the cards life dealt him. Though I find it quite funny that he chose a religion so strongly based on the idea of reincarnation. Herman used to speak so condescendingly about peoples' belief in reincarnation. He'd say" — she lowered her voice in imitation of the way Herman Wind spoke — " 'From a *scientific* point of view, it's impossible. From a *scientific* point of view, it's obvious God doesn't exist.' As if he hadn't noticed Einstein's belief in God and mystery. As if he wasn't aware of the astrophysicists who went into their profession because they wanted to see what God had created. But Herman isn't interested in mystery. He's interested in earthly things. He has a need to *eliminate* mystery — that's why *he* went into science. He even tried to turn *love* into a science. Does Buddhism do that too, Daniel?"

"I don't know. I don't think so," Daniel answered, but then he remembered how surprised he had been to discover that Herman was now married to a young tennis ball– whacking wife who seemed quite happy with the man, and all at once he felt defensive for the woman on the other end of the phone, and added: "Maybe the way he practices it."

There was a pause. "I know I've been talking a lot — too much — about Herman. And you wanted to know about my son. Isn't that why you called me?"

The tone of the question suddenly suggested that she knew *everything* about Aleksandra — knew precisely why he had called her. "That's all right," he replied unconvincingly.

"No. I owe you an apology. I've found that you can sleep and even fall in love with other people, but there will always only be *one* other real parent to your child. It's a hard bond to break. It must be so much easier to move on from someone if you've never had kids with them."

Daniel remained silent.

"Be careful, Daniel. The trap of feeling wronged. I've spent almost forty years in it. Humiliation can be a strong crutch. You start to need it — need whoever caused you to feel it — to believe that you're good. You search for answers, keep asking why, and it's easy to convince yourself that the questions somehow make you a higher person. But what you figure out, way too late, is that you're drowning in pride."

Daniel, still in the kitchen, reached for the edge of the table and eased himself down into a chair. He felt uncomfortably hot, as if he was suffering from a fever, and his throat was constricting. She seemed to be waiting for him to respond.

"I'll try," he muttered feebly.

"It's very sad," she said. For a brief moment he was certain that she was referring to Aleksandra — he feared that she would now force him to talk about her — but she returned to the topic of Herman Wind, and he was grateful. "I still don't understand a person like Herman. I never met a single member of his family. He left them all behind. And as soon as *I* became family to him, as soon as the reality hit him — the reality of having a baby, and of what that meant — he left me too. I fell in love with him because he was a loner, I suppose. I thought there was something romantic and tragic about him. Something sad. Now I realize it was probably more like anger, even hatred. There was nothing romantic about it at all. He was completely, completely alone. And it was all his own doing. I even feel sorry for him now, as much as I still hold so much anger about how he abandoned Benjamin and me. I mean, really, what makes a man want to sever every tie he has to the people who matter the most?

Tell me, Daniel. What makes a man just walk away?"

FALLING

Is she Josef's whore? The question troubles Hannah all through her unscheduled prenatal exam the following afternoon. But the baby is fine, and her relief clears her head. She is actually happy at the sight of Josef, who meets her outside the hospital entrance. Even the bad news he shares with her — that they are no longer permitted to ride the tram — leaves her unperturbed. They walk home, besieged on nearly every street by bright posters berating Jews or celebrating the Reich's victories in the East. Hitler decorating his misdeeds. Yet she and Josef speak of pleasant things: the fine, discreet sky; the "Sunrise" string quartet by Haydn; possible names for their child (if it is a boy, she likes Herman Johannes, after her great-grandfather; if a girl, Amalie). Of what passed between them in bed during the night no mention is made.

It is, nevertheless, the first thing that

343

comes to her mind when, after he opens the door to their flat, she sees that his paintings of lovers have all been restored to their original places on the walls. Josef's cruel joke? Or a *tender* one? No sooner has her gaze finished tracing these lustful figures than it lands on an actual figure in the flesh, or rather in a suit, reclining on their bed: Josef's father. She and Josef come around to face the man, who is on his back asleep.

"He must've convinced Hörler to let him in," Josef says, referring to the building superintendent. Disdainfully, his eyes inventory the contents of a suitcase lying open at the foot of the bed: a change of clothes, a face cloth, house slippers, a history of the Romans, and a toiletry bag, much used — the remains, apparently, of his father's worldly possessions.

"Don't *hate* him, Josef," Hannah whispers, focusing her compassion on Herr Pick. But the slumbering man's large hands, folded over his chest, are so plump with repellent vigor that she almost cannot bear to look at them, and the truth is that she too harbors animosity toward him because of all she has heard from Josef. Ashamed, she sputters: "You can't hate a parent once you've seen them *sleeping*."

"Yes — you can."

Toward evening Herr Pick wakens with embarrassment for having fallen asleep in their bed. He sits up, straightening his jacket, and offers an apology for his abrupt move to their flat, a result of his inability to live another day "in a sardine tin filled with Jews." Josef begins to insist that he is welcome (it is a strained effort, painful to watch for Hannah), but his father stops him with a wave of his hand. *"Please,"* he tells Josef, "I know how wearying every new meeting with me is for you. We are both difficult men. Resentful. Stubborn. You are, finally, a Pick."

As it does Hannah, this last assertion clearly catches Josef by surprise. It is insolently self-flattering, but its undertone is conciliatory, as if the man is backpedaling, distancing himself from his disinheritance of his son, perhaps even trying to bring their years of jousting to an end. "Any child who is exactly as a parent wants him to be," the man adds, holding Josef in careful regard, "would be unbearable."

Josef meets his eyes, they consider each other warily, two old enemies converging on a mountain path, but the new ground they have gained is too perilous, it seems, for a pause, and Hannah can see that together they must move on, move around this delicate turn.

"You hung up my paintings," Josef says.

"Why were they facing the wall?"

By this question Hannah is not threatened: she knows Josef can hear no real curiosity in his father's voice, a trailing interest at best. Herr Pick looks at the paintings abstractedly, and it is unsurprising that he does not wait for Josef to reply. "I wanted to see what my son has been doing with his life," the man asserts, though, predictably, this proves to be nothing more than a pretext to discussing himself. "More than *I've* ever done, this much is clear to me now. What was I doing but serving as custodian to the fortunes of men whose hatred of me, bottled up for so long beneath a tight seal of Austrian manners, was finally liberated courtesy of those German monsters? My oldest clients, who only a week before Hitler's arrival were asking me to lunch, or inviting me to their villas in the country, were suddenly demanding to have their accounts transferred to Aryan overseers. But that was nothing — one almost can't blame them, anyway. People become pernicious when their money is on the line: they were afraid to have their assets associated with a Jew — even a baptized one — under Hitler's regime. No, it was my colleagues who surprised me the most. On the morning I was forced to clean out my desk — to throw my few personal belongings from the office into a sack and carry it out myself — they celebrated as if overtaken by an ecstasy of morality. It's all a great irony. . . ." The man sinks glumly into his thoughts, shutting his eyes and rubbing them as if trying to push out a pestilent vision. When he opens them, they resettle on Josef's paintings. "It's unfortunate your mother is too weak to come see these. She would like them. She has a sensual side I've always lacked." There is another pause. Hannah and Josef stand there looking at him while an image of Josef's bedridden mother seems to hover in the air. "You live your life with the hope of becoming someone's memory," Herr Pick says with a snickering sullenness. "Then it turns out you will have to keep *theirs.*"

Hannah and Josef cobble together a dinner and create a separate bed for their abased guest. They give the man every care, but he nevertheless becomes silent and morose after this initial outpouring, relying on gestures and a few grunts of "yes" or "no" to get through the remainder of the evening. If he notices that Hannah is expecting a child, he makes no mention of it, and then it is late and time to retire for the night.

To try to sleep in tight quarters with a parent: what an odd endeavor it is as an adult, and Hannah can tell that Josef, lying stiffly beside her, is particularly suffering. On the other hand, Herr Pick, perhaps grown accustomed to awkward sleeping arrangements from his tenure in the small flat with other strangers, does not seem affected in the least: shortly after the lights are extinguished he becomes talkative again. Hannah tries to pay attention, but she is tired and catches only dim fragments of what the man is saying before his voice starts to sound as remote to her as her own thoughts. One minute he is declaiming lines from a Goethe poem; the next he seems to be speaking melancholically of the Roman emperor Hadrian. Several times she hears him muttering a popular old Viennese adage, "The situation is desperate but not serious . . . desperate but not serious." Soon she is under the impression that the three of them, she, Josef, and his father, are engaged in warm conversation — that they are suddenly genial and free and easy together — and she knows she must be dreaming. Impossible to tell, then, if the last thing she remembers the man saying is real or the result of her mind's nocturnal reticulations: "It isn't the material items I miss. It isn't the money. . . . It's what the money bought me and what the Nazis robbed me of — *privacy*."

She is awakened at dawn by a wild cry, a woman's, which is followed almost at once by the familiar baritone ejaculations of Herr Hörler, the superintendent, both disturbances seeming to emanate from the square in front of their building. She sits up. The flat is cold, filled with leaden light. There is an empty, religious cast to the place. She notices that Herr Pick is no longer in his bed. Abruptly, the man's hazy late-night statements, actual or dreamed, vivify in her consciousness. "Josef!" she whispers, nudging Josef's side and looking around. His father is nowhere in the room. She does not wait for Josef to rouse before going to the window and wiping away the condensation. A small crowd has already gathered below — people are running toward it from across the square. Off to the side at the base of a lamp, Herr Hörler, still in his flannel nightwear, is consoling an elderly woman — a Gentile, obviously, or Hörler would not dare comfort her publicly — who keeps pointing up past Hannah at the roof of the building. It was clearly her cry that pierced the morning air. Only now does it occur to Hannah — why has it taken so long? — that a figure is lying at the center of the gathering. Its limbs are asprawl, or this is her impression — she cannot be sure, too many heads are leaning over it. Someone finally steps back, affording her a partial view. She can just make out a bare foot and part of a cuffed suit pant. But it is enough. *"Josef . . ."*

People make way for them when they arrive below. Herr Pick is facedown. There is little blood. For a moment Hannah wonders if he might still be alive, but a witness, stirred and excited by what he has seen, begins to narrate what happened, mentioning straightaway that the man died upon hitting the ground. None of the ensuing details, including the fact that Herr Pick somehow made his way out onto the building's steep roof in order to jump, moves Hannah as much as the sight of the man's bare feet, and especially his suit, which he must have donned, quietly, terribly, while she and Josef were sleeping.

The elderly woman shuffles off down the street, and Herr Hörler, before going back inside, cautions Josef and Hannah curtly to "take care of it." Among the remaining bystanders a point is soon reached when nothing seems left to be said, and yet they stay there wordlessly watching the dead man. They are, all of them, Jews; the Gentiles do not come out for the suicides, so numerous since Hitler's annexation. Hannah can see the joint worry behind their mechanical stares — it is a flock's fear, involuntary, watchful of the aggregate, driving them to witness this small diminution of Vienna's already thinned Jewish population.

Despite Hörler's warning, Hannah is surprised when Josef bends down and lifts his father into his arms. She is surprised even more by how he carries the body back into the building — with no visible sign that an assessment is being made of the human cost, to himself or to the world, of the man's leap to his death. No, if Josef's face registers anything then or minutes later when he stands in the flat peering down at his father's colding body (restored to the bed from which the warm body crept in the early morning hours), it is *triumph.* The triumph of an entombed thing freed at last. Indeed Josef looks taller, as if he has suddenly grown.

Yet the shell of disdain for the father remains. "He planned to do it this way," Josef mutters. "He sneaked into our life — into our *bed* — just to do this. To sneak out for good."

"*Really,* Josef," she blurts out, unable to cloak her exasperation. "What's so wrong

351

with that?" She looks at his father. "Isn't it obvious he came home to die?"

"This is not his home."

"I think he realized that at some point."

"And still he went through with it. Now you see what a selfish man my father was."

What she sees is the indentation of appalled flesh at the serrated edge of his father's hairline. What she sees are the same thick fingers she saw yesterday afternoon, wondrously still intact, poised as if unaware they will never be used again. What she sees is the collapse of a life, and a son who will one day regret that the hatred within himself treated this dead man so bitingly. What she sees now — after she tells Josef that you cannot hate a parent once you have seen them dead, and he counters that you certainly can — is that the biggest moments rob us of originality, reducing our responses to a repetition of things already done and said.

Max and several of his contacts at the Jewish Community of Vienna help them with the funeral arrangements. Traditional processions to the Central Cemetery have long been disallowed, and although Herr Pick paid regularly into a burial fund for a plot in the Catholic section, they are forced to bury him in an abrupt ceremony at the Jewish cemetery on the north end, among a cluster of tombstones desecrated by Nazi vandals. Josef remains notably mute throughout, and afterward also, rarely exchanging a word with Hannah for the next several weeks. She does not pressure him, and maintains a watchful distance, but she is frightened, because if he has by his father's death become voice-sick, he has at the same time been intrinsically strengthened overall, and not to her profit. And while the greater implication of his new intensity has yet to reveal itself, a more immediate effect is that he again no longer yearns for her. He seems to yearn only for this: hardness.

In late November, with merely a few weeks remaining before she will give birth, the greater implication manifests: Josef makes a final, last-minute push for her to emigrate. He appears one morning with a ticket for a train leaving to Italy that very afternoon, fare for her passage by boat to Palestine, and contact numbers supplied by Max for Jews who will help her along the way. Pressing these articles into her palm, he implores her: "Don't let our child be born here."

She just stands there looking at him.

"Don't need me, Hannah. Don't confuse things."

This man, honestly, she thinks. She has already confused her *life* with his — and everything depends upon it.

She is unable, of course, to carry out what he regards as necessary, and too weak to defend herself against his subsequent wrath. That evening is passed in an atmosphere of cruelty and recklessness. While she rests in bed, Josef, his face pinched with disgust, takes endless turns around the room, filling its corners with denunciations of her attachment to their marriage. He accuses her of having connived with Max to trick him into the marriage in the first place. Nursing his hostilities into the late hours of the night (when he seems *drunk* on her faults as he sees them), he sinks into a vile mimicry of the posters plastered all over Vienna, calling her a filthy Jew, throwing the unused train ticket in her face, yelling for her to "Get — *out!*" And though sobered by the next day's light, he still takes every opportunity that morning to pronounce marriage a thin tissue of error and illusion.

"Then divorce me," she vents at last from the bed.

He is standing at the stove, gathering in her stare. "I should."

354

"Why *don't* you? Why still be married to me if this is how you truly feel?"

"Because, unlike you, I'm strong enough to do what I don't like doing."

For this final meanness, she has no reply, and he certainly has no apology. They have opened themselves to each other indecently, bloodily, and something new and unclean invades them through the wounds. When a freezing afternoon in early December brings on her first real contractions, he accompanies her silently to the maternity ward of the hospital (they risk riding the tram; no one even looks at them) and, just before leaving her bedside, he tells her that he hates her. "Good," she says. "I hate you too." A harsh reply, uttered with heartbroken self-annihilation.

Her labor lengthens into a long one. Appearing in the evening, her mother, still a dedicated defeatist, stays awhile, proclaims that the child will *never* arrive, and then disappears. Several shifts of doctors come and go. Finally she is informed that the baby has decided to enter the world in the wrong position. *Naturally,* Hannah thinks. The world is in the wrong position — how else to enter it but buttocks first? Sixteen hours in, a nurse confides to her that she has rarely seen such difficulty. *Let* it be difficult,

355

Hannah tells herself, thinking of Josef, who, according to the nurses, has been haunting the hallways outside. Let it last for days. Let it destroy her love. She imagines that she is an aperture, widening to pain, welcoming each new wave like a foul cheating lover.

By the time the pushing begins, she is no longer in control of herself. Her limbs have grown wild, needing to be constrained by nurses on either side of the bed. Death cries fill the room, and she realizes they are hers. There is blood covering the hands of the doctor. And her own shit. The vulgarity of it is frightening, even to her. Finally the doctor, who has been shouting, commands her to give it one last push. And she does — straight into the pain. All at once, as if this final depleting effort were a thrust against her excrement, her blood, her hatred, and her whoredom — against everything that has defiled her — there is a baby on her breast, a boy, crimson and crying, a pure and sacred thing, fresh from nothingness. She is crying too, crying over this beautiful creature, and crying for someone to *go–get– Josef.*

When he is let in later, he brings a sharp silence into the delivery room. His eyes avoid hers and go directly to the child. She lifts the baby for him to see, wants desperately to say something, but is so overcome by the moment that she simply hands the protesting newborn over to him. Coddling the boy against his chest, Josef turns his back so she cannot see his face, but his shoulders, suddenly rising and falling, give the lie to his stoicism.

"Can we name him Herman?" she hazards.

With a nod of his head, he assents, but when he finally turns around, his composure cannot disguise his embarrassment, his hurt. He holds the baby aloft, demanding with his eyes that she look, *look* at this child quivering redly in his hands. "You should have gone," he tells her.

If, in the succeeding weeks and months, he cannot love his new son without trembling, neither can he love Hannah without resentment. And he does come to love her again, if only carnally. It happens in March, three months after the birth. Over and above his general unhappiness with her, a certain surprising delicacy on his part has prevented him from initiating contact with her flesh — an awareness, perhaps, that her body, stretched by the labor, sapped by the newborn's ongoing demands, has been slow to recover. But she has noticed him eyeing her of late, guiltily, vigorously, whenever she opens her blouse to nurse Herman. And one damp evening, after the child has fallen asleep in the makeshift crib they have resorted to fashioning inside the washbasin, she disrobes and spreads herself across the bed.

Josef, who has watched from the window, stands there with his legs a little apart, his eyes fixed on her.

"We know ourselves too well to demand to be loved," she says to him, keeping her voice low so as not to wake Herman. "So can we just forget about love?"

His face is a confusion of pride and amazement.

"I won't ask you to come over here," she says.

He begins to undress one article of clothing at a time, drawing out the process, and only when he is finished does he approach the bed. Careful to avoid touching her in any place, he positions himself over her. An awkward moment. Her need to have him is inchoate and deep, but she is distraught and fears she may say something cruel. Something that will prevent even this, this spiritless conciliation, from coming off.

The possession he takes of her is bitter, satisfying. And she can feel only grateful afterward, when the baby repeatedly wakes her and wants her all during the night — grateful to make an expiatory sacrifice of her body to the child. For this kind of caring, this unpoisoned love, she is happy to give herself up. Because what she has with Josef *is* poisoned, she realizes at some early morning hour when the baby is finally asleep and the edges of the church in the square are just emerging from the blue beyond the window. She does not blame Josef solely. He has only presented her with God's qualities in human form: pain and indifference, the ideal with its equal parts beauty, pleasure, and impossibility — and, yes, caring of a kind. How ironic that she has trouble tolerating from him what she has loved in God. She expects more from a human.

The next night is the same, and the next one after that, until it becomes their little routine: a mother and her man, resuming their rough intimacies, throwing their sadnesses at each other on a bed, then the ablutions of breast milk and sleeplessness. She has entered a time, violent and fragmentary, when she so deeply assimilates her baby's and husband's needs that she cannot distinguish them from her own. There is something almost holy to it, this pliancy of hers. Something else also. Josef and her mother and the gestapo officer were onto it. If she is not wholly one, she is at least half a whore.

There is a toll. No woman, no whore can be consigned to a life of emotional austerities without one. Recently, whenever Josef returns to the flat, she has been unpredictable, displaying everything that is ugly in her nature. She often opens the door for him disputatiously, sometimes submitting him to an outrun of opinions she never knew she had. On several occasions her foot catches his as she steps around him at the washbasin; the first time it happens she contrives to fall violently to the floor; the second time she pretends to be knocked unconscious. Once, at the end of a meal, she even regales him with an animated sermon — broken by odd peals of laughter — on the shortcomings of his paintings (which still cling to the walls where his father hung them). He looks at her, these times, with the alarm of an animal trainer who, used to creatures that cover their disaffections with a mask of submission, is astonished when one of them suddenly reminds him it is a wild thing. Because Josef never acts on his astonishment, because he only keeps sidelong watch on her whenever she lashes out at him, she ups the ante of her attacks, accusing him of destroying her, even suggesting that he has already *killed* her. Deep down she knows he is incapable of doing these things. And it disappoints her, oddly, because in her madness she actually feels that he owes her such a crime. If he will not commit it, maybe someone else will. She entertains fantasies of her own downfall: the gestapo breaking into the flat and taking only her; or simply not eating until she narrows into nothingness. She even contemplates killing herself and baby Herman. Perhaps the pageant of her total demise would humanize her husband.

She almost feels saved by these thoughts. They are blind, unreflected, and she sees beauty in their lack of order and restraint, a kind of relief. Their evil flies in the face of the outside evil that is increasingly imposing itself — as if she has cabined herself in a train raging through an alpine night, the year 1940 pitching by as briefly as an undistinguished village glimpsed from a window, the Nazis' noises no louder than pines soughing in the wind.

But the soughing turns to screaming the following February, when the report of guns and roundup trucks echoes through the Leopoldstadt as quickly as word that a thousand Jews have been brought to the Aspang station, there to be loaded onto a train that is no figment of her imagination — an all too real train headed not for the Alps but for a resettlement camp in the East. Several days later, Max appears at their door, ashen faced: yet another thousand people, his father among them, had to report to the gymnasium at Castellezgasse that morning; when all of them have been processed, they too will be taken by van to the Aspang station, where a train already awaits them. Max sits down on the corner of their bed and tells them how he pled to have his father's deportation delayed on account of the man's importance to the economy. " 'Importance to the economy,' " Max says, repeating the phrase sarcastically. "Those exact words were *stamped* on his ID card. And in front of my eyes, the commissar tears the card up. Father's passport as well. The biggest fabric tycoon in Austria and his citizenship" — Max snaps his thumb — "*gone.* The commissar was of a mind to do the same to me. He only decided against it because he knows I hold sway with the city's Jewish youth. Or what remains of them, anyway. He thinks I can still be useful to him." Max relates the story to them again, and then again, as if an endless recounting of his morning will cause it to make sense. He refuses to leave their flat until late that night, when, his emotions overwhelming him in their doorway, he confesses to Josef (with no regard to Hannah's presence) how grateful he secretly is that the commissar spared him having to be transported with his father: "Because I'm not leaving for Palestine, Josef. Do you understand what I'm saying? When they come for you, I'm going to be on that train too."

Max will have to *wait.* That is what Hannah thinks to herself in the ensuing weeks when three more transports leave for Poland, taking with them a number of people from their very street, but not Josef, not them, not yet. Karmeliterplatz 2, their own building, has so far been unvisited by Hitler's miscreants. Still, she feels reluctant to set Herman down anywhere in the flat. Its interior now seems coated with a residue of distress, as if people were indeed removed from it by force. History is coming too close, breathing on its surfaces. The pillows and eiderdown, the lamps, the washbasin and stove, the floorboards themselves — none feels as if it belongs to them anymore. Yet the thought that she most holds in horror is that *Herman* does not belong to them either. Nothing has ever made her feel more like a stepparent to her child than the overwhelming evidence that she and Josef now have no power to forestall strangers from entering their house and taking them all away.

It is one thing for her to feel this, but to see it festering in Josef that spring and summer, to see a man wrestling with his own powerlessness — well, she thinks (and not without shame), it is a sight no woman or wife should ever have to see. For all her acceptance of man's weakness, she realizes she cannot bear to see it in *her* man. In retrospect, she would even prefer the Josef she saw immediately after his father's death: he was disobliging, he was disengaged, but he was not defeated. Now, as the two of them watch Herman evolve daily (his favorite new game: climbing up into the washbasin with the help of a step stool), the words Josef spoke to her nearly two years ago return to her ears: *Don't let our child be born here.* That is what she has brought Josef: a beautiful boy and a dowry of defeat.

Soon they are required to wear yellow stars whenever exiting the flat, making them vulnerable to the fugitive bands of Viennese youth who, exercising some revived Visigoth energy, have been laying siege to every Jew in their path. By October, visas and permits are obsolete: Austria's borders have closed to all emigration. *No one* may leave now, they are as if paddocked animals. Josef never mentions these developments, but in his head they are ranged against her — of this she has no doubt.

When he does finally speak, it is only to inform her that his mother's condition has worsened considerably and to ask that she help bring Herman to the sanatorium so that the enfeebled woman might once more see the boy before she dies. Naturally Hannah does not object: Josef has largely kept her from his mother — the few times she did accompany him to the old-age home on Seegasse, Frau Pick was only semiconscious and seemed barely to take note of her presence — and Hannah is curious to meet the woman again, if only to say good-bye.

They are halfway there, the three of them (Herman in his carriage), in one of the ninth district's remoter side streets, when Josef startles her by coming to an abrupt standstill. It is a Saturday, the lunch hour. The sidewalk is empty and an oppressive air drifts in from the nearby canal. Now Hannah sees the two gestapo officers. They are fifteen paces ahead, standing well within the shadowed portal of a building whose Gothic stories dwarf the elms fronting it; she might easily have missed them but for their eyes, bent firmly on Josef and herself. One of the officers, the tall one, is tawny-haired and fair, while the coloring of his partner — who has an odd shape, small but alarmingly long of trunk — can hardly be distinguished from the dark shadows. The two men confer with each other briefly and then fall silent, causing her reflexively to verify that her yellow star is affixed to her jacket lapel.

But it quickly becomes apparent that Josef's reason for stopping is unrelated to the presence of the officers. The injury on his face is too personal. This has to do with *her,* though he cannot seem to look her way. "It is important to me," he finally says, choosing his words with deliberation, "that my mother have some joy today. I ask only for your cooperation" — he pauses, his lips struggling to formulate what he has to say next — "and that you pretend we . . . we have a real marriage. Pretend that we are —"

Here he breaks off, submitting the two of them to the tyranny of squeaks emitted by the wheels of Herman's carriage, which Hannah nudges nervously back and forth in place even though Herman is not asleep.

"That we are in love?" she asks.

She immediately regrets leading him with the question, and feels betrayed by her rising intonation, especially of the word "love."

The last thing she wants to do right now is cause him to be imprecise. For the moment, she believes she can handle his brutality — as long as it comes with clarity.

When he responds to her question with a nod in the affirmative, though, something in her ceases: her feeling for him. Without warning she begins to push the carriage away down the sidewalk. In response, little Herman cranes his neck and turns to stare up at her, a bundle of uncertainty and concern. Behind her, Josef's shouting. (Someone else's too?) She concentrates on the carriage's speed.

But then her arm . . . .

There is a tug, a wrenching, then a throb shoots through her shoulder with such vehemence that the rest of her must twist toward it — toward Josef, who has caught her at the elbow. Herman begins to cry. She and Josef struggle wordlessly with each other, a tangle of arms and slapping skin, and then the officers are on them instantly.

They are separated, the tall officer taking Hannah by the wrist, his squat partner administering a rough armlock on Josef's neck.

"What is the problem here?" the tall one asks with a hollow theatricality. A smell emanates from him, cologne-tinged and florid, consuming Hannah.

His partner picks up on his tone. "Yes, tell us, Mr. Israel," he says, indicating whom he is addressing by redoubling his lock on Josef's neck. "What could be so disturbing that it requires you to chase your own wife down the street? What, has she stopped spreading her thighs for you?"

In the instant this is said, two things become clear to Hannah. The first is that, earlier, from within the shadows of the portal, the officers were not studying both Josef and her — they were watching only her. The second is that she is going to be raped by the one holding her arm. The two officers know it already. The false solicitousness and the meaninglessness of their questions, the feigned ignorance and the wrinkled brows of concern: their little show, a prelude to the main act. She can feel her captor openly staring at her, his eyes charting her features, while his hand is busy canvassing the small of her back. Where is it going to happen? The Gothic building? While his accomplice restrains Josef?

And then the moment of clarity is gone. In her confusion she turns beseechingly to the officer clutching her, as if he might actually offer her his help.

What an error, her turning to him. Color

runs riot over his cheeks; his lips, tacky and startled into life, part in offense. Obviously he has been surprised, and the delay preceding his reaction is just long enough for her to consider — because she is forced to consider it — that he will be only the second man inside her. A ghastly sight, his palely beautiful face. She cannot remove her eyes from it, the rinsed skin and bright crest of hair, all that scrubbed indecency, that boundless forehead.

His reaction, when it finally comes, proves swift: quitting her back, his hand moves to his holster, then there is a gun jammed deeply into her ear, its pressure forcing her to turn her head away. He is shouting for her not to look at him again, not *ever*. He still has her arm, and yanks her so violently against him that the gun barrel cuts into her ear canal. Instantly she becomes overwhelmed by sound, an oceanic roaring. The metal tip seems at pains to pierce her very cranium.

Now a different kind of noise — brisker and of a higher pitch — strains through the din flooding her head. Only after the gun is withdrawn from her ear cavity, when her wrist is suddenly free of his grasp — only when her eyes are filled with the vision of Herman being hefted from the carriage by her former captor — does she recognize the noise as her own child's wailing. The sound and the vision are as of a nightmare: the officer turning to face her, Herman screaming under his arm, the gun in her boy's ear now, and the man shouting at her to make the boy stop crying.

All at once her clarity returns. She has her instructions, and she will follow them. The officer is waiting for her, holding Herman away from himself as he might a rabid animal, clutching only the boy's jacket collar so that he hangs screaming in the air. She reaches for her son, diligently avoiding the officer's eyes, but when she tries to take Herman from him he refuses to release his grip on the collar.

"It needs to suckle at your breast," he tells her, giving Herman a ferocious shake.

Herman lets out another wail and looks at her through large eyes filled with water and confusion. "But I've stopped —" She stammers: "He's — no longer taking milk from me."

"Really?" asks the officer. He reinserts the gun in Herman's ear.

She shrieks, she assents, she does not know what she says exactly, but, miraculously, there is Herman — in her arms. The officer leads her to a bench, pushes her down onto it, and again commands her to let "it" — Herman — suckle from her breast. Her eyes find their way to Josef. Constrained still by the other officer, he is staring at her firmly. She searches his face for a sign of what she ought to do, but there is something indefinable and severe about his look — if she did not know any better she would call it a kind of stoic challenge. Herman is writhing on her lap. The tall one standing over her is shouting again, waving his gun. Where did the *world* go? She feels squeezed into a narrowing nowhere in which time seems marked only by the throbbing of her ear.

And then, with no application of thought, she just does it. She opens her coat, slips her sweater down over her shoulder, and pulls out her left breast. She experiences no sensation of giving in. Her movement, rather, is one of departure. Already she is at a remove, looking back at herself on the bench with a measured eye. A silence has overtaken the scene. In the middle of it all is her breast, bright and shocking against her dark clothing, nearly unnatural. And there are the officers staring at the breast. Except they are no longer officers. They are men. They have guns. This is what they do for their delight. And so for a moment she

371

allows her breast simply to hang there, making no effort to conceal it, letting them have their look. At last, remembering her instructions, she hefts the breast with her hand and begins to worry it in front of Herman's mouth, brushing the nipple several times across his lips. But Herman takes no interest in it. His eyes barely register it. Eventually she lets the breast fall back against her chest, where it flattens, dumb and inert, a sad human product, worth something only when it was wanted. The tall officer looks at it quickly and away, without comment, as if suddenly embarrassed about the whole business.

Instinctively, she disappears her breast. It is a swift gesture not unmixed with shame, and the officer clearly registers it. He turns to meet the eyes of his accomplice. All the weight and brevity of an unwilled admission is contained in their exchange of glances. Then without warning, as if to reclaim his administrative dignity, the officer extracts a trim black notebook from an inside pocket of his jacket and demands to see proper certificates of identification for all three members of the family.

In the relative normalcy of this request Hannah believes she has discovered a rescue ladder, however rickety, and she hands over papers for Herman and herself. The officer examines her child's documents first, meticulously transcribing HERMAN JOHANNES PICK in his notebook, along with the rest of the two-year-old's particulars. As she watches the officer finish with a practiced flourish by setting down in bold ink a large letter "J" beside her son's information (just like he did for the other Jews registered by his hand on the same page), she is stirred by everything that is annihilating about identification . . . the reek of human inventory, the chilling exactitude of a street address, the futurelessness of any single person's name.

Then the officer gets to her own papers. This time when he writes in his notebook, all trace of a flourish, practiced or otherwise, abandons him. There is a perceptible waver in his wrist action, he plainly struggles with the task of copying down her information, and, awfully, his eyes keep returning to the photograph laminated to her identification card. It was taken in the fall of her first year at the university, while several of her new female classmates were looking on and taunting her; she is smiling directly into the camera, her lips upturned and taut as if bracing against an oncoming laugh, her eyes shining with self-possession. How happy she looked. It is precisely this — her happiness caught by the photograph — that appears to arrest the man's gaze and derail his officialism. When he catches her watching him, he promptly moves his thumb over the picture and takes an exaggerated interest in the card's text, pretending to make an important addendum to his notes. But at a certain point he stops writing altogether and looks up from the documents. As he scrutinizes her with renewed attention — and an untutored wantonness dark under the surface of his gray eyes — she sees that he is not at all done with her.

He pushes her papers back into her hands and demands that she remain on the bench. With Herman clasping her neck, she watches the man cover the ten paces to the elm tree beneath which the other officer is retaining Josef. *"Papa!"* Herman calls.

"Quiet," she whispers. She has to hear what is about to be said.

The officer asks Josef for his identification. His stocky accomplice, proving to be as imperious as he is short, releases his choke hold on Josef with visible reluctance, brushing a sweaty lick of hair back across his brow and stepping away from Josef cautiously — hand on his gun — as if Josef might dare to exact quick revenge. And as

374

both officers repeatedly insist that he produce identification, Josef looks like a man who could indeed strike back. He has planted himself exactly halfway between his two captors, eyes kept contemptuously on their midsections, his mouth red and snarling, a hunted thing.

"*I'll* get his papers," the stocky officer announces, taking a step toward Josef.

"No!" the tall one says resolutely, and he pulls out his gun and aims it at Josef.

Hannah screams. The tall one looks at her briefly, then fixes his gaze on Josef again. "She was fleeing from you only minutes ago," he tells Josef, gesticulating toward Hannah with his gun, "but it appears she wants you to live — perhaps so you can apologize to her for whatever it was you did to her. Are you going to give us your papers, Mr. Israel, or is your pride so strong that you would rather die than apologize to your wife? And believe me, by the time we're done with your wife this afternoon you are going to have a lot more to apologize for."

Josef's eyes flare as though allowing for some wild image to pass into them — then the flicker of movement is over, the image absorbed into his tensed muscles, and his eyes fall coolly on the officer's gun. There is a pause, yet Hannah feels everything proceeding at a terrible pace. She rises to her feet. Her mouth opens to speak but finds no breath. Stupid with panic, she takes a step toward Josef. But at that very moment, he reaches into his coat and removes his papers. He holds them out in front of him, rigidly, at a salient angle, so that they point upward over the heads of the two officers.

With the gun still aimed at Josef's chest, the tall one approaches him, his open palm extended to receive the papers. Josef hesitates, staring at the man's hand as if holding a private argument with it, but he finally condescends to smother it with his documents. "Watch him," the officer tells his accomplice, who is all too happy to level his own gun at their captive. The tall one retreats several paces and begins to examine Josef's identification, copying certain of its details into his notebook. He seems to hit on something troubling and looks up at Josef.

"Artist?" he says with a hint of alarm. "What *kind* of artist?"

Hannah concentrates all of her worry on Josef now. She is certain that he understands what the officer is really asking him: Vienna's artists were rounded up early by the gestapo, who saw them and most of their intellectual friends as an immediate threat to the Nazi agenda — so what is Josef still doing here? Yet something beyond recognition of this seems raised in Josef by the question, and he looks galvanized as he considers it, like a professor about to address a large hall. His reply is indeed laden with a professor's irony.

"A marriage artist," he says.

The two officers stare at him for a second. Then each of them begins to laugh, echoing Josef's answer — not with irony (for how can they possibly know of his painful history with the phrase, reaching all the way back to its derisive coinage by his father?) but with a sarcasm they clearly assume he has intended. "A *marriage* artist!" the stocky officer repeats, nearly shouting. "Not a very good one, are you?"

Josef actually appears to give this some thought, then solemnly shakes his head in assent. "No," he allows softly.

The officers roar again with laughter, and Josef faintly smiles a broken smile. He is letting the officers have their fun, letting them believe he is mocking what is for all appearances his own failure as a husband. And who knows — maybe he is. Hannah cannot read him anymore.

"It isn't easy," Josef suddenly adds, with an afterthought's offhandedness.

"Obviously not," the stocky officer snorts.

"It would be easy for me," the tall officer says, his eyes resting suggestively on Hannah.

Josef follows the direction of the officer's gaze to her, but manages, somehow, not to meet her eyes. "You mean to say," Josef asks, addressing the tall officer, and here he pauses, "that you would know what to do with her?"

What is he doing? Hannah thinks to herself. What in the *world* is he doing?

"That is precisely what I mean."

Josef grins at the man and nods his head — not condescendingly, but, to Hannah's astonishment, rather as if suddenly in collusion with him. "True — it's amazing what a woman's body can do for a man. Her skin and her softness —"

"Her cunt," the stocky one breaks in, his face now reddened and agleam.

"Yes —" Josef responds. He wavers a moment. "Her cunt," he echoes, brightening the word with a bit of anger as the short, dark officer chortles approvingly. And then Josef says it again: "Her cunt."

Hannah is staring at her husband. His eyes have taken on a sparkle — they look crazed. He seems to have given himself over to the moment. Or rather he has given himself

378

over to *them.* But why is he doing it? Has the imminent threat of what the officers are planning to do to her left him so bereft of his reason that he has just joined them?

She is not allowed to contemplate any answers because Josef has turned his crazed eyes on her and is now declaring for everyone to hear: "Her cunt doesn't change — no matter how many times I take it. Morning. Night. Middle of the day. She could be tired. She could be angry. Or maybe she loves me in the moment. These are only details. Her cunt remains the same. So I challenge it. I turn to her cunt to test it, to use it against my own miserableness. Against everything else that's constantly changing, or leaving, or passing away. I circle around her cunt as if it's a god. Something must bear the responsibility for my unhappiness. All my meetings with her cunt are nothing but supplications — desperate attempts to appease it. I go to ridiculous lengths, shaming myself before it, embarrassing myself just to get to it. Sure, I sometimes grow angry with it, like I would with any god. Then I keep my distance, even try to banish it, because I'm hurt it has ignored my needs. I want it to reassure me — to convince me that this life isn't ruled by nothingness. Or if life *is* ruled by nothingness, then I want

379

her cunt to help me disappear without a trace. These desires carry their own kind of failure. Her cunt only satisfies my needs as long as I'm attending to it. That's how it forces me to return. To come back for more again and again and again. And, of course" — here he sighs and smiles at Hannah; he is still wild-eyed, but seems to have stopped speaking for the benefit of the officers and is instead addressing only her — "we fight over this god. Lovers are like worshippers: doomed to protect their little share of hate so they don't drown in happiness. We're still members of the human race. We use our god divisively, evasively. . . ." Now he is looking at her plainly, even pleadingly. "I still don't know you, really. Only what you let me know, only what I think you might be. It's been mostly my doing, this incompleteness. Is it horrible of me to admit that I can't manage us any other way? You must have noticed my silence. I haven't asked you many questions. And you've become careful with me. A stranger. I know how much you want me to paint us a ketubah. But please — don't make me complete my picture of you. I still want to worship you."

All at once he seems undone by his disproportionate response to the officer's question, which he brings to a conclusion by

380

violently looking away. He remains like that, flushed cheek turned to her, quietly opening and closing his mouth as if trying to comprehend how any of these declarations passed through it. When he meets her eyes again he looks crestfallen.

What occurs next seems nearly incomprehensible. For an eternity the officers stand askew on the sidewalk, merely staring at him. They look very confused. They also look spent, both of them wearing guilty, satisfied expressions on their faces, almost as if they have just finished doing the repeated sexual acts Josef has alluded to — or rather as if those things were just done to them. Before Hannah realizes it, the tall officer has given them back their papers and is telling them in no uncertain terms to leave, to get out of sight before he shoots the three of them dead.

It is not until they find themselves battling down a boulevard in communion with Vienna's everyday people now refilling the streets after lunch, not until they have put five solid blocks between themselves and the gestapo officers — it is not until they have finally slowed down and joined the pace of others around them that Hannah, gripping the handle of Herman's carriage so tightly that her fingers ache, begins to fathom what Josef has just done.

What *did* he do? It is the question she asks herself over and over again in the days that follow, because although they are surely counted days, they are the calmest — yes, happiest — she has ever known with him. And the change was immediate. It was already in effect when they entered the murmurous wastes of the old-age home that afternoon. Even disregarding their encounter with the gestapo officers, there was every reason to be overwhelmed by the visit with his mother: the smell of medicine and decay she unloosed whenever she moved her head on the pillow; the raddled flesh around her lips; her insistence that this room be her last; the way, after they presented Herman to her, she stared at all three of them in wonderment and cried, "Abandoning relatives of every age — what a *messy* way to die!"; and the look on Josef's face when it finally struck him that it was his mother lying there, really doing the dying, and his exclamation out in the hall afterward that his mother's eyes had been *his eyes!* looking at him. And yet if anything overwhelmed them during the visit, it was a sudden feeling of happiness against such horribleness, an unspoken sense, and Hannah was certain

Josef felt it too, of sweetness against the sour. She was amazed to find, standing there before his mother, that they did not have to pretend to anything regarding their love or marriage. Whatever sleight of hand Josef had performed back there with the officers, he had also seemed to unpaint every marriage contract he had ever made, and to turn the whole world until their marriage was real. And when they stopped that evening for Herman's benefit at a corner fountain not twenty paces out of the old-age home, she took Josef's hand and drew pressingly close to him. He looked down at her then, smiling, beautiful, slightly stunned looking, and she felt her eyes tear with gratitude. She said, "We're still here." "Yes." "You frighten me." "I know."

Now, as the November afternoons of 1941 thicken and fade, this bewilderment at the incalculable seems to color her otherwise happy hours with incertitude. This, and a feeling that her happiness is a vain thrust against time. Around the three of them an unraveling city looms — the air itself smells hurt — and on the good days when they defiantly leave the flat and journey out for a stroll, they make their way beside the most frightful things. Only yesterday they were walking home down Taborstrasse and spotted a squad of levyers — Jews forced to assist in ferreting out families for deportation — kicking an elderly man who lay crumpled at their feet while a youthful SS corporal stood by. The old man kept crying out for them to take mercy on a mere beggar, he had scarcely a tooth in his head, but his pleas seemed to incite the levyers to increase the force of their blows. To Hannah's surprise, a matronly lady walking a dachshund suddenly knelt down in front of Herman and, in an effort to distract him from the violent scene, asked if he would like to pet her dog (which she kept calling her "little treasure"). The woman's fatalistic sighs, and her unwillingness to speak directly to Hannah or Josef nor raise her eyes above the yellow stars pinned to their breasts, revealed less a Gentile who was sympathetic to Jews than one who was not a great friend of the Nazis. And while Hannah was grateful for the rare passing kindness of a stranger she will probably never see again, she remains disturbed by the encounter, in particular by the envy she felt for the woman's droopy-eared animal: the creature was not only more safe, more free even, than she and her family, but also the object of unambivalent Gentile affection. How upsetting to discover that after all *this*, after everything her mother ever told her about the Gentiles, she secretly longs for their caring like a child, like a dog! What happened to her sober, indifferent view of the Viennese? And, really, comparing herself and her family to a *pet* . . . clearly she is losing her stomach, becoming overpowered by how fraught their situation actually is. Josef and Herman, these two beings she loves more than anything else in existence — it is true: more than God — were brought to her only by chance, and it is chance to which they are all now subject.

Still, she has time. Time to let Josef worship her by day ("Hannah?" "What?" "I don't deserve you." "You can't say such things." "I don't deserve you, I don't deserve you, I don't deserve you." "Okay.") and supplicate her cunt by night ("Hannah?" "I'm here." "When I said you were my whore —" "It's all right."). She has time to chase Herman around the bed (their new game, a gift of their relative confinement), to lift him to the window when the moon rises yellowly behind the Carmelite church, and when they still dare to go outside, to delight with him in talismanic clouds of her own breath, or stomp on frozen puddles until they split into stars. She has time to understand that all she wishes for exists. And to love these days as the fortune of her life.

But when, one early December afternoon, Josef does not return from trying to secure potatoes for them, when he does not arrive by evening, nor at any point during the night, she has no time. Or rather she has too much time, time that spreads and swirls, grows as undirected as her tired thoughts. The night's darkness nearly drives her mad with its silence. Yet the morning's vacant hours prove to be the most difficult, filled with such wild speculation that, lying there in bed beside her sleeping Herman, she falls into a kind of catalepsy that prevents her from lifting her arms. Never has the sun's return to the sky been so cruel; she watches it crest the frozen roof of the church across the square and penetrate the flat as if commanded to shine its cold light on Josef's absence. Herman wakes and she throws herself into routine, proceeding through the day as if it is any other, all the while knowing that what prevents her from going out and looking for Josef is a fear of discovering the worst. And yet it occurs to her later while playing with Herman that some part of her might actually fear discovering the *opposite* of the worst: that Josef is still alive. Was it not she this morning, who, despite how unimaginable the death of her husband seemed, went ahead and imagined it? Was it not she who experienced a sudden leaking of emotion — a frightening, electric feeling of release at the thought of finally being *done* with him?

When a knock comes at the door, and she opens it to find not Josef standing there but Max, with a stricken expression and a scarf as dark and twisted as her fears, she instantly has her answer. It was not she. It could *never* have been she who entertained such thoughts.

Max steps into the room. "They took him, Hannah."

"You mean — he's alive?"

She brightens all at once and Max, misreading her, answers with a mocking smile: *"Yes,* he is *alive."* The scathing eloquence behind his sneer . . . she has forgotten he could be this mean. But now he turns despondent. "We still don't know where he will end up — somewhere in the East. They put him on the train at the last minute; no one can understand it. They didn't ask the Community to provide his name. Didn't send anyone to apprehend you and Herman. They refused adamantly when we used our usual ploy of asking that he be held back until his family could join him. And when I tried to get on the train with him they wouldn't let me. Doesn't make sense at all. It's as if someone wanted to get him. Like they were determined he go alone."

Hannah suddenly thinks of the gestapo officers and emits a very quiet *"No."*

"What?" he asks.

The only response she can muster is to stare into his indignant eyes. His face hardens then into a mask of hatred, and his words come spitting out in wet, plosive gasps: "What did you *do,* Hannah? Tell–me– what–you–*did."*

This anger of his, undiminished by his sadness over Josef's deportation, frightens her into sobriety. She tells him about her rash flight from Josef with the baby carriage, about their subsequent fight — how it gave the officers an opening. She explains what the tall officer wanted to do to her, and how he discovered that Josef was an artist ("He had a *black book,* Max — I saw him make note of it in there!"). She recounts every- thing, leaving out no detail, neither her bared breast, nor her cunt cataracting down through Josef's speech (Max winces at her mention of the word). When she is done, they stand there avoiding each other's gaze. His silence feels terrible to her, more unbearable than his outbursts. "Do you think," she ventures nervously, "do you think he'd still be in Vienna if I hadn't stormed away from him like that?"

In answering this question, Max, his eyes flashing demonically, seems to draw on all the reserves of his history with her. His reply is long and foul, all the more fierce because heartbroken, and in the end he succeeds, on a small verbal scale, at what Josef prevented the officers from doing that day — raping her.

When he exhausts himself and abandons the flat without closing the door, it is merely her ghost who shuts the door on the assembling shadows in the stair landing and turns to find that Herman has climbed up inside the washbasin. Perched like a lookout in the crow's nest of some ship, the boy stares at her with wide-eyed expectation. Josef is *gone,* she thinks blankly. What did she ever really have of him? All that trouble, their love, those days . . . it was just a taste. For a moment the thought seems to satisfy her. "That's *it,*" she says to Herman across the room, detachedly, as if she were a custodian who, coming out to sweep after a puppet show, notices a child still trying to get a glimpse of the marionettes and tells him there is nothing more to see — show's over. Herman just looks at her. She looks at him. There is a pause. And only then does she see the horrific truth of her words. She rushes to her son, lifts him to her, and wails the words at the empty room: *"That's — it!"*

Days pass, and she hears nothing. They will come for Herman and herself — she knows it is only a matter of when. Even Herr Hörler tells her so, in a sorrowful tone (though neither the superintendent's sorrow, nor his certain knowledge that he will be the one who opens the building for her takers on that day, deprives him of the frivolity of filling the stairwell with his daily whistling). She thinks of the tall officer and wonders if he is the force driving this quietus, drawing out the days on purpose. He was a cruel man but probably no stranger to love's regional backbone; in some German village there must be a wife pining for his return, dispatching letters of longing to him. Surely it is a universal truth, Hannah tells herself, that one always suffers more intensely from the beloved's absence when forced to remain in the place where love was a habit. If this separation of hers from Josef is, in fact, part of the officer's design, then the man has succeeded: she is hurting.

But he has also failed, in a way. Inadvertently he seems to have erased what she thought was the limit of her caring. The physical distance between herself and Josef, whatever it is (*wherever* he is), has become the new measure of her feeling for him. Her moments of contemplating him are no less full for being spent without him. And although each hour has its pressing duty — finding food, or attending to Herman — it seems to matter little, anymore, how it is actually passed. She is no longer moving in one direction. Rather she is moving in all directions — toward Josef, who, being only "somewhere in the East," is everywhere for her. Some days she thinks of herself as an expanding sea, whose entire surface is his skin and eyes and hair. Other times she feels as flippant as a single wave casting loose before being immaterialized by a granite seawall. The burial of Josef's mother, for example. The poor old woman was finally granted her wish: she left the world while lying in that room on Seegasse. And though Hannah's journey through the city to the Central Cemetery turns out to be halting and perilous, she hardly takes note of it. The cemetery itself proves to be a refuge, its Jewish section wonderfully empty but for the rabbi and two workers from the Community, its frozen grass — the last green in all of Vienna on which Herman is allowed to run free — almost filled with expectation.

If she expects anything at all, surely it is that Max will soon reappear at her door, not out of a desire to apologize but in answer to a silent trilling in his head that she imagines must be beckoning him back to the one person left in Vienna through whom he is connected to Josef. Then a postcard from Josef arrives — a very strange postcard — revealing where Josef is (Riga, Latvia, says the postmark) and where Max is too:

11th of January 1942

My Dearest H. ——
Do not worry about me. Max arrived here by train today. There is no need for you to join. I am well, though I wish I were still painting ketubot like I was before I left. Sorry to leave you the task of closing down the studio, but I think it's for the best. The good news is that my picture of you will remain incomplete.

Forever,
J.

In an effort to see past its brevity, to see

through a cryptic formality clearly meant to elude Nazi interest, she reads the card many times over, imbuing its words with more meaning than was perhaps intended, but nevertheless allowing various of its odd features to anger her (Max got himself there? . . . what *canine* devotion), confuse her (Josef's lie about painting ketubot before he left means that other parts of the note, the fact that he is well, for example, must also be lies), frighten her ("closing down the studio"? — surely he is enjoining her to abandon the flat as soon as she can), and cause her to cry (that last line, and the closing "Forever," which she cannot help but see as an addendum to it, so that it reads "my picture of you will remain incomplete forever"). Of one thing she is certain: the conditions in Riga must be terrible, and Josef wants her to avoid pursuing him. In the past she would have taken this appeal as a sign of his diminished feelings for her; now it comes to her as a concentration of love that has crossed through the thickness of a fallen world. It is not lost on her that this is exactly how she used to believe God's mercy came to people — briefly, cryptically, and from far away. Either God is acting through Josef, or Josef is God, or more likely there are no gods, there is only evil to make a man into one.

She prepares to move Herman and herself to her mother's that very afternoon. The flat ought to appear as if it was abandoned in haste, she decides, hoping, probably naively, to convince whoever finds it first that she and Herman have already been deported. It occurs to her that by relocating to her mother's small room on Rembrandtstrasse she is not just violating the ruling that no Jew may change residences unless instructed to do so: she is also going into hiding. And, as she empties a cloth sack of Josef's old painting supplies and fills it with a few changes of clothes for Herman and herself, she is aware of the clutch of terror at her heart. She is as rootless now as the particles of dust seething up out of the sack.

Before she knows it she is on the landing, ready to lock up. Herman in one arm, her few possessions in the other, she pauses at this threshold through which she has passed for four years. She should just close the door and go — this she understands more clearly than she does anything else at the moment. But having come this far, she loses her fortitude and risks a last glimpse at the room. She *envies* Josef for being apprehended and sent off without having to take leave of the place. How is she to bear for both of them the vision of the makeshift bed with its two unmade mattresses on which they did *everything?* Or the washbasin, whose worn surfaces greeted their fingertips, their water, their newborn. Even the women in Josef's paintings stare at her with reproach and horror. On *them,* finally, she closes the door, but not without a bittersweetness. And when she turns to face the descending stairs, there is nothing to stay the flood of her emotions. Her shoulder somehow finds the wall, and in the shadow of the landing she begins to cry, uncontrollably, as if someone has died.

From then on, everything, right up to the last thing, runs as fast and straight as the street, Rembrandtstrasse, where she and Herman rush into hiding that evening. The daily, meaning-filled looks of her mother. Herman's acquisition of new words and other burdens ("Clap, Mama." "I'm clapping." "Another time, Mama." "Fine." "Another time, Papa." Silence. "Another time — Papa." "I'm clapping, Herman." "No another time — *Papa!*" "I'm clapping . . ."). The shooting of a Jewish boy, merely a teenager, in the courtyard of their building. The breaking down of her courage. Her mother's astonishing disinterest in

Herman. The postcard in June from the Central Office for Jewish Emigration, instructing her mother to present herself in two days at the gymnasium on Sperlgasse: FOR DEPORTATION TO AN ELDERLY PERSONS RELOCATION CENTER IN THE FORMER CZECHOSLOVAKIA. Her mother's melancholy, more from being counted as "elderly" than from the prospect of having to leave Vienna. The sudden appearance of a family of five Jews, young and hungry looking, who have already been "assigned" her mother's residence. Hannah's desperate flight back to the Karmeliterplatz flat, where she and Herman are barred entry by Herr Hörler ("Why are you still in Vienna?" he shouts, exhaling hurt and venom as if she and her son are unjustly reminding him of some suppressed injury, then he smooths his fiery-dark hair into place, asking her if she has gone blind, asking her, "Can you not *see* there is a new tenant living here?"). The disheartening return to her mother's flat, where the five strangers, having already unpacked, having already filled the small room with their things, stare at her and Herman with the alarmed eyes of animals defending a hole. Her decision to try to stay together with her mother, no matter what. Her mother's tears of joy. Her own tears of defeat. The tumult of the collection center on Sperlgasse. Herman's delight at all the new faces. The commissar's mocking of her stupidity ("Why should I let *you* board a train full of geriatrics?"), his acceptance of her identification papers anyway. Her mother's fingers finding the hem of Hannah's coat as they leave the commissar's table. The truck ride to the Aspang station. (The obscenities of onlookers.) The confusion of Jews, nearly all of them old except for Hannah and Herman, crammed into the equally ancient passenger train. The thirsty madness of the night. The long walk, after arrival, after being slapped and stripped of valuables, into the Jewish ghetto of Theresienstadt. The loud, harsh voices of the Nazis, different than in Vienna, where the city's soured majesty must have had a civilizing influence (here, the Nazis speak as if addressing not people but rather forces, such as the ghetto's sickness, its universal reek of decay). Her mother's dissatisfaction with their barrack and its dimly stacked bunks ("They're turning me into a baby." "What?" "Either that or a body. The beds! These aren't made for *sleep!* They're built for birth, or death!"). Herman's incessant crying for food, and Hannah's own shrinking reflection, pale and alien in the dusty ghetto windows. Her smell. The absurd hunger inside her for Josef. The rumors about camps to the east — camps much worse than "Spa Theresienstadt" — circulated by women mostly, their beautiful voices reeling off unspeakable stories, the word "gassing" exploding in the damp summer air to the collective disbelief of their listeners. Her own disbelief, a difficulty in imagining what Josef might be going through in Riga (now that she is in a camp, his experiences seem both more proximate and more impossible to conjure up; for some reason she finds she can only picture the disasters of strangers). The moment when she realizes the rumors are true, the overheard detail she must have missed earlier: that, on admittance to the other camps, everyone — man, woman, and child — is shorn of their hair. (Nothing she has heard before so powerfully attests to death. Cold hair, wisest of the body's parts, knows what the warm flesh can never know until the end: the temperature of eternity. By removing the hair, the Nazis are depriving each person of their living permanence.) The constant burials outside the fortress walls. The ghetto's initiation of deportations to the east. The panic blowing through the barracks every time the Council of Elders releases the names of deportees they have been forced to choose. Hannah's fantasy — surely a death wish — that she might be sent to where Josef is (if, in fact, he still *is*). The afternoon in late summer when her mother, fresh from checking the new list, looks hard at Hannah once and retreats to her bunk, and Hannah's awareness then of the cement floor (because all of a sudden she feels she might fall to it), and her fixation on a knot of beetles near her feet — fellow kin of the night, dying in their black armor — as she struggles to prop herself up against the fact that she and Herman and her mother will be on a train heading east by sundown tomorrow. And then.

Then the long walk again, this time in reverse, between the ghetto and its distant train station, through fields flush with a sickly sweet odor, through thick air, orange and warm, riotous with grasshoppers, through the conspiring decline of the summer and the day. And her mother's complaints, as they gain a small rise near a glowing oak stand, about the heft of her luggage, revealing, for the first time Hannah can remember, a secret optimism: the old defeatist's suitcase is filled to brimming (Hannah's is nearly hollow — *her* great weight is Herman, and not just his body pressed to her shoulder). Then, at dusk, heaving into view from behind the station, the awaiting freight train — a long, low document of wood and wheel cutting into the field — and their orders, shouted at them on reaching its open cargo doors, to climb aboard at once. And the enormous arm reaching down for Herman, extended by a man who, having hoisted his own three sullen children up into the car, takes it upon himself to assist Hannah, and her hesitation to let go of her son — it is too soon to let go of her son — and the charge beneath the man's tired red gaze that frightens her into handing Herman over and following his two tiny kicking feet up into the car. Then the smell, it hits her right away, a urine-tinged fug whose source is not animal, and the closing of the door, which envelops her in a black waste where nothing can be distinguished, and which leaves her feeling in the seconds before her eyes have time to adjust that she has been hurled into nothingness. Then the train's sudden movement, setting off a panic inside the car to which she contributes her own share of outcrying, and still worse the fight, somewhere erupted between two men, that causes her to be jostled this way and that by unseen bodies. Then the vain calls to Herman in the darkness, and the image before her of his small head already shaven, and her useless realization that there are too many people, that the inside of the freight car is all organic wildness. Then the cry, by a youth staring out of the car's one barbed wire–covered window, of the name — meaningless to Hannah — of a village being passed, and another cry (anything but meaningless) belonging to Herman, whom she somehow finds in the black violence. And her son's refusal to be calmed, as if he knows what she knows, knows what the fighting is for, what the lamentations and divine entreaties are about, as if he knows that the car is a swaying coffin and that the train is conducting them to death. Then her frantic path through the car to the window, lured by its purple glow and the hope that it might quiet her son's wailing (and it does: when she holds Herman up to it he stares transfixed at a smear of low villages retreating into the gloom, and by the time the last of the day's illumination leaves the sky, and the indistinct land becomes all lands, and the sound of the wheels click-clacking in the blackness becomes all sounds, his eyes are closed).

Then, then the hole she notices ripped open in the barbed wire before her, a gap narrower than her shoulders, wider than her head. And the hole ripping open her heart when she sees what she is going to do. And the waiting for the train to pull within range of a lone farmhouse, and the calling of its cultivated plants glinting faintly in its floodlight. And the wash of lilac-scented air that suddenly carries off all of these moments since she and Herman vacated the flat on Karmeliterplatz (perhaps since she first laid eyes on Josef Pick) — blows them away out the window, as if they were mere breaths that did not so much happen as expire. Only *this* is happening. The whispering of instructions in Herman's unconscious ear, the words of Josef whorling like a dare in her own ("unlike you I'm strong enough to do what I don't like doing"), the worrying of her son's slumbering body through the gap in the wire, the tearing of her flesh, the trembling of her extended arms, the vision of her son aloft in the blowy void . . . hanging there in her hands . . . his sweater billowing in the slipstream . . . his limbs already pointing down at the raw earth sliding by, the sudden opening of his eyes, the held second of incomprehension, his bearing of terror, and the last thing, the end of everything, the wind's snatching away of his protest and then his person.

■ ■ ■ ■

There is no thinking immediately afterward.

There is only the cool night air caressing her face.

The sound of the tracks.

The heavenly vault.

If she feels anything, it is a vague sense of relief.

The weightlessness of having finally put down a heavy object.

For a few seconds — a few strange, lovely seconds — the sensation is not unpleasant.

But the space where Herman hung between her hands remains without him being there, and into that space her conscience begins to pour its poison, forcing her to recognize as real what she did not think possible.

She pulls in her arms and turns from the window, noticing right away two eyes burning at her. It is the father who helped her lift Herman up into the train. She cannot bear to look at him, and her legs begin to give out. She sinks to the hard floor between two women — one of them sleeping, the other murmuring prayers — and closes her eyes. Instantly, she succumbs to visions of Herman's unknown fate. He keeps dying in her mind, only to be resurrected so that he can die in a different way: his neck breaking from the impact of hitting the ground head-first; his chest being crushed under the wheels of the train; shots — from an officer in the rear of the train — nudging his body across the dirt. She tries to imagine him landing perfectly on the plowed earth, sliding a bit, perhaps tumbling a time or two, but none the worse for the wear. She tries to picture him lying there this very moment, maybe even asleep, the stars watching over him. But her mind will not rest there. No, it forces her to see the worst vision, the absolute worst, more terrible than any vision of his death, the one she simply cannot bear and yet seems destined to bear during each endless minute of the train clicking on through the night: it is the vision of a lone boy, her son, sitting up on the cold, hard ground in the middle of a field, watching the caboose's single red light disappear into the blackness, and calling out to his mother.

She tries to sleep. Time is not on her side, maybe sleep will be. She manages to lay her head down behind the praying woman. But she is only visited by sleeplessness, which stands vigil over her agitation, ensuring that it grows. Lying there on the wood floor, she finds that she is filled with rage at Josef for

404

leaving her to make such decisions by herself. She is angry with him for ever implying that she was selfish in clinging to him and not leaving Vienna when she still could. He could not call her selfish *now.*

Or *could* he? What made her hold Herman out the window? A selfless concern for his life? A desperate bet with the universe that he would have a better chance of surviving if she dropped him from the train (assuming he came through the fall in one piece, he might be taken in by some compassionate farmer) than he would if she kept him? If this was true, then her motherly instincts, far from telling her to hold on to her child at all costs, actually *drove* her to abandon him. But what if nothing *motherly* made her do it and instead a more base instinct, such as self-preservation, did? What if some animal part of herself saw Herman as a hindrance to her *own* survival? Or, and this is what really frightens her, what if it was an entirely conscious, simple human selfishness — oh, God, even self-*pity* — that not only led her to hold her son out the window but also to do the final condemning deed and let him slip from her hands?

Madness. In her confusion about her motives, she clings to the only thing she has left: her parting words to Herman. Whether

405

they registered in his unconscious, or she was acting out of an irrational desire to rid herself of her freighted responsibility for him, there was *goodness* in what she breathed into his ear.

Why, then, is she so haunted by her instructions for him to get away from the train and the tracks and the Nazis who could shoot him from other passing trains? Why do her very last words to Herman leave her shivering in the darkness?

"Walk away from it all."

■ ■ ■ ■

WE WILL ALL
BE WEDDED

■ ■ ■ ■

GHOSTS

Toward the end of May, roughly three months after their phone conversation, Daniel received from Francine Wind an envelope in the mail containing a photograph of Benjamin standing beside a Jewish grave with a rose in his hand. Her son had sent her the picture, she explained in a brief accompanying note, after the trip he had taken to Europe to learn about his father's real family — and Francine thought the two names etched above a Star of David in the modest tombstone might mean something to Daniel, or, if not, then, as she put it, "maybe you can do some research on it for your book about Benjamin." No research was required for Daniel to recognize instantly that the snapshot had been taken by Aleksandra, on the same trip during which she had captured the image of Benjamin and herself huddled before a dim European doorway. Benjamin was wearing the same outfit, and the print itself was made by the lab Aleksandra had always used; Daniel was sure that he was holding in his hands one of a number of prints she had personally given to Benjamin as mementos of their "vacation."

Yet the names on the grave were a mystery. And Daniel, when he could finally manage to remove his eyes from Benjamin Wind's grinning face in the photo (still another glimpse of his happiness with *her* — how many more was he destined to catch?), was intrigued by the fact that both persons listed on the dark granite tombstone — Leopold III and Ada Pick — had been buried in the graveyard after Hitler had begun his official campaign against Europe's Jewry. Leopold had been the first to go, in October of 1939, while Ada, the man's wife most likely, had lived on another two years, until January 1942, when things in Europe had really heated up, for no one more than its Jews — and the qualitative difference in how Ada Pick's inscription was carved into the stone seemed to provide subtle testament to the unfathomable terrors of the time: the letters and numerals appeared thinner, shallower, they held shadow more diffidently, suggesting hasty chiselings, hounded buriers. . . .

But who were these Picks? And what had

they meant to Benjamin?

There likely remained only one person who could answer these questions — the man who had sent Benjamin to this mysterious European gravestone in the first place: Max Wiener. The old man had not returned Daniel's calls from winter, but Daniel decided to phone him anyway. Unsurprisingly, he was greeted by the answering machine, on which he left merely his name and a single question: "Who were Leopold and Ada Pick, Max?"

Half an hour later, Max called him back. "You have no idea, Mr. Lichtmann, how good it feels to be able to speak to you," he told Daniel.

Daniel waited for elucidation, an explanation of the man's three-month silence, but none was immediately forthcoming, and it catapulted Daniel right over the question of Leopold and Ada Pick and back to the one that had been burning in him all this time: the question of Max's real relation to Herman and Benjamin Wind. With all the anger and self-pity of someone who had been deceived, Daniel said: "You're not really Herman's father."

Max's interminable silence was an admission of the declaration's truth. It also was a reminder of how high was the cost of truth, indeed of speech itself. You were forced to produce more words, even when you had no desire to do so.

"So who *is* his father?" Daniel persisted.

"There is a person you need to know about."

"Clearly."

"Please. You are unhappy with me. But you must understand I never received your messages, Mr. Lichtmann. Carmen — you met her in New York, do you remember? — she only spoke of such messages today — after your call, do you see? It is not her fault — do not be unhappy with her also. Each day, she worried I could die. I have been at the hospital, Mr. Lichtmann — what, I should be bothered with more of these questions about my son? she thought. You cannot blame her. She has helped me so much. More than you know. She is the reason why I am here — in my house — talking now to you, instead of stored away in that freezing hospital bed where the doctors want to keep me until I die. I am flying to Vienna, Mr. Lichtmann — *this* is why I got out. It is my last chance to see it. I have never been back. The doctors — they are telling me I will not make it if I try to go, so you see they are not on my side. What do they understand of what I need? I need to go back, Mr. Lichtmann. I am asking you to come with me. *There* I will answer your questions. I hope I will find answers to my own."

Daniel tried to beg off, feebly so, because the truth was that he *did* want to join Max, for so many reasons, on the man's valedictory trip to his city of origin, and he was relieved when Max told him that he had already, in the half-hour interval between Daniel's call and this one, had Carmen purchase a plane ticket for Daniel. Early June was the departure date, and though it would not work out for them to be on the same flight (nor even the same airline), they would arrive within hours of each other and rendezvous at the pied-à-terre of an old Viennese friend of Max's, recently deceased, whose main residence had long been Tel Aviv, and whose Israeli children had kindly offered Max use of the apartment during his Vienna stay since it was vacant and they were preparing to sell it anyway.

To his magazine Daniel had turned in a respectable clutch of reviews over the previous months, and he was enjoying a rare if tenuous solvency that would allow him to make the trip (and, importantly for Daniel, reimburse Max for the cost of his airfare). There remained only the okaying of his

413

three-week absence with his editor, a chore that Daniel put off literally until the last minute, out of a nervousness that turned out to be unjustified. When he started to apologize for having to be away, his editor interrupted him with a nonsense-implying wave of his hand and a reassurance of what they both knew anyway: that the art world essentially went into hibernation all summer. Still, the man's nonchalance about the matter, such a reversal of his earlier frustration with Daniel's commitment to his post, nearly bordered on being flip, and Daniel was followed out of the magazine office's doors that morning by a lingering suspicion that, in so many words, he had just been granted a permanent furlough. But the feeling began to diminish later that afternoon as he sat in the back of a cab hurrying him to Newark International, and when he landed in Vienna (was it really a whole day later?), whatever remained of the sensation was soon wiped away — if not right there in that capital's clean, yellowly lit airport, then on the train that efficiently whooshed him toward its center — to be replaced with a jet lag–erasing recognition that Aleksandra had made this very same journey with Benjamin, and with a belief that they or their ghosts were out there somehow, somewhere, in this old imperial city, into whose atmosphere he was already being drawn by an ache for something that had been lost.

Max's directions led him to a quiet residential neighborhood in the purlieus of the Habsburg monarchs' summer palace, the Schönbrunn, where Daniel, laden with laptop and other impedimenta, trudged his way along Wattmanngasse, a linear brick-paved lane lined with chestnut trees and polished metal plaques bearing the names of doctors and professors and the street's famous dead. Something about its three-story apartment buildings, their even profile, or the way the afternoon sun goldened the pleasant ocher-tinted facades, filled Daniel with a subtle melancholy — it was the same sensation that sometimes came over him when on certain Mediterranean beaches he would glimpse a perfect row of unrented umbrellas — and he was looking forward to seeing Max and a familiar face. When he rang at the specified address, he was nervously greeted by the building's manager, a raven-haired frau of middle age who began struggling in her thick Wienerisch to communicate with him. Daniel politely interrupted, calling on his best university German to announce that he was an expected guest of Herr Max Wiener, but it only seemed to drape a veil of frustration over the woman's face. Now her forehead was scored with anger, and Daniel found himself in that unpleasant position that so often attends foreign travel: that of standing chastened but, due to the confusions of language, uncorrected. It was only as she ushered him up the stairs that he was able to unknot her remonstrative word torrent, enough anyway to gather that Max's assistant, Carmen, had phoned, and that *they* — Carmen and Max (the German pronoun "sie" could mean either "she" or "they") — would have to delay their flight to Vienna by at least a day, possibly two, while Max recovered from the complications of a cold. The second-floor hallway was unlit, and the manager came to a halt before a door at its far end. Handing Daniel the key, she looked embarrassed all at once about her little sprain of anger, which in retrospect appeared less the result of a collision with him than with a patch of emotional underbrush that had gathered itself around something else entirely, like a bad marriage, a disappointed life. She hastily took her leave.

The apartment was darkened by books and old wood furnishings, but it had the advantage of a bird-rich plane tree that grew on this side of the building, and as Daniel stood there in the tiny kitchen getting his bearings, the branches and birdsong seemed to come laughing into the room like an offering of much-needed reassurance. He set down his things finally in the master bedroom (if it could be called such a thing), for the simple reason that it had only one bed, whereas the apartment's other bedroom, though less roomy, contained two, and he wanted to avoid any awkward decisions when Max and Carmen arrived. The smallish living room did have a couch, and he would of course offer to relocate to it when the time came. For now, he seemed capable only of lying across his bed. Vienna was warm, his lone window stood open to its moist air, and he felt as if he were sinking into the eiderdown in glum concert with the dimming of the room by cloud shadow.

He tried to take several honest soundings of his state, but the only feeling to keep coming up was the magnitude of his disappointment over Max not *being* here. Disappointment was too weak a word. Heartbreak was close; heart terror even closer. He was in a tired state of terror. And the elephant in the room was death: what was traveling all this way to find no one waiting to greet him but a rehearsal of going to his own? Big departures he was good at, and life was a farewell anyway, to the degree that one's earthly chore, or part of it, was to learn how to say good-bye with grace. But arrivals? Concerning them, the important ones at least, the onus was on *others* (beginning with one's birth; on whom the onus fell to greet one in death was a matter for believers and atheists to fight or weep over — Daniel mostly wept).

He knew he was in a peculiar frame of mind.

His bird friends were no longer helping. The ebb and flow of their melodies, their endless recapitulations — these had to be the very same songs heard by people long departed from this earth. It almost seemed to him that the flittering gray things meant to re-alert him to death with some sort of knowing bird haughtiness, the insolence of longevity.

But it was not all in his head. He *was* staying in the apartment of a recently deceased man, an academic (the books were a giveaway) who, to judge by the framed photos on the wall of him in a displaced persons camp, had been a Holocaust survivor. And the man's doorless closet *was* displaying a pair of worn walking shoes, binoculars, and an umbrella — purposeless objects now, and an unspeakably sad sight.

Daniel fell asleep in his clothes, and when he awoke it was dark out, he had no idea what time it was, though it felt as if he had been sleeping forever. He remembered only that he had been wondering, right before he had lost consciousness, who the last Holocaust survivor would be, and it reminded him now of an article he had recently read in the *Times* — about a solitary whale that for the last twenty years had been tracked by the navy using the same acoustic instruments they employed to monitor enemy submarines. From the whale's distinctive basso profundo voice, which had apparently deepened significantly as the animal aged, experts were able to say with near certainty that no other whale of its kind was left anywhere in the world's seas. Some believed that the whale was aware of this fate, but that he nonetheless continued to try to communicate to a world empty of his own, roaming the frigid North Pacific waters year after year with no better hope than calling out at regular intervals that he was there.

Daniel was afraid of remaining alone any longer in the apartment, and so, grabbing only his money and a map (it was too hot for a jacket), he quietly left the building and went out into the street. The nearby cathedral, wrapped in darkness, lifted a modest tower above the rooftops; he had passed it on his way in from the airport and was now drawn back toward its Gothic gloom. He found the cafés there to be recently closed, the paved square still warm and fragrant. It was almost five in the morning if a clock on a bank's stone face was to be believed, and he turned onto the main street to walk and wait for the sun. Several couples were finding their way back to the enormous old hotel directly opposite the Schönbrunn, which had been built by Emperor Franz Josef himself, and where, as Daniel read on the plaque, Thomas Edison had enjoyed staying. Farther down the street, entire trays of bread and pastries were emerging from a tempest in the kitchen of a small, brightly lit bakery. The world was as living as ever.

But Daniel was not after the living. He was hungry for ghosts. And Vienna readily trafficked them to him, starting with his own, which every shopwindow reflected back to him as he walked through the empty streets. When he randomly boarded a tram in front of the ugly modern train station straddling the River Wien, he was somehow unsurprised to see the ghosts of Aleksandra and Benjamin already sitting there in the first two seats. They patiently accompanied him — or his imagination — through a series of seemingly haphazard connections that took them across the entire city, and even stayed on when, for reasons he himself did not understand, he rode the southbound Simmering tram nearly its whole length, deep into the outskirts of Vienna, through alien neighborhoods afloat in the hazy dawn, past building after building in which he would never in this life set foot and that therefore filled him with sadness. Only when he caught sight of a headstone company that fronted the main road did he recall drawing a red circle around the Simmering tramline on the map he had studied during his flight across the Atlantic, and suddenly the morning lost its aura of aimlessness, and he became aware that all this time he had been unconsciously taking himself to the Central Cemetery.

And just like that, Aleksandra and Benjamin vanished, he could no longer conjure them, and when he disembarked at the north gate of the cemetery he was on his own, except for three ravens picking at something in the road. What could Aleksandra have been feeling when they had come here? What had she wanted? Had it really been as simple, and inevitable, as her fate becoming linked with Benjamin's due to a shared sense of an immediate and above all pressing Jewish-European history? This did seem an obvious answer, especially if there was any truth to the notion that when we love we are not really looking to see something *new*, but rather our own ideas embodied in the other person — qualities that awaken echoes already resounding in us. Had Benjamin's struggle with his new identity, which must have been fierce, revived something dormant inside Aleksandra? After all, his was likewise a story of displacement — possibly on an even grander scale, personally and historically. And the two of them must have suffered equally the trauma of immigration: she from her childhood escape from Russia, he much later from the discovery of who he really was. Perhaps in him she had found her own identity, made more dramatic. And, of course, he would have needed her to help him *through* it — to make sense (to make art?) of all that he bore undeveloped in him.

Daniel stood there, holding up the photograph she had taken of Benjamin somewhere inside the high walls of the cemetery. What had prevented her from just telling Daniel what she was doing with Benjamin? Telling him what she *needed* to do? Could their marriage have sustained it? Could *Daniel* have sustained it?

Maybe. No. Probably not. Love, at least theirs, made too little room for frankness anyway.

The morning was breaking. Here and there clouds parted, and a thick atmosphere of summer pervaded the road. When Daniel passed through the open gate he was confronted not just by grass and graves, but also by the history of the twentieth century itself. To his left, the Christian section looked intimidatingly neat and trim; its flowered, manicured, carpetlike lawn ran sweepingly into the distance. To his right, separated from the Christian graves by a double-wide dirt path and crammed into a corner of the cemetery, was the Jewish section, largely unmaintained and badly overgrown. Its headstones and monuments, many of them toppled, vandalized, or simply buried beneath tangles of weeds and wild shrubbery, seemed to speak of Gentile malice, perhaps even of damage wrought by some of the very souls who, by virtue of their final real estate just across the dividing (and divisive) path, made posthumous claims to the brotherly love of their particular god. Daniel penetrated the Jewish section with trepidation, because the horrid condition of the place, when contrasted with the sheer size and health of its Christian

423

counterpart, put all the ancient threats before him, to such a degree that another outbreak of anti-Jewish violence among the locals did not seem to him, suddenly, to be out of the question. It sickened him that the city of Vienna, here in the twenty-first century, could let such a disparity stand. If there were no Jews left to maintain the graves, was it not the responsibility of the descendants of those who had *removed* the Jews to care for them? He kept looking over his shoulder, as if they — *they:* Daniel had benefited from a contemporary American existence that had given him very little reason and still less occasion to employ and feel that word in its most threatening sense — would at any moment come for him.

No one came for him. No one came for any reason. Alone, he walked the Jewish cemetery for the rest of the morning, getting lost among the graves, among his thoughts too. But he never grew more comfortable.

And it seemed that he would never find the tombstone beside which Benjamin had stood in the photograph. He located plenty of Picks — the place was roiling with them — but no Leopold and Ada, and he began to think he had the wrong cemetery. He began to tire also — from so much walking, and certainly from hunger (he had not eaten since the plane) — but his exhaustion was not merely physical: his close examination of every name on every stone was having its spiritual side effects. Toward what end, he wanted to know, were names stamped into stone in the first place? Was it not, in any case, a writ of near-instant obscurity — one generation, two at the most, the job complete? There was something desperate about all these deep-chiseled Felixes and Fritzes, these Heties and Hermines and Hildas staring out at the world expectantly season after season. The dead were supposed to be pure: present in our imagination and real only by their absence. They were meant to lie beyond our reach, never asking anything of us, never answering us either, terminally silent and therefore ultimately useful, each one a god.

But then, just as he had written off the value of eternizing a name, he saw, on a stout little stone, his *own*. It was his last, Lichtmann (though not his first: one Aron Lichtmann had been interred here on the 19th of May, 1903), and it froze his thoughts — and his blood — on the spot. As though casting a spell on him, the letters of his own name abducted his eyes, filling them with terrible visions. He saw that he had already been dead once, for a very long time (though not an eternity), right up until his conception. He saw that his life was but a brief illumination of his eternity, and that when it ended, he would simply be eternal. And he saw that he was mistaken to be so interested in himself, when he so easily could have been born someone else.

He could hardly hold himself up — his blood sugar was low — and his only concern now was to decamp quickly and locate something to eat. Afraid to let his eyes land on any other names, he began to walk. And this was how he found Leopold and Ada Pick — by not looking. A felled tombstone tripped him and brought his shoulder and side down hard across its broad diagonal surface. When he righted himself, there it was.

The grave, already so familiar to him from the photograph, lay several feet from where he had fallen, well off the path and hard by a thicket of berries that must have prevented him from spotting it earlier. To get to it, he had to pick his way through a jumble of languishing graves and chunks of marble and granite. He spotted the remnants of the rose at once . . . the one Benjamin had been holding in the picture. Pinned beneath a cairn of small stones at the base of the tombstone, its petals had long ago shriveled into themselves and mostly disintegrated away, and Daniel had to sit down immediately and take what was left of the dried thing into his hand. Surely Aleksandra had been the one to bring it to the grave for Benjamin to place there. It was almost impossible that he was here holding the same flower.

The beauty of the spot, and the soft, canopy-like bed of grass and brush that lent it a privacy, slowed his breathing, and despite his hunger he sat there quietly looking at nothing in particular, following the odd gnat or butterfly with his eyes, staring off into the dust-filled lances of light. It came over him gradually that this was precisely the kind of place where two people who were newly in love, and who were caught up by soul-shaking emotions — by the confusion that any real confrontation with mortality brings on — would seek the resolving and consolidating comforts of each other's bodies, and it forced him to consider the possibility that Aleksandra had made love to Benjamin right here. But the effect of his imagining it — of picturing and picturing and picturing them in the act and then lying side by side afterward on this same patch of earth, their chests respiring together — was completely unforeseeable: Daniel found himself praying for the first time in his life. Praying to be forgiven for indulging in this (albeit nightmarish) fantasy, for coming here not to pay respects to the spirits of Ada and Leopold Pick but for his selfish pursuits. He prayed to be forgiven for his *own* desecration of the dead — those buried here in this hallowed ground and Aleksandra and Benjamin too.

Daniel's petitions skyward notwithstanding, Vienna had further sorrow to supply. And more ghosts. He had been to the city once before as a college student but was so enthralled by the Klimts and the Schieles — by the music halls where Mozart and Beethoven and Brahms had premiered their own compositions — that the city's Jewish past had made little impression on him, even when he toured the State Opera House, where Gustav Mahler, the most emblematic of Vienna's Jews and certainly one who had captured Daniel's interest and ear from an early age, had brought all of his prowess and perfectionism to bear on the best-conducted operas the world had ever known. But this time Daniel was being sucked into an alternate Vienna, a town denatured, deracinated, a parallel world of unpersons. Where were the Jews? That the few overtly Jewish institutions — including a preschool — required around-the-clock watch by machine gun–toting guards only rejuvenated the feeling he had experienced at the cemetery that he was unsafe here. Indeed, each second he spent inside the Jewish museum, where he had decided to eat, found him tense. The silence in there was not the usual museum hush. It was a fellowship of sadness. And a collective holding of breath — as if the place could be invaded, or bombed, at any moment.

Yet according to the guide he purchased on his way out — a pale pamphlet bearing the names and addresses of the vanished — the real Jewish museum of Vienna was not a museum at all, but a section of the city called the Leopoldstadt, which Daniel wandered at length. Not that there was much material evidence on display. Bland housing projects stood where inconceivably beautiful temples had once risen; the great Yiddish theaters were now adult education centers or banks, the prayer houses Internet cafés. Nearly everything Jewish had been excised from the place. Though not from its soul — you could not delimit the dead — and nowhere did Daniel sense this more stirringly than when passing beneath the gray apartment buildings driven densely into each block: their glaucous windows seemed to hold a sixty-year sadness. It was only appropriate (Daniel felt) that the neighborhood now had an undecided, transitional feel. Its present occupants — immigrants, mainly, from Africa, the Balkans, and from Turkey, of course, from places more vibrant and vigorous than modern-day Austria — appeared to be stunned (or was it fatigued, the exhaustion of two worlds having impinged?). And yet they were hungry. Certain of the men (and occasionally their progeny) peered out from their doorways, waiting for something that might rid them of this odd European disease, a melancholy of the over-municipalized. Did any cure exist for history? They were living in a destroyed altar, and every one of them stared expectantly at Daniel as he passed by, as if wanting him to tell them what the new republic had done with happiness.

What could he tell them, when his own hurt for the place was so strong as to border on grief, as if he had destroyed it himself? A Turkish doner kebab, purchased at a bustling, aromatic grill tucked beneath some tracks transversing the Prater amusement park, did him much good. It did him no good too, because it only reawakened his appetites — none more than his appetite for ghosts. The day seemed to be exhaling, its light already thickening toward twilight, and Daniel, thinking he should return to the Wattmanngasse apartment to rest and see if Max and Carmen had arrived, was walking back through one of the Leopoldstadt's curved streets when, having passed a corner bar whose red velvet drapes billowed from its open windows, he was treated to a whistle and then a Hallo! — a low, incantatory, *female* Hallo. It caused him to stop and look. There behind him on the sidewalk, slight of figure, bedizened with glimmering accoutrements and glistening dark hair that fell to her bare shoulders, stood the ghost of Aleksandra — inhabiting the body of a young woman who was calling him back to the bar, calling him to engage her services (if he understood her correctly). From the moment he had first set foot in Vienna, he had felt that he was treading not actual city streets but the contours of a death cloak, or rather a scrim that covered everything. It was through the scrim's coarse weave that this woman was now gazing mischievously at him, a curl to her lips, as if she had already made him a once-in-a-lifetime promise and was threatening retraction. Yet there ran through her eyes a countercurrent to this playfulness, a darker stream that suggested such confidence was short-term, abortive. Her face still shone of a girlhood only recently ended, but its disappointment sonars seemed finely tuned. What prevented Daniel from walking away was her unignorable resemblance to Aleksandra, and the thinness of her skin that revealed the armature underneath. Her skull gave every indication that it was about to take its turn staring out at the world, and he was defenseless against the vision. It seemed to answer to an unclosed hurt in him, and touch off emotions that Vienna, starting with its cemetery, had been imposing on him all day. Because the truth was that he harbored a latent fear that Aleksandra had been taken irretrievably from the middle of her life for no reason. And no reason was ever evil's reason. The removal of the Jews from Vienna? No reason.

It only proved that a certain sort of hopelessness hid behind every person's best qualities, because in the end it was his empathy, and a surpassing hopelessness, that made him turn from restraint — from order and propriety, his usual caution and purposefulness — and walk back toward this living ghost, toward the bar inside, where before he knew it he was buying the two of them drinks, showing her his guide-book, and telling her about death and Jews and this crazy, fucked-up city. By way of responding, she lit another of her perpetual cigarettes and asked in German if he was from America. "Would that explain every-thing?" he said sarcastically into the leer of her perky, thinly veiled breasts, which held him in their level regard like two widely spaced pupils. And then he followed her real gaze to a large fellow at the opposite end of the bar, a representative of the aggressive gum-chewing caste, who smiled skeptically at Daniel, and who was obviously impatient for them to strike a deal (but not enough to interfere — a politic pimp). She named her price then — an exorbitant, planetary price that Daniel paid without argument, and soon he was laboring up a wood staircase behind the bar, convinced he was carrying the dead with him, and following her into a room whose tiny space was so hot, so consumed by an unshaded lamp's despotic globe of light, that he felt as if he had climbed all this way only to tumble into a declivity of fire.

Now the woman began to undress, and her exposed flesh, what there was of it anyway, shone translucently in the light like something dreamed. She sat naked and facing him on the room's one narrow bed, but the space between them might have been a gaping hole in the flow of time. Daniel felt himself brushed by the breath of Aleksandra, the *real* Aleksandra, the last woman he had lain with. Perhaps it was this remembrance that caused him to begin assuring the woman on the bed that he was not just another man but a messenger from the vanquished realm, who was only going through with this because of some need to desecrate himself. He had never done this, he promised her, had never done *any* of this — whatever it was that he was doing here in Vienna. She listened to him with the dryness of one listening to thin-sliced arguments. A mannish impatience briefly seized her lips, but then her eyes grew eloquent of experience, of common sense and male weakness. She took him into her arms, and he felt ashamed and stupid as she helped him to undress. Somewhere along the way a condom was freed of its wrapper. When he could arouse none of his native vigor, she was kind about it, generous with her mouth, and he began to weep because he could not avoid thinking of all the women throughout history, now long gone, who had found it necessary to build tender, tough careers out of this kind of resourcefulness, and for a moment as he watched her brown head of hair bob gently against his abdomen, he tried to project all the solemn tragedy of those women onto this one.

But this one, as it turned out, would have none of it. When it became clear to her that, in spite of her resourcefulness, he would never be able to perform, she resisted tragedy — his and that of her profession — with vulgarity, with anti-Semitic slurs, with an angry exit. Gathering his clothes, he told himself that he would need to be good, truly good, from this moment forward, without exception. And he dressed urgently, as if the dead — who were still in that room with him, he felt — depended on him alone.

If it was goodness that he was after he could not have come across a better sight than the tableau of Max's and Carmen's toiletries ranged neatly along the bathroom counter in the darkened Wattmanngasse apartment when he returned. For a minute he stood there taking in the toothbrushes and razors, the pill boxes and deodorants. The vision was not entirely a consolation, but it was a light.

Light. When he opened his eyes the next morning, his room was permeated with it.

He threw on fresh clothes and went out to greet his roommates. The bathroom was occupied, and he found Max in the living room, sunk into a corner of the couch (*pressed* might have been more accurate: if the old man had been frail before, there was even less of him now). To judge by the smile that erupted across Max's face, he had been waiting for Daniel.

"Come, sit," he said, directing Daniel to a plump chair abutting the couch. "Excellent! Do not be shy — push my wheelchair out of your way if you have to."

Max looked awful. Emphatically awful. He appeared barely to be finessing life, as though the odds might tilt against it — his life — at any moment. *"Please,"* he said as Daniel sat down, "take my hand, and stop this silly looking at me as one looks at some man in the grip of death! It is a different spell I am under anyway" — the old man suddenly stared at Daniel with such intimacy that it caused Daniel to blush — "but almost as strong! I am speaking of the spell of seeing you again, Mr. Lichtmann. Ah, I made you smile. Good. It is true. Seeing your face, my eyes are refreshed. You remind me of someone who was very important to me. Someone who carried the planets on his back." Max shook his head then, as if trying to shake loose a thought. "But this is the problem with getting old . . . all the remembered faces! There becomes no room in the heart for fresh faces. Anyone new I meet seems to have stolen their smile from one of my dusty old photo albums."

Daniel let it slip that he had visited the gravestone of Leopold and Ada Pick the day before. Then he added: "The person I remind you of . . . on the phone you said there was someone —"

"I will tell you everything. This I promise. But I do not have the strength yet. What was I expecting coming here like this? Last night — just one glimpse of the city and I thought I was to die in the back of our taxi. The old places grow stronger! They call for you. This place is screaming for me, Mr. Lichtmann. I am not convinced I will be able to leave it in one piece. You see, I have spent most of my life enjoying not only the freedom of America but also the freedom of *memory*. But last night, when we drove past a building I have not put my eyes on in more than sixty years, I saw that I have paid for this freedom with my life. Would you believe, Mr. Lichtmann, that I have no idea where my youth went? I only know that I miss it. Not because I miss all the young I knew then, but because I miss the old.

When you are my age, there *are* no old. There are just more of you. This is what else is terrible about aging — there becomes no more mystery about other people! Do you understand? When you are young, you feel a mystery about your grandfather, your great-grandmother . . . it gives you a comfort, these mysterious older persons. But as you age the difference in years between you and the oldest living persons decreases — until *you* are the oldest living person, and the only difference of age to speak of is between you and the young. And the young, well, you have *been* them! The truth is I don't even know *how* my great day came and went — where was its sunrise? Where was its sunset? Here, look at our hands" — the old man held up their clasping hands shakily for Daniel to see — "and what can you see? Why do you think my grandson's last sculptures were like this — holding the hands? Wait! You wrote of this precise question. I remember. It was to make dying more tasty, you said."

"Palatable," Daniel corrected him.

"Yes! But no. They were already *dead,* these people in the sculptures, you see? They were holding hands too late. *This* was the irony that my grandson, my young, young grandson saw. It is how I know his heart was broken when he built these sculptures. He was in love — the real love that is all pain — but he was not happy. If he was happy, he would not have made such wise things. The happy are not complete. They have everything, except . . . what is the English word? Except *being.* Unhappiness — do you not see that it is only this *one quality* which lets you know you have been alive during the last second? Unhappiness made the sixty years since I left this city into two hundred years! Unhappiness! And not just any kind. I am speaking of a variety that in my day we could *not* speak about. It had to wait for the future, and even now the world only whispers or yells about it. I mean male love."

Max met Daniel's surprised gaze with an illumined look then. His eyes were shining with significance. The old man was evidently enjoying the moment, the disclosure: he had nearly exclaimed the last two words, as if trying to shock the decorum of the apartment.

And Daniel had indeed been tossed into a state of embarrassment, not so much by the revelation itself as by the fact that the old man would trust and honor him with one that was so *defining.* It left him with a thrilling lump in his throat. His eyes returned to

Max's spotted hand and to his own, the joining of which had suddenly taken on a new significance. What was to be his response? He had already allowed too much time to pass without offering one, and he searched his brain frantically for some way to cast off the heavy air of the anomalous that had surrounded their conversation.

"Was there a particular man?" he asked impulsively, pretending to modern frankness and flexibility.

But the question came out like a breach, and Max immediately withdrew his hand. Daniel was left to sit there, ashamed by his forwardness. The truth was that he still hardly knew the old man. He offered several apologies, each of which was met — to his growing alarm — with silence. When Max's eyes began to swell with something that looked a lot like sorrow, Daniel realized that he had not offended him. He had caused Max pain. He had brought back an old face.

It was at this exact moment, when the two of them were sitting there foundering in a sphere of damaged looks and elongated silences, that the bathroom door opened and Carmen entered the room. Her almost-black eyes moved quickly between their faces — an instant analysis that surely told her he and Max had been speaking of wounding things. She began to look at them as if they were *both* invalids, not as a doctor or nurse might, but as one whose care was much closer in. Daniel was put at ease by her caressing gaze, and stood up to greet her, feeling grateful all at once to be un-alone with Max.

Then she came near, and he was confronted by the elegance of her figure. Her particular displacement of space was unmistakable, and, leaning over to feel Max's forehead with the back of her hand, she (and her pale blue summer dress) inhabited the room in a way that he could only think of as ruinous. She had just showered. Her skin still had a glow to it. And although her dark hair had been pulled back, water had caught a few of its strands and pressed them stirringly to her neck.

As if she had been alerted to his thoughts, she straightened and took hold of him with her eyes. It unnerved him to such a degree that instead of just saying hello he introduced himself to her — inanely — reaching out to shake her hand and explaining — *very* inanely — that she might recall they had met briefly once before.

"I would hope so," she said without meanness. "Max and I spent most of the flight talking about you."

He felt himself redden. They were face-to-face. He was staring at her lips. And now her color changed, and she let go of his hand.

"How do you like Vienna?" she asked, averting her gaze.

What was happening here? Or rather, what had already happened? Because, within a few seconds, they had *discovered* each other — not just with their eyes, but also with other senses conscious and unconscious. First a major revelation from Max, and now another revelation: *Carmen.*

How did he like Vienna? That was the question, and he found that he could answer it, now, in the past tense. "It was filled with ghosts."

"Real ghosts?"

She looked serious. He could not manageably take his eyes off her. "Yes. One of them."

"You must have been frightened."

"I ran from her, actually."

He noticed how she caught at his mention of the ghost's gender. Her brow rose slightly at it, though her smile was beautifully undisclosing.

"Oh? Did she chase you?"

"She'd already walked away from me."

Now her expression was scrutinizing, and

he was surprised at his own daring, this odd willingness to talk, even obliquely, about Aleksandra's ghost. Why was he doing it? Was he trying — already — to make her jealous? Or was it that he was for some reason unashamed in front of her? Her presence did exert a mysterious de-barbarizing effect on the transgression he had committed the day before — to the degree that he felt comfortable enough to offer her a furtive confession dressed out as amorous play.

Max, who, having all the while been absorbed in whatever private pain Daniel had accidentally reanimated in him, appeared only to pick up generally on the fact that they were discussing ghosts, because, out of the blue, he sighingly asserted that people filled the world with ghosts so they would not be all alone. Daniel's and Carmen's eyes met over the comment, as if they were each trying to assess how relevant or incongruous it was to the drift of their conversation. But then Max added something that simply *ended* their conversation. Something that would have ended *any* conversation. He said: "Jewish America — it clings to the ghosts of six million Jews so it will not feel alone. Europe — it ignores these ghosts. That is why it is the loneliest place on earth."

Daniel joined Carmen in attending to this with respectful silence, until she said: "I'll make eggs."

"I'll help," Daniel offered.

Soon they were both in the tight kitchen, pulling from the refrigerator the few things Carmen had picked up the night before, taking stock of what was already in the cupboards, throwing themselves like two overeager actors into the distractive theater of cooking breakfast.

"How long have you worked for him?"

This was Daniel, as he scrambled six eggs in a bowl.

"I don't."

"Then you're —"

"I'm here because I want to help him. Do you beat milk into your eggs?"

"What?"

With a mock-inconvenienced expression, she held up a small carton of milk. "To make them fluffier?"

Dutifully he took the milk from her and poured a little into the bowl. "He doesn't pay you?"

"Oh, you don't know me very well. And you don't know *him* very well either. You're not beating those correctly." She appropriated the bowl and fork from him and gave the eggs several vigorous whippings. "You

444

need to aerate them without blending them to death."

She nudged him out of the way with her hip, and Daniel, charmed by the maneuver (it was unstudied and affectionate), stood aside and watched her pour the properly beaten eggs into a pan on the stove. "What's *this?*" he asked, pulling a pack of beer from a grocery bag on the counter.

"I'll take some of that."

"For breakfast?"

"They're good — local — I had one last night. There's an opener in that drawer."

This compelled him to take a fresh, favorable measurement of the woman before him, and to serve her a drink as fast as he possibly could. He located the opener, unlidded a bottle, and was mining the cupboard for two glasses when she grabbed the beer from the counter and brought it directly to her mouth. The move surprised him, in a good way, as did how she proceeded to drink in an unreconstructed American-college-girl fashion, clutching the bottle by its throat. And, somehow, right there in that very moment, Daniel saw that life was beginning to happen to him — again. Carmen was happening to him. It was too fast. *He* was being too fast. And yet Max's regret-filled speech about getting old had frightened him, and if ever he was ready for a looser handling of the art of living, it was now. In the chaotic shambles of Aleksandra's passing, death had been allowed to construct itself too neatly around him, and here was Carmen, within ten minutes helpfully disarraying death. It was not that it had disappeared from his vision, but it was death with a difference, or Daniel with a difference: with a prospect. He and Carmen drank, they laughed, and the deeper they were drawn into the soft-footed intimacy that their cooking together implied, the more conscious he grew of enjoying her nearness, her wit, her benign culinary corrections, and the obvious gracefulness with which she handled everything. And it did strike him that she was handling *everything*: a whole paraphernalia of travel practicalities, of Max and his heavy power wheelchair and his afflictions of body and spirit, of personal beleaguerments hinted at but so far undisclosed, and of Daniel himself, the delicate tangle of getting to know a man. He did not tell her that he was in love. But he could have.

Breakfast was about ready, yet Daniel wanted to stay in that kitchen and satisfy his sudden interest in every part of this woman's life. Grasping for an excuse to keep her there longer, he picked up the thread of their earlier discussion and asked: "So, you *aren't* his assistant?"

Even to his own ear, the question sounded random, if not abrupt. Its effect on her was subtle but immediately apparent in the spark of doubt in her eyes. She had been pulled out of the rhythm they had established — just enough to hear its hasty composition. And the fact that this slight verbal misstep could blight what had otherwise been a fine first conversation seemed to remind them both that love was erected less on what two people said than on what they each divined of the other.

"I help him with the big battles," she said at last.

"He seems to be waging more than one," he hazarded, thinking of what Max had let fall right before she had come out of the bathroom.

She was quick to read the meaning behind his tone. "He *told* you?"

"You find it surprising?"

It was like watching someone labor valiantly to ward off their own embarrassment. "I'm the only person he'd ever confided in about it," she quietly admitted, and then, as if Daniel were arguing against her opinion: "You need to take it very seriously . . . no, I

447

mean it — very seriously because he's old and he's gay and . . . and that means there's a double mystery to his purpose. I've known Max for a long time. He'll say things that can be upsetting. He has his prejudices. But you have to judge someone like him by his echoes, not by what keeps clipping his wings."

Daniel could see that her worry for Max was authentic, it was an impulse of her being, independent of any principle of goodwill, and he felt like taking her hand then — the one she was using to hold herself up against the counter. But his intuition was to leave her alone — her emotions were running high, she was still working with sharp tools — and so he just stood there and stared in admiration, trying to understand where a young, highly modern American woman had learned so much humanity. It was plain to see (or rather hear) that she was educated, but hers was not the kind of knowledge they dispatched in graduate school; it was the kind that one kept in the hollow of one's palm, the freer, better kind that came from the substance of life. Her words answered to experience, and Daniel heard in them an honorable response to a past that must have had its due of discord.

For a brief instant, she looked as if she

was going to say more on the subject.

"I'm sorry," she said instead, eyes lowered, and then she took up two plates of food and went into the living room.

After breakfast, Max announced that he felt strong enough to venture out and see his old city ("What: I came *all this way* to house-sit my dead friend's apartment?" was his final word on the matter). Daniel had to bear up the old man in the elevator while Carmen folded the power wheelchair to fit into the tiny space and then unfolded it in the lobby below. Traversing the town itself with a wheelchair-bound charge did not turn out to be as difficult as Daniel had feared. Once they had emerged from the subway into the center of the city, Max powered through the ancient streets, uttering each of their longish *gasse-* or *strasse-* ending names in the unmodulated tones of a priest performing a sacred act of remembrance. Or was it an act of reconnaissance? The old man was noticeably restive in his wheelchair, especially as they went along the more crowded pedestrian thoroughfares, often pitching his upper body violently to one side or the other in order to get a glimpse between passersby of some particular doorway, or abruptly twisting around to give a certain storefront a double take. And all the while he wore a militaristic air of being on permanent alert, vigilantly inspecting each shiny face as though it might be an enemy's. Perhaps he was simply saying farewell. Daniel did have the feeling, on many a street, that the old man was taking final leave of everyone and everything in it.

He was not, however, taking leave of his memories. When, having just finished a lunch of paprika-rich finger sandwiches, they rounded a corner and were suddenly confronted by St. Stephen's Cathedral, Max looked up at the fawn-colored south tower with a bitter set to his mouth, as if gazing across the gulf of years. Daniel followed his eyes to the small Gothic windows at the top, and, without even knowing the details, had the disembodying sensation of holding another man's memory. That the cathedral's tile roof was being restored seemed particularly to bother Max, and after several minutes he demanded to be taken away from there. Whether it was this encounter — with the capital's most important symbol of Christianity — or the one they had shortly afterward with a nearby window where the defenestration of one of Max's friends had occurred at the hands of Nazi brown-shirts, a sudden trembling need arose in Max to see the Vienna Synagogue — the only temple, he explained, to have "escaped the Nazi bastards' handiwork during Kristallnacht."

The synagogue was hidden from the street, deep inside a nondescript residential building, and getting into it turned out to be an ordeal — not because of Max's wheelchair, but because of one impassive security officer, a product of Israel's anti-terrorist outfit, who came preinstalled with an overweening sense of mission and refused to offer Daniel easy admittance. Daniel was separated from Carmen and Max and taken to a windowless room no bigger than a closet, where the devoted young fellow, whose English sounded impeccably American, ran him through a sequence of pharisaical questions — what were the Jewish holidays? to what synagogue did he belong and when had he last attended a service? how much Hebrew could he speak? — that seemed fairly rote even as they caused Daniel, whose answers to the latter two questions in particular were less than satisfactory, to feel like a recusant member of the tribe (in his shame, in his exasperation, and surely not to his own benefit, he ended up informing his stone-faced inquisitor that he was "simply a bad Jew"). Then things got weird. That the officer acknowledged no Jewish consanguinity with him may have been part of the job, but why he began to suspect him of strong Arab ties (he kept asking him to name the Arabs he was staying with while in Vienna) was beyond Daniel's understanding, especially given that Daniel's surname was Lichtmann, and that he was escorting an eightysomething-year-old former Viennese Jew around named Max Wiener. But the weirdness began in earnest when his interrogator submitted him to questions about Carmen, and it finally occurred to Daniel that it was not *him* this guy was interested in, but her. It did not help that Daniel hardly knew anything about Carmen, and it was a surreal experience to have this intractable Israeli warrior bring home to him just how much dew was still on his connection to her. "You don't even know her last name?" the officer asked him. "No." "Yet you're staying in the same apartment with her?" "Yes." "Are you her lover?" A pause. "We just met." "In Vienna?" "No — in America. I met her once before at a funeral." "An Arab funeral?" "It was Unitarian." "Was it held in a mosque?" "No, it's a church that accepts every religion." "Islam too?" Another pause. "Yes."

This was obviously a grave demerit: the

officer left the small room, ordering Daniel to remain. He returned five minutes later with a small notebook, to which his eyes repeatedly went during the rest of the interrogation. "What did you discuss with Carmen last night?" "Nothing. She was asleep." "In your bed?" "In another room." "She never came into your room?" "No." "What did you discuss with her this morning?" "How to cook eggs." "What is her last name?" "I told you I don't know." "Where is she from?" "I don't know." "Did you fly on the same plane as she?" "No." "Why not?" "We didn't know I was coming until later." "Did she arrange for your flight?" "Yes." "Will you fly back on the same plane?" "I don't know. I don't think so." "Why not?" "Because they were booked at different times. The flights fill up. It's summer, right? It's very simple." "A woman whose last name you don't know buys you a ticket to Vienna. She flies on a different plane but sleeps in the same apartment. Is this what you call simple?" "Yes — no." "Which one: yes or no?" "We are helping an old man see his hometown before he dies. He's a Jew. *I'm* a Jew." "Is Carmen a Jew?" "I don't know." "Is she an Arab?" "I don't know." "Will you see her when you return to America?" A pause. "I think so." "You don't know?" "No." "Why not?" "She's a woman. In America you can't make a woman see you." Daniel thought (hoped) that this would bring a smile, some sign of fellow feeling, to the guy's face. Nothing. "What did you drink this morning?" *What?* "What did you drink this morning?" Another pause. "I had some beer, actually." "Did Carmen drink beer?" "Yes." "You saw her drink it?" "Yes."

And then, very abruptly, it was over. He was let out of the room and handed a yarmulke — he was in. And there was Max in the dark neoclassic antechamber, smiling at him from his wheelchair. Thank God for *beer,* Daniel thought: as obvious a demarcator as any between the Islamists and everyone else. And thank God Carmen had suggested they drink it for breakfast.

But just as he finished these irreverent thoughts, a different door opened, and a different Israeli officer stared out of it at Daniel as Carmen emerged, looking shaken and white. Only then did Daniel understand that the two of them had been interrogated concurrently. He was too stunned still to say anything, but the effect of seeing her again after what he had just been through must have been mutual, because as they accompanied Max into the synagogue's hushed inner sanctum, they kept exchanging wayward, reckless glances that promised to evolve into a full-blown love affair. Their interrogation sessions had been clarifying, strengthening, emphasizing; what had been emphasized was *them.* The sessions had also been accelerative: to have been questioned about each other with that kind of intensity, that kind of gravity (as if their very lives had been on the line: the officers had had guns holstered to their belts), to have been unexpectedly removed from a tourist's existence and then isolated in separate rooms for the sole purpose (it seemed) of being *confronted about each other* . . . it was as if a whole year's worth of caring and worrying, of examining and probing and considering, of struggling and fighting and negotiating — the kind of serious work that gets done between any two people entering into a relationship that is going to matter — had been accomplished in ten minutes. And then to be sent together afterward into that secret sacred space, whose narrow escape from evil and destruction more than half a century earlier had been secured only by its absolute concealment — to stand together under its domed Prussian blue ceiling — was to experience an ineffable feeling of solidarity: with the good, with the lasting, with each other. Daniel felt that it had all amounted to a ceremony of sorts, what with their having gone up before the state (the state of Israel!) and outfaced the questions of its officious ministrants. They might as well have been *married.*

Was Carmen of Arab descent? It did not matter much to him, certainly not as much as it had to the Israeli guards, but he put the question to her anyway, after they had finished with the synagogue and were re-grouping out in the hot afternoon street. "Me?" she replied. "No. Mexican. Spanish. I told the guy who questioned me that it'd been five hundred years since the Moors had left Spain, but that didn't seem to go down very well."

And with this, Carmen set the easy, lifted tone of their talk — Daniel's and hers — which continued unbrokenly, as they started their trek toward the Leopoldstadt, where Max wanted to go, and in the course of which they became themselves again, ap-proximately. Something between them was being adjusted, even settled; they were beginning to tell each other of themselves, which alone seemed to make their words mean things that they did not mean openly. Even Max appeared to pick up on it: what-ever their words meant to each other, they clearly meant something pretty different, and pretty unpleasant, to him. With a new expression of indignation, he kept falling behind them, only so that he could register some sort of inaudible verbal protest as he passed them again — or at least it seemed to Daniel, who was going to ask the old man about it before his attention was drawn away by Carmen's stunning revelation that she had been married until recently — to a highly regarded professor.

What a *relief* to learn that she was divorced. It gave them big-top failure in common. And although she said the words "my ex" as though no resentment were attached to them, a competitive part of him was pleased at the emergent picture she painted of a man who had exacted a heavy price in exchange for the favor of "making her" — of taking a precocious, gifted, apparently barrio-bred girl from Arizona and helping her not only to realize her academic potential (she admitted when Daniel pressed her a little that she had graduated summa cum laude from Princeton, and had been several years into a PhD in history at Columbia before she took a leave of absence), but also to avoid falling into the narrower margins of identity to which well-meaning academics often confined what they liked to call "women of color." If Daniel was seeing the picture correctly, the professor, an overbearing black hole of narcissism with appointments and apartments in New Jersey, Manhattan, and Berlin, had succeeded in taking from her everything except her disposition to be kind.

"Just say it," Daniel chided her as they made their way down the cobbled Fleischmarkt. "The guy was an asshole."

"I'll say this: it takes a lot to fill a small heart."

"That's it?"

"I have a hard time saying bad things about other people."

"You must be hard on yourself, then." When she merely smiled in reply, he kept on: "Sounds like he turned you into his slave."

"I was more his aide-de-camp."

"Not fun."

"It was awful."

"And it was wrong of him. In every way. He took advantage — not only of you being a student but also of your obvious selflessness."

"I'm not *totally* selfless," she said. She was looking straight at him.

"No?"

"A woman learns to be many women. The

458

one he turned me into, I left with him."

It was attractive, the way she said these things. Her eyes had an exceptional shine to them, and though they kept threatening to fill with tears, she still seemed to believe that happiness awaited her. He found it impossible to take her at her word that she was not entirely selfless, especially when she explained that, after abandoning graduate school and the professor — it had happened all at once — she had moved back home to Phoenix in order to support her parents and help out Max, who had employed them for many years after they emigrated from Mexico. Where on the path this woman walked did her ego, her airs, her own interests, find any purchase? It killed him that she had experienced a single setback, and on Rotenturmstrasse he told her as much, eliciting a laugh from her. "It wasn't *completely* bad for me," she replied. "Not in the end. I owe my ex, you know. It's amazing how much you can learn from the smallest of people. I really do feel that I owe him now for what was wanting in him. We all carry around debts like this, I think."

Without making too much of the matter, she changed the subject — when they were halfway across the bridge spanning the Danube Canal — from herself to him,

inquiring about Aleksandra in the unmistakable language of earnestness, and with a
restraint that moved him. She kept her eyes
on him while he spoke, and even when he
let on that he had actually been married
once *before* Aleksandra, they were never
judgmental, but instead full of understanding.

If there was a sour note to be heard in all
of this, it was a silent one, and it sprang
from neither of them. Max was its source.
At the opposite side of the canal, they asked
him if he wanted to stop for a rest, but he
refused hotly — like a child — and it was
with a sore, defeated face that the old man
powered onward. By now Daniel understood that he had again managed to wound
Max, and that Max needed something from
him, or rather something *of* him: all the way
down Taborstrasse the old man kept taking
measure of him, as if he wanted to tilt the
whole of Daniel's being into a gaping want
in his own heart. And every attempt Daniel
or Carmen made to speak to each other
now seemed only to draw his scorn.

"What's *wrong?*" Daniel finally whispered
to Carmen, his eyes glued to Max, who was
advancing before them.

Her answer was vague, and it struck him
that she was being careful. "It started after

460

the synagogue," she said.

At a square called Karmeliterplatz, the old man commanded them to halt in front of a modest empty café that fronted the square. But as Daniel drew closer, he saw that it was not the café before which Max had stopped, but a door to the side with a "2" on it. Max turned and looked up at him with a triumphant anger.

"Recognize *this?*"

Daniel did. And the recognition was rough on him: rough, and disordering. It thrust him from the present into a place where life, and light, and even the speech of reason had no more concern. He was in the freezing, frozen nonspace and nontime of a photograph, and Aleksandra and Benjamin were there with him, bundled in their parkas, pressed against each other. There was the slate-gray wall. There was the massive stone masonry of European origin. He was finally *here.*

For some reason, Max was drawing his attention to the pavement. Daniel could only stare at it from an inhuman distance, as if he were looking through a telescope.

"This morning you asked me, Mr. Lichtmann, if there was a particular man." Max was panting, shaking, and yet he looked somehow exalted as he spoke. "His name

— was *Josef!* Josef *Pick.* He had the gift of making himself hated and loved by the same person. It is why people fell in love with him so easily. If you cared about him at all, you were pulled right into a tragedy. And it was from this spot" — the old man jabbed his finger toward the ground — "that he lifted his dead father, the man whose grave you visited yesterday, into his arms after the man had leaped to his death, and carried him up into that building" — Max pointed at a row of windows above the café — "where you are going to carry me now, Mr. Lichtmann, so that I can show you where the greatest artist of the twentieth century lived."

Buzzers were pushed in the doorway, none of them eliciting answers, until a young bald man came out of the café and asked if he could help them. Max spoke to him in German, gesticulating at a particular window above, and the man, who sported the fashionable rectangular glasses favored by architects the world over, surprised them all by asking Max if he was Jewish. At once, Max's defenses rose, so sure was he that the man meant to traduce him, and he proceeded to unleash a tempest of abuse on the fellow, drawing from the finest obscenities that the German and English tongues had to offer.

Daniel stood there, immobilized. He was still stunned by where he was, and by the confrontation unfolding before him. He was also disconcerted by a vague awareness that Max was redirecting to the fellow in the glasses some of the hurt that Daniel had apparently caused the old man this afternoon.

It was all cleared up soon enough: the fellow turned out to be the owner of both the café and the very apartment that Max wished to see, and he explained that he had recognized Max's unique, anachronistic accent from other elderly Jews who occasionally patronized his business during their return visits to Vienna. Max's display could not have been pleasant for him, and his glasses were slightly askew on his nose, but he clearly felt terrible about having upset the old man, and was at pains to convince all three of them to sit down and order anything from his menu. Max, who was still humid and upset and now making a point of speaking English to the man as if he did not deserve to hear the old dialect of the Viennese Jews, insisted that he only wanted to see the apartment. "It belonged to a part of my family," he added.

"Then you must be related to the man

who came to see it maybe two years ago," the café owner remarked, "with his wife."

Carmen turned to look at Daniel. Daniel found that he could not meet her eyes.

"That was my grandson," Max said tersely. The owner obligingly fetched his keys and unlocked the door, telling them, before he returned to his café, that his apartment was open and to take as long as they needed. Then, as if she sensed the enormity of the moment for both Daniel and Max, Carmen managed to somehow remove herself from it, while continuing to help them. This extreme courtesy would be fully appreciated by Daniel only later, when the moment and the demands it placed on his attention had passed. He hardly noticed that she was the one who held the door open while he carefully scooped Max into his arms and carried him into the building, and his awareness of her after that was routed by other more pressing awarenesses that came over him as he entered the narrow darkened hall: there, he was revisited by all the heaviness — of heart — that he had experienced the day before when gazing up at the apartment windows of the Leopoldstadt. The heaviness had regathered into something more powerful now that he was actually on the inside of one of the buildings — more

powerful, and more personal. He was burdened with the knowledge that Aleksandra
and Benjamin had breathed this hall's same
musty air. Burdened too with an ailing old
man in his arms, and with that man's
imperiled memory of the people he had
known who had once lived here. Max was
weeping unrestrainedly as they mounted the
stairs, sending forth echoing laments into
dank shadows that turned their ascent into
a solemn procession. Yet except for the
name "Josef" that was repeatedly invoked,
the words hardly reached Daniel. He was
aware only of the sound of the old man's
sorrow, which merged with the creaking of
the wooden steps until the entire stairwell
seemed to exhort Daniel to accept his
proper place in the history of things, seemed
to tell him that he had been born so that
one day, following the footsteps of his
deceased wife, he would carry this man up
these stairs. Suddenly, the story Max had
told below of Josef Pick carrying his dead
father up the very same stairs sent a chill
through him. It was as if the past, so utterly
unconjecturable most of the time, were
reclaiming the present, fortifying itself by
these mysterious repetitions. Daniel did not
want to believe it. He feared it would mean
Max was going to perish very soon —

perhaps even on this day. He told himself, as he approached the dark landing, that Aleksandra had led him here by accident. He told himself that Max had not come to Vienna to die.

The apartment, even by Daniel's New York standards, was shockingly small and sparsely furnished. In the center of the wood floor lay a futonlike bed that took the back side of a low modernist dresser as its headboard. There were a desk and chair before the window, a stove and old enamel sink in the far corner. An iPod sat in its dock atop a vertical upmarket speaker, and, except for two wall-mounted halogen lamps and a flat-screen television, that was it. Daniel set Max gently onto the bed (there was no other choice: the bony Bauhaus desk chair was *not* an option) and sat beside him while the old man drank the room in with his eyes, saying nothing. Carmen was there, but she remained a silent and invisible presence.

"You have had many problems, Mr. Lichtmann," Max finally said in a voice from which all of his earlier emotionalism had fled, "but at least yours have *changed.* I have lived with the same problem for sixty years — and it began here in this room. Everything looks almost exactly as it did then.

And it kills me all over again."

Daniel turned and looked at him. "What happened here, Max?"

To this, the old man, refusing to meet Daniel's inquiring gaze, had a remarkable reply. "What happened here is what is happening to me again with you and Carmen."

If such a thing as a missed heartbeat really existed, Daniel experienced one then. "Nothing is happening between Carmen and me," he said. It was a lie, and it was risky, because he knew that Carmen was somewhere behind them.

"Do not!" Max said, nearly shouting. "Just please do not! Enough. I know what it is to be a bystander to love that is blooming. Do not take me for an idiot, Mr. Lichtmann. And you must understand that I do not blame you. After all, I am the one who introduced you to Carmen, just as I introduced Josef Pick to the woman who married him, the woman who took his heart right here, where this bed is! *Everything* comes back to me as I sit here today. Do you realize this is where Herman was conceived?"

"Herman . . . he's —"

"He was born Herman Johannes Pick."

"But why did you say he was *your* son?"

"Because he *became* my son — after the

467

war ended."

"Josef Pick," Daniel said automatically. "He didn't survive the Holocaust?"

"Do you think *that* is what we were calling it at Riga? Do you think, when we managed to survive that lovely place, only to be put on a train for Birkenau, we turned to each other and said: 'How unfortunate that we are caught in the Holocaust.' There was no name for it then, Mr. Lichtmann. It was these persons being marched into a room, this warm flesh being pulled out."

"You were *there* with him? You saw him die?"

"Do you not understand? I am still alive. So no matter how I try to describe what happened to Josef, it will be changed by the gratitude we all secretly have — you, Carmen, even myself — for being allowed to breathe this air today after such things have occurred in the world. This secret relief that no one talks about — it turns what happened there into the long ago, even into something beautiful, and it was not beautiful. This is why I hate these historians, anybody who writes about such things — they are all masturbating to their beautiful images of horror! What an abandonment of the dead! — who have no defense against such persons. I know *nothing* about the dead."

"What about Josef's *wife?*" Daniel said, trying to see the whole picture. "The woman you introduced to him? Herman's mother — did she survive the war?"

Max nodded. "She came to America with me. We raised Herman together."

"You — did you *marry* her?"

The old man turned and met his gaze miserably. "On paper. Yes."

"So . . . is she still alive?"

Max held perfectly still.

"She is dead."

Daniel thought a moment. "And Benjamin? Did he know all this?"

"I told him everything!" Max said defensively. "I told him all about his real grandfather. I told him to come here, to this apartment, to see where his grandfather painted all those beautiful marriage contracts!"

"Marriage contracts? What, ketubahs?"

"Ketub*ot!* The finest that had ever been made."

Now Daniel's interest was even more piqued. A connection was being forged in the back of his mind, where he kept picturing those last sculptures Benjamin had made, the flung figures, the entwined fingers. . . . "What did they look like, Max?" he asked abruptly.

"Like nothing you have ever seen, trust me."

"Well, did *Benjamin* see them?"

"*No one* has seen them."

"Why not? What if Benjamin found one? What if that was what led to his final show?"

"What led to his last show, Mr. Lichtmann, is something that I told him."

The declaration arrested Daniel's thoughts — his pulse too. He fixed his eyes on the old man, who was staring back at him defiantly. "What did you tell him?"

"What I have never told anyone. I told him what his grandfather did at Birkenau. I told him of the extraordinary thing Josef Pick did that led to his execution."

It was obviously too much for Max to fathom again, let alone speak about, whatever it was that Josef Pick had done all those years ago. With the help of the café owner, Daniel found a service willing to pick up the three of them plus the wheelchair, and during their cab ride home Max began to feel unwell, as if the very act of summoning the memory had depleted him of that last invisible barrier by which his ancient body had remained defended. To watch him shiver and curl away into himself against the seat was to watch an aged wild animal choose a patch of earth on which to become quarry to chaos, the decaying forces that always lay waiting to filch a life. Daniel suggested they find a hospital, but as they whipped onto the fast-moving Währinger Gürtel, Max surprised them by throwing his door open and threatening to leap from the cab if they did not take him back to the apartment on Wattmanngasse. Carmen, who was riding in the rear seat with the old man, finally convinced him to pull the door shut, but only after plying him with assurances that there would be no hospital, and that they would do everything in their power not to let him die in Vienna. And even then, Max, his cheek pressed weakly against the window, felt compelled to say: "You cannot allow it! This is the last thing that I ask of the two of you. Sixty years ago this city wanted me dead. I–*will*–not give it the satisfaction!"

Once they were in the apartment, and Max was safely in the bedroom, both Daniel and Carmen got on the phone to their respective airlines to see about early return flights to America. As it turned out, no seats were available the next day — in either of their cases — but each of them managed to book a flight leaving the morning after that. Max would have to survive one more full day in Vienna.

Only as Carmen was freshening up in the bathroom — she was about to head back out to get dinner for all of them — did Daniel, who had settled with a book in the living room to be within earshot of Max, admit to himself how grateful he was (Max's fast-deteriorating health notwithstanding) to be given another day in this woman's presence. In less than twelve hours it — her presence — had changed everything. It had filled everything . . . his vision, his mind, the surrounding air — even when, back in the Leopoldstadt, he had been swept up in the moment. And it had revealed what a solitude his life had become after That Day: sure, there were his mother and his friends, the colleagues at work; there were people on every side of his life, but there had only been one person *in* it, and she was no longer living. Yet with Carmen a reconfiguration had occurred, one that promised to attenuate his secluded state. Or this was what he felt anyway as he listened to her getting ready. The plash of water in the sink, the sibilance of a brush being pulled through hair — recognizable sounds in themselves, but thrilling and alive in his fresh connection to them. They took the dust off a disused feeling. To hear them now felt like a completely new way of needing someone.

Her awareness of *his* presence, at least now as he sat in the living room, was evident by the haste with which she suddenly burst from the bathroom and tried to leave the apartment — by the way she awkwardly avoided his eyes and restated that she was going out to get dinner. He rose to his feet and tried to intervene, he tried to slow things down by offering to buy the food himself, but she refused from outside in the hall, and suddenly the front door was closed.

She was still out when Max's cry came from the bedroom. Daniel found the old man sitting up in bed with no glasses on, staring at the reality of the room as if at a nightmare.

"It was my fault, Mr. Lichtmann! *My* fault!"

"What was, Max?" Daniel asked, sitting down on the edge of the bed.

The old man pushed his glasses onto his nose and for five seconds peered glumly into the sheets covering his legs. Then he leveled his head and looked straight at Daniel. "Josef's death."

Daniel was about to ask him about it, but Carmen came into the apartment with dinner in two bags, and the old man made it clear that their conversation had come to an end.

There must have been some mutually felt measure of guilt that drove both Daniel and Carmen to insist on eating dinner — a panoply of Austrian starches and meats — in the bedroom with Max, and as long as the old man was awake they went out of their way not to be alone together for more than an instant. Max, for his part, for all his weakness, tried to *stay* awake as long as he could, reminding Daniel of a little boy determined not to miss out on the perceived pleasures of adult doings.

Adult doings increasingly came to occupy Daniel's mind as the evening progressed, particularly while he sat there in the darkened bedroom, holding, at Max's request, the old man's impossibly thinned hand as he struggled to sink into sleep, thinking all the while that Carmen was somewhere out there in the apartment . . . the couch? the bath? Daniel's bed?

She was in the living room, and with wine, when he finally emerged. It was a great sight, the best he had seen in, well, a very long time. As he sat down beside her on the couch she poured him a glass and asked about Max — was he finally asleep? how

was his temperature? did he seem okay? —
and Daniel was sure, with these questions
answered and out of the way, that they
would at last really begin to talk. But before
he could exert any influence on the conversation, she brought up subjects that were
very careful, and carefully chosen, it seemed
to him, to avoid paths that might head
toward *them*. It made him nervous and self-
conscious, and soon he was locked in a
frustrating partnership with her, striving to
keep their topical talk from dying, doing his
best to steer it safely around the only thing
he wanted to discuss. As for topics, Max
was the plain choice, an easy one that
seemed to hang there on the wall opposite
them like a serviceable piece of art to gaze
at while they fingered their wineglasses, so
that they would not have to gaze at each
other.

Not that Daniel found any of her thoughts
about the old man uninteresting. Her theory
about why he was having such a difficult
time in Vienna, for instance, informed by
both her intimate knowledge of Max's life
and her learnedness in the field of history,
captured his attention. A complicated picture of exile began to emerge as she spoke,
a rich and dramatic portrait of a man whose
Zionism had sprouted in his youth exclu-

sively from European soil — a man who, if he had been granted an Israeli visa after the war, may very well have been cured of his Zionist nostalgia by the realities of that country, but instead was given a visa to America, where, suffering the exile's disease of loneliness and displacement, he went to extremes to preserve an idea — a *Jewish* idea — of where he had come from, only to return here at the end of his life and watch his memory of the place be pauperized by reality. His misfortune, Carmen explained, was to find Vienna just as he had left it — but stripped of the deeper significances, the layers of associations that sixty years of reflection had added to it.

But it was the *extremes* the man had gone to — and the way they had merged with a changing America — that lit up Daniel's imagination, and as Carmen spoke about them he was reminded of certain things Herman had told him about Max, the way he had held on to every object, for example, as if trying to arrest time. Nearly a fourth of one of the old man's storage facilities, Carmen said, was dedicated to preserving objects and memorabilia that reminded him of his Jewish, and moreover his Zionist, youth in Vienna — room after room, locker after locker, filled with furniture, art, relics, photographs, even tools and clothes. According to Carmen, Max's enormous storage empire had its roots not only in his early Zionist longings to preserve Jewish identity but also in the old man's survival of the camps, where, for a price, he had organized secret places to store prisoners' valuables, to the point where he had even come to be called "Herr Storage." Yet its success, said Carmen, its fantastic, unforeseeable success, had everything to do with timing: Max, who out of the ruins of his prewar existence was already assembling his "repository of sadness," as Carmen called it, got the idea to start his own storage company when he grew tired of paying so much for a tiny locker in New York City, where he lived immediately following the war — but it was not until well after he had relocated his family and business to the West Coast, in the late sixties, when the age of divorce began in earnest, the age of self-fulfillment and lifestyle and getting what you wanted, that he saw the true potential of self-storage. "Getting what you wanted meant movement," Carmen said, lifting her wineglass to her lips but not drinking yet, "movement from the house you'd been living in to some new place, an apartment, a commune, a geodesic dome. What were people to do with all their things? People were free, but they still weren't free of their stuff — and their stuff was *them.* Storage allowed them to remain free while keeping their sense of selves, their *histories.* And no one understood this need better than Max, because he'd lost *all* of his stuff — the Nazis had taken it away from him and his family. So here he was, using storage to maintain a piece of his old world, while building facilities to allow Americans to hold on to a piece of their brutal and transitory *new* world. The Old World and the New World, all contained right there in storage." Carmen took a sip from her glass and set it down. "And the land was cheap," she added as if afraid to stop talking. "It was everywhere on the outskirts of towns and cities. The most inexpensive parcels by far were along freeways. So Max bought. He bought parcels so fast it took him years to fill them with storage places."

There was a natural break in her story, but the silence that expanded to fill the room then was anything but natural. Why were their silences so awkward? Daniel stared at the floor as if the answer might lie there. When his eyes sought hers, he was surprised to find that she was looking at him — with that deep, quieting gaze of hers.

Then she said, "He's in love with you, you know."

It was Max she was referring to, but Daniel hoped that she was sublimating, really expressing how *she* felt about him. "It's not *his* romantic interest in me that I care about," he said.

She took up her glass and almost imperceptibly turned her back toward him as she drank.

He could hardly breathe, watching her. "I hope I haven't offended you," he said.

"I don't know yet," she stammered. "Conversations usually upset me days later."

"Well, then, I'm safe," he insisted, trying to make light of it. "I won't be around days later."

She was still a little angled away from him. "I feel like I'm confusing what you came here for," she said.

"What I came here for — I can't measure anymore, or even understand," was his reply, but he was unhappy with how pat it sounded, so he went with the simple and the concrete: "The truth is, I came here because Max invited me to come."

This brought her around to face him. "It was *my* idea that Max invite you."

She set her glass down and rose to her feet then, placing the full force of her shapely figure before him, only to take it away toward her and Max's room, very slowly, so that Daniel could assimilate the severity of her abandonment as it was happening, his eyes absorbing all the meanings that a departing body could bear.

When she was gone, he went to his own room, where, by turns exultant and filled with doubt, he lay on his bed running through every word she had said, every expression of her face, every posture and attitude that her figure had struck during the day. Sure enough, for his body and his thoughts alike, it turned into a night of twisting and untwisting. He hardly slept an hour.

Max seemed no stronger the next morning, and Daniel feared that his condition was as bound to his recent confession as it was to any organ. His moans and complaints were, for the most part, pointed not at his own ailments but at his failures, and, as in that dank stairwell the previous afternoon, they frequently narrowed to simple sighs of "Josef!" It was clear enough to Daniel that he was a man who was finally doing the work of blaming himself, sifting through whatever he had done to cause the death of his closest friend — with all the severity of someone who, to judge by the evidence, had put great effort into checking memory and then sealing it, someone who had apparently spent a lifetime directing blame elsewhere (at Herman Wind, at Vienna and the Nazis, at time itself). Throughout the morning and into the afternoon, Daniel and Carmen strove to help him, but the job he was trying to finish required solo work; it would suffer no assistance if it was to be done correctly — and it needed to be done correctly if it was to be done at all, if it was, finally, to be *done.* Sometime in the late afternoon he ordered them both to leave the apartment. If this was not symbolic of an essential change in the old man's psyche, then nothing was.

They very reluctantly did as commanded, leaving Max alone, strolling out under the warm, wide-skied expanse of the Schönbrunn's imperial gardens. Their worry about Max dominated their talk, but the shame they seemed to share in taking this unexpected opportunity to be exclusively in each other's company did not prevent them from pausing by the neatly ordered rows of pollarded trees, by a fountain dedicated to Neptune, by a Baroque greenhouse filled with palms. Eventually they discovered, perched on a hill, an ornate temple called the Gloriette, where they turned to look back over all of Vienna.

"I've fallen for you," Daniel said.

"I know."

"It's not what you'd bargained for." He felt compelled to tell her this, unable suddenly to banish the thought that she had only come with Max to help him see his old town, and here she was, stuck with a widower. "I know I shouldn't expect anything of you."

"Don't," she said, nearly inaudibly, and he was forced to steal several glances at her just to get a reading on her meaning.

Her forehead was bunched in supplication as she stared out beyond the palace at the steepled horizon, but it was her pallor, and her delicate temples so marbled with fine blue veins, that hit him like a presentiment. He saw a faded majesty in them — he saw her as an old woman — and as he tried unsuccessfully to refocus on the view he realized that he was going to remain with this person to the end. "Don't what?"

"Don't try to say anything about how I feel or what I expect."

"I'm sorry."

"You have no idea."

He saw that her lips were trembling. "No, I guess I don't."

"I thought I was in love with Benjamin," she said without looking at him.

He just stared at her. The earth's gravity had suddenly seemed to double its pull.

But then it halved itself, or almost, when she added: "This was before I'd ever met him."

"Then how?" he asked, unable to form the rest of a question about how yet another woman in his life had come to love Benjamin Wind.

"How did I fall for him? Well, that's the thing, Daniel. Brace yourself. It was from all the reviews of his work that I'd read aloud to Max."

Daniel involuntarily blew air out between his lips. "*My* reviews?"

"Just listen to me until I'm finished. I met Benjamin — when I went with Max to meet him for the first time. He courted me very heavily while we were still staying there in New York."

"Great!" Daniel said impulsively. He could not help himself. It was too much.

"Please," she said to him. "It was awkward. He was a mess from what Max had revealed to him. And I had Max to handle — he was in no great shape either."

Daniel was incredulous. "Did you go *out* with Benjamin?"

483

Her immediate answer to this was a silent look of understanding that only made him angrier. She took his cold hand in her hot one and squeezed it. "I saw him a couple times," she finally admitted.

He drew his hand away from hers.

The maneuver quickened her talk, injected it with passion and pleading. "He was an impressive man — you know that. I wasn't dating anyone at the time. But I quickly realized it wasn't *him* I'd fallen in love with — it was the words that'd been written about him." She had taken his hand again. "I was *seeing you,* Daniel. Each new review that came in . . . without even being aware of it, I was getting to know someone who was more impressive to me than Benjamin Wind, and when I finally laid eyes on you that first time at the service I thought, 'There goes the loneliest, most sensitive and beautiful man I have ever seen.' "

Daniel was listening. But he found that he had to look away from her, as though her words had generated their own physical force, a gust of air that pushed against the side of his face.

"And then what you said to Max at the end when we were in that church rec room — the way you consoled him by praising Benjamin so generously. That couldn't have been easy for you. It broke my heart how loving and forgiving you were."

"Why didn't you say anything to me?" he asked.

"Were you in any kind of condition to deal with some strange woman approaching you in that church and saying, 'Excuse me, you're going to think I'm crazy, and I know we've just met and that your wife just died, but guess what? I read your work and I'm totally in love with you.' I knew what'd happened to you, Daniel. I saw what you were still doing to yourself. I was very careful around you that day. It's why I was so careful with you *this* time."

He turned to her then. "But you're not being careful anymore?"

She seemed to really think about it. "No."

They might have embraced then, they might have even kissed, but the moment passed, or Daniel *made* it pass out of a sudden fear that stepped between him and his discovery that he was — cared for. "Maybe you *should* be careful," he plunged on, knowing, as they left his lips, that these words would not serve him, they would not serve love.

"Why?" she asked, looking firmly at him.

"Because I've disappointed the women who've loved me the most."

He had used the plural — wom*en* — but he was thinking only of his second wife, of Aleksandra. And amazingly Carmen seemed to see right into him. "I'm going to tell you something, Daniel. It might be hard for you, but you need to hear it. I can understand why a photographer like your wife would have fallen for Benjamin."

Daniel could feel his eyes interrogating her with a minatory intensity. But she continued: "For the very reason Benjamin was all wrong for me, he was probably all *right* for her. There was no fizz between us. I'm not a woman who detaches herself from life. I don't look at it from a distance like I'm not part of it. It's not a carnival to me, and not a nightmare either. I respect your wife's work — I think the world *should* see pictures of people on both sides who survive violence in the Holy Land, just as it should see art like Benjamin's that somehow makes us feel what it's like to soar above suffering. But there's no restless need in me to capture the dangerous shadows of life. He needed to be with another artist. And maybe your wife did too. I don't question that you disappointed her. But it wasn't all about you, Daniel. It never is. So give me a *good* reason why I should be careful around you."

Her look was so suddenly stern that he

486

felt he had to provide a reason just in order to mollify her and to defend the validity, however irrational and unfounded, of his original statement. "Because I've behaved badly even *here,*" he shot back. "That ghost I ran from? She was a prostitute."

Carefully, he watched the play of thought in her face. There was due interest in what he had confessed to her, but, incredibly, no alarm. It was more a process of deciding and then dismissing. "Did you sleep with her?"

"I couldn't."

"Then what are we talking about?"

She was winning. And he was starting to understand that he needed this from her. He *wanted* her to win. Whatever it was that was doing the fighting for him had to be put down, put to rest for good. But it seemed determined to make one last stand, if his answer to her question was any indication: "We're talking about how impossible a person I am to love."

Her two almond eyes reached out to him then, not with condescension, but with real pity. "Then good. I'm a veteran at loving impossible things."

From a Sicilian Café not far from the apartment, they brought Max pizza: Margherita,

487

his favorite. He nibbled at a slice, then wanted to be left alone again to rest. He was still doing the work.

They turned on a light in the living room and finished the entire pie, breaking out the remaining bottles of beer. What awaited them at the end of their dinner was a decision. They both knew it, and their delay from minute to minute — every new subject raised up for discussion — was a kind of uncomfortable ceremony in which they each felt compelled to participate, a big, fat confession that neither of them knew what they were going to do.

"Well," she finally said. "It's late. I guess I'm going to pack."

So this was how they were going to avert a decision.

"Good idea," he said.

They smiled at each other sadly, and for an instant another opportunity seemed to present itself to them, but they did not grasp it — they did not grasp each other — and then they each stood up and went to their separate rooms. Daniel hit the light and stared angrily down at his suitcase for a good five minutes. It was ridiculous to have the kind of afternoon they had had and then part in such a manner. He was just finishing this thought when Carmen came into the room and closed the door behind her. She would not meet his eye while she performed a little tour of the room, taking in its dishevelment in a way that made him ashamed. She had smoked a cigarette since they had parted in the living room; it was on her breath. And suddenly her breath was on him, and in him, as were her lips, her tongue, her teeth. Then he and she were pressed against each other in the hard light, two new believers squeezing through a tight temple door, until everything broke up, violently gave way, a switch was hit, and together they were spewed into the darkness where they recklessly gave and received.

At dawn they dove into the abyss of packing. Her flight was an early one, and Daniel, who did not have to leave for another few hours, helped her prepare Max as far as the old man could be prepared for the assault of travel that yawned before them. Repeatedly Daniel's eyes met and held hers, and a hundred words must have died on their lips — none were spoken. He was the one who called for the cab. It had to have been the most flameless request he had ever made.

Much too quickly, the three of them were out on the sidewalk, stiffening themselves for what was about to come. The cab having arrived, Daniel lifted Max up out of his wheelchair, embraced him, suspended him, kissed both his cold, wet cheeks, and put him into the backseat. There seemed little else for them to say but the one thing they each did not want to say for fear it would be the last, so Daniel did not tell him good-bye, but he did tell him that he loved him.

When he turned back to the sidewalk Carmen was standing there, laden with bags, in a green dress she had thrown on with careless grace. He went and picked up the suitcase at her feet, and straightened before her.

"What now?" he asked.

"We're separating. Now we'll discover what connects us." And she kissed him, biting a corner of his lower lip as she pulled away.

That bite, her valedictory gesture, accompanied his thoughts as he left Vienna himself, a task that proved more taxing than he had anticipated. There he was, several hours later, riding a bus through the gray city toward the airport and suffering hard from subtraction. What went hardest with him was not so much Carmen's absence — she was an addition. It was his ghosts. He looked for them on street corners, in the wide boulevards, through the windows of passing cafés. And when he could not conjure them — when he could not conjure Aleksandra — he finally understood: with that bite, life was letting him know. It was finally divesting him of the dead.

Yet there are certain places that lag behind life, they acknowledge a different schedule, as Daniel was to learn. Arriving home in New York, he found waiting for him a letter that had been written two months earlier by Clifford Fatheree — from Rikers Island prison. It turned out that the man Benjamin Wind had mysteriously thanked in the catalog of his final show was an inmate serving his second sentence there in as many years. His single-page letter, a response to the note and the review clipping Daniel had sent to Fatheree's publicly listed address, had only come to Daniel now via the inmate's wife, who had mailed it from the Bronx. And it was a zinger. It kindled the old questions. It reanimated the dead.

The salutation and date were typed, but the body of the letter, soiled with solecisms and misspellings and erasures, was written out with a blunt graphite tip in a halting and uneven hand. All of it, save for its last two sentences, was consumed by Fatheree's circular explanation of how his wife had

491

taken "her sweet time" bringing him Daniel's letter on one of her apparently infrequent visits, and how he had read Daniel's review of Benjamin Wind's show not just once, but many times over. The note seemed to bear out this last claim — in its only error-free sentence, it even quoted the question posed by the review: "How did this offering, possibly the best showing of art by a living artist this reviewer has ever seen, come to be?" But the letter took a dramatic turn with its penultimate line, which suggested that Clifford Fatheree knew exactly (perhaps even had intimate, insider knowledge of) how Benjamin's show had come to be. The last line seemed to confirm that improbability. It also caused a chemical event in Daniel's gut, something roily and electrical and cell splitting, with its present-tense evocation of Benjamin and its uncanny echoing of some of the first words Max had ever spoken to Daniel. It said:

I know Mister Wind so well every thing you rote about that mans art is wrong just dead wrong.

THE ATHEIST OF LOVE

He has never been told that he was dropped from a moving train. When he asks about the war, he invariably hears the story of his mother's rescue: how, after she had been forced to march across half of frozen Germany by prison guards in retreat from the advancing Russian army, an American soldier suddenly pulled alongside her in a jeep and asked, "You want a lift?" She was so diminished of body and mind that she had not noticed the Germans' abrupt absence, nor had she spoken English since gymnasium. Looking up, she said to the soldier: "Yes. Please. I would like to be lifted."

It is supposed to be a comforting, even humorous, family anecdote — a joke on his mother's Englishing of a German verb conjugation — but it always leaves him dissatisfied, and with the feeling that he is being engaged by his parents in an enterprise, the enterprise of not telling him things.

And his intense young intelligence is right.

The ten-year-old boy has never been told *many* things about the war, including its most important fact: that it robbed him, Herman Johannes Wiener, of his real father, and that it robbed both of his parents — his mother and Max — of the man they loved.

And how can they possibly tell him now, his parents, when for five tendentious years they have been steadfast servants of agreements, the stated and the unstated, that were struck between them immediately after the war? How can they tell him anything when they have not even told *each other* what compelled them to seek out such consequential, such devastating agreements in the first place? How can they ask Herman to understand that he has been living inside an invisible hole left by a father he has no idea existed, when they cannot even ask themselves what led them to believe they could cram a child unhurt into such a secret?

What compelled Max to look for Hannah, following his liberation from Birkenau, was an overtopping desire to say three words to her. For fifteen months and eight days, they — the three words — had been as present to him, had been as vivid a part of the camp climate, as the lank limbs of his fellow inmates (the standing and the prone), or as the skies that sometimes teemed inconceivably with birds above the barracks. They were also as difficult to integrate into his understanding of life's fairness. The first word was "Josef" and the third was "dead." To contemplate the second word in any combination with the first or the third was, even after the reinvigorations of being liberated, too taxing for him — it had been potentially *life ending* in the camp, where, in order to conserve energy, his mind had borne down on a reduced, virulently literal version of reality. How, went Max's pruned and punctilious thinking, could "Josef" be used with "is" when Josef *wasn't?* How could "is" be used with "dead" if being dead meant you could not *be?* In this way was Max's a fractured brain, indeed was Max a fractured man. But he preferred it this way. The opposite only caused him to bristle with soul-scattering anguish. Whenever, on waking in the barrack, or later in some transit camp run by the Red Cross or American army, he was for a few seconds whole again, the three words in their malevolently logical sequence never failed to possess his ear, really all his being, and he was prone to weeping tears his parched body could hardly afford to lose.

So he quietly carried his three words all over the fallen German empire, hearing them everywhere, delivering them nowhere, like some ignored herald bearing the news that the king was dead to an unworthy world that did not even know it had had such a king. And what Josef had done back in Birkenau did seem, in retrospect, in death, to make him into some sort of lord, his subsequent execution into a kind of crucifixion. But Max could no more withstand contemplating his friend's last worldly deed than he could say aloud the three words that represented the deed's consequence, and despite being the only living witness, he was *not* an apostle: he would never share with the world what Josef had done, and in particular he would never reveal it to Hannah, because, even though fate had allowed him and not her to enjoy the concluding and perhaps most important and profound days of Josef's life, he still hoarded bitterness toward her for taking Josef from him, and he knew that, no matter how he spun it, any account of Josef's deed would give her the final satisfaction. And he could never grant her that. This piece of Josef was still too painful for him to

think about — and might always be so —
but it was *his* to hide, his to have, his to
hold . . . to the end of his days.

There was thus nothing altruistic about
his search for Hannah, which he privately
conducted while working for a Jewish relief
agency that ministered to displaced persons
camps scattered all across the American-
occupied zone of Germany. Nothing noble
motivated him to make the difficult journey
— by train, truck, and tread — all the way
back to Vienna and, when she was not there,
to travel the length of Austria and Germany,
scouring each message board, each camp he
came to, for any sign of her. He went to
such effort not because he felt she deserved
to know the fate of her husband, but because *he needed* her to know the fate of her
husband. Because he understood that if she
was still alive, she was carrying around an
unexploded bomb in every part of her body
and being, and that the three words he had
to say to her would set it off. He persisted
in looking for her because he wanted someone else to hurt for Josef as much as he did.
Mutual pain was his lodestar.

But what he had not anticipated was that
when he found her — and find her he did,
in June, ill and billeted in a DP camp
hospital in Bamberg — she would actually

be *relieved* by his three words, relieved to finally know what she had suspected for an eternity of days. "He's died to me so many times since the last time I heard from him," she whispered from her bed (it was all the volume she could muster), "and I've died to *myself* so many times because of it. Now we both can stop dying." Nor had he foreseen that, against his protests that his job required him to leave, she would beg him to stay with her: "But you're the one who introduced me to him — you're the one who told me he's no longer living. You *have* to remain with me now, Max."

He did remain with her in Bamberg for several days, during which she repeatedly expressed her belief that he would leave her, never to return, and her words acted as some kind of spell on him: he found that he could not leave as long as she kept saying he would. Then one afternoon she revealed to him that she had thrown Herman from a train — it took her nearly an hour, it took all her strength, to finally get it out — and that she wanted him to go looking for her son, who she hoped might still be alive somewhere, perhaps in the Polish country-side to which she had abandoned him. Max doubted that the boy still lived, but he was grateful for any pretext to get away from this woman, and he went through the motions of asking her for Herman's birth certificate or any photos, knowing full well that she had no proof even of her son's existence. Feverishly she composed a letter for him to take with him, a plea, intended for anyone who might know of her son's whereabouts, to help restore her son to his rightful mother; the note contained Herman's biographical details, a brief account of when and why (and vaguely where) he had been released from a train, and a description of the birthmark behind his left knee. Sure enough, when Max went to say good-bye, she looked up from the bed with those intense dark eyes of hers and, before curling away from him, said: "You're not going to come back. What would compel you to do so?"

He did not believe anything would compel him to do so. The letter she had given him was folded and forgotten in his trouser pocket. As if it were the only way he could put distance between himself and her, he quit his job for the relief agency and applied at once for a visa to Palestine. No decision was expected until August at the earliest. For a week he wandered the devastated Baltic cities to the north, but the waiting went rough on him, the damp summer days seemed to stretch out interminably, and by each twilight, when he returned to some blighted DP camp where he inevitably ended up, his emotions were often disordered, as if time itself were testing them. His nights, though enlivened by the talk that swathed the temporary camps in tales of survival and woe, were passed in increasing isolation and self-counsel. What began to crystallize in his mind was that Palestine had been his dream when Josef was still in the world. Palestine *was* Josef. Palestine was out. Word had spread that the Austrian government was welcoming back its Jews, who would be rehabilitated without discrimination if they would help to rebuild the country. But just being in Vienna for a day and a half during his search for Hannah had been all he could bear of the place, and it decided him now against going back. At an immigration office in Hannover he at last put in for a visa to the United States (where he had a cousin who could vouch for him), but a feeling of homelessness — it ran deep, it sank down to the soul level — followed him out of the building, and he left Hannover half an hour later, catching rides on any vehicle that was headed east, though it was not until several days afterward, as he crossed into the northern tip of Soviet-occupied Bohemia in the back of a farmer's truck and pulled out for the first time the letter Hannah had composed, that he realized he was on a path toward Josef's son.

Poland, wherefrom he had fled only a few months earlier after liberation, did not exactly welcome him back. Everywhere, he met resistance, he met anger — he nearly met his death at the hands of an abstracted landowner who harbored misbegotten ideas about the Jews, who he claimed (as he pointed a hunting rifle directly at Max's forehead) were primarily to blame for allowing the thieving, raping Russians into his homeland, where they had "spread like the damp." Yet Max did encounter kindness that amazed him: Poles here and there who, at the bidding of their moral consciences or their visions of a child without its true parent or simply their curiosity at Hannah's letter (which he kept producing), were assiduous in helping him track down leads. And there were more than a few leads, just as there were apparently more than a few Jewish children who had been cast out into the countryside: Herman had not been the only Jewish star to fall from the heavens and land on Polish soil during the war. Because neither of them clearly was the child he was looking for, Max had to turn away from two who were still there, living with families who had discovered them — an inalterably sad moment, both times.

And then he came upon the lead that took him one afternoon to a drowsy railway halt not far from the Czech border called Trzebieszowice, where he dismounted a train and made his way to a matted hut of a house that lay just north of the tracks at the far end of the hamlet. A boy who had been found abandoned nearby during the war, and who matched Herman's general features and age (Herman would now be five and a half), was said to live in the tiny place with a peasant couple who had rescued him. Max's knock was answered by a wiry, lint-haired lady who took one glance at him and seemed to know at once why he was here. She nevertheless asked him what she could do for him, first in Polish, then in Czech, and then, when it was obvious that he could understand neither, in a coarse and unconfident German. Perhaps she was simply trying to delay the inevitable, and there *was* an awkward bit of ceremony in her question, though none of the formal kind that so naturally attended the German language, and it certainly was not the usual attempt to discountenance a Jew by implying that he had no business addressing a Gentile.

He told her he was looking for a boy, and it gave him gooseflesh to say the words, because he had the feeling, for the first time since he had reentered Poland, that Herman was alive, that he was here.

He was still standing at the door when he gave the woman Hannah's letter. For several long minutes she stared down at it, her expression a mixture of fear and irritation, until she handed it back with some embarrassment and asked him to tell her what it said. He read it aloud, and, through several of its details, including Herman's date of birth, and his light brown hair and eyes, she maintained a kind of sangfroid. But when he came to the part about the night Hannah had released the boy from the train, and when he named the specific date, several painful involutions of thought passed through the woman's face. When he read off Hannah's precise description of the rectangular birthmark on the back of Herman's left knee, her lined and ruddy cheeks were glistening with tears. She invited Max inside then, and the boy in question (if there was any question remaining) was promptly produced. Max recognized him at once and spoke to him in German, telling him, for practical reasons, that he was his father. There was a vehemence about the boy's eyes, which held steadily on Max, and Max wondered if the child could possibly have remembered what his real father had looked like. He decided to inform him of his true first name (the peasant woman called him Mały, or "Little One"), and suddenly Herman's face became enlivened. At this point, and not without displaying her painfully conflicted feelings, the woman urged Max to take the boy away as soon as possible — before her husband came home from the fields and stopped him. She warned him not to wait for a train, because the station was the first place her husband would go looking for them, and he might do something terrible. Max wanted to ask her if her husband would not hurt *her* when he discovered that she had allowed the boy to be taken away, but he decided against it due to the exigency of the moment. The boy was extremely reluctant to go with him. Surely he would not have relented had he known the truth of who Max was — or rather who he was not. But after an excruciating farewell that nearly caused Max to change his mind about the whole thing, Herman's Polish mother committed him to Max's care — forever, as her agonized face made clear. And this was how Max came that afternoon to complicate Herman's young life, and to take him from the poor woman and her absent farmer-husband, whom the boy had loved as his own parents without complication. Max, heeding the woman's warning, his arm curled around Herman's shuddering shoulders, avoided the station and hastily left that low, peaty land the same way he had entered it: dwindling through the fragrant decay of summer fields in the back of a truck burdened with hay and a little extra human hurt.

The boy's restoration to his mother went hardest on Hannah. It was more than merely his aloofness. It was more than the difficulty she encountered in persuading him to consider her his true mother (a task complicated by the boy's poor command of German: he wielded what little he had managed to pick up in that remote outpost on the fringes of the former Austro-Hungarian Empire with the same flouncing Slavonic-inflected dialect that his Polish mother had used). It was, as Hannah privately conveyed to Max one night when the boy was asleep, that all this time she had imagined, as a mother naturally does when separated from her child, that he was more spiritually bound to her, and also more well behaved, more happy, more pleasant — even, she had to admit it, more beautiful — than he actu-

505

ally was. Max told her that she was simply frustrated and tired, and still recovering after all, but he did not believe his own words. He had never seen such catastrophic disappointment on a woman's face. Over the next few weeks, she occupied herself with her son, but she did not win him back, and, more painful to watch, the boy did not win her back.

And then came two decisions that would change everything. The first, which led inexorably to the second, was prompted by the boy's multiple attempts to flee the Bamberg DP camp where they were still staying and return to the peasants who had raised him for the last three years. Max and Hannah agreed not to tell Herman who Max truly was, for fear the boy would run away for good. Then Max, whose application for a visa to the United States had been approved, proposed, against everything his life had pointed toward so far, that Hannah and he marry, and immigrate with Herman to America. The proposal, which implicitly and explicitly offered a solution to the problem of lying to Herman about Max being his father, elicited the first smile out of Hannah that he had seen since he had found her. "You're going to stay with me," she said with surprise.

He was. Though what he could not tell her was that it was *Herman* he felt compelled to stay with. Herman — his and Josef's son.

A natural consequence of these decisions, aside from the marriage ceremony (which *was* an aside: it was civil, it was swift, and it was secret), was that on the way from Europe to America, like so much ballast being shed into the Atlantic, something totally dropped out between Max and Hannah: Josef. This was one of their unstated agreements. It was to become the most devastating by half. Ever to be in their thoughts, he was never again to be in their talk. They covered Josef up for their new lives, just as they covered the tattoos on their arms for the New World. And it made them into permanent immigrants, as immune to New York, their first home, as to Los Angeles, their second. Their new existence shaped itself not on the climate or the culture around them but on the breaches between them, on the one big omission of their marriage, and finally on Herman, who evolved into the painful symbol of that omission — a reminder of the hole, of him whose name was never mentioned. For this last reason, it was to Herman, more than anything else, that they each quietly applied their mental and emotional resources, abetted by a hope that a steady confrontation with the problem of child rearing might cancel what the camp chimneys had failed to burn out of them. Never had two parents so separately and privately invested themselves in the hum-drum dramas and details of raising a child. Never had a husband and wife so wanted daily life to loosen them from love.

And what a reminder, what a problem, Herman was. Individually, they held their own understandings of the cards life had dealt the boy. They also knew what they had each toiled to give him. The knowledge that eluded them was what, exactly, he had absorbed. It was why he so frightened them. It is why he still frightens them now, several years on. And he sees that he frightens them — with all the awareness of any ten-year-old anxiously looking out for his effect on the adult world. He sees the worked surfaces of his father's face when he catches the man gazing at him. He sees the suppressed unease whenever he enters his mother's presence, and not just when he pretends to hit her.

That, pretending to hit his parents, is a spectacle he has been performing as far back as his memory can reach, but the fake beatings have grown more elaborate of late;

he is maturing, perfecting his act, infusing it with more flourish. Location is important: he likes surprising his mother near the living room window where she often reads, or sneaking up on his father in the study. And he has learned to pull his punches within an inch or two of their jaws, their noses, their midsections — the parts of their bodies he considers his private property. But the sound of drawing his other fist, the one he is not using to throw the jabs, hard against his chest has been his big discovery: it makes his flailings sound so real — or even better than real, like the woody, echoing punches thrown by the cowboys and the cops, the gangsters and the Martians who populate his favorite radio shows. His parents always seem at a loss for how to make him stop, a fact he enjoys so much in the moment (though never for long; it never lasts, the feeling) that he often revels around them after his mock displays of damage, hands raised in victory and self-congratulation. They pretend to laugh, and, sometimes, he laughs with them, but then he sees the fear they are trying to hide, and he ends up loping away as though he is the one who has received the blows.

That they never touch on the subject makes him suspicious. Why are they letting him get away with it? What have they done, what has been done *to him,* that they are so hesitant to say anything? And this is precisely what they are being with him: hesitant. It would seem they are throwing up no barriers, and yet he is not stupid, or rather he is a child, and therefore possesses a child's savvy that tells him his existence is subject to unseen barriers, the outer edges of an arrangement — one not worked out by him. And the arrangement harasses him well into his early teens, producing sensations for which he has no words, such as the stricken silence that follows him into any room occupied by his parents, the sense that something is about to be said — *should* be said, just to make the room sound right — but at the last second is not. What he hears is more than simply silence: it is renunciation as a sound. It gives him the same uncomfortable feeling, a kind of ache in his chest, that pierces him whenever someone goes to suck in air before holding their breath.

Nor does he perceive with his hearing alone that, long ago, something beyond his knowledge took place, something that matters a great deal still. Regularly, he is confounded when he asks his parents the essential questions: Where was he born?

510

How did they fall in love? Why was he separated from them during the war? With respect to all of these questions his mother and father are either mute or at variance, causing the past, when he tries to picture it, to look as indistinct as the future. And it contradicts what Herman understands about families. Families express themselves. They say and portray themselves. The chirpy mothers and fathers on television (his father recently brought one home, their first), the vocal sons and daughters and relatives on the radio . . . they describe everything about their feelings and lives. He has not failed to notice that the same tendency is general among his friends' families as well. Whereas *his* family: they are not being depicted.

If his parents have worked together all these years to prevent him from seeing something, theirs has been a frosty collaboration, one that is growing colder with time: when he used to broach the subject of the past, they would look at each other portentously, but now they only sink into their own spheres of anger or despair — or worse. It has become obvious to Herman that what his father feels toward his mother cannot be shrugged off like some spell of rage. He hates her in a silent, physical kind of way. And it manifests itself in his change-ful moods, the way he turns his eyes from her whenever she opens her mouth to speak. Yet he appears to possess something that cannot do without her.

She certainly cannot do without him. Her-man can tell by how often he has heard her cry for him not to abandon her, cry for him to touch her — pleas she makes at night in their bedroom, loud enough for Herman to hear from his own room down the hall. She seems to need his father so much that he causes her to cry even when he is not around: more than once, and with humilia-tion, Herman has watched her suddenly tear up at the market while he and she are wait-ing together in line to buy eggs; she does not even bother to wipe her cheeks when she hands money to the staring cashier. But even more embarrassing are her new public flirtations with his middle school English teacher, Mr. Stanton. During evening school events, with his father standing right there, she involves herself in long, intense discus-sions with the man, discussions in which she flaunts her new mastery over the English language (the fruit of all her reading, her radio listening, the language courses she has taken). They speak passionately of poetry (he shares her love of Hölderlin), of obscure

German novelists who preceded Thomas Mann, or of Plotinus and Montaigne and Pascal, topics that prevent the other parents from participating, and his mother makes sure to sprinkle her talk with one or two metaphysical revelations that leave Mr. Stanton speechless. The first two times it happens, his father slips in the car afterward and asks her if she is satisfied with "her comic little performance," to which she offers no reply, and the two of them fill the front seat with something hard and permanent — what looks to Herman like a sourness that will last as long as his life — until they get home and his father retreats to his study, where Herman, looking on from the doorway, observes him picking up each object in the room, from among the old things he has collected and put on display there, as if it were a single fragment of himself.

The third time, however, everything changes. They are attending a back-to-school night. As his mother talks on and on with the rapt Mr. Stanton, Herman watches anger harden around his father's features like a cast, until his father, who has been pacing the classroom, comes to a halt five steps away from her and stands there, frozen. Only his eyes move, and where they land frightens Herman down to his bones. He has never seen his father look at her like this. It is neither at her eyes nor at her face that he glares. It is at her body. And his way of looking is not *kind:* there is no admiration in it, but something else, like resistance, and meanness. Ominously, the man says nothing the whole way home, and, instead of taking refuge in his study like before, follows Herman's mother into their bedroom and shuts the door behind them. The house is dark. No words make it down the hall, none of the usual hushed arguing. For five minutes Herman cannot hear a sound. Then a very quiet "no" — his mother. And another, this time with more volume: *"No!"* The third "no" causes Herman's eyes to well up. It is less a word than a physical catching of pain. The no's that follow (and there are many of them) come at regular intervals, decreasing in volume until they are all but inaudible, and as Herman stands there shaking at the end of the hall, they wash over him like vanishing echoes rising up out of a deep hole in the earth, causing something in him to turn irreversibly against his father. But when he suddenly sees the man before him in the darkness, and throws all his weight into six straight punches, real ones meant to connect and hurt, nothing is there to meet his fists, and he has the sensation of falling into the hole.

It is not a new sensation, falling. He has felt it and feared it all of his life. In the past the feeling would come over him suddenly, for seemingly no better reason than his face was being buffeted by wind rushing in through the lowered windows of his school bus. It always faded, the feeling, as abruptly as it had arrived. But it does not fade after the Night of No's, as he comes to think of it (and think of it he does — he is never not thinking of it). And this time he is amazed to find that he savors the sensation of falling. He is at home in the descent. No longer is it fear that follows him into his downward flight, but rather anger, and excitement, and freedom — a thrilling vertigo of emotion to which he gives himself up eagerly. Eagerly, because he senses that he is falling away from something.

But from what? At first, all he can think of is his father. And he does want to deal the man a lasting blow. But he is unhappy with his mother too — not just because she has disappointed him by behaving as if the Night of No's never happened (she has even returned to pleading with his father not to leave her), but also because the truth is that he has felt a deep, hidden animosity toward his mother ever since he reunited with her after the war. He has no explanation for this anger of his toward her. Sometimes he feels that he is waiting for her to explain it to him.

It must be the two of them, he reasons, whom he wants to escape. But how to actually *do* it? How leave your own family? He remembers running away from them when he was little — they only caught him and brought him back, and they would surely do the same now. His trips into the Sierras with the Boy Scouts take him hundreds of miles from his parents, but never for long enough. No, it would have to be an inner escape, and yet one that still made a mark on them, made them know that he was gone.

What rises at last to meet the problem is a remedy Herman never saw coming. He never saw it, because it involves leaving behind something he never saw to begin with: Jewishness. Of course, he has always been peripherally aware that his family is different from the others on his block. When has he not known his mother and father to have a talent, seemingly unavailable to his playmates' parents, for taking each of life's trivialities as an assault? It has something to do with the war, of that much he is certain:

the Knudsens next door, the Langleys on the other side, the Bauers and Buckleys and Earnhardts across the street — none of them came through it as he and his parents were forced to do (a few of the fathers fought *in* it, yet they appear at ease and even pleased with the fact). And he remembers having to get used to the way the other parents speak to their children, the dry deliberateness of their reprimands, the bland detachment of their praises, whereas his own parents are incapable of suggesting even a fun outing without flinging color — usually dark — over the proposition. But for most of his life he has known too little about the world not to take these differences as his due, just as when, for the first year or so after he and his family arrived, he did not question the glaring discrepancy in size and strength between himself and his American-raised friends of similar age (everyone seemed *monstrously* built; as far as he was concerned, even the girls had masculine hands and feet). No one ever said anything to him about it — they accommodated him the way America seems to accommodate most of its aberrant citizens: easily, indifferently, confidently. They certainly never said anything about his being Jewish, right up to this very day. No, it has taken a *Jew* to do that. It has taken Shirley Molotnik approaching him in his life sciences class and suggesting that they become lab partners (because, after all, they *are* the only Jews in the class) to tell him who he really is, and, crucially, who his parents are. It has taken Shirley Molotnik to show him what happens when he acknowledges no Jewish loyalty, no difference between himself and everyone else ("You shoulda been killed by Hitler!" she told him after he declined her offer by insisting that it did not matter who was Jewish). It has taken Shirley Molotnik's hurt and Shirley Molotnik's anger — neither of which has subsided for going on three weeks now — to illustrate how to properly and permanently turn against his parents, to reveal precisely how to sever ties with a Jew. In order to fall away from his parents, he had really to find them.

And he finds them, all right. He finds them in the dozens of books about the Jews that he checks out from the library, books *written by* Jews that inadvertently identify everything he has come to loathe about his parents, books that yield up all manner of pithy, useful phrases with which to salt his talk at home, allowing him to express, for example, his distaste for his parents' "slavish survivor mentality" and their "out-

518

moded, isolating tribalism," his impatience with their "stealthiness and secrecy fertilized by an exaggerated sense of being put upon."

His father's reaction is swift: at the local synagogue, he enrolls Herman in two study courses, Intensive Hebrew Language and Jewish Religion & Culture, with the intention that Herman, already approaching his fifteenth birthday, will read for a belated bar mitzvah. But beginning with his very first class, Herman is the despair of his Judaic teachers, putting his recent self-education on all matters Jewish (to say nothing of his reading of Zola, his anthropology textbook from school, and the science fiction magazines he has been devouring) together with a burgeoning grasp of astronomy to argue that religion has been one headlong retreat from lightning and multiple gods to an abstract god that cannot possibly exist. Word of his recalcitrance at the synagogue reaches his father soon enough, and a series of confrontations ensues at home, but these arguments eventually cool and draw out into something more entrenched. For nearly a month, his father imposes his silence on Herman with such force that Herman feels the man is attempting to cancel his existence. When finally his father decides to speak, it is only to take up his cause again, and Herman immediately rejects his father's renewed exhortations to embrace his Jewishness, informing the man that there are only two things he will embrace from here on out: reason and science. As if to prove it, he brings Heinlein and Asimov to the dinner table, he brings *The Dying Earth* and *Farmer in the Sky* and *Amateur Telescope Making*. He brings, more than anything else, an increasingly formal response to anything his parents put forth.

And they put forth a lot — to him, and to each other. When his father, who seems to have suddenly increased his religiosity in response to Herman denying his own (Herman cannot recall the man ever speaking so frequently about God), speechifies one evening on the need for increased ritual in the house, his mother finally ends her silence on the whole matter and, to Herman's surprise, goes on the attack. "Can you not see, Max, that your rituals are useless? Useless to him" — she gestures at Herman with her napkin — "and useless to God, who couldn't care less about whether or not we light some candles, or God forbid, work on a Saturday. And it hardly matters that your son has rejected God — if ever faith finds him, it can do so through disbelief. In fact, it is better through disbelief. *Let* your son use science and doubt to purify himself of false consolations. All his skepticism puts him closer to the reality of God anyway. God either takes possession of you or He doesn't. You cannot get to Him through some silly observance. You cannot *get* to Him at all. There is no *seeking* God — there is only refusing your love to all that is not Him. And your son is already doing a fine job of that."

His father accuses her of holding harsh beliefs that no one could possibly live by. Her God is unobtainable, he yells. Her God is not even a god! And then he yells at both of them: "You are both the same! Harsh, impossible people! I should have gone by myself to live in Israel!"

It marks the beginning, that evening, of his mother's own retreat, one that in some ways comes to mirror Herman's. And the look on her face at the end of that dinner never completely goes away again. To the degree that Herman notices, she seems exasperated by her own impotence in the house, and slowly she draws away from everything that keeps it running, leaving Herman and his father to take over the chores, the shopping, even the cleaning.

Certainly, she draws away from his father, bringing what little talk there has been between them to a virtual end, and choosing to sleep nights in the third bedroom. That she hardly speaks to Herman represents little change from before. But it is where she retreats *to* that comes as the biggest surprise, because it succeeds, at least for a while, in superceding even Herman's recent efforts at severing ties. His mother begins taking the bus — almost daily — to St. Francis of Assisi, a Catholic church, of all places, there to escape her Jewishness, apparently, and worship her godless God.

Then Herman does her one better. In the summer of his seventeenth year, on a Boy Scout trip to Montana, he spends five days on the Blackfoot reservation, participating in a powwow, befriending Blackfoot boys his age, joining their families for meals, and camping out on their land, which seems to reach endlessly into the hot, aromatic plain. It rekindles something he tasted as a young boy, when his father moved the family to California and they drove through the Indian nations of the desert Southwest. On that trip, his parents were drawn at once to the Hopis, whose dense vertical rookeries, scattered grudgingly across several mesas, reminded them of the apartments and tenements in which they had spent their whole lives. But Herman was fascinated by the Navajo, invaders from the north who for many years had held the Hopis to ransom, levying tribute from them and meanwhile spreading out all over the land. Their lean, low-lying homesteads, isolated and sleeping in the sun and the dust, seemed then the antithesis of the confinement Herman had known in New York City. Now, the Blackfoot seem the antithesis of everything Herman hates. The children are hardly ever in their homes: entire days are spent stealing down a river's edge, pausing here and there on a precipitous rock, then time and again leaping out under vaulting canopies of clouds, only to be enveloped in cool mountain water. When they do come home, there is none of the emotionalism of Herman's family life. Everyone, the mothers and fathers included, is calm, well mannered, perhaps a little grave, which suits Herman just fine. And they are very good-looking, even the males — Herman admires their hair in particular, which, to a man, is dark and fine and not so different from Herman's own. It is this similarity of trait and temperament that gets to Herman, and when, as he and his troops are packing up to leave the reservation, their Blackfoot benefactors announce that they have made them honorary members of the Blackfoot nation, Herman takes it to heart.

He takes it to Hole-in-the-Wall, a remote Rocky Mountain roost high on the Continental Divide, where his troop spends the next week in camp, and where, just to look out over the granite edge at the thousand-foot drop is to feel like you are falling. And there in that hole, surrounded by snow-balded peaks, with the whole planet beneath him, Herman experiences the sensation of falling as he never has before. That secret stone place, out of phase with the rest of the world, answering only to wind and rock and a million dead stars above, suddenly reveals to him the secret of all life, which is the hunger for *more* life, the longing to be more than just ourselves. He has caught glimpses of it before, peering into the telescope he built at home or the petri dishes in his biology class. He even felt its vague presence in the protagonists who threatened to leap out of their lives and out of the novels he read by Hugo and Balzac, Norris and Sinclair and Dreiser. But only now, only here, does the secret take possession of him, or rather does *he* take possession of it and fall away from who he is — fall away from his father, away from his mother, away from his Jewishness — and into his new life as a Blackfoot.

And he takes it home, where he announces that not only will he no longer do religion, he will no longer do Jewishness either: not the talk, not the classes, not the food, not the names. He will make no concessions whatever to the requirements of being a Jew. And as soon as he is old enough, he will change his last name from Wiener to Wind. None of this, he tells them, is up for discussion. If they try to discuss it with him, he will discontinue speaking while in the house, until the day, not so far from now, when he will leave it.

All of this is conveyed during dinner. His father, by now trembling, glares at his mother, as if expecting her to say something, but she continues to eat quietly. "*Wind?* What kind of name is this?"

"Blackfoot," Herman says.

His father turns to him. "Black *what?*"

"They're Indians."

A tense pause. "And what of your own history?"

Herman looks him straight in the eye. "I don't know my own history — you've never told it to me."

"Jewish history! *Jewish* history!" His father is standing up now, gesticulating with

525

his arms. "I'm talking about the history of your people!"

"They aren't my people anymore. I've already told you. It's over." As if to put a point on it, Herman leaves the table for a moment to refill his glass of milk.

His father follows him wildly into the kitchen. "A Jew without *history?*" he shouts. He looks back at Herman's mother. "Did *you* put this thought into his head?" Now he is shaking a finger at Herman. "A Jew *is* his history. Slavery, the Exodus, the destruction of Solomon's Temple, the Babylonian Captivity and the return to Israel — this is not some story. . . . It is our *religion!*"

Herman ignores him and returns to the table. His father remains standing there by the refrigerator for at least five minutes, silently staring at him. When finally the man leaves and disappears into the study, Herman's mother sets down her fork.

"Do you love us?" she asks quietly.

He reaches for his milk, lifts it to his lips, and drinks.

The question never gets answered, not for his mother, and not for him. He is uncomfortable with the question, because he is uncomfortable with the concept of love to begin with. What is love? He is not even sure

526

he believes in it. And this is what he does not approve of: one has to *believe* in love like a god, or it will not exist.

There are things he *likes,* of course. He likes eating the same cereal — corn flakes — every morning. He likes contemplating other worlds. He likes the concept of satellites. He likes analyzing soil in the laboratory at school. He likes blowing glass, and taking notes about data, and measuring things to within five significant figures.

And he likes Lana Vining, a willowy blonde who agrees to wear his jacket — he has lettered in varsity tennis, another thing he likes — at the beginning of their senior year, until Bob Burklane — who lettered in football — takes her away with his convertible Corvair and his jaw. Convinced that his last name — still *Wiener* — played a part in her departure, and spurred by Sputnik and a longing to help America overcome the Russians in the race into space, he retreats from social life for the rest of the year and submerges himself in his science studies with the goal of gaining admission to a top-flight university program.

He gets into Berkeley, where almost everyone seems to be in a process of denying what determines them, where he thus quite naturally becomes Herman Wind, and where, in his very first semester, he meets Francine Anderson, one of only two women in his freshman chemistry class. Francine is no Shirley Molotnik, and when she asks him to be her lab partner he is thrilled. When she invites him back to her bungalow — a bungalow her parents are paying for, a bungalow with no roommates — he cannot believe his luck. Unlike anything he ever wanted before in his life, it happens so easily. At her tiny kitchen table they talk all night, conversing on chemistry, and covering everything from Calypso to communism, from the defeated dreams of Adlai Stevenson to their own dreams of themselves. And that, Herman's dream of himself, seems to flow as freely as the gin and tonics Francine keeps pouring for them. Out of his five days on the Blackfoot reservation, he fabricates nineteen years, an entire past. He tells her of the "big sky back home," of the mountains, the rivers, and the rocks. He speaks about his Blackfoot family, and then, in an inspired bit of extemporaneity, adds with remarkable feeling that his mother and father are dead, applying to those factitious parents a passion he has never felt for his own. It never seems to occur to her, as he talks, that he is not an Indian of any description, because his description — of his plight, and the plight of his people — is so convincing. The deeper he gets into his fairy tale, the deeper her apparent investment in it. His own investment in it deepens too, to his dismay. *To his dismay,* as he fills in a picture of "the Blackfoot's triumphant surmounting of successive hardships" (about which he knows next to nothing), he finds himself employing perversions of the very phrases he fired at his parents in his assault on Jewishness. He boasts proudly to Francine of his people's "survivor mentality" and their "fierce tribalism" — of how "put upon" they have been, and the necessity of adopting an attitude of "stealthiness and secrecy" in their dealings with the American government. Encouraged by drink and by her impassioned assurance that she stands foursquare for Indian rights, he concocts a long and gloomy inventory, none of it real, of the injustices committed against his tribe. It is a foolish move, but one that he sees he will get away with, as she is already off and running, at least her mouth is, passing harsh judgment on the human race. When she finally falls quiet, he frowns and pretends to a homesickness that he has to wash down with another gulp of gin, and then, just for effect, he adds a shade of complication by reclothing his feelings about his Jewish family in buffalo hide, telling her that he came to Berkeley because he had to put distance between himself and where he came from, because he felt held back by life on the reservation, because he was chafed by the narrow, deep-rooted expectations placed on him by the tribe. Francine takes his hand then, her face flushed with alcohol and understanding, and for a moment he *believes* everything he is saying — believes it so strongly that he tells her something truthful for once, tells her his *real* dream. Tells her he wants to go up into space, despite a fear he has always had of falling. At this her eyes well up — she grabs his other hand and declares that she feels with all her heart that he is going to be the first American Indian into outer space. He is touched, but hearing his lie on her lips (that he is an American Indian) pulls him right back down to earth, pulls him down to Francine, and to her bed, where to his surprise she gives herself to him, and calls him her "Blackfoot boy," and where, lying beside her afterward, he feels so grateful, so relieved, that he already begins to calculate their future together.

It is a calculation that continues over the next four years, during which he refines his

530

measurement of her, until he is convinced that he cannot let her get away from him. She is a free spirit and she is smart, a great one for science and sex, and, most important, she is a Gentile — a long, slender, blond, green-eyed Gentile who has no idea who he really is. When, on the day of their graduation, he asks Francine to marry him, she has only one question for him: does he love her? He falters for a moment, because it carries him to a question asked of him five years earlier, carries him back to his mother, whom he has not seen since he left for college. *Is* it love? He is no more comfortable with the question now than he was then, no more at ease with the concept of love than he is with any belief system. But he needs Francine like other people need their God. He wants to lose himself in her. He hopes to be released. So he throws himself into the ritual and the religion of love. He throws himself at her feet . . . a reluctant practitioner, entreating a woman for her hand by saying all the old words.

The ceremony is held that summer, high above the Berkeley campus (where he is staying on for his PhD) in a small eucalyptus-packed park overlooking the bay. Herman's mentor, a professor of chemistry and ordained Buddhist monk, marries them in front of her parents and a smattering of the scientific community. Appropriately, all religious references are jettisoned from the proceedings, to be replaced by scientific shibboleths and insider jokes about the "physical chemistry" between the bride and groom, about the organic reactions or electron pairing or chemical bonding that will occur later that night in the conjugal bed. When it is over, as he and Francine head hand in hand down the hill, she keeps declaring how happy she is, and when she finally asks if he is happy too, he says that he has never been so happy in his life. It satisfies her, this answer, but it does not satisfy him. He wishes he could share the real reason for his happiness: that their wedding was a burial ceremony, that his long battle against lineage has at last ended here on this hill. He wishes he could tell her that Herman *Wiener,* a man she never knew, is finally dead.

For the next several years, Herman Wiener rests in peace, allowing his murderer to enjoy productive days in the lab and pleasurable nights with Francine. Then one morning he is unexpectedly exhumed, by another of the dead brought back to life. The exhumation begins in the basement of the chemistry building, in "The Crypt," appropriately enough, where the graduate students gather to grade exams and commiserate, and where Herman is interrupted by a new secretary from upstairs who pops her head in to ask if he ever goes by the name of Wiener . . . because there is a woman on the telephone, as she explains with a puzzled expression, who is claiming to be his mother — the mother of Herman Wiener.

He is unprepared for his mother's call, since neither she nor his father have attempted to contact him in almost three years, a result of several brisk, hostile rebuffs he subjected them to shortly before he wed Francine. The phone conversation, already awkward for being conducted at the desk and in the presence of the secretary, is instantly unsettling to him — as unsettling as the sound of his mother's staggeringly thin voice.

"Have you married?" she asks straight-away.

He grants this a reluctant grunt in the affirmative. Then, defiantly, he says: "We're having a child."

There is a long pause.

"Are you going to stay with them?"

The question truly catches him by surprise. At first, he is shocked by it. Then he is only angered by it — so angered that if the secretary were not right in front of him he might have yelled into the receiver. Instead, he holds his silence.

"*I'm* not staying," she offers vaguely, as if detecting his anger and trying to soften it. "I thought you should know."

"Dad?" he asks, confused. "You're *leaving* him?"

For a moment, there is only the sound of her breathing on the other end. She seems to be steadying herself. "Max is not your father," she says with audible effort. Again the breathing. "Your real father didn't survive the camps, Herman."

He stands there, holding the receiver to his ear. The secretary, impatient to have her phone back, gives him an unsmiling look.

"But Max has been good to you — he loved you as his own," his mother adds. "Try not to walk away from everyone."

He hears a click — the connection is dropped, and with it, to his astonishment, so is he. Afterward, he roams the campus in a daze, wondering at how, for all his effort to get away from his mother, he feels so overcome with a feeling of being left behind.

Who was his real father? What was he like? Why did Max step into his place? And why was Herman never *told?* These are the obvious questions, but if, during the following weeks, he yearns for answers to them, he does not admit as much to himself. Rather, he uses his mother's revelation — that Max is not his father — to justify keeping Max in the grave for good.

And against her parting wish, he *will* walk away from everyone.

He thought having a child with Francine would cement his victory on the mountain. He thought recklessly breeding with a non-Jew would further dispossess him of his parents, but then suddenly there is Benjamin, difficult, crying, screaming Benjamin, who, in his effect on Francine, in his effect on *Francine and Herman,* single-handedly revives every last strand of Herman's filial history and hatred. How is it possible that his wife, this free spirit he married, could suddenly transform into a needy, melancholic woman whose dependency on Herman reminds him grotesquely of his mother's desperate love for Max? The nightly pleadings, which begin when Herman starts to come home later and later from the lab, even *sound* the same as his mother's old cries from the bedroom: "You can't leave me now, Herman," she tells him, or, "You haven't *touched* me in so long."

He has not touched her in so long because

she is too tired to have sex with him, and because, well, because he is touching other women who *will* have sex with him. It starts with Digby, a brunet postdoc who is also spending late nights in the lab. His interest in her, already as robust as the braless breasts she freely bounces around the lab beneath her cotton tops, increases dramatically when he learns how much older she is than him (seven years), and especially when he discovers that she is working on a satellite that, with any luck, will be sent into space to record images of Mars. It is through this — the topic of space — that he earns her ear, her time, and then her breasts, which, over the course of that spring, he ends up handling as frequently as any other equipment in the lab, and which become as familiar to his mouth as the pipette tubes he uses to suck fluids out of flasks. In time, Digby introduces him to Connie, a physics PhD student she is working with, and in Digby's attic apartment down by the bay the two of them introduce him to the thrills of a threesome. And then there is Barbara, the wife of an associate professor, who places her mouth over his one night in her kitchen during a department poker game, and who invites him to visit her the following afternoon when her husband is teaching. That visit turns into a fuck, and then into a regular thing. One day when they are done, she tells Herman that it is time they have a talk. Her husband has been informed of their trysts, she explains, and he is fine with it, fine with her idea of taking her own apartment too. She wants Herman to know that she is forty-one, she is childless, and she is liberated: she could care less if he continues to sleep nights at home with Francine and Benjamin, so long as he comes to see her regularly during the week, and perhaps spends at least one weekend night with her in her new apartment in North Berkeley. She asks to speak directly to Francine about the arrangement, and wants to offer her help in raising Benjamin, now going on one and a half years of age.

About all of this, Francine knows nothing, and the meeting between the three of them, held in the bungalow after Benjamin has been put to bed, begins awkwardly, with Francine emerging from the bedroom and rather irritably asking Herman why he needs her to talk to the wife of one of his professors on a night when she is so exhausted from a difficult day with the baby. Then, as though foretasting a hierarchical shift, she decides not to join Herman and Barbara in claiming one of the living room's three seats and instead sits below them — literally — on the floor. Before Herman can even start to answer her question, Barbara informs Francine that she and Herman are lovers and that they would like to continue to be lovers without breaking up the marriage. Barbara sees no reason why she and Francine should not become friends as well — perhaps even best of friends — and, after telling Francine a bit about her life, suggests that the three of them have something to drink to celebrate their new relationship.

Herman waits for Francine to look over at him, but her eyes land on everything in the room except him as she digests what she has just heard. Then, to his consternation, she stands and goes to the kitchen, her movements robotic and dutiful, as if she is operating under hypnosis, and soon she is back, handing Barbara and him cans of beer. She returns to her place on the floor and leaves her own can untouched while he and Barbara converse forcedly about the politics in the chemistry department. It makes him so uncomfortable that he is actually relieved when she finally raises her placid face toward his, looks at him assessingly, and, in the most heartfelt and heartbreaking voice he has ever heard her use, asks him to explain why he is sleeping with

Barbara.

And explain he does. Many as the advantages of marriage are, he begins, it does not enable the exploratory elements of life. Marriage, he declares, has halted him halfway down his road. He joins Francine on the floor then, and, taking her hand, says: "You've been halted halfway down *your* road too, Francine — you just don't see it yet. You and I . . . we can't allow the religion of monogamy to prevent us from traveling to wherever we need to go."

"The religion of monogamy," she echoes.

He tries to find her eyes, but they have contracted, withdrawn to a different sphere. *"Yes,"* he insists. "We've been taken in by it, *brainwashed* — all of us! First they fed us the religion of family. Then we were forced into subscribing to love so we'd get pulled right back into worshipping the family even after we finally left it! And then they had to go and invent the religion of monogamy to ensure that we *stay* in it. What Barbara and I are proposing, Francine, is freeing ourselves — and *you* — from those childish, outdated beliefs."

For the longest time, her gaze remains frozen on some nonexistent mote of dust that moves in the air before her. But at last her lips form a smile. "Oh," she says mysteriously, raising her can of beer to her lips for the first time. She nearly empties its entire contents. Barbara exchanges glances with Herman, then makes the suggestion that the three of them go into the bedroom. "No, I want to sleep with my husband alone tonight," Francine replies matter-of-factly, and then she turns to Barbara. "I'd like you to go home now."

Barbara hesitates before leaning over and embracing her — for far too long, in Herman's opinion — and then she stands, and Herman and Francine do the same. On her way out, Barbara kisses him on the lips and gives him a hug from which he is quick to extricate himself. "I'll see you in the morning," she tells him so that Francine can hear.

Before the front door even closes Francine is pulling him into the bedroom with an air of expectancy that is so sober, so inanimate, that it scares him. Yet soon enough their naked bodies are churning the bed, lurching toward something at once familiar and foreign. And *that* is what he has done to her, he sees: by introducing other women into his life — into *their* life — he has made Francine as foreign to him as she is familiar. He has given her a new negative need, one that he cannot, or will not, pacify — not in bed (despite feeling

that he is in the full noon of his virility) during the long night that follows, and certainly
not in the morning when, confronted by her
hysterical insistence that he not leave her in
order to see Barbara, he finds himself shockingly emulating the same coldness that his
father — Max — displayed in front of
feminine hurt and want. The ensuing fight
is a terrible one, and it happens in full view
of baby Benjamin, who screams from his
playpen until Francine, desperate to plead
her case to Herman, tosses a box of Cheerios into the pen in order to shut him up.
And the boy does shut up, taking the Cheerios one by one into his mouth and sticking
them wetly onto the wall. It is then that
Francine levels her final threat: if he goes to
Barbara's, the marriage is over. He stares
right at her for a moment, and then calmly,
brutally, turns toward the door.

To his surprise, he has time on his way
out of the house, he has the coolness of
mind, to note what is transpiring on the wall
behind Benjamin's pen: the Cheerios are
aligning into patterns — magnificent patterns as beautiful as any cluster of stars he
has ever seen. And as if his son's artwork
were *that* powerful, as if Herman were once
again a boy humbly gazing through a telescope into the heavens, he suddenly feels all

the arrogance, all the scientific rigidity and coldness, leak out of him. What replaces it is this vision — a terrifying vision he knows he will never forget — of what his son created at the very moment that he, Herman Wind, destroyed the only goodness he ever made. The miracle of beauty in the face of such ugliness is almost enough to make a man believe in something — some*one* — larger than himself. And what an uncanny sensation: to walk away from your own child, and feel only a longing to be saved.

THE LAST WEDDINGS IN THE WORLD

It was still summer. He was in New York, he was in the light, he was in love (safely in love, past all recall), but, despite a new industriousness that had firmly reestablished him at the magazine, some unfinished business still beckoned to him from a dark place. And was it really so unaccountable — as it had seemed to him when, after his initial shock, he reread Clifford Fatheree's note with a sober eye — that the missing answers to his questions about Benjamin Wind's final show (his final *days? Aleksandra's* final days?) were held by a prisoner in Rikers Island? The longer his visit to the prisoner and the place was delayed, and the greater the difficulty he encountered in obtaining permission to visit an inmate with whom he had no blood relation, the more he became convinced that an indissoluble link existed between this man Fatheree and what he wanted. What he wanted — the

truth about Aleksandra and Benjamin —
had been equally impossible to penetrate,
and as he stared down at Fatheree's note
during endless calls to lawyers and the
Department of Correction, its words began
to transform before his eyes into truth, its
erratic letters into recognizable marks of
pain. When at last the call came, informing
him that he could have half an hour with
Clifford Fatheree at three o'clock the following day, Daniel felt a sharp restriction in
his chest, as if he had finally been granted
visiting rights to view his dead. And on a
dry, glorious August afternoon, after weeks
of waiting, he headed to the prison like a
man anxious to get his life back.

The journey was not an easy one. Three
bus rides were required, the second one fer-
rying him across Queens and giving him a
distant freeway view — his first since the
funeral — of the cemetery where Aleksandra lay buried. Closely bound with her as
his thoughts had been and still were, he was
chilled by the sight, all that terrible stone,
the immovable rows. What an *illusion,* her
closeness to him: she was not, was no
longer, near. Uncertainly he boarded the
final bus at a place called Queens Plaza
South, and joined the other passengers — a
crush of women and their children, stoically

venturing to see their incarcerated men —
in staring out the windows at the grim commercial strip commanding the corner. Half
an hour later, after tracing a path through
the leaden outskirts of LaGuardia Airport,
the bus crested the long Rikers Island
Bridge that separated the free from the
forgotten, and Daniel caught his first
glimpse of the vast penal colony. Known to
him previously only by name and reputation, the complex, with its sprawling bone-
white buildings and glinting coils of razor
wire, seemed, beneath the jets that were
constantly taking off over it, to lie on a
meridian of invisibility, an impression
italicized by the surprising proximity of the
skyline of Manhattan, a city that, though
served by Rikers Island, refused to consider
the place one of its own.

And it *was* a dark place, at least what
Daniel saw of the inside of it. Not that its
interiors were unlit; on the contrary, every
hall and room was fluorescently unshad-
owed. It was more that the place appeared
to be penetrated by no natural light, neither
from the sun nor from the eyes of the souls
who worked there. To a man, the officers
who scanned him in had expressions of
purposeful vacancy, as though they were all
listening to a gripping speech just beyond

hearing. But it was the guards in the visiting room to whom Daniel had trouble adjusting, and not because of the decidedly ungallant language they used to address the inmates. They menaced him purely by means of their glacial stares, their inhuman ability to mix an absolute devotion to their duty with obliterative uncare. What a relief to finally face Clifford Fatheree through the security glass. Though he seemed to share with the guards a stolid disposition, he was eager to speak openly to Daniel, and in fact the first thing he said was that, in addition to committing petty theft, he had been a drug user and dealer, for the latter of which he had been reincarcerated. None of these confessions were requested by Daniel, who felt they were being offered as a sign of good faith, and sure enough Fatheree let him know that he was now clean. If such radiant, richly brown skin was any indication of what was going on inside the body, he must have been. He was an extremely pleasing young man to look at: tall, high-cheeked, with flecked, wide-set eyes that carefully avoided Daniel's own. That avoidance was the aspect of his demeanor that most struck Daniel in the initial minutes of their meeting. Clifford Fatheree's was a blunted grace; the impassiveness, the reticence — they seemed to be affectations, shaped less by his nature than by his determination and, in all likelihood, the exigencies of prison life. Yet when he began to speak of Benjamin Wind he gave himself to it utterly, his voice loosening out into a beautiful galvanism. "He done it, mister," Fatheree said, shaking his head as if at some inner amusement. "Fooled all y'alls. But you're talking to the right man — finally. I know where that show come from, 'cause I helped him make it."

The statement astonished Daniel, and he leaned in closer to the glass. "How? How'd you help him make it?"

"Told him all about Hart Island."

"Hart Island? The *potter's field?*"

"I was on burial detail there during my first incarceration. Back there again now. Earned it for my good behavior."

Daniel was familiar with Hart Island, having written the catalog preface for a career retrospective of an American artist who photographed the place. He knew that it was home to the only separate cemetery still serving a major city's unclaimed, unacknowledged, and undesirable dead. He knew that it sat out in Long Island Sound, not far from New York City itself, and that it was essentially unchanged since the birth of the country. He even remembered that its potter's field operated under the auspices of the city's Department of Correction, and that inmates from Rikers volunteered — with the hope of working outside in its open, largely undespoiled setting — for the job of filling its mass graves with the babies and adults dispatched each week by the city morgue. He knew these things. What he did *not* know was what any of it had to do with Benjamin's show, though the prospect that it was somehow connected to, perhaps even the source of, the artwork that changed everything (for Benjamin, for Aleksandra, for himself) set off a minor tumult beneath his rib cage.

"When did you meet Benjamin Wind?" he asked.

"Don't know — couple years ago, maybe. Right after I started on Hart Island. He just showed up there one day."

"On Hart Island? What was he doing there?"

Fatheree adjusted his shoulders in a manner that evoked a shrug without suggesting weakness. "People come for different reasons. He only said hi to me that time — we ain't allowed to talk much while we work. I just thought he was one of the ones come to pay respects to a family member he finally found. But then he showed up here."

"Benjamin came *here* to see you?"

"Three times."

A second volley of fugitive heartbeats fired in Daniel's chest. "Forgive me for putting it this way, but how'd he even find you here? Why *you?*"

"Told me he saw my name tag. Saw me digging and burying and wanted to ask me about it."

Daniel pressed him: "I need to know exactly what he asked you."

Fatheree scratched his ear; he was staring at the floor. "He was kinda shocked by it, that's all."

"By what he saw out there?"

"Yeah. How come so many were buried like that? How come the only witnesses were us prisoners? He was trying to get a grip on it, you know?"

"Of course," Daniel said, probably a bit too impatiently. He *was* impatient, because all at once the connection Clifford Fatheree was trying to draw between Hart Island and Benjamin's show was looking like so much speculation. "So . . . what: you think the potter's field influenced the work? Did he tell you that?"

"No, mister. Didn't influence the work. It *was* the work."

Something about Fatheree's tone frightened Daniel. "What do you mean?"

Fatheree paused. His gaze was still downcast; he seemed to be considering. When he spoke, it was in a lowered voice. "I mean the bodies."

Daniel looked at the guards. One of them was staring right at him. When he turned back, Clifford Fatheree was staring at him too.

"Those were *sculptures*," Daniel insisted, though he was suddenly less than confident.

"Yeah."

"Made from wax."

"Yeah."

"Plaster and pigment."

"I know."

He searched Clifford Fatheree's eyes, and guessed that the young man was withholding — not because he wanted to; rather, because he could not speak freely. Daniel glared at the two-way speaker embedded in the glass. He had forgotten the obvious: conversations could be listened to.

"Are you telling me those sculptures are based on some dead —" He stopped himself. "Are you saying he took casts out there?"

"Ain't saying anything except he visited me three times wanting to know about the grave markers and boxes —"

"What boxes?"

"You know. The wood ones."

"That the bodies come in? What about them?"

"Just how they're screwed closed — how we organize them in grids in the ground so's later if a family comes wanting one of their own we can find the right one. That's why the boxes got numbers on them."

"He asked you about all that?"

The young man let out a quiet snicker. "Tryintell you."

As Daniel sat in silence, attempting to adjust to the implications of what he was hearing, Clifford Fatheree explained how he had been unable to get Benjamin out of his head after the man had stopped visiting him, and how he had started poring through every newspaper that he could get his hands on, searching for something — anything — about Wind, until one day he saw the obituary, and then later, a lot later, his wife finally brought him Daniel's art review. Fatheree appeared to grow restive and severe at his own mention of what Daniel had written, and suddenly he put his mouth right up to the two-way as if it were a receptacle for his overflowing disquiet. He began to speak up against the review, in angry defense of himself and the other prisoners on burial detail at Hart Island, all of whom now revered Benjamin Wind for creating pieces of art that seemed to answer an ache that working out there among the mass graves had fastened on them. Wind's final show, according to Fatheree, was still a topic of intense discussion among them, even though they had never seen it; all they had to go by were the few descriptive passages, related to them by Fatheree, that had been embedded in Daniel's otherwise inaccurate (according to Fatheree) review, and the tiny accompanying image that merely reproduced a detail of one of the sculptures — the rest they had been forced to imagine.

That Benjamin Wind's work enjoyed a secret society of admirers among the Rikers Island inmates amazed Daniel as he sat there listening. So did the aptitude for textual recall that Clifford Fatheree, enlivened by outrage, was at this very moment displaying to him: in his effort to set Daniel straight, the young man kept quoting lines from his review, and the longer he went on the more obvious it became to Daniel that Fatheree needed this meeting as much as Daniel did. Daniel evidently represented for him the outside world's indifference to Hart Island, and for five minutes, maybe more, Fatheree, his eyes fixed accusingly on Dan-

iel, worked to dilate the disinterest — real
or no — by arguing that he and the other
workers were the caretakers of what belonged to Daniel and every other American
without them even knowing it: the dead on
Hart Island were their common property,
because they were *no one's* property. The
hard-won beauty of this reasoning, which
returned Daniel to feelings he thought he
had left forever back in Vienna's cemetery
and the haunted suburbs of that city's sur-
round, made him utterly vulnerable to the
upbraiding he was receiving from Clifford
Fatheree — not only to its content but also
its tone. A tone that was shifting, he noticed:
the anger seething through Fatheree's voice
was dissolving into a defeatism that nearly
broke Daniel's heart. Fatheree seemed to
concede that this dressing-down of Daniel
would change little. At the most, like the
quiet show of respect he and the others tried
to apportion the nameless dead they buried
every week, it constituted a minor correction in the cosmos, a cosmos that had
somehow allowed them and the dead — lost
souls, all — to end up together in that
forgotten place.

Fatheree looked bereft, embarrassed by
his outpouring, and as if to save his pride
he suddenly recovered the thread of their

original conversation. "Last time Mr. Wind come here he asked me which graves had a temporary cover on them and where they were. Ain't saying I told him," he said defensively. "Mr. Wind also asked about docks and dogs and electric fences. Ain't saying I told him about that neither."

Daniel was frustrated that the two of them could not speak freely, and he knew that his allotted time with Fatheree was almost over. "What *are* you saying?" he said with insistence.

Clifford Fatheree grinned then. The smile was his first of the day, and it was characteristic: most of it was suppressed, so that only a small corner of his mouth lifted.

"I'm saying I know the sound of a man planning a break-in."

On the bus ride back into Queens, Daniel asked himself if it could have been possible for the artist to steal onto Hart Island, at night, say, when no one was there, and make quick casts of some of its recently interred dead. The answer was certainly yes. Daniel knew enough about modern casting compounds — about silicone spray and brushable polymers, about the speed with which life casts could be made using accelerators (death casts were even quicker, when the heat of instant solidifying was no longer an issue) — to estimate that Wind could have made a number of casts in one night, theoretically limited only by the difficulty of accessing the bodies themselves.

And it was from the macabre promptings of this last thought — a vision of the artist, alone at night in America's largest repository of anonymous dead, prying open box after box of the nation's strangers — that form was finally granted to what had been very vague in Daniel's mind ever since That Day. All along, he had sensed that the answer to why Aleksandra had left him for Benjamin Wind was to be found in the artist's final works of art, but now he saw that it was not simply a matter of Benjamin being a great artist, or even of how phenomenal his last pieces were. If Clifford Fatheree was right, if the artist had, in fact, committed a "break-in" at Hart Island, then Benjamin had not just captured, as Daniel had speculated in his review, the likenesses of anonymity in general with those sculptures; rather, he had gone and done something entirely more astonishing and profound. In the process of immortalizing some Jane and John Does and a horde of other disinherited dead who were buried on Hart Island when he conducted his clandestine fieldwork

555

there, Wind had risked everything — he had (again, Daniel was forced to think of Vienna's cemetery) desecrated graves! It must have been *that*, his willingness to aim toward the extremes — toward death — that drew Aleksandra to him. After all, she too had consistently put herself in harm's way for her art, particularly while venturing into certain parts of the Palestinian Territories to capture her pictures. Benjamin Wind's lack of fear, the impetuosity that took him to the point of diving into evil for the sake of his work, must have felt like a life ring to her. Carmen had been correct about the two of them: his vitality, and hers, was fed by a proximity to the dangerous shadows of everything alive. Whereas Daniel had always kept a safe distance — from all of it, really — until That Day. The fate of Aleksandra and Benjamin and himself? In a way, darkness had decided it.

Although he could not distance himself from any of this, Carmen certainly could and did when he phoned her later at her parents' home in Arizona (as he had every evening since they had parted in Vienna) to tell her how right she had been. She was, in fact, entirely uninterested in what he had to tell her. And when Daniel thought about it, he realized that it was not a new development. Though she had continued to assure him in their last four conversations that she loved him, she had at the same time permitted herself a series of uncharacteristic displays of indifference on the phone. It was only as she began to speak of the recent and steep (and probably final) decline of Max's health that he understood: in tending to the dead, Daniel had been neglecting the living and the dying.

He offered to fly out to see her and Max, adding that it did not make sense for her to be alone during such an ordeal.

"I'm not," she insisted quickly. "I have my parents."

He girded himself. He inhaled twice. "I can be there by tomorrow afternoon," he put forward, attempting to sound cheerfully at ease.

"I don't know."

"Really?" His voice — God, how he hated its highness, its hurt. "You don't want to see me."

Her reply was a release — of boldness and breath. "I'm not *ready* to see you."

"I'm coming," he gulped.

"Daniel?"

"I'll call you when I land."

"Okay."

The following morning there was a slight

mortuary feeling to his flight. All the executives who filed past him down the aisle in their dark suits reminded him of a funeral procession, and indeed Daniel had packed a black suit of his own, anticipating that a funeral-going was in the cards for him. He knew it was going to be good-bye to Max. He hoped it would not be good-bye to Carmen. The Phoenix airport did not augur well for him: it had been renovated, he discovered, so that after recovering his luggage he emerged not out onto the bright desert plain, but into the bottom of a deep, funereal furrow that had been cut into it. There, in that cement-encased desert ditch (sarcophagus?), he pulled out his phone and dialed the digits to which all his hopes and fears were now pinned. He wanted a restoration of Carmen's caring voice, and he got it — with a twist: "Daniel, I'm pregnant. Max is dying. We're at Tempe St. Luke's Hospital. Hurry."

Had one minute from the next ever been more happily contrasted for him? No wonder she had been distant — she had been carrying a lot, lately, literally, out here in Arizona. Rising up out of the trench in his rented car, he was aware that Circumstance, the artist, had just added an immense inlay of tile to the mosaic of his little destiny. It merited a call to the original artist. His mother, who had (from all that Daniel had shared with her) been predisposed in Carmen's favor, was noisily, tearfully thrilled when he broke the news of Carmen's pregnancy. Still, he needed her nudging.

"Tell me this isn't a bad thing," he said, pulling onto the expressway.

"*Please.* You're going to have this child with her. I just hope it won't be the last."

"I'm not even sure we're together, Mom."

He could hear her sniffling, the hiss of tissue being torn from a box.

"What was the last thing she said to you?"

"She said, 'Hurry.' "

"You're together."

"She's not Jewish."

"Are you *happy,* honey?"

At moments, as always, his mother had a way of *getting* to him. Happiness? For a man who had just fallen in love, he was averagely happy, he supposed. For a widower, he was averagely unhappy. He was average. Average was good. "I'm all right," he said.

"Then you're ahead of where *I* was. Your birth saved me, Daniel."

Daniel hesitated. "What was so special about having a child?"

"It's the greatest conversation I've ever had."

He had not been expecting *that* answer.

"When you used to scream for my breast, and later such reasoning, such fighting! But all of it, right up to here on this phone with you . . . I miss your father every day of my life — I still turn to his chair twice, three times an evening to ask him a crossword question, or tell him an interesting tidbit about someone we both knew, this crazy world of ours. But this conversation with you. It's the only one where I feel all of me is hanging from the words."

At the hospital, a receptionist rang Max's room, spoke to someone, then told Daniel to go on up. Carmen met him in the corridor as he came off the elevator, her face shining with that exhausted beauty that follows from a lot of crying. When they embraced she squeezed hard and told him that she loved him. Then she squeezed harder.

"I haven't decided if I want to marry you yet."

His reply was several seconds in coming. "All right."

"We'll talk later."

"I know."

She relaxed her grip on him, but he held a second longer, inhaling her hair, his eyes closed, trying to envision what was growing inside of her, the beginning of another greatest conversation ever.

Still they were in a hospital, those air-conditioned empires of cosmic balance, where conversations and beginnings must be paid for with their opposite — and at Carmen's urging, he left her in the hall and entered the little white room nearby in which a race was being run. Max lay there in the bed, horribly diminished, chasing air. Daniel thought how numberless breaths seemed until you saw them done like this. He thought that was the difference: breathing was no longer happening of its own accord, it was being done.

There was another difference. Pain. It was established baldly on the old man's face. And yet Max was lucid, uniquely so: one was alive in this way only once in a lifetime. His eyes followed Daniel with a despairing vitality, and he grasped Daniel's hand vigorously with his cold, damp fingers. As though he and Daniel had already been discussing the matter at length, he said, "To Carmen I am giving *all* my money."

Daniel could not assume that Carmen had told Max of her pregnancy, but he thought he detected an avuncular tone in the declaration, as if by extension the old man were going to take care of *him* as well. "You know she won't keep it, Max," he replied, lowering himself into a chair at the bedside.

Max blinked once — slowly — in acknowledgment of the statement's obvious truth. "She will give most of it to her parents. I am counting on this. The rest to charity. On this I am counting also."

"Have you considered that she might give all of it to Herman?"

"Are you referring to the Hebrew Indian who refuses to come watch a Jew die? Are you referring to the scientist who does not recognize death? The man who believes technology will help us all leave life *reasonably!*"

The old man was shaking, gasping for breath, and Daniel regretted having raised the specter of a long-estranged son before this dying father. It made him realize that he would not, as he had considered doing, raise before Max another family specter, Benjamin — and all that Daniel had recently learned (and hypothesized) about the artist's tanglings with the mass burials of Hart Island. Why trouble dying with more death?

"No, I have *not* been thinking of Herman!" Max said in adamant response to Daniel's silence. "The advantage of old age is that you barely think of others at all."

Daniel made no answer.

"But I have been thinking of his mother," Max went on, "and there is something I need you to bring to her."

Daniel straightened up. "I thought you said she's *dead.*"

"Hannah Engländer is dead *to me!*" the old man replied angrily, his voice faltering. He worked his lips. He tried to gather himself. "She is dead to the *Jews,* whose faith she abandoned. And dead to the *world* also! — all these years, living in one of these, these . . . *nunneries!* Cut off from the phone, from communication!" Max pointed his trembling finger at a large black folder resting on the air vent behind Daniel's chair. "*Please* — open it. When Carmen informed me that you were coming, I asked her to get it out of storage."

Daniel took up the folder — which turned out to be a weathered artist's portfolio — and, untying the string fastener, splayed its two leaves across his lap. What confronted him then was so incredible that his lips let out a loud profanity — *twice.* He recognized immediately that he was looking at one of the Jewish marriage contracts — the ketubot — that Max had told him about in Vienna, the ones that had been painted by Benjamin's grandfather. In the next moment, he realized that it was for Josef Pick's *own* marriage. And Max had been right: Daniel had never seen a ketubah like this. The entire thing was drawn in pencil, and with haste, though not to its detriment. Dimly shimmering over its surface, leaving cuneate footprints in their wake, were advancing ripples of misshapen, semitranslucent skeletons — some clambered over walls, others tunneled under towers, a few fugitives worried their way through the ketubah's thinning Hebraic words, which were ranged so sparingly across the page that their attachment to it seemed perilous. Indeed, each letter could hardly claim kinship with the word in which it convalesced, and several pairs of them — particularly those letters that found themselves close to a passing skeleton — seemed, as if advised by the dead to do so, to reach out toward one another. There were only two letters that actually touched. They were in the absolute center of the page, and they were not Hebraic. One was the lowercase "r" at the end of the bride's name, Hannah Engländer. The other was the capitalized "J" that began the groom's name, Josef Pick. From this central touching point, the two names curled up and away from each other, in arcs of such sweep and, somehow, sadness, that Daniel felt he was seeing a lost love lifted out of the paper's coarse fiber. And this, the piece's emotional exposure, was what struck him so deeply. Of course, he recognized its sophistications: the confident, loose, nearly despotic handling of line and pencil pressure, the residuum of light in transition that lent the drawing an absolute unworldliness, the fleshly disemboweling of perspective, the sheer brinkmanship brought to what, in a lesser artist's hands, would easily have been insoluble problems of composition, the aesthetic prevaricating that paradoxically turned a work into truth. But it was the triumph of love, or rather of love's innocence (and this was the biggest surprise — how had the artist *done* it?), that made the piece sublime. Everywhere was death, and everywhere was death declined. It was a mortal recitation, but God seemed to be sighing on high. And with good reason: a quick glance at the backside of the work revealed that it had been drawn on ledger paper obtained (illegally, no doubt) from within a working Nazi concentration camp.

"Christ," Daniel said for the third time.

"He betrayed me," Max said weakly.

Daniel held up the ketubah. "With *this?* But it was made in the camp, right? Weren't they already married by then?"

"He refused always to make one for her.

Josef broke my heart when he drew that."

Only then did it occur to Daniel what was really being asked of him. "You never showed this to her," he said with rising alarm.

The old man briefly met his eyes, then looked away, lost in some sort of attenuated shame.

"Max, is this" — he indicated the ketubah in his hand — "what got Josef Pick executed?"

A minute must have passed before Max turned his gaze back on Daniel, but by then it was already dissolving into tears. "It was part of it."

How much of the rest of it would Daniel tell Hannah Engländer when he saw her? It was a question that, like the astonishing things themselves that Max revealed to Daniel before he left the old man's bedside that afternoon, had haunted him all through his visit afterward with Carmen's parents in their tiny Tempe home (her mother was courteous but formal; her father rose *heavily* from his chair to greet Daniel) and had still not been answered two days later when he drove the car he had rented at the Seattle airport onto a ferry bound for a remote island in the San Juan Archipelago where

Ms. Engländer was still (after nearly thirty years, according to Max) living in a Benedictine monastery. Daniel was suffering from the sensation of having suddenly broken with everything in his life — an effect less of arriving in a part of the world wholly unfamiliar to him than of being on a boat whose plodding engines seemed to churn up nothing so much as his life, until he was forced to reckon with what lived at its depths, and take note of which way the current was carrying him. To stand there deckside in the mineral wind as the ferry throbbed away from the landing, to face the fingers of placid blue water that seemed to hold the distant islands in their grasp, to passively witness his own removal from the peak-punctuated mainland, was, particularly in light of the last two days (during which nothing, neither the immediate fate of Max nor of Daniel's future with Carmen, had been settled), to feel the full anguish of the unknown.

And though Carmen had wanted him to carry out Max's wish (it was she who had pushed him to leave Arizona so soon after he had arrived, claiming that it would allow her time alone to think), he could not help feeling that he was in some strange way being unfaithful to her. She was carrying his child, and here he was: journeying a thousand miles to see another woman about love. Granted, Benjamin Wind's grandmother was a stranger to him, and it was not *his* love pressed onto that remarkable page now lying improbably in the trunk of a Hertz rental car two levels below deck. But Daniel could almost feel the energy of Josef Pick's original act of creation driving him to complete this journey — the ketubah's journey — sixty years later. It seemed to prove that love never perished once it was put into the world. And to bring such a thing to *any* woman was surely enough to turn even the most distracted man into a lover, if only for a few quixotic moments.

The monastery, a cluster of cubical, almost Japanese-inspired buildings, was at the far end of the island, nestled in a stand of pines on a promontory that allowed the nuns to survey the strait to the south and their three hundred acres of farmland and forest to the north. Daniel had been instructed ahead of time by the abbess (with whom he had communicated by e-mail — he had been allowed no direct correspondence with Hannah Engländer) to wait by the fountain should he arrive early (he had), and, having left the ketubah in the car, he went and stood there with some uneasiness, listening to the intimate Gregorian chanting coming from the chapel and trying to discover what, exactly, was fueling his vexation at Ms. Engländer's choice of digs. That she had selected such an isolated spot in which to spend her years was not what nagged at him; in this respect she was hardly different from the rest of her family. All three of the eldest — Max, Herman, and Hannah — had sought to retreat from the world, mainly by escaping its most onerous force: time. Max had frozen it, put it away in storage; Herman had simply eliminated the evidence and, through his newfound Buddhism, any attachment to the future and the past; Hannah Engländer had, from the looks of it, sought the timelessness of God in cloistered life. But in the human realm, time tangled with responsibility — the resulting dance was generally called history — and as Daniel stared at the cross mounted to the chapel's cedar facade, he wondered if Ms. Engländer had not, in converting to Christianity, tried to sidestep the responsibility of being a Jew who had survived the Holocaust. What was she doing *here?*

A few minutes later he got his answer. Sort of. A tall and elegant elderly woman emerged from the chapel and, taking both of his hands in hers, hovering before him with a modest grace, said that she was Sister Engländer but that he could call her Hannah. After a strained introduction, they began walking down a gentle slope — slowly: she was hindered by a painful-looking limp — to a garden that was hers to tend. He explained that Max had sent him, withholding for the moment the reason why, and, when she responded only with silence, he expressed an interest in what had driven her to the monastery.

"It's not that I want to be here," she told him with the faintest trace of a Germanic accent. "It's that I don't want to be anywhere."

If Daniel was having to adjust to the woman's black-and-white habit (somehow, it had not gelled in his mind earlier that if she was living in a monastery she would have to be a nun), he was more stunned by her way of thinking, which, like her ferociously handsome face, was as rawboned and hard as it was noble, and gave an impression of depths beneath it and behind it. He came from a world of irony, where people protected themselves from pressing questions of the soul (even from the *word:* "soul" had been banished from contemporary talk for as long as he had been an adult) and rarely committed themselves to anything more than a half measure when confronted with metaphysical problems.

"You don't want to be anywhere," he echoed respectfully, trying to follow what he believed was the monastic strain of her statement, "because of people —"

"Because of God," she said plainly, stopping and turning to him. "How else can I close the gap with God? If *I* am *some*where, then I can't be where He is, which is *every*where. Religion is really homesickness."

The sparks that flashed in her brown eyes, when he gave her a look of mild confusion, illumined her face so that for a moment it was unseamed by age, and then appeared to radiate to the rest of her person until it too had almost effected a repossession of youth.

"If I am somewhere, even here," she continued for his benefit, gesturing up the hill at the monastery with her hand, "I have to speak to people, whereas what I want is the great dialogue with no one."

Daniel hesitated a second. "You mean — with God?"

"Well, not directly. That would be blasphemous. You can talk *at* God, but not *with* Him. God must remain silent. Otherwise, He can't be *us*."

"You believe He is us?"

"Us and everything else. From our inch of observation, our poverty of cosmic vision, He appears as that 'Thou' or, to be less formal, that 'You' which seems to follow our 'I' around wherever we go. Of course, that closeness is an illusion: He couldn't be farther away from us."

"Because we're *somewhere*," Daniel said. "Because we're here."

She looked at him then with new interest. In her gaze, a tidal world was at work, troubled by fits of thinking. "Are you sure it was *Max* who sent you?"

"Yes. Why?"

He could see that she had been on the verge of offering him an answer but had stopped herself. "Let us check the garden," she said, taking to the path again. "Each day, one should study the garden."

Study the garden they did, though Hannah did not so much contemplate the flower beds as train her eye on their behavior. Daniel knew next to nothing about flowers, but to him this nun seemed to play favorites — there was a preponderance of darks, of black and liverish blooms — as she anathematized the shortcomings of one bright blossom after another, and, with a pair of shears produced from somewhere in the folds of her habit, laid the lovely, defective things to rest. Its misdemeanors corrected, the garden resettled into something masculine and sluggish, slightly humiliated. "I have affection for my flowers," she declared, surveying the beds, "but still one has to deny them one's supreme love." She reached down and tickled the underside of a flower's plum petal with her finger. "These are still a veil. It's where I take issue with Goethe and Schiller and the other romantics who claimed that no evil can touch those who look upon beauty."

"Sure," Daniel agreed, "but one can still take some consolation from it. I mean *look* at this place: the rocks, the trees, the water . . ." He inhaled volubly. "You can at least feel more at one with the world."

"No, Mr. Lichtmann," she retorted, glancing at him gravely. "Unlike my sisters, I find no comfort whatsoever in this place, nor in God especially. I don't *blame* the others. They were all children once — we've all been raised to think we're worth more when someone is looking at us. But God isn't watching us. And that's His mercy. We need to believe in a God who is most unlike ourselves. Sometimes I think the real reason a woman comes to a monastery is to go *un*-remarked by Him. What an unnecessary hardship. It's not God who catches up with

573

you out there in the world — it's an aware-ness of your own wretchedness. And that finds you out well enough in a place like this."

"Then why *come* here?" He was not exasperated — he actually wanted to under-stand.

Her face held serene, but she richly dis-liked the question — this much he could tell. For nearly a minute she stood there as if recovering her memories, her experiences, a body that was no longer hers. "I came here because I wanted all the evil I do to fall only on myself. That's the burden, the cross we should all take up, wherever we are, but I couldn't do it out in the world. I was too weak to resist being pulled into hurting its people."

Daniel felt that she must have been allud-ing to those who had once been closest to her, to family, some of whom Daniel himself had met.

"It's another thing that distinguishes me from my fellow sisters," she went on. "For a time, quite a long time, I tried life. Whereas most of them have spent their adult lives meditating on things they will never do, I — I did it all. Then I came here. I needed to get away from mankind so that I could love it again. And I *did* love it again. I think

I love it in a way that my sisters don't. It helps to hate what is human at least once in your life. I'm not convinced true pity is otherwise possible."

Daniel was penetrated with the truth of this. How *different* this woman was from the rest of her family — save her grandson, whose prodigiousness of spirit was explained by hers no less than his artistic talent was explained by that which had created the ketubah lying out in Daniel's car. And yet Hannah Engländer still seemed to be divided against herself. She still seemed to be, well . . . a Jew.

"And Judaism?" There, he had finally asked.

She met his glance with a sodden expression. "Oh, that."

And then, after taking two steps up the path and turning halfway back toward him, she said: "Of course. You were sent by Max. We'll need the bench for this one."

The bench, as it turned out, was a rain-splintered log that had been planed on its uppermost side for sitting, and that faced a view of some rough coastline. Directly below, idling away the afternoon, was a rookery of sea lions, whose elders watched their pups contend with the current as though viewing the most boring show on earth.

"I imagine my former husband is still railing against my abandonment of Judaism," Hannah said, after they had sat on the log for a good five minutes. "He never was willing to see the subtlety of my reasoning when I tried all those years ago to share my decision with him. It wasn't an easy one, my decision. And though I have indeed been in the Catholic Church now for over three decades, I still find religion — all the religions — unacceptable. Humans hold too much sway over them."

"But — you're here. There must have been something about Christianity . . ."

Hannah's gaze was transfixed on the rookery. She seemed to be searching for something, with a kind of futility, as if her life lay down there among one of the herds, a dark exposed thing lolling on a granite slab, its intention as incomprehensible as the returning tide. "There *was* something about Christianity," she slowly replied. "I realized that it more directly acknowledged what I had felt — I do not exaggerate — since I was two years old: that the soul *is* its sufferings, and yet that there is very little cosmic support for weakness. Weakness: only *man* is left to tend to it. But man is so busy pacing back and forth in the trap of his vigor. He has always been willing to die for the powerful; it nearly makes him drunk to do so — one has only to read Homer, or to reflect on the great wars, to verify this fact. Still, intoxication is not transcendence. It took Christ to show us this. To show us that it is transcendent to die — and live — for something that here below seems weak. Christianity gave man something to *do* with his weakness. And it was something that *I* could do with my dissatisfaction with this world. Max refused to honor this need of mine. He required everyone close to him to be an emissary of Jewishness. He made a cult of Holocaust survival to which we all had to belong."

"Is that why your son turned his back on him?"

She looked at him then, her face lacerated with surprise and emotion. "Do you know my son?"

Once he revealed that he was an art critic who had written extensively about Benjamin, and that he had spent a not-so-distant afternoon with Herman — to test, as he explained to her, several theories he had formulated about the origins of Benjamin's last works of art, and more widely, to fill in a few biological blanks — Hannah pressed him for information about both the son and the grandson (especially the son: she was aware that Benjamin had died, but having never actually met her grandson, she took an understandably cooler interest in him). *This* was not a story Daniel had come prepared to tell, and he struggled to bring the woman up to date on her estranged son (or was *she* the one who was estranged?) while carefully holding his subjective impressions of Herman Wind at bay. It proved not to be enough for her; she seized on each detail with an agitated possessiveness that spoke of the damage caused by a family rift that was far from settled — and then she told him to give her the truth. "Don't soften it for me, Mr. Lichtmann. I'm not unacquainted with my son's malevolence."

So Daniel committed one of the worst breaches of etiquette: exposing a mother to the flaws of her son. He gingerly raised before Hannah Engländer a vision of the self-absorption he had encountered that day in Herman Wind. Bewildered to be the bearer of such news — he felt like a polluting force — he tried to bring his judgments into an alignment with a mother's hurt by expressing his sympathetic dismay at Herman's abandonment of family, of anything to do with his actual past.

Hannah took this in as she had everything else he had told her — with a quiet thoughtfulness. At last, adjusting her habit and looking out over the water, she said, "To see your own child in a merciless light. It's one of the most difficult things one can ever experience. Because what you find is that you're looking obliquely at yourself — a version of yourself, at least. It is your fault, you feel. And I *do* feel this with Herman. I feel it every day of my life. It's not just that he inherited some of my traits, the stubborn adherence to ideas and beliefs, the inflexibility, really. It's also what I *did* to him. When he was very little — it was during the war — I let him go, literally: I dropped him from a train that was taking us to Auschwitz."

Daniel looked at her. "To save him?"

She was shaking her head, though it was not clear to Daniel whether it was in response to his question or to a thought that was troubling her to tears. "Some phrases have the longest fuses," she said. "They only detonate years after they were uttered. I told him to walk away from everything. He was hardly old enough *to speak.* You must have compassion for Herman's rigid response to pain — he encountered it too early. What could he do with it when life hadn't yet

579

covered him in any sort of casing?" She turned to Daniel suddenly. "I didn't just throw Herman out of a train, I flung him out of his childhood."

"Surely you tried later to repair the damage," Daniel said.

"I gave him every maternal indulgence."

"Of course you did."

Hannah smiled at him wanly. "You're very kind. You have real goodness in your heart." She took up his right hand and held it for a moment, then pressed it back down on his lap. "But I will share with you something only a mother is allowed to learn. There is no better way to lose your son than occupying yourself solely with him."

A breeze came up then, filling their ears so that the silence that rose between them was less pronounced. After some time had passed, she asked: "How *is* Max?"

And here we are, Daniel thought. Life had called on him to say what he was about to say only once before — it was his father, that time — and with this, his second time, he was just as tentative, just as slow-tongued, for fear that the phrase might turn from descriptive to proscriptive. "He's dying."

It was nearly intangible, the momentary lapse in her self-possession when she heard these two words. What movement in her expression Daniel could catch struck him as purely transitional, a restoration of equanimity, the face fitting itself to a new kind of repose. But her voice was a dishevelment of bitterness. "Is that why he sent you?" she asked. "To tell me that he was dying?"

He told her that it was not, and then he led her down the hill to his car and showed her, right there with the trunk open, the reason why Max had sent him. When her eyes fell on the ketubah she knew what it was instantly, and tenderly picked it up. Daniel could see she needed to sit down, and he helped her into the backseat of the car with him, where she kept lifting the ketubah with her hands and letting it fall back down to her lap while she cried with her mouth open. Daniel did not speak, except once to say that Max had managed to store the ketubah away in the Birkenau camp until it was liberated, a statement that only elicited another paroxysm of crying. Ten minutes must have passed in this way, until, to Daniel's amazement, she turned to him and asked, "What took you so long?" — and then leaned over and kissed him on the mouth.

If he had worried on the ferry that he was betraying Carmen by going to meet a mysterious woman, the sensation was doubly strong now that he was sitting here in the backseat of a car with Hannah Engländer herself, the taste of her lips on his. She was so much older than him, but she did not fail to arouse something in him, and not just sympathy. But *Christ,* it occurred to him, he was kissing a nun in the parking lot — within full view of the monastery!

Hannah suddenly pulled away and stared at him with what could only have been the shock of recognition. She looked horrified, she looked ashamed. And she also looked beautiful — her wet, shining eyes, her pale oval face . . . they held the beauty of an embarrassed femininity that age could not refine away from her. Daniel was deeply moved by it. What a *triumph* this woman was.

"I'm sorry," she gasped, lowering her gaze to the ketubah. "It's very confusing when what had seemed so dead all these years suddenly blooms before you. It happened even before you showed me this — when I first saw you standing at the fountain. You looked so much like Josef: it's really quite extraordinary. Even the way you talk and think. It may very well be the silly imagination of an old woman. But still, I can't see it as an accident that Max sent you to me. Walking and talking with you this afternoon

— it reminded me too strongly of Josef, of a day we once passed together, in Vienna, after being introduced to each other by Max. I apologize for kissing you just now; I hope you will forgive me for my confusion. This is what happens when the dead return near the end of one's life. It isn't generous of them." She held up the ketubah and stared at it. "And whatever Max told you, this isn't a *gift* from him. I can't help feeling that this is Josef come back, wanting his due. It's not fair. And I was better off not knowing this existed. I was able to look on my marriage to Josef with nostalgia: the key to viewing any marriage in a favorable light. But this — this destroys my selective memory. It destroys my memory, period, by suddenly erasing the distance between me and the past. And don't you see that memory is the only place where no one ever dies? No, this kills Josef for me — all over again. *That* is why this isn't a gift. Max knew what he was doing in giving this to me now. It is his final retribution."

Then she fell quiet, and for a minute or so ran her fingertips over the paper's coarse surface. She seemed to be assembling her thoughts. "You told me earlier that you're an art critic," she said at last. Now she angled the ketubah toward his eyes. "Do you understand what you're looking at?"

Her words were no longer chasing themselves, she was composing them too calmly — he did not trust their control, and he instinctively refused to reward them with words of his own. If she noticed, she gave little indication other than a slight increase in her voice's insistence: "This is no normal marriage contract, Mr. Lichtmann — and not only because it was painted under the worst of conditions, or made years after the fact of our marriage. It's a nightmare of mastery. The work of a man who was doomed, at a very early age, like a musician, to repeat and repeat one initial inspiration — an inspiration that came to him via the very bad marriage of his parents. You mustn't just see this as some declaration of love from a destroyed world. It's a portrait of a destroyed man fighting desperately for a vision of love. And it reenlists me in that most painful of struggles, the battle of love, whose fighters, unlike soldiers in an army, cannot claim ignorance of what they do. It remarries me to Josef, Mr. Lichtmann, ending the wholeness I have enjoyed for the last three decades. The Greeks were wrong about men and women completing each other. The connected are always incomplete."

The woman's arresting admissions sent Daniel sailing out over Carmen, over Aleksandra, over his first wife — the key women in his life — where, from high above, he saw their lives . . . the unreached individualities, the impossible hurrying after perfection, the race to live by the heart. He was at a loss for words, and was relieved when Hannah said she needed to get away from the monastery for a little while, and asked him to take her for a drive.

She moved up to the front with him and held the ketubah in her lap as they drove in silence, the two of them lulled by motion into approximate thought, locating their separate troubles in the tree shadow, in the solemn, low-sunned scenery. The pines gave glimpses now of dark blue water, now of pastoral farmland, and, while Daniel could not deny the general beauty of what he was seeing, he found that he was somehow saddened by the proportion of the place, its island modesty. It seemed to cast a spell on him, a specifically northern dissatisfaction.

They must have been halfway around the island when he caught Hannah with a smile on her lips — she was studying the ketubah. He allowed some time to pass, it was so lovely to see. Then, keeping his eyes on the road, he said, "I need to tell you what

585

happened when he painted that."

There was a balky acquiescence in her eyes when she turned to him. "Yes, I suppose you do."

And so, while they wound their way through a lengthy stand of aspens, Daniel began to recount, as best he could, what Max had shared with him of the ascension and descent of Josef Pick during a few days in November of 1944. He told her how, according to Max, Josef had gradually come to seem oblivious to the misery of camp existence, and how, for most of that dismal autumn, all he could speak of was the fact that he had not painted a ketubah for Hannah and himself. There came a point when Josef finally convinced Max — who had procured a coveted work assignment in one of the camp's inventory buildings — to risk his life organizing paper and pencils, so that Josef, working in increments, stealing a few moments in his bunk at dusk and dawn, could illuminate the contract he had never made for his marriage. To Max he spoke of crazy plans for somehow smuggling it out to Hannah, despite having no idea where she was by that time, or whether she was even still alive. As there was no privacy in the barracks, the ketubah soon drew the attention of the other inmates — who began bringing Josef drawing supplies they themselves had organized so that he could make ketubot for them as well. Many of the men were married and had left their marriage contracts back in their home villages and cities — or they had been forced to abandon them along with the rest of their belongings upon arriving at the camp. They were dreaming of their wives, most of whom were already dead, and wanted new ketubot to commemorate them, to make concrete on the page unions that would never manifest in the flesh again. The men understood that they too would in all likelihood soon be dead. But it was for this very reason that they asked Josef to make them ketubot — something to remind them, even if only for a few days, of what had been. They longed, as Max had put it, to be painted back home before they died.

To judge by Max's account, Josef was resistant at first, insisting that he had stopped illuminating contracts years earlier. "I'm not a marriage artist!" he would shout wildly at the men (as if he had gone *mad,* according to Max). And there *was* the element of risk. Inmates were being shot every day for lesser crimes than making objects of great Jewish significance. Josef had to have been frightened. But he clearly found that he could not say no, because soon he was creating quick ketubot and, if Max was to be believed, even jokingly quoting the old Viennese saying, "One must paint the dead quickly" — while the men shared stories of their wives with him and told him what to put into their contracts. And it was not just the already married who came to him, but also those who had been robbed by the Germans of the chance to wed their sweethearts. He was even approached by one youth — a boy from Prague, who was much too young to have known what love with a woman was — as well as a group of the direst pessimists among the inmates, the ones who had all but given in to the argument that the prevalence of evil around them proved that life was of no value.

"Of course *they* came to Josef," Hannah interjected bitterly. She had turned to Daniel so that her eyes caught the sun as it pierced the trees, the erratic lances of afternoon light causing her irises to flash. "The women's camps had plenty of nihilists too. They're the ones who ended up surviving in the largest numbers, because they were in on the big secret: that you could no longer care about the collective if you wanted to make it. And there's no better way to be in it for yourself than to believe the world isn't worth anything. Josef's creations probably offered those men the only opportunity they ever had in camp to think of someone besides themselves. Certainly that's what love is for. His ketubot showed them something that *had* to have worth. What else has evil ever taken from us but that which we value?"

Daniel was relieved by her interruption, her sudden display of indignation. It appeared to have given her a new fortitude; it lessened his burden. It also gave him a reprieve: her last utterance was less question than philosophical statement — one that demanded no immediate answer — and he let the silence hang. Their circumnavigation of a small, limpid cove seemed to introduce a welcome solitude into the atmosphere of the car, and he even allowed himself to imagine that his duty was done.

It was not done, of course. Hannah sensed it, and said so: "Mr. Lichtmann, what terrible thing aren't you telling me?"

For this, Daniel had to pull over. He parked along the side of the road, a hundred yards up a slope from a boatless dock. Farther out on the water, several mooring buoys were quarreling with their cables, and it was on them that Daniel settled his gaze as he explained to Hannah how, at Max's prompting, with fresh marriage contracts in hand, a number of the male prisoners — including Josef — had reenacted their weddings one night in the barracks, using fellow inmates as stand-ins for their brides. Knowing what their chances of survival were, the men married against death, in what they felt had to be the last Jewish weddings in Europe, perhaps even the last weddings in the world.

And then, because Max had vehemently insisted he do so, Daniel told Hannah the truth about another wedding — her own, to Max. His face burned as he spoke. It was the hardest thing he had ever had to tell a woman, and his voice sounded so unsuitable to the task. He told Hannah that Max had never once considered his marriage to her binding — because he was already married. Because, earlier, on that November night in Birkenau, having volunteered to take *her* place next to Josef, he had walked down the aisle between the bunks, hand in hand with his beloved, realizing a dream he had secretly husbanded ever since a day in his youth, when he had exchanged vows with Josef at the top of St. Stephen's Cathedral.

Hannah, who had been visibly moved by the story of Josef and the other men holding weddings in the camp, understandably stiffened at the revelation of Max's ulterior motive in instigating them. She was, in fact, statuesque — five minutes must have passed during which her eyes never moved from one of the air vents in the dash, and her upper body, canted forward slightly in the seat, never wavered from its rigid pose. It looked to Daniel like some kind of a severe purging ritual . . . death by dormancy, or coldness. Max, to be sure, did not figure in what she had next to say. "Was Josef discovered?" she asked in a level, clerkly voice.

"They were still enacting the ceremonies when guards broke into their barrack."

"And was he —" She broke off.

Daniel paused, but he required *more* than a pause: Where was time's incrustation when he needed it? Did the life of death *ever* curtail? Did its descriptions ever dim? He turned until he was completely facing her.

"They were going to shoot him, Hannah — but he ran out of the barrack, and, before they could, he leaped onto the electrified fence."

Daniel felt such an urgent need to speak to Carmen after dropping off Hannah that he drove only a few dozen meters — enough to be out of visual range of the monastery — before pulling into a dusty turnaround and dialing from the car. He was unsuccessful in reaching her, and tried again from the ferry, and then later from the Seattle airport, and still later (the next morning, in fact) when he touched down in New York, leaving him to assume that she was keeping a bedside vigil for Max, perhaps watching him field his body's final requests for breath (she would have called if he had died). Each time Daniel came to the end of her voice mail greeting, he would find that he was unable to leave a message. It never seemed to be the appropriate moment or forum to express his desire to marry her, and, beyond offering her a few words of support, what would he have said? That it had been a difficult and confusing encounter with Hannah?

It certainly had been *that,* no part of it more so than its final seconds. Hannah had refused to leave the passenger seat when he had pulled into the monastery's lot, and she held him hostage with a silence that he had assumed was a consequence of her finally learning the precise way in which her first husband had died during the war.

But was it? Was it shock that drove her to end her silence by saying she was not sorry for having kissed Daniel earlier? Was she clearheaded when, in the next breath, she alluded to the possibility that, were it not for the vast run of years between them, she and he could have been lovers?

Or was it *he* who was not clearheaded? "The tragedy of time is that it keeps lovers from each other" were her exact words, and, had they not come on the heels of her retraction of regret about kissing him, he might have been certain that they applied to herself and Josef Pick during the Holocaust — that she was lamenting history, how it hewed love in half.

But he was certain of very little, sitting there beside her in that moment. He was not even certain that they — he and Hannah — were *not* lovers, so mangled was his sense of time and place. There was something about having to say good-bye to her after what she had just said — after what both of them had been saying all afternoon, really — that took away all assurances.

Then she kissed him, on his lips, for the second time that day. And because he was already disoriented, because it happened again in the car, he had trouble distinguishing it from his memory of the first kiss, and it frightened him. He was not sure if the woman before him was real, present, *there*.

A moment later, when she moved to pick up the ketubah in her lap, his confusion cleared. But there had been a transitory instant before that — like a flicker between the past and present — in which he saw what memory meant. It was the eternal house. It was where we held each other, forever.

His assumption had been correct. When Carmen did finally call him, it was to share the news of Max's passing. Daniel flew back to Arizona for the funeral, and this time when he returned to New York, Carmen came with him, for good. They found an airy two-bedroom apartment within walking distance of Columbia (where she resumed her graduate studies), and, in their spare time — which did not amount to much, with the art world back in full swing, school under way, and the odd trip to the obstetrician — they began to talk about what kind of wedding they wanted.

The question of how, exactly, Aleksandra had met her death was not resolved in his mind, and it did occur to him, in the months since meeting Clifford Fatheree, that Benjamin's brush with the convicts of Rikers Island — where, after all, no one stayed incarcerated for very long — could have had something to do with it. That remote possibility, of an outside murder, plagued him enough that he actually called up the original investigators in the case and explained what he had learned about Wind's relationship to Hart Island and the inmates who had worked there. The investigators repeated to him what they had said the first time around: there had been no sign of a struggle. No scuff marks on the roof of Wind's building or in his loft. No skin or blood cells beneath their fingernails, no bruises that were not from the fall. There was no case, nothing they could move on. Hart Island and the artist's multiple visits to Rikers? A good story.

In realizing that the greater world would not get involved in sorting this one out, Daniel grew to accept that the story of how Aleksandra came to lose her life — the mostly unknown series of events that began, really, on that long-ago day in Vienna when Max had introduced Hannah Engländer to a talented artist named Josef Pick — would remain *his* story. And the indifference, and unconcern, reminded him that the world had its own story, and it was not ours. We helped it along — with our lives we paid to be players — but rarely were we granted our dreams of speaking parts, and most of us never rose above anonymity. Such were Daniel's thoughts, anyway, when, on a wet and freezing December morning, having finally obtained a media permit from New York's Department of Correction, he stood on a small ferry that took him, a morgue truck, three correction officers, and eleven prisoners (Clifford Fatheree was not among them) to Hart Island — where *only* the unstoried were buried. If he now resolutely held that Benjamin had stolen onto its potter's field and exhumed the dead in order to take casts for his astonishing last show, Daniel had never really asked *why* — why Wind had made the anonymous dead there his dark problem, and then, by universalizing them through art, made them the world's dark problem. Had it been Benjamin's intention to give them, the unacknowledged dead, speaking parts (so to speak)? After all, the possibility of realizing that nearly impossible dream — to play a role, to *count* — was as available to the dead as it was to the living, perhaps even more so. It happened every day that we, the survivors, burnished the dead, finished their unfinished selves, and then, only in their posthumous perfection, made them part of the story. Had Benjamin's final works of art been his way of coming through for those who had no survivors, who had no chance of fulfilling that secret sacred wish every human harbored, in one form or another, of being resurrected? The more Daniel considered these questions, the more convinced he became that Wind's entwined ascending and descending figures had been connected, somehow in the artist's mind, to the millions who in the Holocaust had gone with unchronicled qualities to their graves. Surely Benjamin had seen the ketubah his grandfather had made in Birkenau; Max must have told him about the marriages those men had mounted in their last days on earth. The parallels between his final sculptures and Josef Pick's ultimate marriage contracts were just too close: both artists had honored the dreams of the dead.

But if it was indeed true that Benjamin had never seen *any* of his grandfather's work (as Max had so adamantly claimed in Vienna), then the last things he had sculptured merely proved that certain human undertakings, the ones that carried crucial news to us, were bound to recur in different forms. And Daniel had to admit that this ride to Hart Island — to see the improbable place where the direction of his life may have been decided — did itself feel like some kind of recurrence, whether it was simply that he was making another significant journey to an island by ferry, or that he was again going to see New York's banished (the living among them exiled at Rikers, the dead here on Hart Island), or whether it was the eerie and yet calming sensation, as he stood there staring across Long Island Sound at the approaching landing, that his nerves were Benjamin's nerves and his eyes Benjamin's eyes.

Daniel's first impression of the island, when they reached it, was mussel shells. They were everywhere — on the shore's shallow banks, along the serrated sides of the roads, and even mixed in with the mud of the burial site that lay a little in from the water, below a hill commanded by some old blackened barracks — and the shells' sheer ubiquitousness gave the island a sweet, salty, slightly rotten scent (despite the cold weather) that was a little too close, in Daniel's opinion, to what decaying human flesh might smell like. The current burial grounds were all rutted earth and muck, an amorphous mess save for a freshly dug pit, deep as a man was tall, which, in its general dimensions, could have been a hole excavated for a house. And if the island's overall smell, or its overgrown mass grave markers, or even its discarded shoes (products of a shoe factory that had once been in operation), did not evoke the Holocaust in Daniel's mind, this giant open trench beneath the barracks did. Today was "dead man day," as several of the officers had blandly quipped on the ride over (Daniel was relieved he had come neither on a Monday nor a Tuesday, which were "dead baby day" and "dead woman day" respectively), and no time was wasted in unloading the truck's gloomy lading: numbered wood boxes, adult-size. Forming a kind of human conveyer belt, with two men on the receiving end down in the trench, and still two more shoveling mud that had infilled overnight, the prisoners began to make their sad deposit while Daniel, whose ostensible reason for being there was to write an article for his magazine, stood near an unoccupied edge of the pit and attempted to play the role of disinterested observer.

He was nothing of the kind. This was *personal:* so many reactions came over him while he watched that it simply had to be. What hit him right away was the horror Wind had gotten himself into by coming here — *here!* — to make his art. It could not have been dying that was on his mind. It was *being dead.* The raw reality of wood chambers arranged in the wet, putrid muck of the planet was too clear in its message. What a reminder, all that dirt . . . the unlimited, worthless commodity: of course we went to it in the end! And Wind had addressed *that,* the body's decomposition, directly. Worrying these dead up from such a place — it was as if he had gone back, all the way back, to the primordial ooze. Had it been the only direction he could find to turn from the madness of his family and their hashed history? Had it been worth it? This last question rang rhetorically — and bitterly — in Daniel's ears as he eyed the stacks of pine boxes in the pit. Surely Wind had lost his way in the process (Daniel felt he was losing his way just visiting), and how could he not have, when what he had been pulled into here on Hart Island would seem to have bordered on the demonic? As he stared down into the trench, Daniel saw with absolute clarity, with anger too, that Benjamin had taken on a force that fated him — and Aleksandra — to die. There were consequences for tangling with such darkness. Resurrecting the dead was not a chore reserved for us. And if it *had* somehow come down to an errant ex-convict or two, they were simply evil's servants. Wind had started it. Or his family had, or history had.

How did the prisoners on burial duty *deal* with it? How did these discontented creatures of the shovel bury other arrested lives without losing *their* way? The answer, which came only after Daniel had observed them for the better part of an hour, was a surprise. It was dignity. He had expected an extension of what he had seen at Rikers and even on the ferry ride over: the apathetic stares into space, the sentiment denied. But that distinction belonged to the officers alone, who stood watch over the pit and broke their boredom with a barked command every now and then. As for the inmates, they returned these dead to the dominion of nature with a gravity — and perhaps this *was*, after all, imported from prison — that was entirely germane to the occasion. Even the rare curse or joke, the odd raillery that was uttered as another box passed from one pair of hands to the next, sounded to Daniel like the punctuation of some ancient language that told of what lay in store for everyone, or of the serenity and friction that lay behind. Their brief exchanges seemed to acknowledge the lightness and the darkness of what any one person's portion of life offered.

Moreover, to the degree that these dead had dislodged from their particular ties of blood, the prisoners were, as Clifford Fatheree had indeed told Daniel, burying them for all of us. And the prisoners appeared to know it, even take a kind of pride in it. They were standing knee-deep in the civic slough: the mud at the bottom of the open trench was a sort of solid national sustenance from which the men seemed to bloom, in flashes anyway, like settlers clearing the cruel continent. The image, of men sinking shovels into the wild New World, forced Daniel to look up, past the pit and out over the distant sound. To the east lay the privileged corners of the Great Neck peninsula; to the south, beyond the bridges spanning the East River, Manhattan lifted its towers into the sky. Each was an emblem of America's vulnerable idealism, and perhaps even its principal glory. But they were also half-truths. To view them — the mansions and the metropolis — from this mass grave was to see a nation's projection and its reality all at once, how it dangled and denied promises at the same time. In the pit there was no projecting. The earth was not our echo. The anonymity of the dead said as much. Their deaths without distinction set an example, a model for how to die, and, in this sense, if the prisoners were burying them for all of us, they — the dead — had died for all of us. And that made this place, Daniel suddenly saw, the nation's truest holy ground.

It caused him to shiver, this realization, because it opened to his view a completely new understanding of Benjamin Wind's genius: as the source of his final work, it was possible that he had found the last American place in which the earthly and the divine were fused. And if not, he had fused them with those sculptures of his, like some latter-day god.

WHERE THEY RESIDE

They have just finished conducting their dreams when shouts erupt outside the barrack. Someone, the Kapo perhaps, has betrayed them. Within seconds, four guards enter, ketubot in their hands, demanding to know who made such Jewish trash. There is a silence. And then he steps forward, walks uncertainly across the floor. One of the guards removes a pistol and aims.

He runs, then. Shots ring out, yet he has a blunt awareness that he is still alive. Miraculously, he *persists.*

His fellow inmates, so much suddenly abstract humanity: faces and shapes, a blurred multitude, retarded by fear and standing in his way. Their meaning to him a thing of the distant past.

Or *not?*

Their names, at least some of them, make the list of marriages he starts reciting to himself as he breaks from the barrack and runs toward the electrified fence. Enumerating the names — it helps him not to look back at the guards who are shouting that they will shoot. He is so frightened. The fence is so far.

He remembers all the couples his ketubot have joined. They are there with him now, running around him, hurrying him to the fence. Their names cause him pain, of course. That is okay. He wants the pain — as much as possible. Maximum sensation, before none.

The names take him. And he goes willingly — forfeits himself to them like a soul finally finding its idea — because in the instant before he *becomes* them, he sees that they speak of something much larger than everyone for whom he painted. Larger, even, than the mass grave of the gone — the sum of those he has survived. These vanished brides and grooms, hidden memory of the race . . . they were a selection of the world's hope.

The fence is within reach, now. The guards are going to let him do it to himself. At the last moment he leaps, he transitions, leaving being behind. He is all physics and force, the pride of the external laws. No longer does he understand the names, though they remain distantly crucial, something missed, pieces of advice in a foreign language:

Liselotte Toch
Minna Briefwech-
  sler
Herta Königsberg
Auguste Jellinek
Sabine Last
Hetie Platz
Else Hendel
Charlotte Beer
Sofie Trost
Isa Buchbinder
Josefine Inslicht
Rosa Löwenthal
Helene Pisk
Amalie Klein-
  fischel
Eva Liebenwalde
Aloisia Deutsch
Hanna Subak
Friederike
  Antscherl
Kamilla Teltsch
Taube Aschkenasy
Gusti Bock
Yella Werdesheim
Franziska David-
  sohn
Lotte Mischkönig

Ignatz Wallisch
Emil Marcuse

Leopold Glass
Joachim Schöngut
Lev Israelsky
Egon Ullmann
Werner Rosenfeld
Hermann Luft
Florian Warkany
Emmerich Holz
Julius Adler
Oskar Strobl
Chaje Bloch
Moritz Wie-
  selmann
Benno Munk
Sigmund Löbl
Eduard Beinhacker
Sandor
  Schwarzbartl
Jonas Fuchs
Ludwig Engel
Simon Blümel
Alexander Besner
Karl Zernik

Alfred Slatkes

Hanna Banaschek	Georg Koralek
Anni Hamlisch	Erwin Arnsfeld
Friede Asch	Ferdinand Stempelberg
Illona Chasin	Max Blumenthal
Rebekka Wienowitsch	Wilhelm Rosenwasser
Blanka Aron	Hermann Zlowski
Thea Prager	Kurt Bodner
Gisella Schmul	Zdeněk Birkenfeld
Olga Hajek	Siegfried Erant
Lissi Neuländer	Peter Simon
Grete Wolf	Egmont Lewin
Lina Abramsohn	Otto Sabatzki
Kamilla Schiff	Viktor Fodor
Fany Caminer	Herbert Vogel
Alois Lederer	Arnold Baer
Lilly Rynerzelski	Paul Tannenwald
Irma Kopfstein	Theodor Lewinski
Cilly Minkus	Heinz Grünwald
Wilhelmine Noah	Adolf Preusz
Malvina Zunderstein	Leo Münster
Eda Thalmann	Franz Saalmann
Cäcilie Helft	Josef Mautner
Rosalie Zug	Hugo Rabinovitz
Taubilla Ziegeltuch	Arthur Wald
Hildegard Loheit	Heinrich Rubel
Lisbeth Krausz	Reiner Stöhr
Trude Weigl	Isidor Cohen
Selma Wronker	Jaroslav Goldstaub

Ricka Ehrmann	Harry Schnapp
Elli Jakobsohn	Joachim Spronz
Magdalena Herlitz	Helmut Kantoro-wicz
Judith Berendt	Markus Donner
Leonore Mendl	Wolf Michten-hauser
Mathilde Morgen-roth	Maximilian Amster
Brigitte Keil	Ludwig Göllner
Zipora Perl	Israel Heilpern
Flora Moranz	Werner Anschlow-tiz
Agnes Stux	Julius Lewy
Gutta Rippel	Adolf Gotthelf
Minna Goteswilen	Arnim Knecht
Blanka Toch	Leopold Phlipp-sohn
Marion Fisch-grund	Meier Frydman
Pauline Salz	Artur Hesky
Valeska Töpffer	Paul Justitz
Katinka Leinwandt	Egon Levysohn
Edith Lojef	Johannes Band
Louise Molnar	Herbert Israelo-wicz
Feodora Rendel-stein	William Löbel
Eva Kübl	Joseph Beer
Auguste Lorsch	Jakob Werblowski
Henny Schafranek	Theobald Nim-häuser

Zilla Glückstadt

Margot Freimuth

Amalie Kerfunkelstein

Emmy Novotny

Ludmilla Blau

Aurelie Bader

Hannalore Tschupik

Sibylla Last

Hannah Engländer

Manfred Heilbronner

Anton Popper

Abraham Wasserzug

Horst Sonnenschein

Aron Engl

Moses Weiner

Edmund Kolinski

Felix Michelsohn

Josef Pick

ABOUT THE AUTHOR

Andrew Winer is the author of *The Color Midnight Made*. A recent recipient of a National Endowment for the Arts Fellowship, he teaches at the University of California, Riverside, where he has directed the MFA program in creative writing.

The employees of Thorndike Press hope you have enjoyed this Large Print book. All our Thorndike, Wheeler, and Kennebec Large Print titles are designed for easy reading, and all our books are made to last. Other Thorndike Press Large Print books are available at your library, through selected bookstores, or directly from us.

For information about titles, please call:
  (800) 223-1244

or visit our Web site at:
  http://gale.cengage.com/thorndike

To share your comments, please write:
  Publisher
  Thorndike Press
  295 Kennedy Memorial Drive
  Waterville, ME 04901